Driven by ambition, divided by greed, the Stockwells' bitter rivalries threaten the very foundation of their dynasty...

The multi-throated gasp that filled the church hall caused Buffy Stockwell to turn around. Focusing, her eyes turned to angry, smoldering slits. James Linstone Stockwell was walking slowly down the aisle of Gotham Memorial Church toward the front pew and beside him, her arm in his, was Vanessa Brewster!

Buffy was furious. When James had said he would take care of the Vanessa Brewster matter, she'd never dreamed that he would do it in a way that would publicly degrade her. Now all America would know that Vanessa Brewster had been accepted by the Stockwells as a friend of the family.

You'll pay for this, James, she vowed silently. If there was ever a chance at compromise over the estate, you have just killed it. I will get what is rightfully mine, and if I can destroy you in the process, it will be all the better. Yes, I'll drag you and the Stockwells through every court in the land, and smear the Stockwell name in every newspaper, on every TV newscast, that I can.

With this thought, Buffy's fury took a sudden detour. Wait! What seemed a public humiliation might be just the advantage—in disguise—she'd been seeking. By insulting her this way, James might have made a serious tactical mistake. Indeed, he just might have unwittingly supplied the means of his undoing...

RIVERVIEW

BITTER LEGACY

KATHLEEN FULLER

IVY BOOKS • NEW YORK

To Harriet Gottfried,

Peace and Love

The author of this work is a member of the
National Writers' Union.

Ivy Books
Published by Ballantine Books

Produced by Butterfield Press, Inc.
133 Fifth Avenue
New York, New York 10003

Library of Congress Catalog Card Number: 86-91835

ISBN 0-8041-0013-6

Manufactured in the United States of America

First Edition: May 1987

The Stockwells

Governor Matthew Adams Stockwell: Former Governor of the State of New York

Mary Linstone Stockwell: His first wife, mother of his children

Brenda "Buffy" Cabot Stockwell: His second wife

James Linstone Stockwell: Governor's eldest son, widowed

  Patrice Stockwell O'Keefe: His eldest child, divorced

  Matthew Sykes Stockwell: His eldest son

  Michael Stockwell: His youngest son

  Lisa Stockwell: His youngest child

Alice Stockwell Lewis: Governor's eldest daughter,

David Lewis: Alice's husband

  Mark Lewis: Alice and David's oldest child, deceased

  Michelle Lewis Carter: Alice and David's daughter, married to Andrew Carter, mother of Daniel and Robin

Jonathan Charles Stockwell: Governor's youngest son

Ellen Smith Stockwell: His wife

  Peter Stockwell: Jonathan and Ellen's only child

Terry Stockwell: Governor's daughter, deceased

  Holly Stockwell Millwood: Her daughter, estranged from husband Christopher Millwood, mother of Nicholas

Susan Stockwell Wells Gray: Governor's youngest child, divorced from first husband Gary Wells, widow of Lawrence Gray

  Decatur "Deke" Wells: Susan and Gary's only child

The Tylers

Sara Stockwell Tyler: Governor Stockwell's eldest sister, mother of twins, John and Alfred

John Tyler: Her son, Governor Stockwell's nephew, deceased
Elizabeth "Lizzie" Tyler: His wife
  Paul Tyler: John and Lizzie's only child
  Margaret Tyler: His wife
    Elizabeth and Caroline Tyler: Paul and Margaret's twin daughters

Alfred Tyler: John Tyler's twin brother, widowed
  Maxwell Tyler: His eldest child
  Diana Tyler: His eldest daughter
  Louise Tyler Papatestus: His youngest child, married to Spiro Papatestus

BOOK ONE

1

THE MAN STRIDING up the rocky, hillside trail that ran from his family boat house on the Hudson River to Riverview Manor was no longer young. But there was a determined energy to his walk that defied the years. Squared shoulders and a square, jutting chin told them to get out of his way; he had no time for such nonsense, no time for aging, no intention of having his life interrupted by anything so banal as dying.

From the stables that had been converted into garages to house the Stockwell family's various limousines and sports cars, two servants watched as he started up the rise to the broad lawn in front of the porte cochere, Riverview's main entrance. He was straining a bit, and scowling up at the carved gargoyles decorating its eaves, as if defying them to interfere with his progress. There was a certain similarity of expression—a disregard for the weathering and ravishings of time, perhaps—between his visage and the fierce masks of the gargoyles.

"He thinks it's San Juan Hill and he's leading the charge." The older of the two servants, not much younger than the man climbing toward the manor house, leaned on his garden hoe and shook his head at the characteristic energy of the climber.

"Sure, I never knew he saw action there." The younger servant was sporting the unbuttoned tunic of a chauffeur's uniform and a cap tilted with off-duty rakishness.

"He didn't. That was Teddy Roosevelt. Different governor. Different family. Different time. Our Governor was too young for that war." The gardener watched the climber pause with a look of annoyance, catching his breath. "Too young then, too old now," he observed.

"Don't you believe it," the chauffeur told him. "The Governor's still got energy to make lads half his age turn shamrock green with envy."

"Oh, he's got the spirit, all right. But the flesh . . .?" The gardener raised a wizened eyebrow reluctantly familiar with the shortcomings of flesh.

"The flesh is it now?" The chauffeur laughed knowingly, cocked his cap still further over one eye and winked. "Well, there's surely no lack of willingness there for the Governor."

"The man is over seventy!" the gardener reminded him.

"And with the glands of a Killarney goat!"

"You're pulling my leg."

"That I am not," the chauffeur reassured his older companion. "Sure, and aren't I the one takes him to and from his—umm, trysts, is it?—with ladies so young and toothsome as to have their pick of many a young man just as wealthy as the Governor."

"'Trysts,' you say?"

"Or 'assignations,' is it?" The chauffeur's nod was both confirmation and admiration."

"Assignations," the gardener repeated with awe as he watched the Governor clear the last rise and round the corner of the white Ossining marble facade. Then he vanished from sight in the direction of the large, octagonal turret at the north end of the forty-two-room mansion. "At his age!"

Matthew Adams Stockwell had not been chief executive of New York State for many years, but everyone, even members of his immediate family, still addressed him by the courtesy title Governor. Though he recognized it as a conceit, it gave him pleasure. There would have been even more pleasure if it had been "Mr. President." But that was a long-ago disappointment—yesteryear's cold ashes, albeit still smoldering in his heart.

It was a heart that did not reveal itself easily to the members of the Governor's large family. The one exception was his granddaughter Holly. Now, as he rounded the corner and trudged the length of the west wing of the mansion, she viewed his progress from her vantage point in the north tower studio. Intense blue eyes peering over the rim of her reading glasses, she smiled at his purposeful stride.

Grandpa always looks like he's bound for some important meeting, Holly thought, even when he's heading no place in particular. His age was starting to show, she mused, but it was no match for his stubbornness. Her sigh was one of recognition, of identification.

That stubbornness! It's in the genes. We all have it. It's what makes us tough, and vulnerable. It was a hindrance —that stubbornness—in the Governor's relations with his family, his two wives, his children and grandchildren— except for Holly. She was grateful for this distinction, and, even now, disconcerted by it. He'd always acted differently toward her; Holly had always been special to him. It was as if, somehow, by making herself set aside his stubbornness, he might succeed in making at least this one family relationship genuine. Or perhaps he thought his tender, truly loving treatment of Holly would somehow make up for the turmoil that had marked his relationship with her long-dead mother—his daughter.

Holly sighed. Poor Grandpa. It wasn't possible, of course. And yet because he'd tried, Holly had grown to adulthood feeling loved as few children do.

Her grandfather's love had made her a warm and caring adult—vulnerable herself, as recent events had shown, but nevertheless truly sensitive. She'd grown from a straightforward child into a woman who was not devious, nor even manipulative. Even now, grown-up and with a child of her own, there was a certain ingenuousness about Holly that sometimes led people to regard her with undeserved skepticism. Grandpa's love had not allowed for fear, and so, being fearless, Holly had been open; and being open, she had inevitably learned the hard way that

3

there were things that passed for love that were not really loving at all. She had been hurt, and even now was... well, healing, she hoped.

But though Holly had not become devious or cynical, experience had taught her not to wear her artlessness on her sleeve. Lately she'd started using her sharp intelligence—cultivating a quick, sometimes ironic wit—to express her personality.

She was changing. As always happens, there was a lag among those around her in catching up with the changes. This was particularly true with the Governor, with whom Holly shared love, but—at least lately—not closeness. They had fallen into a bantering relationship, the tone of which expressed what they felt for each other while allowing them the comfort of staying on the surface.

This was probably just as well as far as Holly was concerned. One of the changes she'd deliberately fostered was a judgmental quality, a self-protective device she felt necessary to her emotional survival. She recognized, with some sadness, that it was a barrier to being loving and open, that it might push some people away. But she needed it. Holly measured people more strictly now; the results were often disillusioning. Unhappily, such was the case with the Governor.

And yet... and yet... Holly Stockwell loved her grandfather very much.

His granddaughter lost sight of the Governor as he entered the mansion by the French doors at the base of the octagonal turret. The velvet draperies were open, the library bathed in early afternoon sunlight dancing with dust motes. The room rose two stories to a trompe l'oeil ceiling designed to give the impression of a dome's interior. Remarkably, the ceiling was quite flat, set at right angles to the oiled and aged Tamarack pine-paneled walls.

Slowly, but with his customary determination, the Governor mounted a circular mahogany staircase which had once adorned the inside of a lighthouse off a Scottish peninsula. Emerging on the second floor, which actually corresponded to the third floor of the main house of Riverview, he heaved a sigh of relief at his escape from the trompe l'oeil optical illusion. The Governor disliked being

4

deceived. He believed that architecture, furniture, and people should always be what they appeared to be. He clung to that belief even though he'd been fooled many times, particularly when the people were women.

Being fooled had not, however, disillusioned the Governor with women. He genuinely liked them, and in a way uncommon among most men of his generation. It wasn't that he didn't share—and even far exceed—the carnality of his masculine peers, but that his feeling for women had another dimension, one of genuine interest and concern. While this was not calculated, it had gotten him sixty-one percent of the women's vote the first time he ran for governor, and sixty-nine percent the second time. And if later the woman's vote had perhaps also denied him the presidency, well, that was politics.

Entering the airy, eight-sided studio at the top of the circular staircase, the Governor saw Holly curled up on an upholstered Duncan Phyfe Directoire bench, sitting sidewise to an antique Shaker table on which various papers had been carefully arranged. There was an odd rightness to the stylistic contrast between table and bench, he thought, a tribute to the long-dead artist—Holly's mother —who had selected them.

Earlier, when her grandfather had moved out of sight, Holly had gone back to her manuscript. Now, her glasses halfway down the bridge of her nose, her golden head bent over what she was reading so intently, she was unaware of his presence.

The intensity of her concentration gave the Governor pause. That ability to focus on one subject and shut out distractions was a quality common to their blood. A real Stockwell, he thought.

Holly had resumed using her maiden name almost a year ago, when she left her husband and returned to Riverview with her three-year-old son Nicholas. "Won't the boy be confused by having a different name from his mother?" Holly's grandmother had asked, and Holly had reassured her that she would explain it to the boy without causing him any trauma.

The Governor thought that Mary, his ex-wife, had a point. Still, he was secretly pleased to have Holly drop

5

Millwood and revert to the family name. It seemed to symbolize her special place in his heart.

Now she raised her eyes from the papers in her lap and gazed out the bay window at the Hudson. As far as she could see, the woodlands and the riverbank were part of the Riverview estate. Indeed, it continued far beyond the horizon, more than three thousand acres of prime, fertile Hudson Valley farmland and forest. And most of it, she thought to herself as her blue eyes fondled the view, is the same now as it was in pre-Colonial times. There was something very reassuring in that, and Holly's sigh reflected her feeling.

The sigh was misinterpreted, however, by the Governor. "Things can't be that bad," he said, still standing at the stairway landing behind her.

Holly turned with a start. "Grandpa." She smiled, pleased to see him. "I was watching you come up the path, but I didn't know you were coming to visit me. And then I didn't hear you come up."

"The deafness of brooding."

"I wasn't brooding. I was reflecting. Thinking back on the history of Riverview. What made you think I was brooding?"

"A sunny day, a world full of handsome young bucks, and my beautiful granddaughter shuts herself up in this mausoleum. If you're not brooding, why aren't you out having fun at some disco in the city?"

"In the middle of the day?"

"Irrelevant. You're young and you exude hormones." The Governor leered suggestively. "Why aren't you out exercising them?"

"In the first place, Grandpa, hormones are not what you exercise. In the second place, I really am enjoying myself right here, soaking up the history of Riverview. And in the third place, *I* am not the grandchild who is going to carry on the libertine legend you've established. Don't confuse me with my cousin Michael."

"Can't depend on your cousin. He's—what's the modern phrase?—cleaning up his act. Says he wants to go into politics."

"Well, going into politics never cleaned up your act, Grandpa."

"The younger generation! No respect."

"I respect you, Grandpa. And I love you, too. She stood up and reclined toward him, kissing his craggy cheek. But I do see you clearly," she added. "Right through the charisma that seems to blind everybody else."

"Ah." The Governor was pleased. "You think I have charisma?"

"Oh, yes."

"Like Franklin? FDR, I mean."

"I suppose."

"And like Johnny Kennedy?"

"Mmm."

"Then tell me, Holly, how come they got to be president and I didn't?"

"Maybe because they didn't go around flaunting their affairs, Grandpa."

"Ha! Everybody in Washington except Eleanor knew about Franklin and Lucy. And the round heels wore out the White House carpets when Johnny Kennedy was in residence there. No, that's not it."

"Then what was it, Grandpa?"

"They were Democrats." The Governor winked. "The people expect debauchery and war from the Democrats."

"And what do they expect from the Republicans?"

"Unemployment and Depression, of course. And like the Democrats, we rarely disappoint them."

"Is that the way politics really is, Grandpa?" Holly knew his cynicism was only part of the banter, but she sensed that at heart he believed what he was saying.

"Oh, yes."

"How can you stand to have spent your whole life involved in it, then?"

"I loved every minute of it, Holly," the Governor told her truthfully.

"And you wouldn't live your life differently?" Holly blushed suddenly, realizing what an impertinence, even an insult, the question was.

The Governor, however, did not take it that way. "I didn't say that," he told her. "If I had it to do over, I'd do a lot of things differently. For one thing, I'd be a Democrat."

"A Democrat? Why?"

"They get elected. Also, they have more fun." The Governor thought a moment. "Or I'd stay a Republican, and instead of starting out as a businessman and newspaper publisher, I'd head for Hollywood and become an actor."

"Then you really think Reagan will win the presidency this time around?"

"Oh, yes. He has one unbeatable asset."

"Nancy," guessed Holly.

"No. I'm not sure Nancy is an asset at all."

"What, then?"

"Why, Jimmy Carter, of course. If I'd had an asset like that, even I could have been president—despite everything."

"Do you really regret it so much?"

"Not at all." The Governor was sarcastic. "I could not have undertaken the duties of office without the help and support of the women I loved."

"If you loved her so much, Grandpa, then why—" Holly broke off the sentence and bit her lip.

The Governor looked at her until she lowered her eyes. Then it was his turn to sigh. There were some gaps he could not seem to bridge with anybody, not even Holly.

What was it, he wondered, that made the young so prissily moralistic toward their elders? They applied standards they would never inflict on themselves, and it seemed they would approve the harshest punishment for their sinning seniors.

Or was it not her youth so much as her femaleness that made his darling Holly look away from him in this condemnatory fashion? Did women truly look at weaknesses of the flesh differently than men? he wondered. More puritanically? In his youth, along with his male peers, he had certainly believed that. But today? When women seemed as liberated sexually as men? Shouldn't that liberation have softened their judgments?

Perhaps it had, he thought. Perhaps Holly was out of sync with her sex and her generation. But there was little comfort in that. He truly loved Holly and he worried about her. In a few weeks she would be thirty years old— and she was turning herself into a recluse.

When she'd returned from England, it seemed she went out of her way to avoid people, particularly those her own age, like her cousins and their friends. The only people she appeared at ease with were the Governor and his ex-wife, Mary. Holly hadn't been comfortable with his present wife, Buffy, although Buffy was neither as young as her cousins nor as old as the Governor and Mary.

Holly had doted on Nicholas, which the Governor and Mary agreed could not be good for the child. He and Mary not only discussed such matters, but the Governor sometimes thought there were more areas of agreement between them than between him and Buffy. His divorce from Mary was far in the past, the scars faded, and they had rediscovered a fact key to their relationship from its inception—they liked each other. The Governor did not always like Buffy.

But even Mary had been unable to pry out of Holly what went wrong with her marriage to Christopher. It had lasted four years, and now Holly would only say that it was over. "Do you think she's still carrying a torch for him?" the Governor had asked Mary. But Mary didn't know, and didn't want to speculate.

The Governor thought if that was the problem the solution might lie with Holly's dating other men. The Governor had long ago come around to the view that fillies were as entitled to oats as stallions. He only regretted that he hadn't realized this when his daughter Terry, Holly's mother, was alive. If he had, things might have ended very differently between him and his favorite child.

Mary appraised their granddaughter's situation more sensitively and to a certain degree—accurately. "The thing about Holly is that she really is as fragile as she looks," she told her ex-husband, unaware of Holly's recent efforts to alter that picture.

At first the Governor had wondered if that really could be true. There was indeed an unusually fragile quality to his favorite granddaughter's appearance. She was tall and slender, what used to be called willowy, and though she had not been an unhappy child, he recalled how she could be emotionally bent out of shape from her earliest years when her feelings were touched. As easily as a willow in the wind, he thought, picturing her: tall, slender, her golden hair worn short now, the consistency of fine silk; her wrists and ankles unusually delicate; her movements quick, a little nervous, calling attention to the romantic

9

delicacy of her beauty. Her translucent pink-pearl complexion and fine clear, blue eyes heightened Holly's aura of vulnerability.

More recently the Governor had witnessed Holly guarding this vulnerability with an intellectual shield from behind which she fired her bantering arrows. With her grandmother, Holly might let down her guard but with everyone else, including him, he realized painfully, she acted differently. He worried about the changes he saw in Holly since the breakup of her marriage. A woman, a person, could not live happily by brains and wit alone. Equal, if not more important, parts of life were the emotions and the libido.

Usually he agreed with Mary's perceptions and judgments, including her recognition of Holly's vulnerability. But, though he rarely disagreed with Mary's handling of their grandchild's situation, in the matter of Mary's solution to the problem, he did. To counteract the emptiness of Holly's existence after she returned from England, Mary had pushed her granddaughter into researching and writing a history of the Hudson River Valley. On the surface, the project made a great deal of sense. The Governor saw that. Holly had majored in American History at Bryn Mawr and had been fascinated by the history of the Hudson River Valley since she was a little girl. During her marriage in England she'd made many trips to the British Museum to ferret out the backgrounds of the original settlers. She had traveled to Amsterdam to study the records of the Dutch East India Company.

Now Mary offered Holly access to the Charles Stockwell Memorial Foundation, the private family archives dating back to pre-Revolutionary times. Many of these documents had never been viewed by a historical scholar before, and Mary had judged rightly that Holly would not be able to resist the opportunity.

"She'll have to visit the Foundation in Manhattan," she told the Governor, "and if nothing else, that will get her away from Riverview and out with other people."

But the Governor had his doubts. He didn't think that by burying herself in the past Holly would open up to life. He didn't believe it would heal the wound her marriage had obviously left—whatever the cause of that wound was.

It was the Governor's view that behind Holly's new-found irony and wit, she was still the insecure, easily hurt child she had always been. It tore at his heart. "She's beautiful and she's bright," the Governor had said to Mary recently. "So why is she so screwed up?"

Mary had winced at his use of modern slang. She'd never been able to get used to the liberation of language that had occurred over her lifetime. Nevertheless, she answered her ex-husband calmly enough.

"Perhaps," she reminded the Governor, "it is because Holly is the only one of our grandchildren who was born out of wedlock."

2

AFTER HER GRANDFATHER left, Holly was angry with herself. "Damn!" The word exploded from her lips. Why had she tried to rub his nose in it like that? What went on between him and his wife Buffy, him and other women, was his business. He wasn't a young man; he was entitled to his mistakes, his pleasures, even his indiscretions. How much longer did he have, after all?

There was no need for her to have zinged him like that, particularly when she knew how much he loved her, and knew how love is always what makes you most vulnerable. But then, of course, Holly thought with a sigh, it wasn't her grandfather she'd been zinging at all. It was Christopher, her ex-husband.

Tears sprang to Holly's eyes with that realization. She shook her head angrily to rid herself of them. "Enough of that!" she lectured herself. "I won't think about it!" She dried her eyes, pushed her glasses firmly back up the bridge of her nose, and made herself focus on the manuscript in her lap.

It was a remarkable document, painstakingly written in longhand over a period of years in the early and mid-1830s. Time had sucked the moisture from the pages, and so they were brittle and had to be handled very carefully. Some of the edges were charred, evidence of the fire that had almost destroyed the manuscript in 1838, and had destroyed the original manor house. The author of the manuscript, George Cortlandt Stockwell, had lost his life rescuing it from the flames. For more than a hundred years it was assumed that it had been destroyed in the fire, but now, through a series of unusual circumstances, it had found its way into the family archives. Charles Stockwell, the younger brother of George and grandfather of the Governor, had painstakingly preserved and collected all the historical documents he could find after his ancestral home had been gutted.

At first reading, the manuscript appeared to be nothing more than a satirical novel written by a young man who obviously felt bitter toward the world around him and the circumstances that had formed it. But Holly had quickly realized from her other researches into the Hudson River Valley and the Stockwell family that the ironic novel was really a damning indictment by George Stockwell of both his forebears and his immediate family. Indeed, other records corroborated some of the most shocking revelations in George's family "novel."

"You'll line your forehead squinting like that."

Holly looked up from the ancient manuscript and focused on Buffy Stockwell, emerging from the stairwell. She didn't welcome the interruption and barely managed a smile to hide her annoyance. "A lined forehead shows character," she replied lightly.

"Oh, yes. Stockwells are big on character. Responsibility. Integrity. Philanthropy. All the virtues. Except, of course, fidelity. Which reminds me, I thought I saw my husband heading up here."

"Grandpa was here. He left."

"He didn't happen to say where he was going, did he?"

"No."

"Bound for parts unknown then." Buffy smiled unpleasantly. "Female parts, I've no doubt."

Holly had nothing to say to that, and so she regarded her grandfather's wife silently. In her late forties, Buffy was still a remarkably attractive woman. She was beautiful, and she was vivacious, and she was sexy. And when she behaved the way she was behaving now, Holly didn't much like her.

Buffy—really Brenda Stockwell, née Decatur—was the kind of woman that time seems to polish rather than erode. Her complexion, although tawnier, was as smooth as Holly's own. Her hair, a blue-black glory of thick curls, would have seemed foolishly girlish on most women her age, but it was an appropriate crown to Buffy's classical visage. She was as tall as Holly, but where Holly's height sometimes appeared tenuous, Buffy's was never anything but regal. And unlike Holly's slender figure, Buffy was voluptuous: full-bosomed, with generous hips and a firm, rounded derriere. Her sensuality was a magnet to men that frequently infuriated women.

Like Holly, however, she had wit. But it could be tipped with a venom that would always be foreign to Holly's character. When Buffy was younger, she'd perceived that the deck was stacked in favor of men and that any woman who wanted her fair share of life's kitty had best have a card or two up her sleeve. She had never been a part of the feminist movement, and never would be, but her life would follow a path of personal affirmative action aimed at redressing the gender balance in her favor. And if sex was her most effective weapon in this ongoing campaign, that did not keep it from being a source of emotional pleasure and physical satisfaction as well.

"I hope I'm not intruding." Now Buffy read Holly's silence correctly and defused her attitude by naming it.

"Not at all."

"This place is really charming." Buffy looked around her curiously, noting the original paintings on the walls, registering that they were second-rate, wincing inwardly at what she considered to be the decidedly unfeminine absence of frills in the blinds and shutters, rather than curtains or drapes, and the straw scatter rugs on the polished hardwood floor, rather than the patterned Middle

Eastern carpets with which she might have livened up the area. There was too little furniture, and what there was added up to an impossible mishmash of styles. "Did you do it all yourself?" she asked.

'No, very little, really," Holly replied. "It was my mother's studio. Except for the bookcases and filing cabinets, it's pretty much the way it was when she was alive."

"But she's been dead twenty years or more."

"That's right."

"I could never do that." Buffy laughed. "If I don't redecorate at least every two years, I break out in hives."

"I can't believe you haven't been up here before," Holly remarked.

"Oh, I suppose I have. Not often, though. What reason would I have to drag myself up those stairs, after all?" As if to remove the sting from past disinterest, Buffy now strolled around the studio, looking at the paintings on the walls. "I knew your mother was an artist, of course," she said, "but, you know, I don't think I've ever really looked at her paintings before. Her work is really quite abstract, isn't it?"

"Yes."

"It reminds me of Franz Klein and Willem de Kooning." Actually, Buffy detested both artists. To her, art was supposed to be enjoyed, and their demands on her eyes constituted forced labor.

"Well, Mama was contemporary with them."

"Ah, yes." Buffy nodded. "The New York School. I can see that quite clearly."

The hell you can! Holly thought to herself behind her fixed smile. You're not really looking at anything past the mascara on the tips of your eyelashes. Is it really possible, she wondered, not for the first time, that Grandpa was ever fooled by Buffy? Why, Mae West in those old movies was more subtle.

You're missing something, she told herself, realizing she was blessed—cursed, she often thought—with an analytical mind. A man like Grandpa did not sacrifice the presidency of the United States because a woman wiggled her hips a certain way and asked him to come up and see her sometime. There had to be more to it than that, and there had to be more to Buffy than she was willing to see.

14

Still, it was hard for Holly to believe it. Grandpa might joke now, but not since the Duke of Windsor abdicated to marry Wally Simpson had a man of such prominence and potential power turned his back on the ultimate opportunity because of his love for a woman.

That's exactly what the Governor had done back in 1964. Kennedy was dead. In the emotional wake of his assassination, Johnson's popularity had grown. But within the Democratic Party there was still real resistance to committing funds and manpower to his reelection every place but the South and Southwest.

The Republican Party—the Governor's Party—was a different story. Nixon was belly-up in the water, having lost his race for governor of California only two years after his defeat by JFK. Rockefeller was still a dark horse, eclipsed even in his home state of New York by the Governor. Goldwater had solid support on the conservative right but was considered much too far out for rank-and-file Republicans to grant him the nomination. And Romney of Michigan was still trying to get his foot out of his mouth after a trip to Vietnam that had prompted him to the one fatal mistake no politician could ever make—telling the truth. The Grand Old Party needed a moderate and a vote-getter, someone with the charisma to turn Johnson's homespun klutziness against him in the eyes of the voters.

In the Republican back rooms there was solid agreement. Center-of-the-road Governor Matthew Adams Stockwell of New York—like FDR, a patrician with the common touch; too wealthy to be open to the patronage charges, which would always haunt Johnson; proven appeal to women voters; a record not too hard on labor, and a shirt-sleeve persona that communicated directly to working men—he had it all, not to mention the personal fortune to pick up any campaign deficits that might accrue. Why, if the Party played its cards right, Stockwell was a shoo-in.

And then along came Buffy.

She had been Mrs. Nelson Cabot then, wife of the president of a Wall Street investment house in which the Stockwell family held a large but not majority interest. Her husband had gone to Harvard with James Stockwell, the Governor's eldest son.

The two families were friendly, and socialized together. Buffy Cabot was one of the Hudson River Valley's most renowned hostesses. An invitation to one of her parties, on occasion a tad wild for the Tory Catskill region, was considered a mark of acceptance into society among the wealthier young marrieds. Most of the older Hudson aristocrats frowned on such goings-on, but Mary Linstone Stockwell, the Governor's wife, always defended her son's friends and told her peers not to be such old fogies.

"And Brenda Cabot is a genuine beauty," Mary would say. "Beauty and youth have prerogatives. You can't apply the same standards to someone like her as to those of us whose greatest pleasures are in the past."

Mary never suspected that her husband might be among the prerogatives Buffy took unto herself. She was as surprised as the rest of the world when Nelson Cabot called a news conference in his Wall Street office shortly after Governor Stockwell's victory in the New Hampshire primaries, announcing that he was suing his wife for divorce on grounds of adultery and naming the Governor of the State of New York as corespondent.

Events then moved with dizzying swiftness. The Governor, always pragmatic, refused to deny anything, and Buffy was equally brazen. Asked about the discrepancy in their ages, she replied that the Governor was more of a man than her husband—twenty-two years younger—would ever hope to be. Nelson Cabot, perhaps as a consequence, instructed his lawyers to deny Buffy any financial settlement at all.

Then the Governor announced that he was divorcing his wife, and that when they were both free, he and Buffy would marry. The Republican Party then announced that Matthew Adams Stockwell had never really been a serious contender for the presidential nomination, and that Barry Goldwater was not nearly the extremist the liberal, left-leaning press had labeled him. Mary Linstone Stockwell announced that she was going on a round-the-world cruise and would not return until after her divorce from the Governor was final.

16

Both divorces were quickly finalized. The Governor and Buffy were immediately married in a small and intimate ceremony at Riverview, which was nevertheless splashed all over the front pages of every newspaper in the country.

The Republicans nominated Barry Goldwater for President. He never had a chance. Vowing never to send American boys to fight in an Asian war, Lyndon Baines Johnson won reelection in a landslide.

Ah, but that's so unfair, Holly thought to herself now as her unwanted visitor turned away from her mother's paintings. "I really have to be going." Buffy walked toward the circular staircase. "I have an appointment." Though relieved that Buffy would depart, Holly still followed her train of thought. Yes, even if Buffy did snare Grandpa with vampish wiles, it's not fair.

You really can't blame Vietnam on Buffy.

3

A LITTLE MORE than an hour later Buffy walked through the lobby of New York's Plaza Hotel. Heads turned. Men noted the voluptuous body, the calculated rhythm of her hips, the teasing eyes that didn't quite avoid admiring gazes. Knowledgeable women identified her black-and-white de la Renta suit and her Molly Parnis hat.

One pair of eyes that noticed her was more curious and amused than impressed. They belonged to Patrice O'Keefe, another granddaughter of the Governor and his first wife, Mary. Patrice was on her way to the Plaza's Palm Court for a business meeting when she saw her step-grandmother enter an elevator. Grandpa's goose about to enjoy gander sauce, she thought to herself, then pushed Buffy from her mind as she entered the Palm Court.

Although she was a diminutive young woman, unobtrusive in a custom-made light brown tweed business suit that contrasted with her red-brown hair and cinnamon eyes, Patrice was spotted by the headwaiter right away. He smiled and changed direction in order to greet her and escort her to her table. "How nice to see you, Ms. O'Keefe."

She returned his greeting and smiled to herself. His "Ms." salutation demonstrated that the Plaza was not only careful about greetings, but au courant as well. Patrice liked that. It set her apart from all the Westchester housewives taking tea at the Palm Court after shopping at Bergdorf's.

She felt their eyes on her. Her monogrammed briefcase and the tailored suit said she was a business woman. The frilly bow of her blouse, hanging outside her jacket, testified that she had not sacrificed femininity to her career.

Patrice's frilly bows were a family joke. Virtually every blouse she owned had one. It was her taste, not deliberately thought out, but expressive of a softness in her personality which she otherwise kept in the background.

"Beaus, not bows," the Governor had once teased her. "That's what you want, Patrice. Learn to spell. B-E-A-U-S. Those creatures from which women are supposed to select their husbands."

"I had a husband," Patrice reminded him curtly. "He was very nice, too. But I divorced him, and I'm not looking for another, thank you very much."

She hadn't smiled. She didn't like being teased by her grandfather. Indeed, she didn't like the Governor at all.

Patrice smiled to herself as the headwaiter held the chair for her. She was a few minutes early, and her thoughts wandered idly over a wide range of topics. Just as she was wondering once again what mischief had brought the glamorous Buffy to the Plaza, she spied the man she was to meet.

Buffy hadn't noticed Patrice. Her mind was on Suite 514 of the Plaza, and she was already anticipating the greeting she would receive from the man waiting for her there.

His name was Jack Houston, and though seventeen years younger than her, he was Buffy's lover. He was very much a man, not a boy, but in Buffy's presence he had no more control than an adolescent in the backseat of his father's car. This was obvious in his greeting.

Kicking the door closed behind her with his foot, Jack embraced Buffy and his lips sought hers with an eagerness no man could have feigned. His tanned, muscular arms and body became a tactile sensor as he clutched Buffy to him. Opening buttons, undoing clasps, his hands found her flesh and moved over its swellings and roundnesses without restraint. His impatient tumescence made itself known to her.

"Well, hello to you, too, darling," Buffy said breathlessly when the kiss was over.

"I want you." Jack was direct. "I want you now."

"Please may I take my clothes off first? I don't want to leave here looking like I'd been run through a mangle."

"I'll give you sixty seconds."

"Really, darling—"

"One ... two ... three ..."

"Jack, you are such a boy!" But Buffy's heart was pounding wildly. She was not in love with Jack Houston. She did not fool herself about that. But he was young. He was strong. He was eager. He was crazy about her. And he had a natural knack for lovemaking—the sort of knack that's in the genes and can't really ever be learned. Indeed, he was the most magnificent lover Buffy had ever known—except for one.

Thoughts of that one flashed through her mind now as she lay back naked on the soft king-size bed and held up her arms. Matthew, too, had once fallen on her with just such throbbing, rigid passion. The difference had been that she was madly in love with him back then. It was a significant difference. They had been equals, wild and uncaring, adulterers both, heedless of scandal, only their moments of lovemaking of any real importance to them.

Ah, well, that was all in the past, she thought. Matthew didn't come to her that way anymore, nor she to him. It hadn't been like that between them for a long, long time. Indeed, Buffy sometimes reflected, marriage—the connubial rights it conferred, the easy accessibility—had sapped the passion from the most delicious of all affairs.

Youth was a substitute. Not an admirable viewpoint for

a woman her age, but a true one. Jack Houston's youth rubbed off on her when they made love. His obviously genuine passion for her ignited a lust that was loveless, but deeply satisfying all the same. And now that satisfaction was approaching.

"Oh, yes!" Buffy's eyes were randy pools drawing him into their depths. "Yes! Yes! Yes"

"Now?" He was all heat and rippling muscles and adoration.

"Yes, now."

As their bodies locked in a sort of timeless glory, a melting sensation flooded up from her depths to Buffy's large, still firm breasts. Her long lashes fluttered and her eyes went out of focus. Dimly she felt him make the act complete as her orgasm drew his tribute from him.

Later, as she was getting dressed, Jack asked the question he so frequently asked, the question that was both flattering and annoying: "Why don't you divorce him and marry me?"

"You could never afford me, darling."

"I'm not a poor man."

"You're not a Stockwell either. You don't have that kind of money."

"But I'm young, Buffy. I have the chance to make that kind of money in front of me. Why not gamble?"

"Ah, you shouldn't tempt a poor old lady this way, Jack."

"You're not old. But he is. He's really old."

"I suppose he is." But Buffy didn't really think of her husband that way. Despite the many bones she had to pick with him, she knew Matthew would never seem old to her.

"He was old when you married him."

"Not really. The difference in our ages is little more than the difference between you and me."

"I'll still never understand how you could be attracted to him." Jack was sullen, but watchful, a jungle animal denied its prey but not resigned.

"Power, I suppose," Buffy told him, although she knew that while this was true, there was a lot more to it.

"Matthew had great power back then and the potential for more. That is a real aphrodisiac, believe me."

"To women, you mean?"

"To men and women. Why do you think Catherine the Great and Marie Antoinette and Eleanor of Aquitaine attracted so many lovers? Power has the same effect on men as on women. It arouses desire."

"All right, then. So you were attracted to him because he had power, and so you married him. That's no reason not to leave him now. He doesn't have power anymore."

"Oh, no." Buffy laughed. "You really are innocent about some things, Jack. You don't understand at all. Stockwell power is real power. It doesn't have to be seen. It doesn't even have to be exercised. It just has to be there. Governors, presidents—they come and go. But real power, that's a constant. That's the kind of power Matthew has, and he'll have it till the day he dies."

"But it's not an aphrodisiac to you anymore."

"Of course not." Buffy wondered if she was lying. She wasn't sure. "But it is to other women. Young women. Beautiful women. It's not money that attracts them to my husband, and it's not so much that he's famous either. It's that power of his."

"Oh, come on. He just buys sex."

"Never," Buffy told him positively. "Matthew Adams Stockwell never had to pay a woman to make love to him in his life."

"A man his age?"

"It makes no difference. Power is ageless. And it is an aphrodisiac. It really is."

And that sonofabitch husband of mine, Buffy thought to herself, but did not say aloud, uses it to the hilt.

"Tea! Goddammit, Patrice, tea!"

Patrice O'Keefe smiled good-naturedly at Craig Burrows across their corner table. "Do stop complaining, Craig," she told him, "and try one of these scones. They're delicious with the raspberry jam."

"Why can't we have a drink?" Craig's too spanky-clean handsome face slipped into fleshiness with his scowl.

"Because this is a business meeting. I never mix business and drinking."

Business meetings are supposed to be lunch or cocktails, not tea. Who the hell ever heard of talking business over tea, for God's sake?"

"I was busy for lunch, and I'm busy for cocktails. I had to squeeze you in. Tea worked out just right."

"Well, I feel like I'm trapped in some goddamn Dickens novel."

"I'm sorry, Craig. Could we just get down to business now?" Patrice smoothed her shoulder-length wavy, chestnut hair, and put on her tortoiseshell glasses. They turned her usually soft brown eyes cool and professional. Her hand swiftly tucked the frilly bow inside the tweed jacket. She was almost consciously shifting gears, and it showed in the way her posture changed. Even seated, as she rummaged in her briefcase and began spreading papers out on the small table, her petite body seemed to take on stature.

Her ex-husband, Miles O'Keefe, whom she had married the summer she graduated from Holyoke and divorced less than a year later, had just met her at an advertising convention. He'd remarked that she had grown at least three inches since being promoted to senior account executive of Bartleby & Hatch, the Fortune 500 ad agency that employed her. "So now I come up to your chin," Patrice had replied. Her tininess in contrast to his lankiness had become a sexual joke with them all through their short-lived marriage. Still, Patrice thought, there was something to what Miles had said: Business success made her feel taller.

Sometimes, however, it got in the way of the other parts of her life. Like right now with Craig Burrows, for instance. They were meeting on business, but Craig was also her sometime lover, and cool as their affair was, he wasn't used to seeing Patrice in her advertising-executive role. He was obviously having trouble adjusting to it.

"All right," he said, making an effort to banish the stiffness from his voice. "Business now, pleasure later."

"I'm busy later. Dinner with my father. I'm sorry, Craig." He's so transparent, Patrice thought to herself as he absorbed the rejection. He really resents the fact that a woman he's been sleeping with is dealing with him as a business equal.

"I guess friends shouldn't do business with each other," Craig said, unable to restrain himself.

"You mean lovers."

"All right, lovers, then."

"One thing has nothing to do with the other." Patrice patted his hand across the table. "Now, about this stockholders' report and investment prospectus your bank wants us to design for them . . ."

As they started to discuss the details, Patrice banished all thoughts of Craig as a lover from her mind. She plunged into the details, making notes as the discussion progressed. Without realizing it, her voice turned impersonal, her incisive questions divorced her from their intimate relationship. She was only interested in the account of the investment bank he headed and how best to achieve her advertising and public relations objectives.

Forty-five minutes passed in this fashion. Finally Patrice looked up from her notes, removed her glasses, and smiled at Craig. "Well," she said, "I think that covers everything."

"Does it?" Craig was sarcastic.

Patrice was saved from having to make a response by a man brushing her elbow as he passed their table and knocking some of her papers to the floor.

"Oops, sorry." The man, who had a deep tan and outdoorsy crinkles around intense blue eyes, bent to retrieve the papers. He moved gracefully for his size, like an athlete whose sinews had received ballet training. As he handed the papers to Patrice, their eyes met. Without thinking, her hand flicked the bow to the outside of her jacket.

"Jack." Craig recognized the man. "Jack Houston." He stood up to shake hands. "It has been a long time."

"Well, hello, Craig." Houston laughed a toothpaste-ad laugh that displayed very even, very white teeth. "Having tea?" His blue eyes danced over the small Spode cups and diminutive, crustless cucumber sandwiches on the table.

"Unwillingly, I assure you." Craig scowled.

"Too bad. The Plaza serves the best tea this side of Piccadilly. But I forgot—you're a drinking man, aren't you?" Jack Houston smiled conspiratorially at Patrice.

Remembering his manners, Craig introduced them. "The last time I saw Jack," he told Patrice, "I was standing in the middle of the African veldt with a bush leopard charging at me, and he was shooting over my shoulder. Saved my life, I think."

"Whatever were you doing there?" Patrice couldn't for the life of her picture calm, cool, urban Craig doing anything so adventurous as hunting dangerous animals in Africa.

"A client." Craig laughed ruefully. "The only way he'd talk business with me in time for it to mean anything was if I'd go on this goddamn safari with him—my first and my last, I assure you."

"And you?" Patrice looked up at Jack Houston and was glad she'd taken off her glasses, glad her face was no longer in its harsher professional mode. "Were you on safari for business, too?"

"Oh, yes." His blue hunter's eyes smiled down at her. "My business was the safari. I organized it. I had to shoot that leopard because it would have been very bad for business if it had eaten old Craig here."

"Saved by the free market ethic. Lucky Craig." But Patrice was looking back into Houston's intriguing eyes.

"What are you doing here, Jack?" Craig asked him.

"Just passing through."

"Just passing through life? Or just passing through the Palm Court at the Plaza?" Patrice asked him.

Patrice rarely flirted. She couldn't remember having done so since her college days. But she was flirting now.

"Microcosm, macrocosm." Jack Houston replied, and shrugged. "Both, I guess. But I really do have to be going now."

Watching him leave, Patrice acknowledged a little shiver. She did not usually have visceral reactions to men, but she certainly had one to Jack Houston, brief as the encounter had been. She hoped they would meet again, but it seemed unlikely.

After all, except for Craig, they didn't know anybody in common.

24

4

PATRICE O'KEEFE HAD scuttled from the Plaza to the Algonquin for cocktails—another business meeting. Then she'd commandeered a cab and prayed it through traffic back to her spacious apartment on the Upper East Side. Moving quickly, she chopped up vegetables, cubed a steak, and stirred the combination into a pan on a slow flame. Korean, she decided, was how she'd define it if the question came up. While it was cooking she headed for the shower, shedding clothes as she walked through her bedroom, and counting to herself to be sure dinner didn't burn while she was under the spray.

She was dressed in a lavender silk blouse and slacks, her chestnut hair hidden by the towel drying it, when the buzzer sounded and the doorman announced her father from downstairs. The untied strings of the inevitable bow drooped down to define the cleft between her pert breasts. When she let him in the door, she was conscious of her dishabille and of his contrasting neatness, just as when she'd been a child. James Linstone Stockwell was the kind of man who never had a hair out of place, whose necktie was never a millimeter askew. Patrice's fingers raced to tie her bow.

James was as different from his father, the Governor, as two men could be. He had none of the easy ability to relate to people which was the Governor's stock-in-trade. He was neither charming nor graceful. He lacked the common touch. It was shyness that made him seem so aloof, but it was so ingrained by now that informality in anyone genuinely distressed him. It showed in his eyes as they passed over the towel around his daughter's head.

She read the look correctly. "Drying my hair. Just give me a minute." She ran into the bathroom and combed it out. "Fix yourself a drink, Daddy," she called over the noise of the hair dryer.

When she came out, her father was standing with a carefully measured scotch in his hands and looking at one of the many family portraits Patrice had arranged into a sort of picture wall. There was a pained expression on his face. Patrice was not surprised to see him studying the picture of her brother Matt.

"Now I can say hello properly, Daddy." She took the picture out of his hands, hung it back up on the wall, and kissed him on the lips.

James stiffened slightly, and did not quite return the kiss. Still, as he looked down at his daughter, he managed a smile that he meant to be warm. He had to look down because he was six-two to her five-four.

James Stockwell may not have had the qualities to make him a successful politician like his father, but he was nevertheless an imposing figure, handsome, and his body lean and in top condition from a daily game of tennis. With his steel-gray hair and wrinkle-free face, he was considered very attractive by women, although he was far too shy to ever acknowledge this to himself.

Patrice loved him completely. It had taken awhile, but now she saw through his sternness to the man behind it. He was a caring man, a loving man, and unfortunately, a man terrified of letting anybody know it. Once, as a child, Patrice had overheard her grandfather telling his second wife, Buffy, that "the trouble with my son James is he has no *joie de vivre*." Patrice had scurried to her youngest brother Michael's French nursemaid, and when told what it meant, had burst into tears. The fact that it was true didn't matter. She had never forgiven the Governor for talking about her father that way, and she'd never forgiven Buffy for laughing.

Still, Patrice had wondered why her father was so cold, so stiff. Unexpectedly, and not so very long ago, she'd learned the reason from her Grandma Mary. There was a real tragedy in her father's life, one that dated back to his childhood, and when his daughter had learned the details of it, she'd remembered her grandfather's remark about *joie de vivre* and been struck all over again, only this time harder, by its callousness.

26

That's when Patrice decided she really didn't like her grandfather very much. The Governor charmed everybody, but he didn't charm her. As far as she was concerned, if he could not have enough compassion for his eldest child to hold his tongue, then he would get no love from her. Patrice had gone out of her way to avoid the Governor ever since.

"How's business, Daddy?" Patrice asked James when they were seated at the dinner table. It was not a casual question. Patrice was genuinely interested. From her father she'd inherited her own fervor to succeed in the business world.

Quietly, with no fuss but with a great deal of expertise—and a mind that accepted the juggling of details as entertainment—James administered a dozen multinational corporations in which the Stockwell family held the majority of stock, as well as several smaller companies and diversified ventures in which their interest was considerable, if not controlling. His mind could shift from oil wells to railroads as agilely as a Grand Prix driver changing lanes. In the filing cabinet of his brain, the details of a newspaper chain were arranged as neatly as those of the trade-offs to be decided upon for the Stockwell-owned football franchise. Without blinking, his mind could summon up those personalities key to whatever venture he was considering.

Yes, when James Linstone Stockwell discussed business, he came alive. He was truly happy. And his daughter Patrice, whose business dealings were small potatoes compared to the vast empire her father presided over, was one of the few people genuinely interested enough to listen to what he had to say.

He was genuinely interested in her career as well, though he admitted to himself that he would have been happier if one of his sons—Matt or Michael—had taken an interest in business the way Patrice had. Yes, one of the boys could have taken over from him and run one of the twenty largest financial empires in the world. But Michael was leaning toward politics, following in his grandfather's footsteps and Matt...ah, Matt. He was a breeder of horses, which was all he wanted to be. As always, when he thought about it, James could not understand his unconventional second child.

Patrice was compensation. He listened carefully now as she described her business situation. "I'm one of the youngest senior account executives on the Street," she told him, taking for granted his knowing that the Street was Madison Avenue's Ad Row. "Being a woman didn't hurt. The last thing Bartleby-Hatch wanted was for some hip Ad Row feminist to accuse them of unequal promotions for women. So I really was in the right place at the right time."

"Don't sell yourself short. You've got a lot of talent. What I hear is that you've done a hell of a job for them. There's a lot of interest by the financial community now in Bartleby and Hatch. And the interest is because of what you've done with the investment banking accounts you've been handling."

"Well, I hope you're right. Just being a woman isn't going to get me up that next rung on the ladder."

"Which is?" her father asked.

"Vice president. Trumbull is retiring. Everybody moves up a notch. The trouble is, there's five of us scrambling for that particular notch."

"Well, you're still young, Patrice. Even if you don't get it, there'll be a next time."

"I haven't got time to wait, Daddy. I don't want to just be a vice president. I'm not shortsighted. I have my eye on other things."

"Such as?"

Patrice took a deep breath. "My own firm. A really major operation."

"Is there really room on the Street for another big firm?"

"No." Patrice was frank with her father. "There isn't. If there was, I'd have borrowed the money long ago and set myself up. But that's not the way it has to work. I have to get control of an existing firm if I'm going to get where I want to go."

"Bartleby and Hatch?"

"Maybe. Maybe not. But if I'm a VP with them, other outfits will take notice. Batton Barton, J. Walter, even

MCA. Sooner or later, if I'm any good, there will be an offer."

"And then what?"

"What?" Patrice leaned back and laughed. "Why, then I take over the industry, Daddy."

"You're serious." James saw through his daughter's laugh. "You really mean it. You really think it's possible."

"Sure. What do you think?" Do you think it's possible?"

"Oh, yes. You're my daughter." James smiled a thin-lipped but genuine smile. "If that's what you really want, you'll find a way to get it."

And she will, he was thinking. She really will. How much like me she is—her mind, the way she plans, her determination. God, how wonderful to have a daughter like Patrice! And immediately there came the other thought, the one that cast the familiar shadow over James Linstone Stockwell's face.

Why couldn't my son Matt be like this?

5

MATTHEW SYKES STOCKWELL, named after his grandfather, was out in the barn examining the colt's left rear hoof that night when he heard the sound. The colt had been running off stride, and Matt saw now that the problem was the shoe. It would have to be replaced.

The sound was a dull thump of collision. Something moving had come up against something stationary on the road in front of the ramshackle house. The house and barn both belonged to Matt, but the barn was in better condition because with Matt the comfort of the horses always came first. Neither, however, was in anything like the mint condition maintained by the groundskeepers and staff on the Riverview estate five miles west of Matt's horse-breeding farm.

The horse farm, inland from the river and taking up only five acres of undesirable hardscrabble land, was not part of Riverview. Matt had bought it with his own money, painstakingly saved for that purpose during his years in Canada. He had not touched his trust fund. He'd wanted to come back to where his roots were, to live near his family, but *near* did not mean living off them.

Now, responding to the sound, he strode quickly up to the road. He saw the car first, a five- or six-year-old Plymouth with its left front fender half wrapped around the giant bole of a hundred-year-old oak tree. Then he heard the girl, sitting on the grassy shoulder and reciting a stream of idiosyncratic profanity in alphabetical order. She was up to *gamahouche* and *harlotry* when she looked up and saw Matt standing over her.

"Are you all right?" he asked.

"My cohabitating ankle is broken and my oedipal car is wrapped around a tree. How could I be all right?"

"Let's see." Matt knelt down, pushed her jeans above her ankle and had a look at it. There was considerable swelling, but it didn't look broken. He manipulated it gently. "Only sprained, I think," he told her.

"Are you some kind of fellatio doctor or something?"

"No. But I doctor my horses sometimes, and I can tell a sprain from a break."

"Are you a veterinarian?"

"Not licensed. No."

"Oh, great. You're not a doctor. You're not even a vet. And you're diagnosing me. What kind of anal passage do you think I am? Why should I listen to you?"

"I don't mind being cursed at," Matt told her mildly. "But why so archaically?"

"I'm a student of linguistics. The terminology comes naturally to me."

"That," Matt told her, "I seriously doubt." He ran his fingers up and down from her shin to her toes.

"Feces!" She winced.

"Put your arm around my neck and let's see if we can get you on your feet." He circled her waist and drew her up easily. But when she was upright, the ankle buckled under her and he had to support her.

"Scatology!"

"Ice." Matt lifted her off the ground altogether and started back down the path.

30

"Where are we going?"

"My house. It's right over there. I want to get some ice on that ankle before it swells up any more than it has."

"Oh . . . thank you."

"It's nothing. Any old sphincter would do the same."

Inside the house Matt set her down on the sagging living room couch and put a frayed cushion under her foot. He went in the kitchen and wrapped ice cubes in a clean dish towel. Then he returned and packed the ankle.

In the light the girl looked young; college age, and probably just beginning at that. She wore faded blue jeans and a man's white shirt with the long tails hanging out. She was healthy looking, with a pronounced bosom that had bounced all the way to the house, and a compact body that wasn't plump, but solid, firm, and strong. Her hair, worn in a ponytail, was bright red, almost an orange color with gold highlights, and her face was alive with the kind of freckles that come from too much sun.

Returning his gaze frankly, she was more openly appraising. Her eyes recorded a man in his late twenties with long, very dark hair that looked like it had never seen a blow dryer and velvety brown eyes which were strangely tender and vulnerable. She had felt his strength when he carried her, and now she saw the long ropelike muscles of his arms ripple as he moved to readjust the homemade ice pack on her ankle. He was too thin, perhaps, but there was nothing weak about him. His face was handsome, she decided, and she liked his smile because it came so easily and because it was real and not just polite.

"I'm Kathleen O'Lunney," she offered.

"Matt Stockwell." He had a sudden realization. "O'Lunney," he said. "You must be Kevin's daughter."

"That's right. My father's your grandfather's chauffeur. And I know all about you, too." Kathleen grinned at his confusion. "You're the prodigal son."

"Well, at least you didn't call me the cohabitating black sheep."

"I've run out of obscene linguistics." Kathleen grinned up at him. "At least for the time being."

"That," Matt laughed back, "is a relief." He went into the kitchen and returned with two beers. He handed her a glass, but drank his straight from the bottle. "You must

31

have been on your way to Riverview when you tangled with my oak tree," he said.

"It was the tree's fault. It should have honked. Yes. I'm home for intercession from SUNY Purchase college."

"How come I haven't met you before?"

"My father and mother split up. I was raised by my mother until she died, and then I went to a Catholic boarding school. Now I've come to stay with Dad a wee bit."

"And it's a wee bit of his brogue you've picked up, too, I see," Matt teased.

"You should have heard my Mom!" Kathleen rolled her eyes. "And what about you?" she said. "How is it that you're here instead of at Riverview?"

"That's a long story."

"I've heard it," she remembered. "Dad writes long letters. You're the one who dodged the draft."

"Simplistic, but accurate," Matt admitted.

"Toward the end, wasn't it?"

"Yes. Seventy-two. I went to Canada." Matt sighed.

"I'm sorry. I didn't mean to be rubbing your nose in it."

"That's okay. I'm not ashamed of what I did."

"Why did you do it?" Kathleen caught herself. "I'm sorry. It's none of my business. It's just that I've always had this curiosity about your family, hearing about them from far away all the time I was growing up and all."

"I don't mind telling you." He sat down on the couch. "When I was a boy, my cousin Mark and I were very close, particularly as teenagers. Mark was a little more than a year older than me, but a lot more mature. I really looked up to him. He read a lot, struggled to form his own opinions, developed convictions. This was all back in the sixties, and youth and commitment sort of went hand-in-hand anyway—along with long hair. Anyway, Mark decided the Vietnam War was all wrong.

"It wasn't an easy decision for him. He really agonized over it and talked to me about it a lot, too. Anyway, he was draft age by then, and he decided he wasn't going to hedge his convictions with a college deferment or by running to Canada. When he was called, he was going to declare himself a conscientious objector and go to jail if he had to." Matt took a long pull from the beer bottle. "I

32

really admired that. When Mark reneged, I was devastated."

"He reneged?" Kathleen shifted position on the sagging couch. "How? Why?"

"His father leaned on him. My Uncle David is a very, um...strong personality. Mark never could stand up to him. Uncle David pulled out all the stops. The shame for the family. The effect on the Governor's career, when he was just beginning to make a comeback from the divorce scandal. Uncle David's having to admit to his friends and associates that his son was a coward. He hammered away at Mark until Mark finally gave in. He went in the Army. Fourteen weeks later he was in Vietnam."

"What happened to him?" Kathleen asked the question to give Matt a chance to compose himself. She already knew the answer from her father's letters.

"He served eleven months and nineteen days of his year's tour of duty. Then he went out on patrol and was killed by friendly fire."

"How awful." Kathleen reached out and squeezed Matt's hand. "I think I understand now why you went to Canada."

"Senseless," Matt said. "It was so damn senseless. We had no business in that war. Mark used to write me letters. Half the time they didn't know who was friend and who was enemy...He was scared all the time."

"Maybe that's what heroism is," Kathleen observed. "Being scared and doing what you have to do anyway."

"Only Mark's trouble was, he was more scared of his goddamn father than he was of the Viet Cong," Matt replied bitterly.

"But Mark wasn't you," Kathleen pointed out. "You had the courage to stand up to your family and go to Canada."

"Well, I didn't have Uncle David for a father."

"Still, your father disapproved. That's what my father wrote me, anyway."

"Yes. He did disapprove. But he didn't disown me or anything like that. My father is a strange man—not warm, not very demonstrative. He disagreed with my decision, and he let me know he disagreed. We had one very painful, long discussion about it where he told me bluntly—

bluntly for Dad, anyway—how he felt about it. And then he said I was his son no matter what I decided, he'd stick by me and there would always be a place for me at Riverview when I wanted to come back."

"What about the rest of your family?"

"My mother and sister Patrice understood. My other sister, Lisa, was more interested in dating at the time, as I remember it, and my brother Michael was too young to really understand what was going on."

"And your grandfather? The Governor?"

"Well, at the time the Governor was in a holding position. Nixon was in and Watergate hadn't happened yet. A second term was taken for granted, so a Republican with high ambitions like Grandpa had no choice but to play the waiting game. I guess you could say he was downright cynical about my cutting out for Canada. Slapped me on the back and assured me his hawk views were well enough established so nothing I did could really hurt him. 'Matter of fact, fella,' he told me, 'you even might pick me up some of those muddleheaded anti-war votes.'"

"At least he didn't condemn you."

"True." Matt smiled without humor. "Of course, Uncle David, Mark's father, was a different story. He called me a coward, a disgrace to his hero son. It's like Mark's early convictions about Vietnam and war in general never existed as far as he was concerned. Yeah, Uncle David sent me on my way to Canada with all the loathing and contempt he could muster. And since I've come back he's refused to talk to me. If there's a family gathering and I come into the room, he leaves."

"That must be painful for you."

"Yeah. Well . . ." Matt shrugged, indicating there was really nothing more to be said about it. He got to his feet and smiled wryly at Kathleen. "I'll drive you home," he said. "Your father will be wondering what happened to you."

"I would appreciate a lift." She sat up, swung her legs to the floor, and winced as she put her weight on her injured ankle. "But Dad won't be there. I called from the gas station on the way down here, and he'd already left to drive the Governor to the city."

Matt glanced at his wristwatch. "Well, maybe he's back by now."

"No. He was going to wait and drive the Governor back from the office."

"The office?" Matt assumed Kathleen meant the Governor's penthouse office atop the Stockwell Building. "I wonder what Grandpa is doing there at this time of night."

"I wonder," Kathleen echoed, although from her father's letters she had a good idea of what the Governor might be doing in the Stockwell Building after closing hours. Indeed, she knew at least eight proper linguistic dictionary synonyms for what the Governor was probably doing.

6

VANESSA BREWSTER HAD a Ph.D in anthropology from Columbia and a master's in art history from the University of Florence. She'd done her field work in New Guinea, where she had lived in the interior for two years. While at Columbia she'd shared a bed for a brief time with a visiting professor from Zurich, a world-renowned philosopher some twenty years her senior. In Florence a well-known modern artist, also somewhat older than her, had been her lover. In New Guinea she'd gained invaluable insights into the mores of the aborigines by having an affair with the fifty-five-year-old shaman of the village. Vanessa was not only drawn to men of renown and power; she was turned on by older men.

When she met Governor Matthew Adams Stockwell at a private showing of the Stockwell family's most recent acquisitions of Minoan artifacts, Vanessa was thirty-four years old, had never been married, and looked a timid twenty-four. The Governor was exactly forty years older. In no way did this age difference dim his recognition of the interest he read in her green eyes.

Since the crumbling of his marriage to Buffy some years ago, the Governor had not been drawn to obviously sensual women. He'd come to appreciate subtlety, to seek it out, and to value the process of discovery. And he'd learned to perceive the potential for passion in women whose image—unlike his wife's—did not convey obvious lust.

Vanessa Brewster was such a woman. Her figure was voluptuous, but she did nothing to draw attention to that fact. Even her New York clothes smacked of the bush, running to loose fits, the sort of long skirts that guard against brambles, and a lack of any sort of decoration that might snag on jungle vines. Tans, khakis, and pastel greens were her customary colors—hues that faded into the off-white backgrounds of the institutions, museums, and galleries she frequented. She wore her long, light brown hair in a top knot designed to keep it out of her face and to save her the time she might otherwise have had to spend having it styled in beauty salons. The knot almost hid the highlights in her hair, dimming any luster it would have claimed from either sun or electric bulb.

It would, however, be a mistake to think that any of this stemmed from Vanessa's wish to go unnoticed. On the contrary, when a man attracted her, she expertly insinuated herself into his presence and made sure he took notice of her. She was able to do this by force of personality, and by a sort of carefully controlled release of her sensuality designed to pique the man's desire.

Vanessa did not exactly flirt. But when she bent attentively, her loose blouse would display a curve of full, golden breast which would make any man gasp. And later, when the preliminaries of courtship were over, her ego was always delighted by the response to her large, shapely breasts and hips and bottom; her long, clutching legs; and the small, sinuous waist that had been concealed by the camouflage of her clothes.

A sophisticated man, the Governor guessed at the delights of Vanessa's flesh the moment he saw her. For her part Vanessa knew who he was, and his aura of power was palpable to her. She had never slept with a man quite as old as the Governor, but it never occurred to her that his age might interfere with his virility. Some things a woman knows instinctually, and anthropologist that she was, Vanessa had a healthy respect for instincts—particularly her own.

She understood immediately what the Governor had in mind when he suggested that she meet him at his office in the Stockwell Building some evening so that he might show her some of the choicer pieces of his private collection, not on exhibit for the general public. "I'd love to see them," was her immediate response. "When?" was her next, practical question. And so they had arranged a time.

When Vanessa arrived, a doorkeeper-watchman admitted her to the Stockwell Building and showed her to the private elevator which ran only to the Governor's penthouse office-suite. He was waiting to greet her when the elevator doors opened. After showing her some truly remarkable specimens of undeciphered Minoan stone seals, he offered her Crystale champagne and wafers with Beluga caviar over which lime twists had been squeezed. The first hour of her visit passed very quickly.

The second hour began with a kiss. It proceeded at a rather more rapid pace than the first one had. Indeed, there was an almost instantaneous passionate rapport that had them clawing at each other's clothes without thought of comfort or restraint. In no time at all Vanessa found herself lying flat on her back on the Morrocan leather office couch, her sensible cotton panties dangling off one ankle and her plain beige shirt up around her neck.

Not that she minded. The Governor's impetuous assault aroused her to respond in kind. Looking up at his visage, ruddy with lust, the Governor's years melted away in Vanessa's eyes and she saw only a man who wanted her very much and who aroused a surge of warm, answering desire which spread over her body.

As her large breasts rose and fell quickly with little, shallow, eager gasps, she reached for him, found him, guided him. He filled her then, and there was nothing dessicated about that part of him at all. "Ah," she sighed, rising to him, descending with him, rising again.

The rhythm mounted. Vanessa felt herself mounting to the crest of the wave. She arched her body. "Ah," she said. And then, louder, "Ah! Ah!"

37

Years of experience were behind the Governor's thrustings now. They testified to his determination that Vanessa should not ride that crest alone. Pulses pounding in his forehead, blood rushing to his face, he lunged to seal their lovemaking by mingling his own release with hers.

Vanessa closed her eyes, savoring the moment, striving for the mutual ecstasy, and then—Suddenly the Governor pitched forward and there was an inert weight pinning her to the couch. It was a moment before she realized he'd stopped moving. She spoke, but he didn't answer. She shook him, but he didn't respond. In a panic, she slid out from under him and got to her feet.

Vanessa put her hand on the Governor's naked chest. She felt nothing. She bent and laid her ear over his heart. It was still. She stood up again, looked down at the Governor, and admitted to herself what she believed. Still, she wasn't a doctor. Perhaps there still might be a chance to revive him with a pulmotor or whatever it was they used.

Crossing quickly to the desk, she picked up the telephone and dialed the police department emergency number, 911. "I'm at the Stockwell Building," Vanessa told the voice on the other end. "In Governor Stockwell's office on the top floor. I think the Governor's had a heart attack. I'm not absolutely sure, but I think the Governor might be dead."

BOOK TWO

7

DEATH IS A MAGNET, Holly thought as she watched two sleek black cars emerge from between the twin rows of tall oaks flanking the entrance road to the estate. It draws the bereaved from all over the world, and like filings they come together, held by a force they don't understand.

The Cadillac and the Rolls-Royce Silver Cloud slowed for the sunken stone circular driveway, then came to a halt in front of the mansion. These were only the latest arrivals in a procession that had begun early that morning and would continue all through today and tomorrow morning, until the funeral service. The clan was gathering. A patriarch had passed away; the mighty would assemble, and the powerful would pay last respects to one of their own. The rest of the world would pause and bow its head for a moment of silence.

Holly was sitting with her three-year-old son Nicholas on the edge of his small bed. They were looking out the window of his room. It was less than twelve hours since the late-night call had come, notifying the family of the Governor's death. Holly had just finished telling Nicholas.

People had been arriving all morning, filling up the huge house. The telephones had been ringing, there were uniformed state troopers stationed around the grounds, and downstairs people were huddling in small groups everywhere and speaking in hushed tones. A telegrapher had been installed in a study in the west wing to receive the messages of consolation directly so that Western Union would not disturb the family by delivering them. Very important people, Stockwells and others, were wiring, telephoning, and arriving by limousine.

"Who's that, Mommy?"

Holly looked below. A medium-sized man, in his early forties, well tailored to hide a slight pudginess, was emerging from the Cadillac. Her Uncle James and his younger son Michael, her Uncle David and Buffy were all grouped at the front of the portico to greet him. Clearly the gatekeeper had called ahead to announce the man's arrival.

Behind him Holly's Uncle Jonathan—James's younger brother—and his wife Ellen emerged from the Rolls-Royce Silver Cloud unnoticed. Their son Peter got out after them and quickly moved to join the group in front. Even from her vantage point, Holly could tell that Uncle David was annoyed at Peter's presumption.

"That's Zelig Meyerling." Holly answered her son's question. "Before you were born he was Secretary of State of the whole United States. He was the youngest Secretary of State in history."

Nicholas thought about that, but it didn't mean much to him. "Is he an uncle or a cousin?" he wanted to know.

"Neither, darling. He's not related to our family at all. He was a protégé—well, a sort of friend, in politics and personally, too—of Great-Grandpa's."

Really a sort of divining rod, Holly thought to herself. He makes people reveal what's under their surface. She watched, slightly amused despite her grief, as the tableau under the colonnade unfolded.

Uncle James acted courteously toward Meyerling, respectful, admiring perhaps, but certainly not fawning. Uncle David's head, however, was bobbing at Meyerling's expressions of sympathy as if they were policy papers he was eager to initial to show his agreement. Michael's handshake lingered, his other hand cupping Meyerling's elbow, a politician's ploy to force rapport, one Michael had picked up from the Governor. His cousin Peter undermined Michael's gambit by exchanging amused glances with Meyerling.

With Meyerling momentarily between them, the contrast between the two young men was even more marked than usual. Square-jawed, blue-eyed, golden-haired Michael embodied the tradition of Hudson River Valley aristocrat turned politician; Peter, with his powerful, wide-shouldered body and dark, brooding features would have looked more at home on the Brooklyn docks with a baling hook in his thick-fisted hands. Meyerling's presence highlighted the different ways the two ambitious young men went after what they wanted, bringing out both Michael's smoothness and Peter's steamroller personality.

As they vanished from view, Holly was recalling the first time she'd met Zelig Meyerling, shortly after she returned from England. He'd been Holly's dinner partner at a formal dinner the Governor had hosted at Riverview.

"A fascinating man, Holly," her grandfather had told her in advance. "Truly, history may well remember Meyerling long after I'm forgotten. Only two kinds of men succeed in politics—those who anticipate events and those who shape them. I am—no false modesty, eh, Holly—one of the nation's great anticipators. But Zelig . . . Zelig is one of the great shapers of our times."

Such praise was rare from the Governor. Depressed and lethargic as she was feeling in the aftermath of her crumpled marriage, Holly's curiosity was nevertheless piqued. Besides, all over the world people were fascinated with Zelig Meyerling. Who was she to cling to apathy in his presence?

Along with Henry Kissinger and Zbigniew Brzezinski, he was one of the Teutonic Triplets—a misnomer since the three men had respectively been born German-Jewish, Polish, and Swiss—so-called because of their media image as Europe's hard-line gift to American foreign policy. Kissinger and Brzezinski were products of the Rockefeller Foundation think-tank via Harvard. Meyerling had also gone to Harvard, but he'd been snapped up by the Stockwell Institute, where he quickly rose to prominence as would-be President Matthew Adams Stockwell's chief foreign policy advisor.

When the Governor blew his presidential chances, he'd passed Meyerling on to a Republican rival, accompanied by a calling in of certain favors. As a result Meyerling, like Kissinger, had eventually moved up from Assistant Secretary of State to National Security Advisor to Secretary of State. Currently he was out and Brzezinski was in, but he was nevertheless consulted by the Democrats whenever the Russians tipped what was perceived to be a balance. "Of course," Meyerling told the Governor, "if it involves China, they call Henry. Poor Zbigniew," he would add, "is truly haunted."

Two days before he died, the Governor had spoken at Columbia University in connection with the conferring of an honorary degree on Meyerling. He had said that it was a dreadful loss to the United States that Meyerling, because he was foreign born, could never be its President. "All of us," he said, "those who succeeded in attaining the highest office as well as those of us who failed, would pale beside the achievements of this man of genius and compassion if fate had not denied him to our country."

The Governor had been completely sincere. Holly knew that. His admiration for Meyerling was boundless. His faith in the Swiss-born expert's advice concerning foreign policy was absolute. He'd made that clear on the occasion of the Stockwell dinner party.

That dinner party. A wan smile appeared on Holly's face as she recalled it.

Her reminiscence was abruptly interrupted by the ringing telephone. "Hello," Holly answered, her voice soft.

"There is a call for you, Miss Holly." The voice belonged to Berkley, Riverview's butler for over twenty years.

"Is it a member of the family?" Holly knew that Berkley would have screened out casual sympathy calls, journalists, strangers.

There was a long pause on the other end. Berkley, ever discreet, did not quite know how to answer the question. Finally, he was direct. "It's Mr. Millwood, Miss Holly." Berkley did not say "Mr. Christopher," as he once might have.

Holly caught her breath audibly. Nicholas looked up at her questioningly. She patted his small hand and managed to keep her voice steady as she responded. "All right, Berkley," she said. "You can put him through."

There was a crackling in her ear, and then she heard Christopher's cultured British tones. "Hello, Holly. I read about the Governor in the paper. Rang right away."

"What do you want?" Holly's voice was even, free of hostility only by a tremendous effort.

"To pay my respects, love. What else?"

"I don't know. You tell me. What else?"

"I'm truly sorry, Holly. I wanted you to know. I had a genuine fondness for the Governor."

Holly knew that the Governor had always detested her husband. Her grandfather had made that plain before she married Christopher. He'd hidden it afterward, but Holly had always known. Unfortunately, it hadn't stopped her from marrying the man. In his younger days the Governor might have tried to stop her, but by the time Holly was grown, he'd recognized that everyone was entitled and bound to make their own mistakes. "Thank you for your condolences. Now if there's nothing else—"

"Hold on, love. This isn't a time for scrapping, now is it? Oh, no. This is a time for family solidarity. Past ruckuses forgotten, or at least put aside. All stand together to see the Governor to his final resting place and all that."

"What are you suggesting?"

"I just wanted you to know I'll be up on the morning train for the services."

"You're in New York?" Holly's voice rose. She hadn't even known he was in the United States. When she'd tried to have him served with the divorce papers in London, he'd been in Scotland. And when she'd tried to have him served in Scotland, he'd been in Yorkshire. But with all the chasing her lawyers had done, she hadn't known that Christopher had left the British Isles. Now she didn't wait for him to answer. "Don't come up here." For the first time her voice trembled. "There's no reason for you to come."

"Of course there's a reason, love. I'm a member of the family."

"That's a technicality. If you'd stood still long enough, you wouldn't be anymore. Please don't come."

"Not be present at the funeral of my wife's grandfather?

43

Simply not done, love. I'll be up on the morning train. Do arrange to have one of the cars meet me."

"Christopher—"

"See you in the morning, love." He hung up.

Holding the receiver helplessly, Holly stared into space for a long, silent moment.

"Mommy?"

With the sound of her son's voice, she hung up the receiver. "What is it, Nicky?"

"Who was that, Mommy?"

"Your daddy," she told him. "That was your daddy." And, Holly thought to herself, hurting, he didn't even ask about you. Oh, yes, death is a magnet all right, a magnet drawing the dross with the iron.

8

THE "IRON" WAS gathered in the Governor's downstairs study. The group was small, and all male, save one. The exception was the Governor's widow, Buffy.

Her presence was resented for many reasons, not the least of which was that it kept the men from their Havanas. She was aware of their resentment, particularly as regarded the cigars, and it amused her. It also amused her that widowhood forced them to grant her a status they had always denied her as the Governor's wife.

Buffy was truly grieved at the Governor's passing. She was also furious. It wasn't that she minded his infidelity with some trollop less than half his age, but she objected to his having the execrable taste to die in mid-coitus and leave her open not to mere scandal, but to being a laughingstock as well.

This was the subject currently under discussion. Snifters had been substituted for the cigars. Jonathan Stockwell, least among equals, sipped Napoleon brandy older than his son Peter, and gave vent to his emotion. Alone among those present, he was not pragmatic.

"The goddamn *New York Times*!" Jonathan's voice trembled. "I shall write a letter."

"Not to the editor, I hope, Uncle." James's son Michael winced at the possible effect on his budding political career.

"Of course not. To Iphigene." Iphigene Ochs Sulzberger was matriarch of the family that owned the *Times*.

"Iphigene has not been active for some time," James told his brother gently. "Punch—"

"Then Punch shall hear from me. In the strongest possible terms! 'All the news that's fit to print' indeed! A newspaper's motto is a solemn pledge to its readers. That story was definitely not fit to print!" Jonathan's narrow face turned a deeper shade of red as he looked at his older brother for confirmation.

The story had related the circumstances of the Governor's death. It had dealt with them circumspectly, which the other New York papers, the wire services, and the television network news programs had not. The *Times* had mentioned the presence of Vanessa Brewster, and that was all. It had not speculated. It had not allowed innuendo to creep in, as had the rest of the media. But the *Times* was the paper of record, and so Jonathan was outraged.

"The *Times* story was nothing. And the other coverage is only the beginning. Live with it, Dad." Peter, Jonathan's son, was as usual direct and brutal, and lacking in familial respect. "The Governor was an old roué. Another sort of death might have blurred that, but not this one—not with the tart still warm."

"How very graphic." From under her long eyelashes, Buffy's gaze disintegrated Peter.

"Your words are not well chosen, Peter." The tone of James's voice was neutral. He did not like his stepmother. He had never forgiven her for breaking up his parents' marriage, but there were proprieties to be observed. This was not the time to rub her nose in the infidelity that had led to the Governor's demise, and Peter's words were not respectful.

James did not really understand Peter. His nephew was one of that new breed of young, aggressive, effective businessmen whose fast track had no stops for compromise, courtesy, or consideration. James admired young Peter's acumen, but his methods and his personality rubbed him the wrong way.

Presently, Peter was in charge of overseeing the considerable Stockwell real estate interests. At twenty-five, he was young for the job. Still, there was no denying that he handled it very well.

When the Governor had originally assigned various aspects of the Stockwell holdings to his sons and his daughter's husbands, Peter's father Jonathan had been entrusted with real estate. But Jonathan had no head for business, particularly not the complexities involved in the buying, selling, building, and leasing of the many family properties. Surreptitiously, without hurting his brother's feelings, James had gone over everything he did, making alterations where necessary.

All this had changed two years ago when Peter, fresh from Harvard Business School, had gone to work in his father's offices. Very soon James had noticed a remarkable improvement in the real estate operation. Successful deals were accomplished without snafus, and shrewd investments were made. Properties were sold and bought in a way that increased the value of the Stockwell real estate holdings by thirty-five percent in one year. A remarkable accomplishment for anyone, let alone a man who was twenty-three at the time.

Peter had simply pushed aside everything in his way and taken the reins. His feelings toward his father had been formed in childhood. His mother, not happy with Jonathan's weak position in the family power structure, had repeatedly expressed her discontent with her husband to her little boy. It was up to Peter to show up the Stockwells, and her close relationship with her child had not only cut him off from his father, but the rest of the family. Consequently, he grew up with a fierce desire to earn the respect or fear—if not the love—of the Stockwells.

In the beginning Peter had always deferred to his father when there were others present, although privately he was contemptuous of Jonathan's ineffectuality. Jonathan had recently recognized that contempt and the wide gulf that lay between him and his son, and it had saddened him, rendering him even less effectual than before. He was groping to bridge that gap, and allowing his son full rein was the only way he knew how to do it.

At first only Jonathan knew the extent to which Peter despised him. Today, however, there was not even a pretense that Jonathan was anything more than a figurehead. Peter had eclipsed his father and made sure that throughout the real estate world it was known that if you wanted to deal with Stockwell Enterprises, Peter Stockwell was the man in charge.

Lately, James noticed, Peter was taking an interest in the other components of the Stockwell fortune. He asked questions—sharp, knowledgeable questions—regarding the stock portfolio, the companies held outright, and those in which the family jointly held controlling interests. He wanted to know about the football franchise, the Brazilian coffee plantation, the oil wells, the Stockwell-owned Canadian lumber mills supplied by the timberlands he supervised, the publishing combine with its prestigious magazines that lost money and its successful slicks with triple-A ad ratings. Indeed, there was no area of Stockwell Enterprises and its many subsidiaries and investments in which young Peter Stockwell was not avidly interested.

His Uncle James had cooperated with Peter. There was nothing to hide, after all. Peter's Uncle David, however, was not so obliging.

David Lewis, husband of James's and Jonathan's sister Alice, never forgot that he was not born a Stockwell. He was charged with the Stockwell estate's insurance holdings: three major companies owned outright, controlling interests in three others, and substantial stock in twelve more, including Met Life and Lloyds of London.

David also handled the Governor's extensive art collection. All the other Stockwell holdings increased and decreased in worth with the ebb and flow of the various markets to which they were subject, but the art collection grew steadily in value, doubling, and then doubling again, and yet again. David knew—and James strongly suspected—that the paintings and sculptures constituted the most valuable part of the Governor's considerable estate. They had been acquired by the Governor's full-time staff of curators. Only his collection of moderns—estimated value in excess of fifty million dollars—had been selected by the Governor personally.

Now David Lewis was regarding his brother-in-law Jonathan impatiently. He neither liked nor trusted his nephew Peter, but he found himself forced to agree with him. "There are more important things for us to concern ourselves with right now than the *New York Times*," he told Jonathan testily.

"More important! More important!" Jonathan sputtered. "What is more important than that the Governor's good name not be tarnished for posterity?"

Buffy had heard enough about the Governor's good name. She looked pleadingly at the one man in the room who had not yet spoken. Her violet eyes asked him to put an end to the discussion.

Zelig Meyerling spoke softly, deferentially, implicitly acknowledging that he was not a member of the family. "If you would like, Jonathan," he said, "I will call Punch Sulzberger."

"I would appreciate that, Zelig."

"More to the point if Rupert was called." As usual, Peter was blunt.

"Mr. Murdoch would not accommodate me." Meyerling spread his hands palms up. "He will not tamper with the policy of the *New York Post*—all the news that is *not* fit to print." His eyes met Buffy's. "I do agree with David," he said. "There are other things which the family should be discussing. Perhaps if I left—"

There was a flurry of comments reassuring him that he was not intruding.

"Thank you." Gravely, Meyerling accepted their confidence. "I think you should know then that I have spoken with Washington and the Fed is nervous." He meant the Federal Reserve Board of the United States. "The Chairman is concerned about interest rates."

"His concern is premature." James responded quickly and precisely. "With Father's sudden passing, it's only natural that the market should fluctuate."

"As you know, this is not my area of expertise, but I don't think the Chairman meant the initial flurry," Meyerling told them. "He anticipated a plunge in the Dow Jones. He also expects a recovery by the smart money. No, his

48

concern is the long-run stability of Stockwell Enterprises on the world market."

"Difficult to give assurances." James was thoughtful. "My father's death is a pebble thrown in the worldwide financial brook. The ripple effect will be felt everywhere. No, the future can't be guaranteed. For one thing, the Stockwell fortune is entangled with various trusts. Some of these were held jointly by my father and my mother and their children, including myself. Some specify control by a particular individual—sometimes a family member, sometimes not. Some of the interests are overseen by lawyers, or bankers. The Brazilian plantation, for instance, is controlled jointly by its manager and the former American ambassador. There are other special situations."

"But surely these properties belong to the Stockwells," Buffy remarked.

"Oh, yes. The profits are ours. But Father believed in giving those with the know-how the widest possible latitude in order to manipulate to our advantage."

"I see." The computer in Buffy's head was on-line. The data would be there when needed.

"Also," James went on, "when my mother's parents died and she inherited the Linstone estate, it was combined with the Stockwell holdings, and now these monies are inextricably merged."

"Surely the Linstone estate was not equal to the Stockwell fortune," Buffy said carefully.

"My mother's family was quite wealthy." James spelled it out. "The contribution was considerable. There can be no disposition of the Stockwell assets without taking that into consideration."

"Can anybody here provide me with the name of a good inheritance lawyer?" Buffy inquired.

Everybody smiled politely. Nobody, however, thought that it was a joke. Buffy, they knew, would fight tooth and nail for all that she thought was coming to her.

"It doesn't matter how the pie is cut up," Peter said. "What's important is who controls it."

"I would assume there would be joint control," James said frostily. "Just as there was in the Governor's lifetime."

"We won't know that until the will is read." David Lewis shot a quick, nervous glance at Buffy.

"When will that be?" Meyerling inquired.

"Wednesday," James answered. "Three o'clock in Ulysses Blandings's law offices."

"Good Lord!" Michael reacted. "Blandings is going to read the will? He's over eighty. He stammers. We'll be there forever."

"He was the Governor's personal lawyer," James reminded his son. "Father trusted him absolutely. Both his ability and his discretion. He may be old, but when he reveals the terms of the will to us, you can be sure they are exactly what the Governor wanted." James glanced significantly at Buffy.

Before she could comment, there was a knock at the door. It was Berkley, the butler. "Operator thirty-four has your call, Mrs. Stockwell," he informed Buffy. She excused herself and followed him out.

She took the call upstairs, in the dressing room of her suite. It was comforting to hear Jack Houston's voice.

"I caught it on the morning news." He was concerned. "Are you okay?"

"Okay. It was a shock, but I'm handling it."

"Hell of a note. The bimbo, I mean."

"Don't be a hypocrite, darling. We haven't exactly been writing an ode to fidelity in the Plaza ourselves."

"I miss you." Jack changed the subject. "When can I see you?"

"It's very difficult. Tomorrow is the cremation and funeral service. Monday is the burial. Tuesday is a statehouse service in Albany. Wednesday is the reading of the will. Friday is the memorial service at Gotham Memorial."

"Thursday then." His voice was eager.

Despite all that was happening, despite a grief that was genuine, Buffy felt a quickening of her pulses, a sudden warmth of desire. For an instant she was chagrined. Then she remembered something Matthew had once said.

"Death makes people horny," he'd told her bluntly in the privacy of their illicit Washington hotel room on the evening following the funeral of President John F. Kennedy. "It's a reflex, an expression of the life urge in the face of the inevitable." And that night their lovemaking had been fierce.

"Thursday," she told Jack Houston now. "At the Plaza."

"Not the Plaza. There's a high-tech executive convention there. Make it the Algonquin."

"All right. The Algonquin."

They set a time. "I love you, Buffy," he told her.

"I know."

"I want to marry you."

"I know that, too."

"Your husband's not just too old for you anymore, Buffy. Now he's dead."

"Yes." Suddenly, unexpectedly, Buffy's eyes filled with tears.

"There's nothing in our way. Marry me."

"It's too soon."

"No, it's not. Say yes, Buffy. Or say no. Decide."

"Maybe," Buffy said. And then, quickly, before Jack could object, she repeated that she would see him Thursday at the Algonquin and hung up.

Buffy went back downstairs to the Governor's study. As she reentered, young Michael Stockwell was speaking. "... interest of future public relations that the Vanessa Brewster matter be resolved with a minimum—" He cut the sentence off abruptly with Buffy's appearance.

James Stockwell stood, a gentlemanly reflex, and held a chair for Buffy. "I'll handle it," he told Michael and the others as she seated herself. "I'll see that there's no embarrassment to the family."

His tone said the subject was closed.

9

HOLLY WAS SURPRISED the following morning, Sunday, when her grandmother Mary came into her room already dressed on black. She was a small woman with a figure that was still trim and straight despite her years. As a young woman she had epitomized the Gibson girl, yet she had blossomed to womanhood in the flamboyant flapper era. But the Governor had noticed the quiet girl with the pixie smile and the warm brown eyes, and had wanted her to be the mother of his children. This morning her mouth, usually relaxed and upturned at the corners, was compressed into a thin line that lent her fine-boned features a sculpted look in the early morning sunlight.

But why has she come? Holly wondered. The funeral service at the small church in the village of Riverview Heights was scheduled for two in the afternoon. Holly herself had not planned to dress until one.

"Will you take a ride with me?" Mary asked.

"Where to?"

"The crematorium."

"Oh, Grandma!" Holly was dismayed. The family had conferred, and decided not to attend the actual cremation of the Governor's body. They felt it was a purely mechanical act in grim surroundings and that final respects should be withheld for the funeral, the burial, and the two memorial services.

"You don't have to come inside with me." Mary's face was composed, but the lines of age had been etched more deeply by grief. "In fact, I'd rather you didn't."

"But why, Grandma?"

"I want to say my own good-bye to Matthew."

Holly could see she was determined. Mary had heart trouble; she should avoid stress, and the visit was probably not good for her. But she was not asking permission. She was going. The governor had not been her husband for some years, but she was going to say good-bye to him.

"Give me a minute," Holly said. "I'll change."

"Not necessary. You don't even have to get out of the car. I just want company for the ride." Mary smiled the pixie smile that the Governor had treasured long after their marriage had dissolved. "Somebody to pass me the nitro in case I have to pop a pill," she added with a sad chuckle.

She linked arms with Holly as they walked down the long, circular staircase and exited Riverview manor by the rarely used front door. Mary's car was waiting, the chauffeur at the wheel. He had driven her over from the small cottage she'd built for herself on a strip of Linstone farmland adjacent to Riverview.

As they got into the limousine, Holly noticed a sprig of cherry blossoms on the shelf behind the backseat. They were still dewy, freshly plucked. "The Governor loved cherry blossoms," Mary explained. "He always said it was the real reason he wanted to be president...so he could be in Washington at cherry blossom time."

Holly knew that cherry blossoms didn't grow in the Hudson River Valley. "Wherever did you get them?"

"I have a tree in my greenhouse. It was brought all the way from Japan." A smile smoothed the wrinkles at the corners of Mary's mouth. "I thought one day, when he was more mature, I might lure Matthew back to me with them."

"Oh, Grandma!" Holly was touched.

"It was self-delusion. Matthew was many things, some quite admirable, but the one thing he never was nor could be was mature when it came to women."

They fell silent. Holly held her grandmother's hand. It was a clasp of love. Mercedes springs cushioned the last lap of the ride up the dirt road to the crematorium.

It was an ugly building, squat, stuccoed, without character, but functional. A tall, lean man, who was obviously expecting Mary, emerged from a doorway. He helped her from the car, and reached out to carry the cherry blossoms for her. Mary thanked him, but held onto them firmly. He escorted her into the building, and Holly sat back in the plush rear seat of the limousine and waited.

About a half hour later a cloud of black smoke rose from the chimney. Tears splashed Holly's cheeks and a childlike sob escaped her lips. She felt the sharp knowledge that the grandfather she'd loved and who had loved her so much was gone, really gone.

The chauffeur turned in the front seat, concern on his face. "You all right, Miss Holly?"

She nodded dumbly.

He turned back, leaving her to her grief.

A few moments later Holly's grandmother exited the building, no longer carrying the cherry blossoms. The black-clad man was with her, and helped her into the car.

Mary thanked him and told the chauffeur to take them

back to Riverview. Sighing, she looked at Holly. "Dry your tears, child," she said. "Matthew is gone."

"Yes, Grandma." Holly accepted her grandmother's linen handkerchief.

"I'm glad I went," Mary said after a while. "I'm glad I said good-bye to him."

"I know, Grandma."

"And there's something else I'm glad of, too, Holly. I'll tell you what it is if you swear to never tell another living soul." That pixieish light was back in her eyes again.

"On my honor as a Girl Scout, Grandma."

Mary smiled. "Well, that will have to do, I suppose. It's just this, Holly. I've never really held any animosity toward Buffy, you know."

"No, Grandma?"

"No, child. But still . . ."

"Still, Grandma?"

"I am human, Holly. That young Brewster woman caught en flagrante with Matthew when he died . . . when I heard about that, I immediately thought of Buffy. And do you know what I thought, Holly?"

"No, Grandma, what?"

"Chickens come home to roost, Holly. That's what I thought. Buffy's chickens come home to roost."

"Your husband is here." Holly's cousin Matt, looking awkward in a suit, tie, and a fresh haircut, informed her of Christopher Millwood's arrival when she returned.

"I don't want to see him."

"You don't have to." Matt liked Holly and barely knew Christopher. "He's in the east parlor with my father and Uncle David and Peter."

Holly glanced at her watch. "We'll be leaving for the funeral service at the church soon. I'd better get dressed." She started up the stairs. After a few steps she turned around. "Matt." She came back down to him, her hand trailing on the mahogany rail. "Will you do me a favor?"

"Sure, cuz."

"Ride with me to the service. I don't want to be alone with Christopher."

"Okay." Her cousin's eyes signaled his understanding.

"Thanks, Matt." Holly started up the stairs again, then

turned back. "How long has Christopher been here?" she asked.

"Maybe an hour and a half."

"And he hasn't seen Nicholas, right?"

"Well, he's been with Dad and Uncle David and Peter."

"He never even asked to see his son!" Holly was sure. Angry tears sprang to her eyes.

Matt mounted the few steps to her and gave Holly a hug. "That really stinks," he said. "I know how you feel."

"Do you, Matt?"

"Yes, Holly, I do. I really do."

Holly looked at him curiously. Something in his tone made it more than a casual reassurance. There was an echo of anguish that resonated with her own pain.

"I believe you do." She hugged him back, pulled away, and continued quickly up the stairs. "Fifteen minutes," she called over her shoulder.

It was closer to twenty when she came down, looking classically beautiful in a simple black dress of Walloon satin with a high neck and matching cape. Her short, golden hair was like a gleaming helmet catching the rays from the cloud-hidden sun as she and Matt exited the house arm in arm. She held a small black hat, a pillbox of tulle, in her free hand.

The hat didn't stop Christopher from linking his arm above it as Holly and Matt approached the line of waiting limousines. His kiss fell on her reluctant cheek, but he ignored the chilly response. When Holly entered the car first and Matt quickly followed, Christopher simply walked around to the opposite door and sat on Holly's other side.

In the front of the limousine, beside her father—who was dressed in livery—Kathleen O'Lunney watched the scene with interest. The man with Matt and his cousin Holly certainly was good-looking. Her father, with a County Cork snort, had told her who he was and that he was English, and Kathleen thought to herself that with a polo mallet and a pith helmet Christopher Millwood would have looked the very model of an Empire that was gone but not—at least by the Irish—forgotten.

His hair was as blond as Holly's, but with no hint of curl. His color was high, his complexion ruddy, and his

55

eyes a crinkling green. Although a head taller than Matt, there was nothing lanky about him. His bearing was military but not stiff, his demeanor relaxed but not sloppy.

Upper crust all right, Kathleen thought to herself. Rule Brittania. Cricket calluses and no others for this lad's hands.

Christopher leaned in toward Holly in the backseat. "I forgive you," he whispered in her ear.

"Go to hell!" Holly replied out loud.

Matt was embarrassed. He glanced toward the front seat to see if the driver had overheard. The soundproof glass partition was up, so he hadn't. For the first time Matt noticed the familiar red head beside the driver's.

Rolling down the window, he tapped Kathleen's shoulder. "How's the ankle?" he asked.

"Hi, there." She turned around and gave him a freckle-faced grin. "The swelling's gone down. Dad says that's because you put the ice on so prompt and all." The grin vanished. "I'm awfully sorry about your grandfather."

"Thank you."

"It's very sorry I am for your family's trouble, too," said Kevin O'Lunney from the driver's seat. "He was a fine man, the Governor. If there's anything I can do, Mr. Matthew—"

"There is one thing," Matt told him. "You can just call me Matt. No Mister."

Kevin looked from Matt to his daughter, then back at Matt again. A smile played at the corners of his mouth and then vanished. "Matt it is then," he said.

A few minutes later Kevin pulled up with the other limousines across the street from the small, steep-roofed Methodist church, which was the only church in the village of Riverview Heights. All five of them got out of the car. Kevin and his daughter, along with some twenty-five other members of the regular live-in staff of Riverview servants, would attend this local service for the Governor, along with members of the family and a select group of local people—neighbors, merchants, aging childhood friends—who had known Matthew Adams Stockwell over the years. There were state troopers discreetly stationed around the church to discourage curiosity seekers, but even so, some of the mourners would have to stand through the service.

Kevin walked over to join a group of men in chauffeur's livery, most of them hired specially for the occasion, and Matt fell into conversation with Kathleen. Trying to ignore Christopher's firm grip on her arm, Holly observed the family members in front of the church, waiting to enter.

Although she was related to them, Holly hardly knew some of them. In some cases she could identify faces with stories she'd heard—some of it family gossip, not always savory—but little more than that. Others she'd had contact with intermittently over the years. With these she exchanged glances of recognition and sometimes verbal greetings.

Her cousin Deke walked over and kissed Holly on the cheek. Reluctantly, she introduced her tall, powerfully built cousin to Christopher. He recognized Deke's name immediately. "Will they start you against New York in the opener?" he asked Deke.

For the past three years Deke Wells had been a starting pitcher for the Boston Red Sox Triple A farm team, and only recently been moved up to the Major Leagues. At twenty-four Deke's career was ahead of him—"a new Bob Feller," according to the older sportswriters—and there had been speculation that the Sox would start him against the Yankees in the opening game.

Normally Deke would have been flattered to be recognized, but now he winced at Christopher's question. Two weeks ago he'd pulled a ligament in spring training. Rest hadn't helped it, and the team doctors were talking about permanent muscle damage. Deke was just now facing the fact that his Major League career might well be over before it had really begun.

"They haven't decided who they're going to start yet," he told Christopher in answer to his question.

Deke and Holly exchanged a few pleasantries and then he excused himself. She watched him edge through the crowd in front of the church and rejoin his mother. When Deke had taken her arm, she'd looked up at him with an expression that said she was grateful he was back. Holly knew that they had always been close, but she recognized now that the closeness reflected his mother's dependence on Deke.

Susan Gray was a celebrity in a way that the other members of the Stockwell family were not. Blond, with cool gray eyes, her face was softly rounded, adding to the appearance of untroubled youth. The last-born of the Governor's children, at forty-five she looked young enough to be a daughter of James Stockwell, rather than the sister she was. Indeed, her youthful appearance was such that she was still able to play romantic leads opposite screen actors ten years younger.

Her status as a movie star had always been a mixed blessing as far as the family was concerned. Her early exploits in Hollywood—a nude swimming party, a drug bust, being named as the other woman in a notorious divorce—had been a decided embarrassment to the family more than twenty-five years ago, when political considerations had to include much more moralistic attitudes among the voters. When she had publicly admitted to being pregnant by matinee idol Gary Wells, her brother James had been dispatched to see what could be done to dissipate the scandal. The result was Susan's short-lived marriage to Wells, which had ended just one year after Deke was born.

Subsequently Susan had married Hollywood producer Lawrence Gray, twenty years her senior. She'd continued making movies, but her private life had been tranquil up to Gray's death in 1971. There had been no notoriety until recently. A month before her father's death, Susan's face had once again been splashed all over the front pages of the scandal sheets in connection with a night club brawl involving her escort—a bit actor younger than her son Deke—and a prominent Los Angeles criminal lawyer with whom she had just ended a six-month affair. The attorney was married.

Holly watched as Susan and Deke were joined by Susan's brother, Jonathan, and his wife, Ellen. Cheeks were kissed all around, and then they were swallowed up by the crowd mounting the steps to enter the church.

Following behind them was the Tyler branch of the family, the descendants of the Governor's long-dead sister, Sarah Stockwell Tyler. They had been the last to arrive, and had come straight to the church after being deposited at the Riverview Heights depot by the afternoon train. You couldn't miss the Tylers. Every one of them had the same unique shade of red-gold apricot hair. "If you could bottle the Tyler hair color," the Governor used to joke, "you could make more money than Estée Lauder."

Alfred Tyler, in his sixties—Sarah's only surviving child—and Lizzie Tyler, who had been the wife of John Tyler, Alfred's deceased twin brother, arrived arm in arm. The chubby and cheerful son of John and Lizzie, the prominent heart surgeon Paul Tyler, helped his Uncle Alfred up the steps while his wife Margaret took her mother-in-law's arm. Max and Diana Tyler, Alfred's children, walked behind them, arms linked.

Some of those who greeted Diana quickly skittered away, not knowing quite how to deal with Max. At thirty-nine, four years older than his sister, Max was militantly gay—out of the closet and proud of it. Among the family, there would always be mutters to the effect that homosexuality was one thing, but flaunting it another.

Holly saw that the twins, Beth and Carrie, had been separated from the rest of the Tylers. Paul and Margaret's daughters had been stopped by Mary Linstone Stockwell, their great-aunt, who was clucking over the girls.

It was not the sort of comment eighteen-year-olds receive gladly. Still, Beth was smiling at her great-aunt and looked genuinely pleased to see her again. However, However, Carrie, her twin, appeared impatient and sullen.

They were identical twins, not easily recognized individually even by those in their family closest to them. Now, although their outfits weren't the same, both were dressed in black, and it was only by the expressions on their faces that Holly could guess which was which. But she knew them well enough to know that they were as unalike in character as they were alike in appearance.

Beth Tyler was a serious young lady, a devoted student who would start at Bryn Mawr, Holly's alma mater, in the autumn. A humanist even in adolescence, Beth sought to understand the forces that moved the world and to learn how to use them to make it a better place. "A do-gooder" some already called her, not always reacting kindly to her intensity and social concern.

Carrie wanted to have an impact on society, too, but it was nothing like the one envisioned by her twin sister. Of all those in the large Stockwell-Tyler clan, the person Carrie admired the most was Susan Gray. Like Susan, she wanted to be a celebrity. She wanted to have men at her feet. Young as she was, she was highly sexed, and impulsive to boot. Her virginity had been disposed of without a second thought, and now she could hardly remember the face of the teenage boy she'd seduced into deflowering her. To Carrie life was a feast, experience was the haute cuisine, and sex was the Viennese torte for which her palate incessantly yearned.

Beautiful like her twin, whom she thought impossibly straitlaced, Carrie's yearning was easily and frequently satisfied. Both girls had come to physical maturity early, and now both had the athletic, youthful bodies much admired by men and envied by women—even those their own age. The twins were full-bosomed, long-legged, and coltish; their faces were strikingly beautiful, with high cheekbones, naturally pursed cherry lips, and the long-lashed almond-shaped hazel eyes of the Tyler clan. The loveliness of their visages was crowned by the family's apricot hair, a curled red-gold tumble for Carrie, a neatly combed and tied-back heavy mantle for Beth.

Now the twins trailed their great-aunt into the church. Holly started to follow, but Christopher restrained her. "Just a moment, Holly," he said.

"What is it?"

"Your Uncle David told me before that the reading of the will is set for Wednesday."

"That's right. What about it?"

"I thought it might be best—less embarrassing for you with the family, I mean—if you and I went to the lawyer's office together."

"I don't want you there at all, Christopher." Holly did not bother to make her voice anything but cold and nasty.

His green eyes narrowed. "But of course I will be there, dear wife," he said as he guided Holly firmly up the steps toward the entrance of the building. No further discussion was necessary as far as Christopher was concerned.

Fighting back tears of fury, Holly entered the church on her husband's arm.

They entered a fourth-row pew behind Holly's uncles and aunts. Patrice was already seated there. Holly smiled, noticing that even Patrice's mourning dress had a small, unobtrusive bow drifting down from its silken collar. They kissed warmly. Although they were the same age, had more or less grown up together and actually were quite fond of each other, Holly and Patrice had not seen very much of each other since Holly's return from England.

Patrice's ex-husband, Miles O'Keefe, was seated on her other side. How nice of Miles to come, Holly thought. Well, some divorces are friendly. It wouldn't be that way for her and Christopher. Miles was present out of a sense of obligation and respect to a family of which he had once been a part. But Christopher's intention to attend the reading of her grandfather's will erased any lingering doubts Holly might have had that he was there for any but strictly self-serving reasons.

As they all stood for the opening hymn, "Dear Lord and Father of Mankind," the pastor ascended to the pulpit. He read the twenty-third Psalm and then a passage from the New Testament. The choir sang a second hymn, and the minister introduced Patrice's father, James Stockwell, from the pulpit. James spoke briefly about his father, announced the various memorial services, then introduced Zelig Meyerling to deliver the eulogy.

Watching Meyerling take the pulpit, Holly again recalled the dinner party at which she'd first met him.

Her first impression that night had been one of disappointment. Meyerling was attractive, but his face was heavy and his short haircut too young for him. It gave him a sort of Prussian look sans monocle. And when he was seated, even his impeccably tailored vest could not hide a certain roundness to his stomach.

Noticing, Holly had been amused. Zelig Meyerling had been built up by the media as a ladies' man. He dated young models, beautiful actresses, sleek debutantes, and curried heiresses. In his mid-forties now, Meyerling was considered one of Washington's most desirable bachelors. It was part of his legend that there was always a beautiful woman on his arm.

Meyerling had noticed Holly's quick glance. "The curse of the intellect," he said, and without self-consciousness, had patted his stomach. "The mind keeps so busy, one eats without noticing. And then the ideas generated leave no time for exercise." His eyes approved Holly's delicate blond beauty and her aura of innocence, accentuated by her mid-length gown of white lace trimmed handkerchief linen with its Dutch collar. "Also, I have a gourmet's palate," he told her gravely. There was a sudden unexpected twinkle in his warm brown eyes under straight brows. "I cannot resist Fritos."

Holly had laughed aloud. It was the first time she'd really laughed since separating from her husband, and she was grateful to Meyerling for that. "My first diplomatic top secret," she said. "I can't wait to leak it."

"I am at your mercy. My security clearance is in your lovely hands." There was not even the hint of a lilt, let alone an accent in his voice, but there was nevertheless a precision that said he was foreign-born.

"Good. I can blackmail you for top-secret information and sell it to the Russians." Holly's unaccustomed lightness of spirit continued.

Meyerling's eyes had strayed approvingly over Holly's smooth, long pearl-pink neck and throat. "Just what secret is it that you want me to betray?" he asked, his gaze coming to rest on her clear, attentive blue eyes.

Holly thought a moment. "If Ronald Reagan is elected, will you be his Secretary of State?"

"That's not a very secret secret, and not a government secret at all—only a political one."

"Is there a difference?"

"Oh, yes. Political secrets are devised only in order to be divulged."

"But you're not divulging. You're hedging."

"Not at all. I will answer your question. The answer is no, I will not be Ronald Reagan's Secretary of State."

"Why not?"

"Because he won't ask me. He will not ask Henry. He most certainly will not ask Zbigniew. But most of all, he will not ask me. You see, whatever else Ronald Reagan is, he is an expert at imagery. The image he wishes to convey is one of change, of a bright new future. We—I—are identified with past policies. There will be new faces and new twists in Washington when he is elected."

"When, not if?"

"When." Meyerling was positive. "He is the most . . . um, American—yes, that's it, the most American candidate to come along in years, and he will be unbeatable." His eyes danced briefly under the dark, thick brows. "Now what other top secrets will you extract from me?"

"His hair. Ronald Reagan's. What color is it really?" Holly wanted to know.

"Oh, no. The rack! The pincers under the fingernails! The threats to my nearest and dearest! None of these will push me to betraying this most important of America's top secrets. I will suckle the cyanide from my poison ring first. I swear it!"

"Would you prefer me to pass you the hemlock?" Holly was laughing again.

"Yes, please. Death before dishonor."

"And dinner before both." Holly nodded as the mahogany paneled doors leading to the kitchen hallway slid open and a parade of footmen bearing steaming silver platters advanced on the long dining table set with Baccarat crystal, delicate gold-laced Limoges plates, and George III silver on an antique point de venise lace tablecloth. The setting and Holly's fanciful period gown accentuated her patrician air. Her face surrounded by sprays of orchids, which served as the only floral adornment to the room, took on an ethereal beauty that was somehow glowingly alive.

Meyerling looked ruefully down at his slight bulge of stomach. "I shall restrain myself," he whispered to Holly with a sigh.

There had been a brief pause in their conversation as they were served the first course, a blanquette of oysters with champagne sauce. Meyerling ended it easily. "The Governor has told me," he said, "that you are a historian."

Holly felt herself blush. "Good Heavens, no. I only dabble."

"You have a master's degree in American History?"

"Well, yes, but—"

"What is your particular area of interest?" Meyerling seemed genuinely interested.

"The Hudson River Valley. I've been fascinated by the history of Riverview ever since I was a little girl."

"It is a fascinating place," Meyerling remarked sincerely. "Go on," he told her.

"When I was growing up here, I read everything I could find in Grandpa's library and the local library." Enthusiasm overcame Holly's modesty. "Then, when I was in Europe, I did a little research on my own—trying to trace the original settlers, the conditions that brought them here, that sort of thing."

"They were Dutch, the first settlers, weren't they?"

"Yes. And then later English. Anyway, recently my grandmother has arranged for me to have access to some private family records. They're kept at the Charles Stockwell Memorial Foundation, and some of them have never been seen by a historian before." Holly's excitement lit up her eyes and brought color to her cheeks.

Meyerling noticed. "But then you are not a historian," he murmured with amusement. "So it is all right for you to see them."

"Well, I'm really not. I'm only a dilettante, a dabbler. But I did run across this book written in the 1830s by an ancestor of ours, George Cortlandt Stockwell. It's written in the form of a sort of generational novel, and it's satiric, supposedly fictional, but what I'm discovering from other sources is that a lot of it is true. For instance, the first settlers were Dutch, as you said, but they weren't simply the adventurous spirits and pioneers we've been led to believe. They were refugees, just like the immigrants that came here later. They were running away just like the Eastern European Jews fleeing the pogroms, and the Central Americans today, running from political repression. They really didn't come here to create some great new society or country or anything like that. They just came to escape what they left behind."

"But they did build a new country."

"Inadvertently. Almost by accident. In fact, the descendants of the early settlers in the Hudson River Valley mostly opposed it. The family that built Riverview, for instance, was staunchly Tory."

"Well, they were Dutch, not English," Meyerling remembered.

"That should have pitted them against the English King, except they were wealthy property owners who had a vested interest in the status quo."

"And so"—the bushy eyebrows joined over the twinkle once more—"instead of a march on Washington, Washington led a march on them."

"Well, yes. But you see, it really started much further back. That's what's so fascinating—the have-nots evolving into the haves, and then battling against the have-nots. It's sort of a lesson in history, the beginnings of Riverview."

"Tell me about it, the beginnings."

Holly had focused on Meyerling sharply then. She had a horror of being condescended to, even if it was the result of a man's being attracted to her. But his dark, brooding eyes confirmed his genuine interest. She started telling him about what she'd been piecing together concerning the family that originally settled Riverview. Soon the words were tumbling enthusiastically from her lips.

It was only later, at the end of an evening Holly had thoroughly enjoyed, that she realized she'd succumbed to the famous Meyerling charm without identifying it as such. Its secret was not very profound. He knew how to listen. He was friendly and amusing, and he'd put her completely at her ease. She hadn't thought of Christopher at all during the evening.

Uneasily, she realized that it was something more than that as well. In Meyerling's presence she felt a sexual stirring she'd been deliberately suppressing since leaving her husband. When her marriage had been at its worst, Christopher was still able to arouse her. Sometimes she would be ashamed at the sexual abandonment she felt when confronted with aggressive sensuality. But ashamed or not, she'd burned with passion under its spell. Since leaving him, she'd tried to deny what she sometimes thought of as her wantonness. At other times she had thought of doing just the opposite: of going out and having sex with a man —simple, straightforward, no entanglements. But the thing she was most leery of was feeling an erotic attraction toward one specific man. For Holly, such a feeling would call for commitment and involvement and would no longer be simple erotic attraction. Her attraction to Meyerling was intellectual as well as sexual, and this frightened her.

Meyerling had taken her aside just before he left and asked if he might see her again. Holly realized he was attracted to her. Nevertheless, the request flustered her. In her confusion, she stammered that she was married, and when she realized how silly that sounded—he'd only asked her to dinner, after all—she added that really her life was in a bit of turmoil at present and could she have a rain check?

Meyerling, unflappable, had replied that of course she could. Then he had kissed her unexpectedly and quickly on the corner of her mouth and bid her good night.

Now Zelig Meyerling concluded his eulogy to his friend and mentor, Governor Matthew Adams Stockwell. Descending from the pulpit, he paused to bestow kisses of condolence first on Buffy and then on Mary before returning to his seat. The congregation rose and sang "Rock of Ages," the minister read once more from the Bible, and the service was concluded. Everybody waited while the Governor's immediate family stood and exited the church.

Outside Holly chatted with her cousin Patrice. After a moment they were joined by Patrice's father. "Christopher is determined to come to the reading of the will," Holly, obviously upset, blurted out to her Uncle James.

"I know. He mentioned his intention to David and Peter and me earlier."

"I don't want him there!"

"Why not?"

"I don't trust him, Uncle James."

"I see." His tone registered neither surprise nor alarm.

"Is there any way he can be prevented from coming?"

"I don't see how. He's your husband. Under law that makes him a concerned member of the family. He has every right to be present." His words were practical and to the point, but they were meant kindly.

"The only reason we're not divorced is because he avoided service of the papers."

"Even if you were divorced, Christopher is the father of your son, the Governor's great-grandson. He has a legal right to be there to look after his child's interests."

"His own interests, you mean!" Holly couldn't hide her bitterness. "And Grandpa detested Christopher. He certainly would never leave him anything."

"But the Governor undoubtedly left bequests to you and to Nicholas. I can only repeat that you are Christopher's wife and Nicholas is his son, and that gives him every right to be present. I'm sorry, Holly." James Stockwell excused himself and went to thank Meyerling for his eulogy.

"You really are frazzled." Patrice said sympathetically.

"Yes."

"I guess your marriage to Christopher was not exactly Eden on the Thames."

"To put it mildly." Holly smiled wanly.

"Well, this isn't the time or place, but if you feel like talking about it, my shoulder's tearproof." Patrice squeezed her hand.

"Thanks. I guess I'd like that. I've never really discussed it with anybody. There didn't seem to be anyone around who would understand—anybody my age, I mean. I couldn't really talk about it with Grandma or Grandpa."

"I should have called you when you came back." Patrice was contrite. "But I've been so damn busy at the office. Listen, let's not leave it tentative. Let's make a firm date. This week. I'll buy you lunch."

"You mean in the city?"

"If that's all right."

"Well, yes, it's fine. As it happens, I have some research at the Institute on Thursday."

Holly and Patrice agreed to meet at one-thirty. Ordinarily Patrice would have suggested the Oak Room, but there was some kind of convention at the Plaza, so they arranged to dine at the Rose Room of the Algonquin Hotel.

67

10

THE BURIAL OF Governor Matthew Adams Stockwell was the most private of all the ceremonies following his death. Attendance was limited to the family and only those servants judged by James Linstone Stockwell to have been with the family long enough to qualify as old retainers. Thus the Governor's personal chauffeur Kevin O'Lunney attended, along with his friend the gardener, Gustav Ulbricht, who had been hired by the Governor's first wife more than thirty years ago. But Kevin's daughter Kathleen did not attend.

Internment was in the private family cemetery on a bluff overlooking the Hudson five miles north of the manor house. The limousines pulled up at the foot of the bluff where the road ended. The last half mile was a steep path which had to be traversed on foot.

The ascent was Darwinian. The fittest—which really meant the youngest—reached the open grave site first. Here they waited while their elders huffed and strained to join them, pausing frequently to relieve the ordeal. Holly was among those waiting.

So, too, was the pastor of the Riverview Heights Methodist church, who would lead the family in a simple burial ceremony—in accordance with the Governor's wishes—and would personally place the silver urn containing the Governor's ashes in their final resting place. Now he came forward to greet Holly's Uncle Jonathan and his wife Ellen, the first of the older Stockwells to appear over the rise. Holly, too, came forward to kiss her uncle's dry cheek and her aunt's dryer one.

Ellen Stockwell was six years older than her husband and looked it. At fifty-two she was a colorless woman, long of face and body, curveless. Thinly plucked eyebrows arched over deep black eyes, and her face wore disappointment as if under the misapprehension that it was makeup. It was no secret to any of the family that the source of Ellen's disappointment was her husband.

Before marrying Jonathan, Ellen Smith had been his secretary. She'd turned this position into a motherly role, picking his shirts and ties for him, nurturing his ego, staying late to correct his mistakes, just as his brother James would later. Indeed, it was from Ellen, not Jonathan, that their son Peter had inherited his flair for business.

But Ellen had wanted more than to be just the woman behind the man, his silent buttress. As his secretary, she had yearned after the wealth and position that went with being a Stockwell. She was older, but more important, she was knowledgeable and cunning where Jonathan was naive, and that enabled her to get what she wanted.

She set out to seduce him, and it wasn't hard. Jonathan's experience with women and sex had been limited to undergraduate gropings and visits to discreet bordellos catering to a Wall Street clientele generally much older than himself. He was dazzled by his irresistibility to this older woman as competent in bed as in business. He could not wait to make love to her again—and then again, and again, and again.

Ellen had kept him coming until certain she was pregnant. The family was informed. The Governor had a talk with her, and she made him understand that abortion was out of the question and that a child of hers entitled to the Stockwell name was going to have his due.

"Marry her," the Governor told his son. "She will make you an excellent wife. She has determination." And, he felt, his son needed it. He did not add that she would make his son happy. Indeed, he was quite sure that she would not.

Happiness was not Ellen's lot either. She may have snared a Stockwell, but she soon came to realize that he was the least of the clan—tolerated, condescended to, taken care of, but not respected. All this was clear to her by the time her son Peter was born, six and a half barely justifiable months after she and Jonathan were wed.

To make up for her disappointment with the father, she focused on the boy. He was a Stockwell, and she was absolutely determined that he would also be everything that his father was not. He would exercise the power that was rightfully his, the power Jonathan seemed all too happy to relinquish to James. Now, twenty-five years later, with Peter showing every sign of bringing her ambitions to fruition, Ellen's obsession was out in the open. Resentment, bitterness, revenge—these were the ingredients of the cosmetic painted by time on her sallow, long face.

Like most of the Stockwells, Holly found little to say to her Aunt Ellen, whose responses—while usually carefully polite—did not encourage the continuation of conversation. Now Holly drifted away to the western boundary of the small cemetery and looked out over the Hudson.

The view was spectacular. Under the cloudy sky the river and hills were patterned like a faded tapestry. The Palisades across the river were muted, their greenery dulled, a patina of gray blending the browns to a drab tan and pasteling the wildflowers. Even the normal springtime turbulence of the Hudson was calmed by the bleak effluvia rising from its waters.

Everything that could be seen from the bluff on this side of the Hudson's banks was part of the Riverview estate. The boat house—a two-story structure long as a city block—had lost its white gleam to the fog. In deference to the Governor's passing, someone had thought to lower to half-mast the flags of the three river yachts and those of the smaller craft anchored at the complex of docks. But the flags' lankness on this windless day, and their lusterless colors, expressed sadness more eloquently than their halfway position on the staffs.

Following with her eyes the dull pewter serpentine path winding from the boat house up the hill to the gazebo, Holly thought to herself that there was nothing as unhappy as places designed for pleasure on a day of mourning. The tennis courts had never looked so bleak, the riding paths so deserted, the swimming pools so deprived of laughter as they did at this moment, when she was viewing them from the site of what would be the Governor's grave. He, who had loved Riverview not just for its natural beauty, but also for the many opportunities for pleasure he'd created there, would be buried in desolation.

Holly sighed. Perhaps that was as it should be. Death

was an ending, the most final of all, and endings were not meant to be happy.

The grim thought directed her attention to the other gravestones as she waited for the last of the mourners to puff and straggle up the hillside. She had drifted to the one corner of the cemetery not occupied by past generations of Stockwells. The stones here were all pre-Revolutionary, and they all bore the same Dutch name—Van Bronckel.

Holly's eyes widened with recognition. Lately, in her researches and in George Cortlandt Stockwell's thinly disguised memoir, she had been reading a lot about the van Bronckel family. They were the ones who had settled Riverview, long before the first Stockwell set foot on the property.

It seemed fitting that she should come upon their family plot on this of all days. The van Bronckels had certainly been no strangers to mourning.

Death. It had ruled the hold of the ship on which Dirk van Bronckel left Holland for the New World in 1632. He was fourteen years old, traveling with his mother, father, and two younger sisters.

The van Bronckels were Calvinists from the southern Walloon hinterlands. In the northern part of the Netherlands the Calvinists, revenging themselves for both the Spanish conquest of their country—which had just ended—and for the Inquisition, were slaughtering Catholics freely. But in the southern Netherlands, where the van Bronckels had been tenant farmers, the majority Catholic population had struck back. Here it was open season on Calvinists, and the custom of burning them at the stake was enjoying a revival.

This dissension had been viewed as a much needed opportunity by the directors of the Dutch West India Company. The mercantile firm, modeled after the very successful Dutch East India Company, had been formed to capitalize on the New World discoveries of Henry Hudson. However, it had not been able to inspire the emigration to the New World necessary to develop the lucrative fur-trapping outposts planned for the banks of the river named after Hudson. Now, however, with Catholics killing Calvinists, Calvinists killing Catholics, and refugees fleeing every which way over the countryside, the Dutch West India Company's latest recruitment drive was meeting with growing success.

Dirk van Bronckel's father was one of those attracted by the promises the company made in a handbill which, like the majority of Dutchmen, he could not himself read. He signed on with the Dutch West India Company and received a piece of paper which gave him exclusive trapping rights for a strip of land stretching six miles up the banks of the Hudson in what would one day be Westchester County. He did not know that for many hundreds of years this had been the exclusive hunting preserve of the Iroquois Indian nation.

It didn't matter. Meinjeer van Bronckel did not survive the journey to the New World. Neither did his wife, nor his two little girls. Like two thirds of the passengers in the ship's hold, they died of plague—later identified as smallpox—somewhere in the mid-Atlantic. Thus fourteen-year-old Dirk van Bronckel arrived on the harbor island of New Amsterdam—to be renamed New York when the British seized it—an orphan. His father's sparsely stuffed purse had been taken by the captain of the ship as payment for giving his family a decent burial at sea.

However, Dirk did have the piece of paper—which like his father before him, he could not read—that the Dutch West India Company had issued. It propelled him up the Hudson to the site where one day the Riverview boat house would stand. Here he built himself a rough pine shack and started hunting beaver, otter, bear, and other fur-bearing animals.

The Indians in the region, still mostly Mohawks, took pity on him and taught him skills that soon resulted in his accumulating an impressive number of hides. Twice-yearly he traveled downriver to the company warehouses in the city of Bruecklen, across the bay from New Amsterdam. Here Dirk was paid in guilders for the skins. At first he used the money to buy supplies. But on one of his trips he had an inspiration and bought entirely different goods.

He purchased beads, trinkets, bright cloth, and spangles, and brought them back to his riverbank hut with him. The Mohawks, entranced by the treasures, didn't hesitate to swap Dirk pelts for these items. Soon, all up and down the riverbanks, tepees were decorated with bits of golden Turkish cloth and garlands of multicolored glass necklaces. Now Dirk personally did no hunting and trapping at all. He just called his hut a trading post and exchanged gimcrackery for the animal furs so prized by the burgher's wives in Amsterdam. He was marketing seven and eight times as many pelts as when he'd snared them on his own.

On one of his trips to New Amsterdam, after his trading post had been in operation some ten years, Dirk decided to take a wife. He first spied her in a waterfront tavern, which wasn't unusual since the tawdry pleasures of dockside were as close as he ever came to a social life on his sojourns to the city.

Greta was sixteen years old—a prostitute, of course. Dirk knew that. He didn't care. She was willing to come with him, to marry him, to keep the shack he called his house.

One spring morning Greta gave birth to a squalling, red-faced son with a Dutch head the shape of a building block. Gazing at the boy, Dirk smiled one of his very rare smiles, and named his son Hendrik.

The next day, with no urging at all from Greta, he began to build a proper house for his family on top of the hill overlooking the trading post. It was the first real house of what his descendants would call the Riverview plantation, and it stood on the very site where Riverview manor itself would someday stand.

Hendrik would be Dirk van Bronckel's only son. As the boy grew to manhood, Dirk taught him the fur-trading business, and they became partners. The partnership flourished and continued to flourish as Hendrik took a wife and himself fathered sons. Together, father and son, they became more prosperous than Dirk had ever dreamed he would be.

With the money from the furs Dirk purchased patroon rights to Hudson River Valley land from the government of burghers in New Amsterdam. He leased these lands to tenant farmers in return for a share of their crops. Soon Hendrik found it necessary to organize his father's tenants into a defense force against the Mohawks, who now began to actively protest the parceling out of their ancestral hunting grounds.

Despite the flare-ups of Indian violence, Dirk and Hendrik grew richer. Their lands, which by now Hendrik had named Riverview, soon comprised one of the dozen great patroon estates of the Hudson River Valley. The penniless orphan had become, by the time of his death in 1690, one of the wealthiest landowners in the region. Hendrik and Hendrik's grown sons buried Dirk van Bronckel on a plateau overlooking the Hudson. He was the first of Riverview's residents to be put to rest there.

Dirk van Bronckel's headstone stood there still, the name indecipherable, as Holly looked up from the markers of the van Bronckel family in the Riverview graveyard and watched the ceremony of the Governor's burial begin.

11

"DO YOU HAVE many lovers?"

Holly had her back to the young woman who posed this question. It seemed particularly incongruous in this setting. It was the day following the Governor's burial and most of the family was gathered—milling about, actually—in the entrance hall to Riverview, a high-ceilinged chamber lit by sunlight streaming through a stained-glass window at the halfway landing of the sweeping, circular staircase. The window had been installed by an aunt of the Governor's around the turn of the century. Originally it had graced a Dresden church.

The quasireligious atmosphere was ratified by various pieces of Italian Renaissance statuary set in the spaced marble alcoves lining the staircase and the entrance hall itself. While not religious, a hand-carved grandfather clock—purchased at considerable expense from a Tate auction in London by the Governor's father—affirmed the hallowed aura of the chamber. So, too, did the somber family portraits arranged in the entrance hall and up the staircase of dark, polished oak. These ranged from the formalities of Thomas Gainsborough and Gilbert Stuart to three more relaxed but no less respectful works by John Singer Sargent. Interspersed with the portraits were rich landscapes by Frederick Church and Regis Gignoux, of the Hudson River School.

The Stockwells and Lewises, Tylers and Carters, O'Keefes and Wells-Grays were gathered here because of the sudden showers fulfilling April's promise outside. They were waiting for the limousines to pull up one by one at the front door so that they might embark on the trip to Albany. Governor Hugh Carey, "an Irish Democrat, but a gentleman with a sense for the proprieties nevertheless" in Jonathan Stockwell's estimation, had scheduled a major state tribute and memorial service in the rotunda of Albany's State Capitol building in honor of his predecessor, Governor Stockwell.

"Do I have many lovers?" The flagrant question was repeated and then answered by an unshocked, low-key voice behind Holly. "Not really. Only two, actually. One for weekdays, and one for weekends."

It was true. At thirty-five Diana Tyler—the woman answering—had her SoHo artist's life arranged in an orderly fashion not at all in keeping with the wild compositions— "I paint in defiance of Cubism!" she would laugh—and fauvist colors that marked her work. Her appearance was as rumpled as her canvases, or her long red-gold Tyler hair, but her romantic life was well compartmentalized.

George—weekdays—was a married suburbanite. On Tuesday and Thursday nights, freed from the chains of family, his lovemaking was passionately grateful. It suited Diana deliciously. She wanted no more from George, and certainly no less.

Ernie—weekends—was a merchandising man who covered New England Mondays through Fridays, a confirmed bachelor incapable of hurting a woman's feelings by refusing to make love to her. But always he returned to Diana, and always with some new move, some new fillip, some new technique to pique her erotic interest. Through Ernie, vicariously, Diana felt like some rampaging courtesan of royalist France. And the nicest thing about Ernie

75

was that she never had to leave SoHo to feel that way, and therefore had plenty of time for her painting.

Neither lover, of course, knew about the other.

"Only two? Why, that's practically as bad as being married." The questioner, disappointed, moved away.

Holly turned around and her eyes met Diana's. The painter grinned. "It seems," she remarked, "that an artist's life isn't any more agreeable to young Tylers than old Stockwells."

"Not hard to guess which twin that was." Holly smiled back. "Beth would have been asking you about the obligation of the artist to have a social conscience à la Picasso's 'Guernica.'"

"Oh, it was Carrie, all right," Diana confirmed. "Right down to the white powder on the tip of her nose, which was in no way Max Factor."

"Sugared doughnuts?" Holly was slow on the uptake.

"Not likely. Not for my little second cousin Carrie. Unless I miss my guess, she's been snorting lines in the downstairs bathroom."

"Cocaine?" Holly was shocked. Carrie was so young, and this was hardly the place. "Are you sure?"

"Darling," Diana replied dryly, "I know snow from powdered sugar when I see it."

Before Holly could reply, Carrie's twin Beth walked up to her and Diana. Again, Beth's black outfit—a simple traveling suit—was similar but not identical to Carrie's. "Has Sis been bugging you?" she asked.

"Not really," Diana replied.

"How have you been, Beth?" Things had been so hectic since the Governor's death that it was really the first time Holly had spoken with her.

"Just fine." Beth went on to discuss her plans for Bryn Mawr in the autumn. While the three of them chatted, her almond-shaped eyes kept straying toward the front door, where the various chauffeurs were summoning mourners to their cars.

"Don't worry, Beth." Holly followed her gaze. "You won't be left behind."

"I know that. It's just that I want to ride with Zelig Meyerling. I want to ask him about the nuclear freeze."

"You don't have to ask him." Diana was disdainful. "I can tell you. He doesn't support it."

"I know that. I wanted to ask him why—face to face."

"Do you think this is the time—" Holly started to say.

"I don't mean to start a fight. Not even a confrontation. Just a person-to-person sort of reasoning together. I mean, he is for disarmament, so why—" Beth broke off suddenly and her face turned angry. "Damn!" she said. "Damn her anyway! She knew I wanted to ride with him."

Holly followed Beth's furious gaze. Her twin sister Carrie had linked arms with Meyerling and was following a chauffeur out the door with him. Just before she exited, she turned around, looked directly at Beth from identical hazel eyes, and stuck out her tongue. It was quick and playful, but nonetheless spiteful.

Outside, Carrie allowed Meyerling to help her into the back of the limousine. When he followed her, she reached across him and closed the door. "You can go," she told the driver. "There's just the two of us." And she added, before Meyerling could protest, "I just don't feel up to sharing our car with anyone else right now."

Ever the gentleman, Meyerling nodded and told the chauffeur to follow in with the rest of the procession bound for Albany.

As the Cadillac moved smoothly off, Carrie leaned forward and rolled up the window separating them from the front seat. She knew that the window was one-way; they could see into the front but the driver couldn't see into the back. "I feel like I'm coming apart," she told Meyerling. "I don't think I could bear for him to see me."

"Is there anything I can do?" What a remarkably beautiful girl, Meyerling thought. That extraordinary hair! Very young, but already classically lovely. He didn't know the Tylers at all, and had only the haziest idea of Carrie's relationship to the Stockwell family. He didn't even know that she had a twin sister.

"No." Carrie sighed deeply. Two large tears rolled slowly down her cheeks from her tilted Tyler eyes.

"Oh, my dear—"

A choked sob escaped her lips. Carrie turned toward him, green-flecked hazel eyes brimming now. Her smooth young face was a pleading mask of heartbroken grief.

Meyerling did the natural thing. Obviously this young relative of the Governor's was in need of solace. He put his arms around her and patted her shoulders.

Carrie buried her face against his chest. Her hands went inside the jacket of the custom-made Carnaby Street suit he'd bought on his last trip to London, and she clutched at his ribs through the tailored silk sides of his vest as if she were drowning. He reached for her hands, first because they were tickling him slightly, and second, in order to hold them in his own and perhaps communicate some comfort. Instead he found a firm, young, hard-tipped silken breast, unencumbered by brassiere, nestling in his palm. Embarrassed, he tried to release it. But before he could, Carrie had shifted position and the breast was pinning his hand between them. Meyerling felt a masculine stirring not at all seemly for such a solemn occasion.

He decided to say something, but before he could formulate the words, Carrie moaned and her face slid down against his chest and came to rest on the slight protuberance of tummy, below his vest. Reflexively, he sucked in his stomach. This caused Carrie's face to slip even farther down.

There had been moments before in Zelig Meyerling's life where events so unexpected had occurred as to be comprehended by him with only the greatest astonishment and disbelief. When he was young, scarce out of his twenties, he had been face to face with a shouting Nikita Khrushchev, who had abruptly stopped pounding his shoe, put it back on his foot, bent to tie the laces, looked up at him and grinned. "All right," the Russian had said. "We will concede on the question of Iranian oil." On another occasion, having just completed a five-minute speech praising Henry Kissinger, the President of the United States had turned to Meyerling and asked him sotto voce if he would be interested in replacing Henry. And once, during Meyerling's own tenure as Secretary of State, the head of the Joint Chiefs of Staff, after perhaps one drink too many, had confessed to him that in reality there was no effective safeguard against the pressing of the nuclear button by any one of the number of officers of middle rank who had nothing to do with making crucial policy decisions.

His reaction to such moments was to question their reality. That was his reaction now, in the back of the silently cruising limousine, as he felt the warm breath approach his loins, heard the unmistakably metallic sound of zipper teeth unlocking, sensed the approach of pursed, young lips. Zelig Meyerling did not believe this was happening.

But it was.

It was a New York State good-bye. The nation's farewell would come later. Governor Hugh Carey spoke movingly, making no reference to Matthew Stockwell's public chortling only a few days before his death at columnist Jimmy Breslin labeling him "Limousine Carey." The Lieutenant Governor paid tribute, despite Stockwell's jibe at him as "Milksop Mario" for his deeply felt stand against the death penalty. The Mayor of New York City—his sour pickle face truly bereaved, perhaps more from finding himself in Albany than grief at the Governor's death—did not mention Matthew Stockwell's letter to the *Times* pointing out that if the Koch giveaways to the landlords continued, even he, Matthew Adams Stockwell, would no longer be able to afford to live in New York City.

Naturally the Republicans were even more stricken at the loss of such a valued leader. State Senate chief Warren Anderson spoke with tears in his eyes, and never once mentioned his former rage at the bills Stockwell had consistently vetoed favoring his district. Senator Roy Goodman eulogized a fellow Manhattanite as if Stockwell had not always worked behind the scenes for Westchester and Putnam, Rockland and Orange first, Brooklyn, Queens, the Bronx, and Staten Island second, and Manhattan tied with Buffalo's Erie County running a poor third. And David Rockefeller, a banker after all and not a pol, fell back on quoting his brother Nelson as to Matthew Stockwell's greatness, as if the two had not fought each other head to head down through the years for control of the state and —they had both hoped—someday the nation, too.

Sitting with Buffy, holding her hand to express sympathy, was Governor Carey's wife-to-be, the wealthy, beautiful, and thrice-married Evangeline Gouletas. Matilda Cuomo sat with James, who was a widower. Mary Linstone Stockwell, the Governor's first wife, was flanked by the Harrimans—the aging, but still brilliant Averill, and his much younger third wife Pamela, whom he had first met through her then father-in-law, Winston Churchill. The Harrimans were old and valued friends, even if they were Democrats. Mary was lost in a reminiscence of having been their guest in Washington, along with Matthew, on a long-ago night when the citizens of the nation's capital serenaded Averill Harriman for having negotiated the very first arms limitation treaty with the Russians.

Diana Tyler had not been present on that occasion, but her great-aunt, knowing Diana's political leanings, had described it to her many times. Seeing Mary with the Harrimans, she recalled it now. And later, after the ceremony ended, Diana stood outside the State Capitol building and tried to convey to Holly and Beth Tyler the feelings of hope for all humanity Mary had described to her.

"Yes," Holly agreed. "Grandma told me about it, too. So did Grandpa. You know how cynical he always tried to act, but even he couldn't be cynical about that."

"Oh, yes." Beth's eighteen-year-old eyes were shining. "It must have been such a moment of hope for people everywhere. And there can be other moments like it. There really can be."

"I believe that," Diana agreed with her quietly.

"I hope for such moments." Holly was slightly less sanguine. From the corner of her eye she observed Beth's twin talking to Holly's cousin Michael. The expression on Carrie's face conveyed open interest, and Michael was obviously responding to it. At the same time, Holly caught a glimpse of Zelig Meyerling moving alone toward one of the limousines. "Beth." She nodded in Meyerling's direction. "Here's your chance."

"Oh." Beth smiled. "Thanks, Holly." She moved quickly toward Meyerling.

Standing beside the car, Meyerling saw her coming. Not aware that there were twins, he thought Beth was Carrie, the impetuous young woman with whom he had shared the limousine to Albany. Now, from the eager look on her face, she seemed to be anticipating a similarly bizarre ride back.

Meyerling was no prude, but neither was he an exhibitionist, nor a teenager anxious to steal moments of passion in the backseat of a car. He decidedly did not wish to be alone with this beauty with the apricot hair and the hungry hazel eyes on the return trip.

The passing arm he clutched at belonged to Peter Stockwell. "Peter." He beamed charm. "Why don't you ride back with me so that we can talk?"

Peter was flattered. There was a moment of confusion as Beth came up to them, and they both began saying something to Meyerling at the same time. Meyerling dealt with it by ushering them both into the car with him. When they were seated, he had contrived to place Peter between him and Beth.

She was disappointed. Meyerling was polite, of course, but it was Peter, and not she, whom he was encouraging to talk. Peter was half turned away from her in the car, talking to Meyerling. She would have had to lean around him to broach the subject most important to her—the nuclear freeze—to Meyerling. It was just too awkward to interrupt.

And so Beth sat back and listened. She tuned in on Meyerling in mid-sentence, responding to something Peter had said. "...an odd direction for someone concerned with real estate," Meyerling observed.

"Not really." Peter's voice was confident, glad to have Meyerling's attention but not intimidated by it. "Real estate isn't just land. It's water, too. And air. Naturally that includes whatever rights are inherent in the water and air. And so the truth is that today I'm spending more and more of my time buying up ERC's. I've even started a trading company under the Stockwell umbrella called Oxytron. It's a wide open market."

"Suppose the loophole is plugged?"

"You were in the federal government, Mr. Meyerling. How long do you think it will take the Environmental Protection Agency to do that?"

"I see what you mean." Meyerling laughed. "Well," he said, "I don't suppose Oxytron needs any additional capitalization, does it?"

"I can't imagine that it would. Still, you might ask me again after the will is read. Right now, of course, there's plenty of Stockwell capital available for the purpose."

"Too bad."

"But you're like a member of the family." Peter spread his hands. "Of course I can make room for you to invest if you want."

"Perhaps I'd better check with Interior first." Meyerling was teasing. "Maybe there's pressure building for them to clamp down on ERC's."

"If you find out anything—"

"Of course, my boy."

"Just what are ERC's?" The momentary pause gave Beth a chance to ask.

"Emission Reduction Credits," Peter told her as he turned and smiled.

"Which are?"

"Well, that's kind of technical. It takes a little explaining."

"Well, now, if I lay my apron aside and put down my dolls and listen real hard, maybe smart old you can think of a way to put it simply enough so I can understand." Beth batted her long, red-gold eyelashes like Lucille Ball in the reruns.

Meyerling chuckled softly.

"Whoa!" Peter was affable. "Some of my best friends are women."

"I'm listening very hard."

"Okay, then." He took a deep breath. "To put it as simply as possible, ERC's—Emission Reduction Credits—are pollution rights."

"You're kidding!" Beth's hazel eyes narrowed.

"Well, now, don't jump to the wrong conclusions. Like I told you before, it's complicated. Let me give you an example. Let's say Megabuck Industries in Chicago is brought up on charges of polluting the air by the U.S. Environmental Protection Agency. Okay, they're given six months to put scrubbers on their chimneys to cut down the pollution by, oh, say twenty-five percent. Now for the sake of argument, let's say this costs them 3.2 million—"

"How can you put a price tag on the air people breathe?" Beth wondered.

"Money," Peter told her, "makes the world go 'round."

"How original. Did you just think of it?"

Meyerling squelched another chuckle.

"Anyway," Peter continued, "after the scrubbers are installed, Megabuck Industries realizes it's cut pollution not by twenty-five percent, but by thirty-five percent. It has accumulated Emission Reduction Credits. Now in some cases it will be to a company's advantage to increase production back up to the pollution limit. But in the majority of instances, for marketing reasons, that's not a profitable thing to do. So they try to sell that extra ten percent pollution right—the ERC's—to another manufacturing company that needs them."

"Is that legal?" Beth stared at him.

"Sure. They're transferable. Why not? The EPA has set an air quality standard. If Megabucks is well below that standard, why shouldn't it be able to help out another company that's above it and turn a profit at the same time? The company that buys the rights is going to pay Megabuck Industries a lot less than it would cost them to put in scrubbers."

"I see." Beth's voice was turning cold. "But I thought you were in real estate," she remembered. "What has all this got to do with your business?"

"Say there is no company already in the area to buy up the ERC's. Well, that's where my new trading company comes in. I buy the ERC's and hold them. Sometimes you can buy them up cheap because many companies—particularly smaller ones—don't yet realize that ERC's are assets. I check to see if Stockwell owns real estate in the area. If we don't, I set about buying land covered by the ERC's. Then I seek out a small manufacturer—or a big one with specialized small plant operations—and I sell them land along with the ERC's."

"With built-in pollution rights, you mean!"

"Sure. But within the guidelines."

"But you could have ten percent less air pollution if you didn't resell the rights," Beth said, tight-lipped.

"Well sure, but—"

"I think it's unconscionable!" Now she did lean around Peter, not caring how awkward it was, and stared into Meyerling's face. "The government should do something to stop it."

"I'm no longer in the government." Meyerling held up his hands defensively, his customary slight smile—the one expressing charm and charisma—on his face.

"But you have access. You have connections."

"The environment is not my field. I try not to interfere in it. Besides . . ."

"Yes?" Beth stared hard at him. "Besides?"

"The overall result of the guidelines, despite the resale of Emission Reduction Credits, has been to reduce pollution to acceptable limits."

"Acceptable to whom?"

"To the Environmental Protection Agency."

"Try telling that to some Chicagoan breathing Megabucks' ERC air. Tell it to some poor old lady with emphysema, or a slum kid with asthma, or a pregnant woman passing that garbage down to her unborn baby."

"Automobile pollution—" Meyerling started to say.

"And you're even willing to invest in it," Beth remembered, riding right over him. "You! A man who used to be Secretary of State of the United States of America!"

"*You* invest in it," Peter reminded her quietly, his dark eyes flashing anger. "All of your family, the Tylers, have holdings in Stockwell Industries."

"Not by choice!" she assured him. "And not for long if I have anything to say about it!"

"You are very righteous for one so young." Meyerling regretted the words the instant he spoke them.

"And you, Mr. Meyerling," she snapped back at him, "are an abomination. Peter is just greedy and ambitious and still young enough to change. But you are older and supposed to be wise and supposed to be concerned about the people of this country." Beth took a deep, shaky breath. "Maybe I am righteous," she said. "But you, Zelig Meyerling, are a pig!"

He stared at her, then leaned back and looked out the window on his side. First that brazen assault on the way to Albany, and now this. Yes, she is really crazy.

The three of them rode the rest of the way to Riverview in silence.

12

A S THE PROCESSION of limousines wound its way down
the Taconic Parkway toward the turnoff for Riverview, Matt Stockwell, grandson of the Governor, and
Kathleen O'Lunney, redheaded daughter of the Governor's personal chauffeur, sat facing each other across a
booth in a diner just off a strip of highway outside Albany.
Kathleen had ridden to the Albany services in the front of
one of the limousines with her father. Matt had driven up
by himself in a car of a vintage so ancient as to make some
of the older members of the family wince.

After the ceremony Matt offered Kathleen a lift home,
and she accepted. Both hungry, they had stopped off for a
hamburger before starting south. The burgers were awful,
they agreed, then laughing, wolfed them down and ordered seconds.

"How is it, now, that you didn't come up in one of the
limos like the toff you are?" Kathleen inquired, matching
Matt bite for hungry bite.

"How come you don't spice up your conversation with
high-tone cussing any more?" Matt shot back.

"Sure, I only do that when I meet a fellow for the first
time—to get us over the awkwardness."

"I see."

"Now I'll have my answer," she demanded.

"It's Irish you are today," Matt mimicked, teasing.

"It comes and it goes without my thinking too much
about it. It's sorry I am for the inconsistency, but then we
can't all be high-and-mighty Stockwells, is it?" Kathleen
deliberately came down hard on the Irish accent.

"Stockwell, yes. High and mighty, no. And for what it's
worth, I am head over heels in love with your brogue."

"With my brogue only is it then?"

"Absolutely. The rest of you is all freckles and sass. I
want no part of it."

85

"And a good thing! My faither would nivir approve such goings-on with a Stockwell, not knowin' what he does about your dreadful family skeletons and all."

"Now you really are overdoing it. You'll choke on your hamburger."

"Sure, and that's all it's fit for. But then what would I be expectin'? Date a Stockwell and beware the vittles. Sure and everybody backstairs knows that."

"Beware the vittles!" Matt laughed heartily. "I'm going to take away your television! You've been watching too much *Upstairs, Downstairs*. It's barely tolerable in British, but with an Irish brogue it's positively 'Up the Rebels!'"

"Ah, well." Kathleen giggled and dropped the brogue except for the faint, unconscious lilt that was always part of her speech.

"And this is not a date," Matt added. "I only offered you a lift home."

"I'm sorry." Kathleen clutched at her breast with both hands, a mock-tragic gesture. "I had forgotten the abyss separating our stations in life."

"The date comes later."

"Does it?"

"Like next Saturday night, say?"

"Well, maybe." Kathleen pressed a fingertip to a freckle on her cheek as if thinking it over.

"What does 'maybe' mean?"

"It means absolutely yes, but I don't want to look too eager."

"Of course not." Matt ostentatiously patted a yawn. "Neither one of us is really interested in the other. It's just to pass the time."

"That's right." Kathleen giggled again. "So tell me," she said, "why did you drive up in that wreck of yours by yourself instead of coming in a limo with the rest of the family?"

Matt considered, and decided on an honest answer. "So I'd have an excuse to offer you a ride back, just the two of us, and maybe ask you for a date."

"Really?" Kathleen blushed freckles. "Well, I'm very pleased that you did." She reached across the table and took his hand in hers.

They looked into each other's smiling eyes for a moment. Abruptly, Matt's expression changed. It was so marked that Kathleen dropped his hand and pulled back. He was looking at something over her left shoulder.

Kathleen turned and followed his gaze. A young woman with long black hair and very white skin was standing at the cash register paying her check. Her paleness was incongruous with the multipocketed trail pants, faded lumberjack shirt, and backpack she wore, indicating an outdoors life. She was counting out change to pay the bill carefully, but without embarrassment, her dark eyes intense under unshaped brows as she laid down the coins one by one. The intensity matched the too-thin wiriness of her small-boned body. There was something both timid and wild about her.

"Who—" Kathleen started to say.

"Excuse me." Matt was on his feet, an odd expression on his face as he moved toward the young woman. Startled, her eyes widened and her body tensed as she looked up and saw him. She looked poised for escape.

Matt said something to her; something very serious from the look on his face, Kathleen thought. She was too far away to hear either his murmured words or her soft reply. He spoke again, and put his hand on the woman's arm. She shook her head violently. He tried to continue speaking, but she pulled her arm away. As she started out of the diner, Matt tried to follow.

She wheeled on him. "Leave me alone!" That Kathleen heard, as did quite a few others in the diner. "I'm in a hurry." Her voice was softer now, but audible, and with a note of pleading. "I have to get to Montreal, and I'm late."

"But I can't just let you go again like this. We have to talk."

"I'll contact you. I promise I will. But I really have to go now, Matt." And then she was out the door of the diner and gone.

Slowly, Matt came back to Kathleen and sat down, an expression of numbed disbelief on his face. She waited for him to say something, make some explanation, but he seemed lost in thought. Kathleen felt as if she might as well not be there, but she couldn't be angry with him when he was so obviously in pain.

Unable to stand the silence any longer, she finally

spoke. "Who was that?" Her voice was sympathetic, interested, not resentful.

"Someone I knew in Canada." His tone was flat, unhappy.

"Knew well, I guess."

"We lived together for three years."

"Oh." That wasn't something Kathleen particularly wanted to hear. "I'm sorry. I didn't mean to pry. It's really none of my business."

"That's all right. Running into Wendy was a real rainstorm on our parade. I know how I'm behaving. You're entitled to an explanation."

"Her name is Wendy?" Kathleen didn't know what else to say.

"Yeah. Wendy MacTavish."

"Scotch."

"On her father's side. Her mother was French, only she died when Wendy was small. Her father brought her up, and then he threw her out when he found out she was involved with me. He had nothing but contempt for draft dodgers."

"So Wendy moved in with you?"

"That's right. She moved in. And then one day three years later, she moved out."

"Did you quarrel?"

"Not really." Matt was upset enough to blurt it out. "She got pregnant."

There was so much hurt in his voice that Kathleen jumped to the wrong conclusion. "It wasn't yours?"

"I never said that."

"Oh. Sorry." Kathleen thought for a moment while a silence built between them. Then, hesitantly, she said what she was thinking. "Did you want to be a father?" she asked gently, ready to withdraw the question if Matt indicated it was none of her business. "Did you want Wendy to have the baby?"

"I wasn't sure. I needed time to think." Matt sounded truly wretched. "We . . . we talked about an abortion."

"She wasn't willing?"

"She didn't say. But one morning I woke up and she was . . . well, she was just gone. Vanished. I searched for her for six months, but couldn't find her. That night before she took off was the last time I saw her until today."

"Did she want you to marry her?" Kathleen asked gently.

"She never suggested it."

"Would you have if she'd asked you to?"

"I don't know." Matt took a deep breath and ran his hands through his silky dark hair. "Listen, I know how that must sound, but the truth is I wasn't exactly on top of things at the time." His brown eyes focused on Kathleen. "I'm not exactly on top of them right now either," he realized ruefully. "This is a hell of a story to be telling someone you've just asked for a date."

"That's not important." Kathleen looked at him from level green eyes. "What's important is that Wendy may have had the baby. You may be a father. You may have a child—how old would it be now?"

"Five." There was wonder in Matt's voice. "Five years old."

"You may have a five-year-old child you've never even met." When Matt looked stricken, Kathleen tried to lighten the impact of the realization. "Another heir," she added with a smile, "to share in the Stockwell fortune."

All told, that made eighty-three.

13

MANY, BUT NOT all of them, were present when the will was read the following afternoon in the large pine-paneled conference room of Ulysses Blandings's law offices on William Street in Manhattan. Certain servants who had been with the family for a long time were also there, by the old gentleman lawyer's invitation, and the Governor's bequests to them were disposed of first. As they filed out, Holly caught Kevin O'Lunney's eye and received a brief, sorrowful nod. Her grandfather's personal chauffeur was satisfied with the twenty-five thousand dollars he had received. He was truly sorry the Governor was gone; he would miss him.

After the servants had departed, Ulysses Blandings, speaking with an intermittent stutter in a voice not unlike the rustling of dry leaves in late autumn, read out the Governor's bequests to sundry charities. Largest of all was the twenty-five million dollars he bequeathed to the Stockwell Institute think-tank, the disposition of which was to be supervised by Zelig Meyerling, the person most familiar with its multifarious programs. Along with the Charles Stockwell Memorial Foundation—the historical archives with which Holly was familiar—the Stockwell Museum of Modern Art and the Stockwell Museum of Primitive Art headed the rest of the list, with various other New York State art museums and institutions coming next.

There were outright and generous gifts to the NAACP, the B'nai Brith, and Catholic Charities, as well as to Protestant Welfare Services, an organization with which the Governor's ex-wife Mary had been involved for years. A substantial amount was left to the New York City Public Library system, with a codicil specifying that while the lions of Fifth Avenue—where one of the six greatest research institutions in the world was located—were to be well fed, the greater part of the bequest was to go toward stocking, maintaining, and enlarging the collections of neighborhood library branches around the city, with particular attention to those in underprivileged neighborhoods on the Lower East Side, in Harlem, and in the South Bronx. Special Services—charged with arranging cultural programs for the branches—received a separate gift to be paid annually for this purpose.

The list of charities was long. Ulysses Blandings did not, however, drone on, although all present wished he would. A drone would have been a welcome change from his stutter—a handicap which increasingly slowed down the proceedings. The April light was fading by the time he finally got to the specific family inheritances.

Ulysses Blandings, despite his stutter, was not without a sense of the dramatic. He had been reading wills for a good part of his eighty-odd years. Thus he deliberately worked his way from small bequests to large, quite satisfied that the suspense should build.

One of the first of the smaller bequests went to Louise Papatestus. The Governor had left this granddaughter of his long-dead sister an outright gift of five hundred thousand in various securities. Louise was not present, although she'd wired Diana that she would be flying into New York from Greece for Friday's memorial service at the interdenominational Gotham Memorial Church.

David Lewis greeted the announcement with a snort. "Talk about coals to Newcastle," he observed. To Louise, wife of Greek munitions manufacturer Spiro Papatestus—one of the wealthiest men in the world—the bequest would probably not pay her yearly clothing bill.

"It is the thought that c-c-counts." Peering at David Lewis over the tops of his eyeglasses, Ulysses Blandings managed to look more than ever like a solicitor straight out of Dickens. He now announced that the Governor had left equal amounts to Louise's brother and sister, Max and Diana Tyler.

Diana smiled quickly at Holly. It had been a problem hanging on to her SoHo loft in the face of rising rents. The money was welcome.

"These three b-bequests," Blandings announced, "as well as those immediately fol-fol-following, come with a recommendation from the G-Governor—not a stipulation. I should stress, only a recommenda-da-dation. He suggests that they should remain in the overall Stockwell p-p-portfolio. Held in this fashion, the b-bequests can be voted if desired. And, of course, the p-portfolios will be strengthened, which will in turn accrue to the b-benefit of the inheritance."

"I think not." Max Tyler shook his head of shaggy red-gold hair and spoke out loudly and firmly.

"May I ask why, Max?" James had been taken by surprise.

"Insurance."

"Insurance? But insurance has nothing to do with this at all." James was mystified. "David oversees all of the Stockwell insurance interests."

"I know that." Max deliberately removed the red lumberjack kerchief from the back pocket of his chinos, held it by both hands, spun it to create a tight triangle, put it in the breast pocket of his jacket and fluffed it out with nimble fingertips. His panache in executing this maneuver would surely have secured him the offer of a drink at any of the gay bars in the West Village. In this setting, however, the stylized movements were a deliberate declaration of gay pride. "As a matter of fact, I shall probably use my inheritance to go into competition with him," Max said.

David Lewis rolled his eyes.

"But why, Max?" James was patient and conciliatory. He did not want the solidarity of Stockwell interests to be weakened even by this piddling amount. "Does something bother you about our insurance operations? Our own companies? Our voting record in companies where we hold large or controlling interests? Our incidental blue-chip holdings?"

"All of those."

"Oh, come on." David Lewis was impatient. "Why are we wasting time on this?"

"No. Wait, David." James held up a hand. "I'm interested. What it is that troubles you, Max?"

"You're fag baiters."

"What?" Peter Stockwell did a long double-take at his distant cousin.

"That's right." Max marched his fingers across his knees and back again. "You lure gay men and lesbian women into buying your insurance policies, and charge them higher premiums than everybody else."

"That's ridiculous!" David Lewis was beginning to get really angry.

"No, it's not. I took the trouble to check every insurance company we own or are associated with. They all discriminate."

"Then it must be industry-wide." Peter Stockwell dismissed the accusation impatiently.

"Sure. All the insurance companies shaft unmarried gays and lesbians." Anger lurked in the tilted sockets of the hazel Tyler eyes.

"Wait a minute! Wait a minute!" David Lewis had a sudden realization. "Unmarried. That's the key word here. He's trying to tell us that homosexuals are discriminated against because they pay higher premiums than married couples. But that's true of all unmarried people, not just qu—not just homosexuals."

"Is that right, Max?" James's tone was more kindly than the others.

"I don't deny it. Insurance companies charge higher premiums to all single people. That's true. But the effect is to discriminate much more heavily against the gay community than against straights. And to add insult to injury, they refuse to recognize voluntary marriage commitments between gays or lesbians."

"But it's not deliberate discrimination, for God's sake." Peter's impatience was growing.

"De jure. De facto. The result is the same."

"I appreciate your concern, Max." James was still trying to smooth things over. "But don't you think you're being —um—quixotic? Perhaps even impractical?"

"Not at all. I'm being every bit as pragmatic as all you heavy-duty business types with your compulsively heterosexual orientation. I've identified a market, and now that I have the money, I'm going to go after it. I'm going to raise some more money in the gay community, add it to what I've inherited, and start an advertising campaign to sell insurance at fair rates to gay men and lesbian women."

"And after you've made your fortune in the fruit business," David Lewis blurted out, "what then?"

Max ignored the slur. "A savings-and-loan company for homosexuals," he told them without hesitation. "Loan officers in banks—Stockwell banks definitely included, I might add—are always discriminating against gays and lesbians. Their attitudes alone are enough to keep nonheteros away. Resentment has created a tremendous potential market. I believe that I'll make a fortune."

"So first you're going into the insurance business, and then into the banking business?" James was not unsympathetic, but he was amused. "Well, you really will be in competition with the family. Still, I wish you luck, Max. I can't help hoping, though, that nobody else here has such competitive plans."

"Well, I'm not very competitive." Diana Tyler spoke up, running blunt fingers through her own thick apricot hair. "But from my vantage point, I think Max is on to something. I'd like to invest a large part of my inheritance in his insurance company. Do you have a name for it yet, Max?"

93

"I was thinking of Gay Life Benefits and Mutual Fire," Max told her.

"I do not believe I am hearing this!" David Lewis's disgust was complete.

"If the Governor left anything to me, I'm also going to remove it from Stockwell control." Beth Tyler spoke up for the first time, while her twin looked on with surprise at the uncharacteristic boldness.

The spark of revolt, however, was not in all the hazel Tyler eyes. "That would probably be unwise, Beth," her father, Paul Tyler, reasoned with her mildly. "After all, you don't know anything about business, and Cousin James does."

"I won't use the money for business, Daddy."

"What will you use it for, Beth?" James, guessing that his father would not have left money to the twins at their age without some built-in safeguards, was more interested than worried.

"To buy full-page ads in the *New York Times*," Beth told him. "The ads will ask people to write their congressmen and senators protesting policies by the Environmental Control Agency which allow speculators such as Stockwell Real Estate Properties to buy and sell pollution rights. The ad will detail the activities of one Peter Stockwell by name, and it will mention that former Secretary of State Zelig Meyerling, although well aware of these Stockwell practices, did nothing to alert any government agencies so that they might be curtailed."

"Oh, shit!" Peter Stockwell exclaimed aloud.

"Peter!" His grandmother Mary was truly shocked.

"Sorry, Grandma. But I have never heard such—"

"Listen." Buffy spoke up for the first time. "We are wasting a lot of time on trivial side issues. Who does what with whatever pittance they inherit from my husband's estate may be all very interesting, but time is slipping by, and we do not seem to be getting very close to the nitty and the gritty."

She was right, Holly realized. It was completely dark outside now. They would all be having a very late supper tonight.

"In any c-case, young lady..." Ulysses Blandings looked over the tops of his wire-framed glasses at Beth

Tyler. "The m-monies left to you and your sister will be administered by your f-father until you reach your twenty-fifth b-birthday."

"Daddy?" Beth looked at her father.

For one of the few times in her life, Carrie backed up her twin with a silently demanding gaze of her own.

Paul Tyler looked from one to the other of his twin daughters. His normally benign, round face was troubled. All in all, he would have been happier sorting out the problem of a quadruple bypass. "We'll talk about it later," he told his daughters.

"I should have m-mentioned that the young ladies will receive two-hundred-fifty thousand each, while you, sir, will have t-twice that amount," Blandings told him. "At present the funds are held jointly in a mutual fund with diversified Stockwell holdings in market investments, insurance, and real estate."

"Real estate!" Beth's face contorted. "Daddy—"

"Later." This time Paul was firm. "We'll discuss it later."

"Can't we please speed this up?" Buffy did not hide her irritation.

"I will t-try. The next b-bequests are relatively the same as to amounts and conditions. They concern the Governor's g-grandchildren and g-great-grandchildren. To each of his eight g-grandchildren—Holly Stockwell Millwood, Patrice Stockwell O'Keefe, Matthew Stockwell, Michael Stockwell, Lisa Stockwell, Peter Stockwell, Michelle Lewis Carter, and Decatur Wells—the G-Governor has left a stock portfolio with a face value of t-two million dollars. In addition, to each of the g-g-grandchildren's children born prior to his death, the Governor has left an additional one million dollars in diversified holdings of the Stockwell Corporation.

"The st-st-stocks left to Nicholas Millwood, son of Holly Stockwell Millwood, will be held in a combined t-trust with the bequest to his mother until his twenty-fifth birthday. Those b-bequeathed to Daniel Carter and Robin Carter will be held in a combined trust with the inheritance of their mother, Michelle Lewis C-C-Carter. Both Holly Stockwell and Michelle Lewis Carter are empowered to separate their ch-ch-children's holdings from their own, but not to invest them without the approval of the t-trustee of the estate."

"Just who is the trustee of the estate?" Michelle Carter wanted to know, privately hoping it would be her father, David Lewis. She didn't bother to hide her displeasure at having the inheritances of her two children, Danny and Robin, not in her control.

Her reasons were no secret to some of those present, particularly her father, her uncle James, and her cousin Peter. They knew that she and her husband Andrew Carter—an investment banker with Goldman, Sachs—had been quietly buying up stock for some time in *Elite*, one of the most prestigious and potentially profitable magazines put out under the Stockwell Publishing Company masthead. Thanks to her father's power, Michelle held the position of publisher of *Elite*. "That sounds good," she would complain bitterly to her husband, "but the truth is, it's an empty title. It's Uncle James's goddamn accountants who run the magazine. Even when it comes to editorial, I don't have the control I should. Majority leadership of the stock is the only way I can get that."

Her inheritance of two million would not quite suffice to purchase majority control. If the inheritance of her two children could have been applied, however, it would be enough. That was the reason for her concern as to the trustee who would oversee the Governor's bequests.

"With your p-permission," Blandings said, "I will address the m-m-matter of the trustee later."

Michelle was not the ony one concerned about her children's bequests. Holly and Matt each had considerations of their own. And Christopher Millwood, sitting quietly beside Holly, was silently mulling over other concerns.

Matt spoke. "What about any other children of the grandchildren?" he asked Ulysses Blandings.

"Future progeny are not p-provided for, although it was your grandfather's belief that his children would themselves provide for their g-grandchildren after his d-d-demise."

"I see." Matt stole a quick look at his father, James. "And what about great-grandchildren other than Danny and Robin and Nicholas who may have been born before he died?"

96

James stared at his son. What was this all about?

"If such parentage was c-c-confirmed," Ulysses Blandings replied, "the estate would pay one million d-dollars to any such progeny. The funds, however, would be under the con-con-control of the trustee until the recipient reached age t-twenty-five."

"I thought the parent descended from the Governor controlled it," Matt said.

"N-not in the case of an unknown g-great-grandchild."

"What about the non-Stockwell parent?" Matt wondered. "Would they have any say over the inheritance?"

"Ah, yes." Christopher Millwood sat up a little straighter in his chair and paid attention.

James spoke before Blandings could. "That really opens up a can of worms. In-law rights over the assets of minors is a very sticky business. Indeed, the term 'in-law'—considered literally, I mean—is a strong indication of the conflicts that can be involved." A small, very rare smile played at the corner of his lips as he regarded his son. "I must say your interest in the rights surrounding these monies heartens me. I rather thought you had permanently dropped out of our materialistic world."

"I have," Matt told his father.

"Hard to do when you've just come into two million dollars," his sister Patrice observed wryly.

"Whatever I decide to do with the money, it won't be with the purpose of accumulating still more Stockwell wealth and power. This family has more than enough of that now. I don't want it, and the family doesn't need it."

"I see." James set his lips firmly in a gesture of disapproval familiar to Matt. "Well, it is yours to do with as you want. I had hoped..." He sighed. "As you want," he repeated.

"You could invest in my insurance company, Matt," suggested Max Tyler.

"I don't think so, Max. Gay and rich isn't much improvement over straight and rich."

Christopher Millwood spoke for the first time. "What you were saying about in-law rights being rights in law ... I am, of course, very interested in that. Now, where my son Nicholas is concerned, for instance—"

"Christopher!" Holly shot him a look suited to dueling pistols at ten paces.

"Your son's inheritance is subject to ma-ma-matrilineal control," Ulysses Blandings told him. "It is your wife who has control of the money. Strangely enough, however, as her husband, N-N-New York State law recognizes your interest in her inheritance and by extension, therefore, in that of your s-s-son."

"Ah," Christopher responded—a large male Siamese purring over a saucer of milk.

"So long as the m-m-marriage is intact, that is," Blandings added.

"Um." Holly found some slight solace in the qualification.

"There is also an additional stipend to be p-paid to Holly Stockwell Millwood of eight thousand dollars per month to fin-fin-finance her historical researches into the Hudson River Valley, the Riverview estate, and the b-background of the Stockwell family. There is a note of a, ah . . . p-private nature which accompanies this bequest. I hereby d-d-deliver it to you." Blandings handed Holly a sealed envelope.

She opened it, and shielding the paper inside from Christopher's curiosity, read it to herself. Then, unable to keep from smiling, she read it a second time.

Dear Holly,

You will receive this extra money whether you pursue your project (which seems a very dry endeavor for a young girl to me) or not. I would much rather not. I would much rather have you spent it, and your time, having fun. Go abroad. Take a cruise. Spend more time with people your own age. You are afraid of life, and so you don't enjoy it. Overcome your fear. Meet life halfway. Be wicked. Live so that you will never find yourself approaching old age with the only sins you regret those of omission. Eat hearty, drink to excess, and do not turn up your nose at carnal pleasures. Yes, be wicked, Holly my dearest grandchild. It is not in your nature, I know, but try, really try. Life is a one-time-only ride, so make the most of it. Better mistakes than dull safety. Live while you can, Holly. You will be a long time dead. Take it from one who—by the time you read this—will have reason to know.

Now tear this missive into very small pieces and eat every last one of them lest some snoopy would-be biographer of Governor Matthew Adams Stockwell seeks to regurgitate it as revisionist proof of my true immoral nature. Good-bye, my Holly. All my love from the Beyond.

Grandpa

While Holly was reading, Ulysses Blandings had gone on to the Governor's bequests to his four surviving children: James Linstone Stockwell, Alice Stockwell Lewis, Jonathan Ellis Stockwell, and Susan Stockwell Gray. Each had received fifty million dollars; five million outright in various securities, and the balance in the form of an interest in the Stockwell estate which could only be withdrawn in accordance with very strict conditions. The money in the estate would be under the control of the trustee appointed.

Basically the estate, with its massive and extremely diverse holdings and worldwide interests, would continue being run as in the past. James would have the strongest voice, but David Lewis and Peter Stockwell—a stand-in for his father, Jonathan—would continue to oversee their arbitrarily designated areas of investments and banking, insurance and art, and real estate, respectively. The publishing companies, the forest preserves, the football franchise, the coffee plantation, the shipping fleet flying the Maltese flag, the railroads owned jointly with the Vanderbilts, and the sizable oil investments in companies controlled by J. Paul Getty and the Rockefellers, the Samoan sculpture collection and the Ashcan School art collection and the signed-in-the-stone Hudson River Valley lithographs—all of this and more would be basically unaffected by the Governor's death, according to the wishes expressed in his last testament.

Even adding the two hundred million to his children to the other bequests put only a very slight dent in the total Stockwell holdings left by the Governor. Before revealing what disposition was to be made of the immense remaining fortune, Ulysses Blandings felt called upon to mention the complexities of trying to determine the total value of it. The fluctuation of markets around the world from moment to moment, he pointed out, made it virtually impossible. Also, it was complicated by the merging many years earlier of Stockwell assets with the considerable wealth that the Governor's first wife had inherited from the Linstone family. The Linstone assets and the Stockwell assets had remained merged by mutual consent after the divorce, and they were still merged today.

This had made it very difficult, Ulysses Blandings stuttered into what now was a very attentive silence, for the Governor to know how to dispose of holdings that under law might not rightfully have been considered to be his. The Governor had, Blandings assured them, truly agonized over this problem. Finally he had concluded that it didn't really matter since he and his former wife were in agreement that the mixed assets would in any case go to their offspring and other descendants. Therefore—

"Just a moment! Excuse me! Just a moment!" Buffy was visibly agitated. "Do I understand you rightly? Are you saying that Matthew—"

"I shall n-now read directly from the will." Ulysses Blandings rearranged his glasses. "'To my present wife, Brenda Stockwell, I bequeath a portfolio of securities valued as of this writing at approximately fifty million dollars (see appendix for itemization), an additional trust fund to pay her the sum of twenty thousand dollars monthly, and ownership of our town house on the northeast corner of Fifth Avenue and Sixty-third Street in New York City. As to the balance of my estate, I wish to make clear my intention that she shall have no claim to it.'"

"That sonofabitch!" Buffy exclaimed. "He won't get away with this!"

"Who—" James Stockwell and David Lewis spoke at the same time.

"'The b-balance of my estate,'" read Ulysses Blandings, "'is left in total and without hindrance or reservation to my d-d-divorced first wife, Mary Linstone Stockwell. Nothing in this t-t-testament shall be construed to conflict in any way with my wish made in sound m-mind and considered judgment that M-Mary Linstone Stockwell shall have full possession and control over all of the Stock-well and Linstone holdings of any na-na-nature whatso-ever not designated herein as b-b-bequests. I would like to mention specifically that she is the sole inheritor, without encumbrance, of the p-property known as Riverview, and may reside in its manor house or any other of its b-build-ings according to her desire."

"Oh, Matthew!" Mary was overwhelmed. Tears flooded her eyes, and she bent her head and took a handkerchief from her purse to deal with them.

"Are you all right, Grandma?" Holly knelt beside her and took her hand.

"I never thought—" As the full impact of the bequest came home to her, the blood drained from Mary's cheeks.

"Do you want one of your pills? A nitro?"

"Yes, please, dear. I think I better had."

"I am not going to stand still for this," Buffy an-nounced. "I was the Governor's legal wife. I am his legiti-mate heir."

"I c-can assure you this will is quite legal."

"Matthew's mind was failing," Buffy announced flatly, violet eyes darting from James to Mary.

"That is nonsense," James objected. "Father's mind was clear to the end."

"And we all know how the end came about," Buffy reminded him.

"I can tell you as a lawyer—" David Lewis started to say.

"I prefer to consult my own attorneys," Buffy told him. "And do not for one moment doubt that I shall not do so immediately. I am going to have what is rightfully mine. I am going to break this will."

"It is your p-p-privilege to try, madam," Ulysses Bland-ings told her stiffly. "B-But I do not think—"

"Who is the trustee?" Buffy asked bluntly.

Blandings looked skyward as if seeking guidance. It did not seem to him that Buffy was entitled to that information since she had already announced her intention to chal-lenge the will. She would naturally be in the position of fighting the guardian or guardians of its provisions. It did not even seem proper to him that she should remain in the

101

room under such circumstances. And yet, certainly, she gave no indication of leaving. Quite the contrary.

"Proceed, Ulysses." The look James gave him was reassuring. "It doesn't matter one whit."

He was right, of course. The identity of the trustee could not be kept secret. And even if it could, the first injunction Buffy secured would force its revelation.

"The trusteeship has b-been put in the same hands as those now ch-ch-charged with overseeing Stockwell Enterprises," Blandings told them. "It will be a j-joint trusteeship of J-James Linstone Stockwell, David Lewis, and J-Jonathan Stockwell. However..." He ignored the rash of raised eyebrows. "However, it is specified that J-Jonathan Stockwell may d-d-designate his responsibilities to his son, Peter." The eyebrows dropped; Peter's mother looked pleased. "All three of the t-trustees—"

"Three!" Buffy snarled. "A troika!"

"All three of the trustees serve at the p-p-pleasure of Mary Linstone Stockwell, and their responsibilities may be c-cancelled by her. In short, she m-m-may dispense with the services of all three, or of any one of the th-th-three."

"A goddamn troika!" Buffy stood, allowed the fury in her dark eyes to register all around the room, turned on her heel and swept out.

It was the signal for the meeting to break up. James, however, had one last observation. "She can make a lot of trouble," he said. "It could be very bad."

"Matthew probably shouldn't have treated her that way," his mother told him. "Why not just give her what she wants?"

"Because there's more to consider than just the Stockwell estate, Mother. What happens with our investments will be echoed throughout Wall Street. The economy will be affected. The country will be affected. And ultimately the world will be affected. There is a responsibility here."

"I truly don't think Buffy realizes that," Mary replied wearily.

"You're probably right, Mother. But even if she did, I don't know that it would give her pause. The responsibilities of money are hard to accept."

Patrice looked at her father sympathetically. Michael looked at him with a mind committed to memorizing his father's phrase for a time when it might serve him best in politics. And Matt mused to himself how hard it was to keep on loving a man—even if the man was your father—pompous enough to believe such total bull.

Matt stood aside from the doorway to let Holly exit behind his grandmother. Then he had to stand aside again as Christopher moved quickly to follow Holly. He thought about going to his cousin's rescue and decided it wasn't really necessary. Despite her qualms, Holly seemed to have the Christopher situation under control.

Matt was wrong. Holly did not have it under control. Outwardly she stood up to Christopher, but inside she was fearful of what he might do. Which is why, as he drew her aside now, she went without protest.

"I think we should make it up," he told her. "I think we should get back together and work at our marriage."

"What you mean is you think I should share my inheritance with you," she responded bluntly, feeling sick.

"There's Nicholas to consider." He ignored the accusation.

"When did you ever consider Nicholas?"

"Well, I'm considering him now. Come on, Holly. It wasn't all bad." He consciously exuded a sensual charm that had once lured Holly, but at the moment disgusted her. "Let's give it another go. What do you say?" He had her in a far corner of the hallway, deliberately pressing his body against hers.

"No!" She pushed him away. "I say no! You're only interested in our money, mine and Nicholas's."

"Even if that's true, I'm entitled. You're my wife. He's my son. We're a family. Families share with one another."

"Leave us alone, Christopher." Holly looked past him, hoping to catch someone's eyes. But the others were down the long, carpeted hallway with their backs to her.

"When families don't share, do you know what happens, love?" Christopher pressed against her again.

"I mean it, Christopher!"

"The one that's being pushed out has to go public with his exclusion. That's what happens."

"I don't care, Christopher."

"Your family might."

103

"They'll survive. They've survived worse. They'll survive this."

"But will you, Holly? Will you survive a custody battle for our son? Will you survive what comes out? And even your family, will they survive that?"

"You bastard!" Holly's eyes filled with tears of rage.

"How will they feel about the truth, Holly? How will our son feel? How will you feel when your secret goes public?"

"God, how I despise you!"

"How will it go down, love, with all the high-and-mighty Stockwells?" Christopher's laugh was vicious. "See you in court." He turned on his heel and strode rapidly away, leaving Holly standing there, fear clouding her clear blue eyes.

14

HOLLY WAS AWARE of prominent eyes looking up at Patrice's trill of laughter and registering recognition before turning back to the cut-glass stemware and silverplate which were the hallmarks of the Rose Room of the Hotel Algonquin. The other diners' celebrity status signified the time, almost three on a Thursday afternoon, an hour when tourists, guests, and lesser business people had finished eating. In their wake, the antique mirrors covering three sides of the dining room reflected luminaries of the Broadway theater, lions of the publishing industry, silver-haired statesmen discreetly west of the U.N., and financiers negotiating multinational mergers well uptown from Wall Street gossip.

They knew the petite young woman who was laughing, in the way celebrities always seem to know one another even when they have never actually met. Some of them identified her politically as a granddaughter of Governor Matthew Adams Stockwell, or financially as a daughter of the powerful James Linstone Stockwell. To the few who followed the rising of comets on Madison Avenue, she was Patrice O'Keefe, a comer, a woman to watch.

Many eyes, however, quickly passed over Patrice's auburn hair and crisply tailored navy gabardine suit to linger on her less familiar cousin. Holly's blond slenderness, stylishly elongated by the simple sapphire blue sheath she wore, added up to the sort of cool image of elegance that artist-designer Oliver Smith would have wholeheartedly approved when, in the late 1970s, he restored the Rose Room to its original Edwardian splendor. Yes, the decor and Holly went extremely well together.

"But how on earth did you find out?" Patrice wanted to know now, in the aftermath of her laugh.

"I've been doing historical research on Riverview," Holly replied. "It's mentioned in some of the archive material. The records describe the Stockwell turn-of-the-century town house on Fifth Avenue and our neighbors the Vanderbilts, the Rockefellers, and the Whitneys, and how in the late 1880s we all stabled our trotting horses right here in a carriage house where the Algonquin stands now. And then today, when I was coming to meet you for lunch, I saw this plaque. When you face the Algonquin facade, it's to the left of the entrance and down."

"I've been here a hundred times, and I never noticed it."

"Well, it's there. And so I copied it down." Holly read it to Patrice, line-for-line.

"So the Algonquin Hotel, where the elite meet to put on the feedbag, really did start out as a horses' stable!" Patrice laughed again.

"Oh, yes. There were actually stalls for trotting horses where we're sitting right now, in the Rose Room." Holly's gesture took in the hushed opulence of the crystal chandeliers and the plush red-velvet banquettes.

"But why doesn't the plaque mention the Stockwells if we stabled our horses here along with the Vanderbilts and the Rockefellers?" Patrice wondered.

"Probably because it was inscribed during the Governor's common man period." Thinking of her grandfather, sadness dimmed Holly's smile. "With his eye on the White House, he was avoiding the Brahmin label when the plaque was put up."

105

"You really liked him, didn't you?"

"Grandpa?" Holly's sorrow was sincere. "Oh, yes. I loved him."

"And he loved you," Patrice remembered. "It was no secret you were his favorite. I guess it was different for the rest of us grandchildren. I know it was different for me." Patrice started to add something even more negative about her grandfather, then thought better of it. She poked at the remains of her Caesar Salad for a moment. Finally she looked straight at Holly. "You've been avoiding talking about Christopher," she said. "Would you rather not?"

"I guess I'm ambivalent." Holly looked down and bit her lip as she thought. All this time she'd kept her feelings bottled up, but Patrice seemed so genuinely empathetic—perhaps because she had been through the breakup of her own marriage—that Holly found herself starting to talk, and then the words came pouring out.

She attempted to be objective, unemotional, but it was painful as well as cathartic for Holly to describe Christopher Millwood. The forces that had shaped her husband weren't simple. He'd been born into the landed gentry of Great Britain, and his family saw him through Eton before the taxes imposed by the Socialist government had eroded their estates. Christopher, however, had not resigned himself to a genteel, land-poor future. Instead he secured a commission in the army and pulled strings to have himself assigned as a military attaché to Great Britain's U.N. mission.

While there, he met Holly, who was in Manhattan for a Bryn Mawr party weekend. He saw in her a young woman of aristocratic beauty who was also a member of a family that had both wealth and prestige. He recognized the vulnerability behind her finishing-school poise, and the unstirred heat beneath the blond coolness. It was a combination, he knew instinctively, that would be most susceptible to his particular sort of appeal.

Indeed, Christopher's appeal was something new in Holly's experience. On the one hand, he had beautiful manners, was always well-groomed, and presented the kind of decidedly British image that impressed her girlfriends. On the other hand, he was privately macho, and sensual with a strength that at times seemed almost animalistic. She had discovered quickly that there was a level of passion to his caresses which both frightened and aroused her. Previously her boyfriends had been her social peers—although some had been awed by her Stockwell name—and none of them had moved her to the excitement or urgency she felt in Christopher's kisses. In fact, she'd begun to worry that she would never fall in love.

On one of their first dates he had pulled his car off the road into the woods near Riverview, parked, and kissed her. Holly had been kissed in cars by men before, and she'd certainly realized his reason for parking, anticipated the kiss, and made up her mind in advance that she would respond. Nevertheless, the rhythmic thrust of his tongue in her mouth, combined with the strength of his hands moving over her breasts, had taken her by surprise.

"Oh, my!" she'd gasped when the kiss was over. "Things seem to be moving along rather quickly."

"That's because we want each other," he had replied in his precise, upper-class British accent.

"Whoa!" Holly had denied the pounding of her heart. "I'm not so sure I—"

"Well, I'm sure." He took her hand and put it on his lap. His penis was a hard ridge bisecting the flannel of his trousers over his stomach. "And I can tell you're not the type to play games."

"I . . . I . . ." Holly felt weak, warm and liquid with desire.

"No. You aren't." Christopher smiled, slid his hand in under hers and unzipped his fly. He showed Holly his bare, erect member. "I'm not going to rape you, love," he told her. "If you're truly offended, tell me and I'll put it away and apologize. But if you're feeling what I'm feeling, then don't deny it. It's rare, believe me."

Holly had believed him—then, if not later. She had reached out her hand with trembling fingers and touched him. She had made no protest when he slid her skirt up over her thighs and probed inside her panties with his firm, sure, knowing hand.

That was the first time Christopher had made love to her. It was both more violent and more satisfying than Holly had ever expected. Christopher was—well, she thought, energetic was the word—and he somehow drew forth responses filled with an energy she'd never dreamed she possessed.

Holly had assumed it was love. It wasn't. It was sex, of course, but it was something more than that, too. Christopher had tapped something atavistic deep inside her. It was this that made her cling to him long after she suspected that their marriage was doomed.

After what looked to the world like a whirlwind courtship, Christopher and she had been married. He immediately resigned his commission. He was a Stockwell by marriage now, and the doors of the business world swung open to him. The one he chose to walk through led straight back to England, and Holly went with him.

Before it dawned on Holly that Christopher had married her because her family was wealthy beyond most English dreams, she was pregnant. In that state she learned that Christopher was not only a fortune hunter, but a philanderer as well. He was having an affair with the wife of a neighbor, a woman Holly had considered a friend.

"I'd been feeling queasy, and so cut short a shopping expedition to London early," Holly told Patrice. "I found them in our bedroom, Christopher's and mine, in our bed, making love."

"Oh, Holly!" Patrice squeezed her hand sympathetically. "My God. What did you do?"

"What could I do? I confronted him. He begged my forgiveness, swore it would never happen again. I believed him and forgave him. My due date was less than four weeks off."

"Well," Patrice said doubtfully, "anybody can slip once."

"Oh, yes." Holly smiled without humor. "Only it wasn't just once. Not one incident, and not one woman. It happened again, and then again . . . a housemaid. A secretary. Even a nanny. We had enormous fights . . . but I forgave him every time. We established a pattern. Christopher would sin. I would find out. He would beg my forgiveness and swear never to sin again. I would believe him and forgive. That's what our life was like for the next two years after the birth of Nicholas."

"You forgave him the first time. That I understand. But

after the second time, you should have left him. That's what I would have done," Patrice assured Holly.

"I'm not like you. I'm . . . gullible. Well, anyway, I was back then," Holly corrected herself. "Despite everything, I really thought he loved me. I realized that he was weak, but if he loved me . . . well, if Christopher loved me, then I could overlook his weakness. I'd probably still be overlooking it if—" Holly stopped short and bit her lip just as she had earlier, when she'd begun confiding in Patrice.

"If?" Patrice prompted her.

"If I finally hadn't been forced to admit to myself that Christopher really didn't love me." Holly chose her words carefully, telling the truth but not the whole truth, not nearly the whole truth. "I finally had to face the fact that it was the Stockwell wealth and connections that were important to him, not me, and certainly not his son. . . ."

"And so you left him," Patrice interjected when Holly didn't go on.

"Yes."

"But you're not divorced."

"I filed for divorce," Holly told her. "But Christopher avoided service of the papers, and so we're still married. You see, the way things were set up while the Governor was alive, I received income from an independent trust fund. Naturally, Christopher had access to it, and also, the Stockwell name was an asset to him that he didn't want to relinquish."

"Well, you know where he is now," Patrice pointed out. "You can serve him with divorce papers now."

"Yes," Holly sighed. "Only now, with my inheritance from the Governor's estate, he's less willing than ever to give me my freedom."

"I don't understand. How can he stop you? You're his wife for God's sake, not his chattel."

"I know. But his cooperation has a price tag. And the price is high."

"You don't have to buy your freedom from him. You have a right to it." Patrice leaned over her salad bowl and shook Holly's arm.

"I know that. The trouble is, Christopher doesn't agree."

"He doesn't have to. The hell with him. Just divorce him and have done with it."

"It's not that simple."

"Why not? My God, Holly, you make it sound like he's blackmailing you or something." Patrice stared at her. Holly had gone quite pale. "But how can he . . . ?"

"There's our son Nicholas to consider," Holly answered weakly, deflecting the question.

She really could not go into this with Patrice. It was too personal. She could not explain a situation that was so involved that she didn't really understand it herself. She could not expect her sympathetic cousin to believe the truth when there was damning proof otherwise.

Holly's distress was obvious to Patrice, just as it was obvious she didn't want to talk about her marriage anymore. Diplomatically, Patrice changed the subject. "Have you been seeing anyone else since you've been back?"

"No." Holly's smile was wan. "To tell you the truth, I'm gun-shy. Horny," she added honestly, with a small laugh, "but gun-shy even so."

"Well, I'm not gun-shy," Patrice responded. "But judging from the ordnance on my firing range, you're not missing a thing."

"Sometimes," Holly admitted candidly, "I think to myself that if I could just meet some stud, spend the night with him and then never see him again, that's really all I want from a man. It's not sex I'm shy of, it's getting involved—a relationship."

"You sound just like the Governor," Patrice told her.

"Why, so I do." Holly laughed with wonder at herself. "I guess all of his talk must have had some effect after all."

"Well, just plain sex doesn't satisfy me anymore. It's more complicated to me. I want involvement. I want emotion. I want love. But sex is easy, Holly. If that's all you want, just go out and have it. There are plenty of men who'd be happy to accommodate you in that department."

"I guess I haven't really given myself a chance to meet them. I've actually only been asked out by one man since I left England," Holly confided. "And I turned him down. But I forgot. You know him. Zelig Meyerling."

"Washington's most eligible bachelor," Patrice laughed.

"You've wandered into the big game preserve. But beware the competition. I hear it's really cutthroat over Zelig."

Holly blushed. "Well, I think he was interesting. Charming, too."

"Oh, yes. The Meyerling charm is a household word from Park Avenue to Georgetown to Palm Beach."

"What about you?" Holly asked, to change the subject. "Are you involved with anyone?"

"In the process of disengaging," Patrice told her matter-of-factly, thinking of Craig Burrows. "I meant what I said before. There's a real shortage of sevens and eights, let alone tens. And if I do meet one, it's ships passing in the night with his engine turned up to top speed."

"You're exaggerating, Patrice. For someone as attractive as you, I'm sure there are lots of desirable and available men."

"Not lots," Patrice disagreed. "But every so often I do meet one that could really turn out to be special." And now the dreamy expression on Patrice O'Keefe's face testified that the image of Craig Burrows had been replaced on the screen of her mind by that of another man, a man she had met only once, and then only briefly—Jack Houston.

At that very moment, in a room four floors above the Rose Room in the Algonquin Hotel, Buffy Stockwell was regarding Jack with conflicting feelings. A man who is nude, erect, and angry, may be viewed by a woman as virile, savage, and sexy. On the other hand, the movements of mixed anger and lust, nakedly exposed, may also be seen as petulant and ludicrous. It is a very thin line indeed that separates the arousing from the comical when a man in the buff counters rejection with temper, all the while retaining his lust.

Buffy's mind, however, was on neither perception. She had already been made love to once, most satisfactorily, and now her concentration was elsewhere. "We really can't discuss this now, Jack," she said, fending off her young lover's demand. "I have an appointment with my banker."

"Postpone it!" Jack's snarl was furious. "This is more important."

"Nobody would believe what a romantic you are, darling." Buffy was calm but firm. "There are hundreds of millions of dollars at stake. It is a simple matter of priorities." She pulled on her silk panties quickly, then stood up and reached behind her to clasp her bra.

"Love—" Jack started to say hotly.

"Is very tempting when presented in your present state." Buffy stretched to pat the cheek under his furious blue eyes. "But it does seem noticeably more urgent since the burgeoning of my financial worth through widowhood."

"That's not true and you know it! I've always wanted you to leave Stockwell and marry me. And now that he's dead—"

"I am much wealthier than I was before." Buffy's glance fell on his thrusting virility. She looked quickly at her Cartier watch and sighed. No, there definitely wasn't time.

"That's an overstatement." Jack's rage was ice cold now. "It's not as if you inherited the Stockwell estate. You're just one heir among many. Your husband saw to that."

"The will can be broken. The will *will* be broken. My lawyer sees many vulnerabilities."

"Damn it, Buffy, it's you I'm interested in, not your money. I want you!"

"I can see that," Buffy murmured.

"Not just now!" Jack demoted his rampant lust. "I want to marry you. I love you."

"I love you, too, darling." Buffy glanced quickly at her watch again. "But I simply must get to the bank. There are papers I have to sign." She finished dressing quickly as Jack, sullen, angry and still aroused, watched her.

When she was dressed, Buffy crossed over and kissed him briefly on the lips. His reaction was urgent. She pulled away quickly and adjusted her small pillbox hat. "Well," she said lightly, "I hate to cheat and run, but—"

"You're not cheating anymore," Jack reminded her bluntly. "Your husband is dead."

"Yes." Buffy felt a genuine twinge of sorrow at the reminder. "So he is." She reached for the doorknob.

"Buffy!" His voice, like the crack of a whip, made her pause. "Just what am I supposed to do with this?" His eyes drew hers down to his erection.

"Oh, I'm sure you'll think of something, darling." And then the door closed behind her.

You'll think of something, darling! Jack Houston fumed. The bitch! You'll think of something!

For their after-lunch brandies, Holly and Patrice moved from the Rose Room to the Algonquin lounge. It was still well before the cocktail hour and the laying out of the hors d'oeuvres, and so they had the oak-paneled, discreetly posh lobby room to themselves. The famous grandfather clock—"nobody knows its origins, not even what country it came from," Holly had informed Patrice—was just chiming four o'clock when they settled into Chippendale chairs across a small carved wood table from each other. Patrice pushed the brass bell atop the table and a stern waiter with steel-gray hair and a demeanor worthy of a Prussian drill instructor took their order for two Grand Marniers.

They sat in comfortable silence until their drinks were served, then Patrice finished what she'd been telling Holly back in the Rose Room. "I have more of a perspective on it now," she said, "but when I was younger it made me feel jealous and angry and unworthy. I mean, there I was, interested and eager and so anxious for my father's approval, and all he wanted was for Matt to be that way. He never even noticed that I was exactly what he wanted, while Matt couldn't have cared less. Business bored Matt. He's always been interested in outdoorsy things, and never cared about money. And he didn't seem to want approval from Dad, either, just tolerance. I was exactly what Dad longed for—in a son." Patrice frowned, before sipping the Grand Marnier.

"Well, you've certainly proved yourself in business." Holly's delicate nostrils quivered as she inhaled the bouquet from her brandy snifter. "Surely Uncle James must see that now."

"Oh, yes. He does. And takes a genuine interest in my career and encourages me, too. But all the same, when he sees Matt, a certain look comes over his face. If Daddy had his druthers, it would still be Matt making his mark in business instead of me."

"What about your brother Michael?"

"Oh, Daddy's attitude has always been different toward Michael . . . and toward my sister Lisa, too. He expects a lot less from them, and he's more permissive, more willing to let them go their own way. Maybe because they're younger . . . although I suppose in some ways he was like that with me, too. It's only Matt he tried so hard to shape, and of course he failed . . . It still bothers me that *my* success won't ever make up for that."

"I think it's terrific the way your career's going," Holly said sincerely.

"Well, I am sort of pleased my—" Patrice broke off in mid-word. Her eyes grew very large.

"What is it?" Holly was startled by the sudden transformation.

"It's him. Over there buying cigarettes. The guy I mentioned before. The man I met with Craig at the Plaza. Jack Houston."

"Where is that composed woman of affairs with whom I was just conversing?" Holly was amused.

"Business affairs! Man-woman affairs are something else. Oh, Holly, look at him. Now isn't that a ten?"

Holly looked. She saw a thirtyish man with a deep tan. His broad shoulders filled a tan suede jacket which was open to display a hairy chest partly exposed by a carelessly buttoned crisp khaki shirt. His body looked lean, hard, and powerful. His face was angular, with a high forehead and jutting square jaw, his blue eyes deep-set and narrowed as if against a blazing sun. He was a type any woman would notice—a graceful machine of a body, an intense visage to pique interest, and an aura of sexuality to melt away resistance and silken underclothes alike. In short, Holly realized with a start, just what *she* had had in mind when they were talking before—a stud.

"Yes," she agreed with Patrice. "A ten."

"Jack." Patrice got to her feet as he started toward the lobby. "Jack Houston." She raised her voice.

He turned around, saw Patrice, and waved casually. His eyes moved to the attractive blonde sitting at the table with her, and he switched direction smoothly, veering toward them without betraying his change of mind.

"Patrice O'Keefe, isn't it?" He greeted her. He knew without looking at Holly that she was looking at him—

and with some interest, too. "The Plaza. Craig Burrows introduced us."

"That's right." Patrice's smile was a lot wider than she meant it to be. She felt as if she must be grinning like an idiot. "And this is my cousin, Holly Millwood."

"Stockwell," Holly corrected Patrice. "Holly Stockwell. I'm using my maiden name." She blushed.

"Jack Houston." He squeezed her hand briefly, but significantly.

"Join us for a drink," Patrice invited him.

"I don't want to intrude—"

"Not at all. Tell him, Holly."

"You're not intruding," Holly told him.

"Well, then . . ." Jack drew up a chair, summoned the waiter with the brass bell and ordered himself a scotch. "Holly Stockwell." His eyes actually crinkled and—as she was meant to—Holly noticed. "You're Governor Stockwell's granddaughter, aren't you?" he inquired carefully.

"Yes, I am."

"I was sorry to hear about your grandfather."

"Thank you."

"I'm a granddaughter of the Governor's, too," Patrice interjected. "O'Keefe is my married name. But I'm not married anymore," she hastened to add.

Holly looked at Patrice. Her cousin's interest in Jack Houston was obvious. Well, she thought, Patrice saw him first. And she was much too fond of her cousin, and too grateful for her sympathetic ear, to compete with her.

"How does the tea at the Algonquin compare with the tea at the Plaza?" Jack asked Patrice.

"We've been having lunch, not tea. In the Rose Room."

"With the ghosts of the Round Table?" Jack Houston wondered.

Patrice looked blank.

"Dorothy Parker. Robert Benchley, Alexander Woolcott. Harpo Marx. George S. Kaufman. The *New Yorker* gang and friends," he explained. "The prime wits of the twenties and thirties. They used to get together once a week and swap bon mots at the Algonquin. Right where you had lunch, in the Rose Room. They called themselves the Algonquin Round Table."

"Except it was the Oak Room," Holly corrected him.

"Later." Jack was pleasant, but positive. "They started out in the Rose Room first, but pretty soon word spread and the Round Table attracted a lot of attention. People would drift in just to rubberneck them. So they switched to the Oak Room. They met there once a week for years."

"It seems you've met your match, Holly." Patrice laughed. "A man who knows as much historical trivia as you do."

"We'll see." Holly accepted the challenge. "If you're so smart, where did the Round Table meet in the summertime?"

"Lake Bomoseen, Vermont," Jack Houston snapped back with a grin. "Woolcott owned an island in the middle of the lake, and they all used to vacation there. They skinny-dipped, and there were protests from the locals and some of the tourists. One summer Harpo Marx painted his bottom blue and mooned the excursion boats going past the island. Later he used to dance around, all painted up like a naked aborigine, while Dorothy Parker sat out on the shore in a big sun hat and nothing else, editing manuscripts. From all accounts, the Round Table reveled in scandal."

"How do you know all that?" Patrice inquired.

"Once, a long time ago, I worked here as a bellhop. I'd get tips filling in the out-of-town guests on the Algonquin celebrities and the scandals of yesteryear."

"Bellhop, safari guide—you've had a checkered career. Still, it does sound deliciously wicked and wonderful." Patrice shook her shoulders slightly—a deliberate little shiver.

Holly took it as a cue. "Wicked and wonderful," she echoed. "Those were the days, all right. And right now I have to get back to them. Or, to be accurate, further back. I've got a list of facts a yard long to check at the Institute, and if I hurry I can still put in two more hours before I catch the train back to Riverview."

"Holly's working on a family history," Patrice told Jack Houston.

"Goes to show you." Jack slipped in the compliment obliquely: "Decorative—no matter how much—is never all there is to a woman."

"Or a man," Patrice was quick to add. "Bellhop or not, I

never would have expected you to know so much about the old-time Algonquin literati and their cronies."

"Proves the point." He answered Patrice, but his eyes were on Holly. "I'm not just a pretty face. I've got a brain, too."

"Don't let his intelligence intimidate you," Holly told Patrice as she stood up. "No matter what he says, it's his beauty that's really important." She held out her hand to him. "Nice meeting you."

"Nice meeting you, too." He clasped her hand an instant longer than absolutely necessary.

"Thanks for lunch, Patrice."

"You're welcome, cuz. Let's do it again soon." Patrice's look at Holly's diplomatic departure was grateful.

"Another drink?" Jack Houston suggested after Holly was gone.

"That would be nice."

He summoned the waiter with the brass bell and ordered another scotch for himself and a Grand Marnier for Patrice. "So you're a Stockwell," he remarked as they were served. "I didn't realize that before. I'm impressed."

"Oh, goody." Patrice clapped her hands. "I've always enjoyed being impressive." She was, she realized, again flirting with him.

"What's it like? Being a member of American royalty?"

"Oh, not really royalty." Patrice tried for blitheness. "Aristocracy, maybe."

"Aristocracy, then. What's it like being a Stockwell?"

Patrice told him about her childhood. She described Riverview and the servants and the finishing schools. She related an anecdotal and somewhat amusing account of her debut.

She kept the story of her marriage light, and her description of her divorce—which she was careful to mention on the off chance he might have missed it the first time—was closer to Noel Coward than reality. "Really," she said, "Miles and I were just two very nice people who didn't quite hit it off in some rather crucial areas." Which was true enough, but in no way conveyed Patrice's disappointment back when she had realized that their marital

117

lovemaking was never going to live up to the promise of their premarital petting.

Jack listened attentively. The way he focused on Patrice was flattering, and the time passed quickly. Soon the lounge was filling up with the cocktail-hour crowd.

Jack noticed. "Time to make room for the thundering herd," he announced.

Patrice's heart sank. The chance meeting was coming to an end. His hand was already heavy on the brass bell, summoning the waiter for a check.

Patrice's spirits revived outside the Algonquin when he said he was going uptown and could he give her a lift. While they waited for the doorman to hail a cab for them, they looked at the plaque detailing the Algonquin's history as a high-society stable. "Holly actually copied it down," she told him. "History is really her passion."

"What a waste," Jack Houston remarked.

Patrice let that pass. She had no desire to go on discussing her cousin with Jack. It was her own passions—and hopefully his—she was interested in, not Holly's.

Her hopes were rewarded in the back of the taxicab. She deliberately moved close to him, making her interest clear. Without asking, he took her hand in his and held it throughout the drive uptown. He might have kissed her, Patrice thought to herself, if it hadn't been broad daylight.

The thought, and the three Grand Marniers she'd had, made her bold. "Would you like to come up for a nightcap?" she asked as the cab pulled up in front of her Gracie Terrace apartment house. Instantly she blushed. A nightcap! It was only a little past five in the afternoon.

Jack was amused. "A nightcap," he said with just a trace of inneundo, "sounds exactly right."

As the door to Patrice's apartment closed behind them, she turned and looked up at him, allowing her desire to show plainly on her face. Jack reacted without hesitation. He kissed her.

Patrice was not prepared for the feelings that swept over her. She'd recognized how strongly she was attracted to Jack Houston, but still thought of herself as a modern woman, self-reliant, clever in business, even possessed of a modicum of that ruthlessness usually identified only with men. She had never been promiscuous, but she'd

118

had her share of love affairs, and she was not without experience where men and emotions were concerned. Her relationships may not have been trouble-free, but she'd always felt confidently in control of them. If she had been asked, she would have said that "swept off her feet" was a phrase from fiction, nothing more, and could certainly never have any application to her. Only that's what happened now. Patrice was indeed swept off her feet.

The attraction was physical, of course, but even as Jack picked her up in his arms and carried her through the apartment to the bedroom as surely as if this wasn't the first time he'd been there, Patrice recognized that what she was experiencing was more than just physical desire. Weak as she felt in the grip of his powerful body, she was aware of a yearning for an affection to go along with the lovemaking promised by the sure touch of his hands as he removed her clothing. As beautiful as the promise of their mating was, Patrice was certain as he positioned her gently atop the spread on the bed, that she wanted a whole lot more than this one-time sharing.

Temporarily, however, a wave of sensation blotted out Patrice's tenderness. The immediacy and largeness of his rigidity took her by surprise. There had been none of the foreplay experience had taught Patrice to expect. He was naked and patently ready with a speed that both took her by surprise and lubricated her own lust. She rose to him eagerly, her limbs clasping him to her, groaning with pleasure at the expert thrust that filled her completely.

Despite his instant readiness, Jack's lovemaking was far from hurried. Inside herself, Patrice all but purred at his knowing explorations and calculated movements. He aroused her with penetration in ways she'd previously associated only with foreplay, afterplay, or solitary acts. And when the rainbow exploded inside her head, he met it fully with an explosion of his own that abided through the last dyings of kaleidoscopic colors.

He stayed the night, making love twice more to her. In the morning she cooked him scrambled eggs and Canadian bacon. Sitting across the table from him in the early sunlight, her heart in her eyes, Patrice was afraid to ask if she would see him again. She didn't want him to think she was possessive or pushy. Behind her smile and loving, interested expression, she vacillated between hoping he would suggest another meeting and anticipating the despair of sitting by the phone and waiting for him to call. They spoke casually of inconsequential matters and ate their breakfast, he heartily, she picking at her food.

After breakfast Jack dressed. It was time for him to go, for them to part. Patrice's smile was ridiculously brave.

Its tremulousness did not escape Jack's notice. He was a complex man in the grip of conflicting motives. Making love to Patrice had been a matter of impulse and opportunity, an act free of the strong emotions she was experiencing. Like Patrice, he had enjoyed their evening, but he rarely let other people's feelings get in the way of his self-interest. And he was interested in Buffy.

Nevertheless, Jack was not gratuitously cruel. He had no desire to hurt Patrice. It was just as easy to part on a positive note as a negative one, to leave her feeling good about herself rather than suspecting she'd been had. And so he put a lot more into his good-bye kiss than he was feeling.

"It was wonderful," he told her. "I hope you're agreeable to doing it again sometime."

"Oh, yes." Eyes shining, Patrice did not hold back. "Say when."

"I'll call you. It'll be a while though. I have to go out of town on business." The lie was meant kindly.

Nevertheless, Patrice's face fell. "When will you be back?" She could have bitten her tongue clear off. Why did she have to say that? Overeagerness, possessiveness—the sure formula for pushing any man away.

"I can't really be sure." It wasn't that he lied glibly, but that one lie bred embellishments which evolved into other lies. "It's one of those business things." He was purposely vague. "I just don't want you to think this was hit-and-run. I do want to see you again, and I'll call you just as soon as I can." In Jack's not inconsiderable experience, after a month or so most woman would meet some other guy, and he would fade from their thoughts. It was the easy—painless, he thought—way to avoid hard feelings.

"I'm glad it's not hit-and-run." Patrice's eyes were shining again.

If Jack had looked into them, he would have seen that

there was more in her gaze than he usually encountered. But he didn't notice as he kissed her good-bye a second time and started out the door. His hand on the knob, he turned and on the spur of the moment blurted out what had really been on his mind.

"If you see Buffy," he said, "tell her I thought of something."

"Buffy?" Patrice looked at him blankly. "You know Buffy?"

"Oh, yes."

"I don't understand. What do you want me to tell her?"

"Just that I thought of something. That's all—like she suggested, I thought of something."

15

T HE ENTRANCE TO Gotham Memorial Church consisted of white block marble steps from Siena carved and fitted into place by Florentine craftsmen brought over from Italy especially to perform the task. The stairway was demarcated by sweeping wrought-iron balustrades fashioned in Rome, shipped to New York in sections, then reassembled under the critical eye of an Italian master craftsman on loan from Vatican City. The huge rounded triangle of stained glass dominating the facade had been blown and hand painted in Venice. The effect was majestic and inspiring. A truly religious aura emanated from the structure. It was overwhelmingly Italian and—albeit accidentally—quite Catholic in its ambience. This was misleading, for Gotham Memorial was actually a Protestant church, and deliberately nondenominational as well.

Holly's researches had familiarized her with both Gotham's architectural splendors and the financial arrangements involved in building the church. She knew the construction had been financed entirely by Jonathan Braithwaite Stockwell, the Governor's father, shortly before the turn of the century. He had also provided an endowment in perpetuity for maintaining it. The endowment was administered by the Board of Trustees of the church, who were also charged with the hiring and, when necessary, the firing of the minister and his assistants, who actually ran Gotham Memorial.

Over the years, Holly recalled with a small, sad smile, the Governor had had occasion to regret both his father's endowment—a financial faucet bearing his family name, but not within his power to turn off—and the choice of minister—a selection likewise beyond his ability to either affect or cancel. At the time of the Governor's death, the minister had been in place some twenty years. During that span his pulpit had become famous for reverberating with points of view every bit as political as they were religious, and more often than not at odds with the public positions taken by the Governor. Thus there was more than a little irony in the fact, Holly reflected, that the Reverend Malcolm Darrow Cabot would conduct the final public services for Governor Matthew Adams Stockwell.

She was relieved that the service would put an end to the week of observances marking the Governor's death. The funeral, the reading of the will, the almost daily renewal of public mourning, had been a considerable strain. Holly had gone through the ceremonies at Riverside Heights and in Albany, knowing they were only preludes, mere dress rehearsals, as it were, to this spectacle. Still, as she mounted the white marble steps of Gotham Memorial, she thought to herself the towering edifice standing aloof from the Columbia University campus on Morningside Heights and overlooking the Hudson was every bit as grand as the Palisades across the river, and a fitting setting for the Governor's final exit.

Halfway up to the arched entrance flanked by huge bronze doors with engraved twin scrolls quoting the bible, the pressure of Christopher's hand on her arm brought Holly to a halt. She hadn't wanted to attend the ceremony with him, but he'd insisted and she hadn't thought it worth it to turn her reluctance into another confrontation; there were far more serious issues between them that would demand she take a strong stand. Now his grip on her arm made Holly look at him impatiently.

122

"Someone to see," he explained. "Wait here for me a moment, love. I'll be right back."

Holly stood to one side and watched him retrace his steps down the white marble blocks. His progress was slow since he was moving against a swelling tide. Gotham Memorial's interior, with over two thousand seats, was already filling with mourners, each a celebrity in his or her own right. Another four thousand, less notable, were gathering outside on the marble steps and sidewalk with heads bared to listen to the eulogies over a sound system second only to that of Carnegie Hall. Christopher elbowed through them and slipped between the blue sawhorses put up by the police to close off the street to traffic.

On the other side of the wooden barricades an elite tactical police force on horseback separated the mobile units of the television networks from the mourners' area. Using zoom lenses, these units would shoot the entrances and exits of the various celebrities in attendance and occasionally succeed in isolating one of them for a comment on the passing of Governor Stockwell. However, for coverage of the proceedings inside the church they were all equally dependent on the one pool crew that had been permitted to set up its cameras behind the second balcony choir loft.

Christopher walked straight up to a square-jawed young man wearing a J.J. Press sports jacket. The young man's blue eyes and immaculately blow-dried coiffure were familiar to eight million or more network television viewers as belonging to the number two anchorman on the top-rated six P.M. news show. He registered interest as Christopher introduced himself.

Holly bit her lip as the anchorman signaled a technical crew and a camera was activated to move in on him and Christopher. Both their faces turned serious, as befit the occasion. The interview was short, and when it was over, Christopher and the TV anchor shook hands. Then, moving with the crowd now, Christopher elbowed his way back to Holly.

"Was that really necessary?" she asked, tight-mouthed, when he rejoined her.

"Oh, yes, love. After all, you don't show any promise of being cooperative. If things should go public, I'm going to need all the friends in the media that I can get."

"You bastard!"

"Now, Holly, don't be bitter. You've got the Stockwell family name, the money, and all that power behind you. All I have to counter your intransigence is my wits."

"And your complete lack of morality!"

"People in glass houses..." Christopher's sunburned, Anglican face spread into a pleasant smile. He didn't bother finishing the sentence.

"What did you say on camera?" Holly demanded.

"Words of heartfelt regret for the passing of a great statesman, spiced with gratitude for the privilege of having known his warmth and loving nature in the bosom of his family through my marriage to the granddaughter of whom he was so fond."

"Is that all?"

"More or less. In any case, you should probably be more concerned with what the interviewer said to me, love. He was most interested in what I thought of the, um, 'circumstances' surrounding the Governor's death. He asked me twice if the family was upset about Vanessa Brewster."

"Christopher, if you've said anything to embarrass—"

"Not to worry, Holly. Not that you deserve it, but I did maintain family solidarity in the face of tragedy. I told my new friend—American paparazzi that he is—that the 'circumstances' were a simple but tragic heart attack, and that Miss Brewster was a professional associate of the Governor's and a friend of the family as well. I even said you and I had entertained her in London."

"Thank you, Christopher." Relief pushed the words out from between Holly's clenched lips. "That was unexpectedly decent of you."

"But I am decent, Holly, if only you'd give me a chance to prove it."

And if I don't, Holly thought but did not say aloud, you'll pillory me to the whole world.

As Holly and Christopher passed into the church, she was aware of the many NYPD plainclothesmen and FBI agents mingling with the crowd, their jackets bulging with lethal hardware. The Secret Service, too, was everywhere. The pervasive law enforcement presence brought home to

124

Holly that there had rarely been so many high government figures gathered together in one place.

The concern was reflected behind her, outside the church, not just on the urban streets, but in the air and on the water as well. Federal, state and city helicopters weighed down with marksmen crisscrossed the skies over Gotham Memorial. Small gunboats—power launches armed to the teeth—patrolled the Hudson for two miles upstream and down from the church. And a special Army unit beat the bushes of the Palisades across the river on the off chance of flushing a sniper. On both sides of the Hudson there was coordination via walkie-talkie.

As Holly moved down the aisle to the front of the church, she exchanged nods of greeting with the minister. He was chatting with Matt in the fourth of the eight front pews reserved for the more than one hundred Stockwell family members and certain honored guests. Back in 1969 Reverend Cabot had counseled Matt, as he had many other young men opposed to the Vietnam War, as to the various alternatives to complying with the draft. Now he excused himself to greet Leonard Bernstein, who would lead a small, select group from the New York Philharmonic in a rendition of the last movement of Beethoven's Fifth Symphony, a tribute to Governor Stockwell.

Music, Holly knew, was to play a large part in the memorial service. The Governor had been a true lover of the art form, and his tastes had been quite catholic. Thus there would be jazz by the Dave Brubeck Quartet, a medley of Scott Joplin rags on the flute played by Jean-Pierre Rampal, a selection of gospel songs by the Abyssinian Church Choir, an old calypso folk song sung a cappella by Harry Belafonte, and traditional hymns played on the organ and sung by all in attendance at the service. Reverend Cabot, whose baritone the Governor had admired almost as much as he disliked his "knee-jerk politics and bleeding heart meddling," would lead the hymn singing.

There would, of course, be eulogies as well as song. The Governor's eldest son would speak once again in tribute to his father. The aging and ailing Senator Jacob Javits would intone the praise of the Republican Party. Coretta Scott King would pay homage to the Governor's contribution to civil rights both in New York State and nationally.

125

Terrence Cardinal Cooke and Rabbi Alexander Schindler would laud his tolerance and his contributions to the Catholic and Jewish religious communities. And Zelig Meyerling would speak one last time of the Governor's many contributions to the country he so loved.

Other luminaries would not speak publicly but would pay their respects through their presence. President Jimmy Carter was already greeting Buffy in the first pew, holding her hand and looking earnestly into her eyes as he offered condolences. On the opposite side of the aisle Vice President Mondale was talking to the Governor's first wife. Democratic senators Edward Kennedy and Daniel Patrick Moynihan were coming down the aisle.

"Death," Christopher Millwood whispered cynically in Holly's ear as they settled themselves in a pew three rows behind her grandmother, "knows no party lines."

Holly ignored him. She noted that the front pew was not yet completely occupied. Her Uncle James, who would really be speaking for the family, had not yet arrived. The services, she knew, would not start without him. There was still space set aside in the first pew for him and one other person.

As Holly's eyes wandered, she spied Meyerling turning around to talk to former presidents Richard Nixon and Gerald Ford while Pat Nixon looked on with a fixed half smile. Treachery, Holly thought to herself. Grandpa had never forgiven President Ford for making Nelson Rockefeller Vice President instead of him. But on second thought she realized that Meyerling wasn't really being false to his fallen mentor. The Governor of all people would have approved all civilities extended to those who'd come to pay their respects at his memorial service.

Many members of the Stockwell family were putting themselves out to extend those civilities to one-time opponents of the Governor. The Governor's second son, Jonathan, was fussing over Chief Justice Warren Burger—whose nomination to head the Supreme Court the Governor had publicly deplored. David Lewis detached himself from his wife Alice, the Governor's eldest daughter, to thank David Stockman and Congressman Jack Kemp for coming. Both men had crossed swords with the Governor over economic policy. Even Susan Gray, who for a long time had been estranged from her father, was putting her best Hollywood foot forward to be gracious to Nancy Reagan, whom she had known years ago as Nancy Davis in California. Along with Ford and Rockefeller, the Governor had worked hard, if in vain, to keep the Republican Party nomination for president from falling to "that extremist ham cowboy actor," Ronald Reagan.

Susan Gray's son Deke was sitting between George Steinbrenner, owner of the New York Yankees, and on-again-off-again Yankee manager Yogi Berra. There had been rumors in the sports columns of Steinbrenner making the Red Sox an offer they couldn't refuse for Deke Wells. Holly wondered if her young cousin's sitting between them now was an effort to make sure that if he was traded, he would be traded up.

It wasn't. Steinbrenner and Berra had just naturally joined Deke because he was a fellow professional and the three of them knew each other. They were there because the Governor had been a staunch Yankee fan who had used his influence to help push through the building of the new Yankee Stadium. For Deke's part, furthering his career was the last thing on his mind. He was only praying he would still have a career left when the medical experts finished poring over the X rays of his shredded ligament.

The pew behind Deke was entirely taken up by the descendants of the Governor's long-dead sister, the Tyler family. Seated in a row, their red-gold hair formed a blazing stripe dividing the front rows of the church from the center. Alfred Tyler, the Governor's aging nephew, and Lizzie Tyler, who had been married to Alfred's twin brother John, sat at either end of the bench. Among them Holly noticed a relative she hadn't seen in many years.

Youngest of Alfred's children, at thirty-three Louise was also the most famous. Her striking aquiline face with its Tyler eyes and hair had graced the cover of *Vogue* and *Glamour* on many occasions before she married Spiro Papatestus and moved to Greece. There, on the Island of Crete, she and her munitions-magnate husband, allegedly one of the world's richest men, had established a social life of parties and yachting expeditions and erotic permissiveness the envy of the haut monde from Palm Beach to the

127

Côte d'Azur. Along with her seemingly ageless sixty-four-year-old husband, Louise's almond-eyed visage now graced even more magazines than when she had been a professional model. Along with Jackie Kennedy and Elizabeth Taylor, she was one of the three most photographed women in the world.

Shifting her gaze, Holly saw that Spiro and Louise Papatestus were not the only family members who had flown in specially for the memorial service. Lisa Stockwell, James's youngest daughter, had returned from France. She looked much as Holly remembered her from their last meeting, when Lisa had passed through London on her way to Paris, where she had informed her family, she intended to settle permanently and write poetry. Holly had noticed with concern then that Lisa had still shown traces of the anorexia that afflicted her as a teenager. Now, twenty-three-years old and no longer anorexic, she was still quite thin, her frailty was emphasized by a birdlike nervousness which expressed itself in fidgeting and sudden movements. Her narrow face was habitually pale, and while her brown eyes were capable of blazing with the rhythms of a newly penned canto, her more usual glance was dull and wary of people.

The wariness did not exclude her two brothers and her sister. She sat with them now, paying no attention to Matt and Patrice's teasing of their brother Michael for his political ambitions. Nor did she respond to the attempts by Miles O'Keefe, who had known Lisa as a little girl, to draw her out. She had always cut herself off from her family. Now she was physically present, but her mind seemed to be filled with the word images that were all that really mattered to her.

Holly noticed that Matt, Patrice, and Michael kept craning their heads in anticipation of their father's arrival. The lateness of James Linstone Stockwell was delaying the proceedings. When Reverend Cabot ascended the small, winding, wrought-iron staircase to the pulpit, Holly thought he might be about to start without her uncle.

The hush that fell over the large church hall was, however, premature. Reverend Cabot was simply arranging the notes for his talk on the podium. The hum of voices started again.

Holly observed with surprise Patrice leaning over the back of Buffy's pew to talk to her. As James's daughter, loyal to him and therefore in opposition to Buffy regarding the battle over the will, Patrice was hardly a likely friend of the Governor's widow. Holly wondered what on earth Patrice could be saying to their step-grandmother.

The answer was simple. Patrice was innocently delivering Jack Houston's message. "He said to tell you that he followed your suggestion and that he thought of something," she informed Buffy.

Buffy's violet eyes appraised Patrice steadily. "I see," she said finally, nodding. "How nice for you, Patrice."

"What?"

"A moral for us both, my dear." Buffy spoke elliptically. "A woman scorned is not the only gender Hell hath no fury like."

"I don't understand." But Patrice's bewilderment was directed now to the back of Buffy's head. Finally, with a shrug, she sat back in her seat and turned to her brother, Matt. "What do you suppose can be keeping Daddy?"

The question was also vexing Reverend Cabot. He looked up from his papers and squinted, careful to keep the annoyance he was feeling from his face. As he gazed out over the pulpit, however, the expression of relief that suddenly spread over his features could not help being communicated to his audience. Many of them turned in their seats to follow his gaze.

Holly turned with them. And with them she caught her breath. The reaction was so marked that the sound filled the church hall as if the acoustical string of a harp had been plucked.

It was this multithroated gasp that finally caused Buffy Stockwell to turn around. Focusing, her eyes turned to angry, smoldering slits. James Linstone Stockwell was walking slowly down the aisle of the Gotham Memorial Church toward the front pew, and beside him, her arm in his, was Vanessa Brewster!

Her appearance, really not so different from what it usually was, gave the lie to the innuendos contained in the descriptions of her in the newspaper accounts of the Governor's death. Her dark gray dress hung from her waist in

129

loose folds that hid her hips and long legs. It did not hide the largeness of her bosom, but neither did it define it. The lenses of the eyeglasses she wore were not thick, but the frames were heavy, durable, more suitable to the knockabout of hard travel than the hush of Gotham Memorial Church. The unfashionable topknot which was her customary hairdo gave her a somewhat dowdy—almost a frumpy—appearance.

Today she looked her age—mid-thirties—no more, but certainly no less. The thousands of curious eyes watching Vanessa Brewster as she came down the aisle on the arm of James Linstone Stockwell could find no flicker of the fire, the passion, the sensuality promised by the circumstances of the Governor's demise in her all-too suspicious presence. As a symbol of immoral, decadent youth corrupting its hallowed elders, Vanessa Brewster was a decided disappointment.

James escorted her straight to Mary. "Mother," he said when he reached her, "here is our dear old friend Vanessa Brewster, recovered from the shock of the Governor's death and come to join us in paying our last tribute."

"Oh, my dear." Mary stood up. "Thank you for coming." And she kissed Vanessa on a cheek that had never known the blush of rouge, the patina of powder.

Up in the second balcony, behind the choir loft, the television crew caught every bit of dialogue and action on camera. Every network would carry it on that evening's national news. All America would know that Vanessa Brewster had been accepted by the Stockwells as a friend of the family. With one bold stroke James was laying the rumors to rest.

As did virtually everyone else in the church, Holly immediately turned to look at Buffy. The Governor's widow stared straight ahead, ignoring the carefully staged tableau on the other side of the aisle. The expression of her face was set, as if carved in stone. She's really furious, Holly realized, not without a twinge of sympathy.

Holly was right. Buffy was furious. When James had said he would take care of the Vanessa Brewster matter, she'd never dreamed he would do it in a way that would publicly degrade her. It was, truly, one of the most humiliating moments Buffy had ever known in her life, even more so than those accompanying the scandal when her first husband had made public the details of her adulterous liaisons with the Governor.

You'll pay for this, James, Buffy vowed silently. If there was ever any chance of compromise over the estate, you have just killed it. I'll get what is rightfully mine, and if I can destroy you in the process, it will be all the better. Yes, I'll drag you and the Stockwells through every court in the land, and smear the Stockwell name in every newspaper, on every TV newscast, that I can.

With this thought, Buffy's fury took a sudden detour. Wait! What seemed such a public humiliation and defeat might be just the advantage—in disguise—she'd been seeking. By insulting her this way, James might have made a serious tactical mistake. Indeed, he just might have unwittingly supplied the means of his own undoing.

As James and Vanessa Brewster took their places beside Mary Linstone Stockwell in the front pew, across the aisle from Buffy, Reverend Cabot spread his arms and raised them toward the arched ceiling of the cathedral. "Let us begin." The gesture was a signal for the congregation to rise for the singing of the first hymn.

Buffy almost missed it. Her brain was still exulting with her sudden realization. Yes, James had erred badly. He had publicly revealed a connection between the Stockwell family and the woman the Governor had been making love to at the time of his death. The alliance opened a door to the claim that Vanessa Brewster, acting in the interest of the family, could have used her sexual wiles on the Governor to influence him against Buffy in the writing of his will. Absolute proof would not be necessary. Insinuations and innuendos alone would powerfully bolster Buffy's rights as a wife to at least half her husband's estate under law. Why, she could even plant the suggestion that James and his mother had stood to gain an immense fortune by luring the Governor into strenuous sex and death through the hussy Vanessa Brewster! What a field day the media would have with that!

Buffy rose to her feet a beat after most of the congregation. The enormous chamber still echoed with the rustle of expensive silks and the subdued tinkle of the jewelry of the privileged. A heavenly light filtering through the

131

white robes of the angels and the halos of the apostles decorating the stained-glass windows, spread over spring-time mink and ermine, custom-made men's suits of dark blue cashmere, Tiffany diamond brooches, and Van Cleef pearl necklaces. Outside there was a purr of Cadillacs and Mercedes' and Rolls-Royces wafting uptown toward Harlem as the chauffeurs periodically ran the engines in order for the heaters to maintain an even temperature inside each limousine.

Manicured hands turned to the page in the hymnal announced by Reverend Cabot. "Let us join now in singing the old Shaker favorite, which was Governor Matthew Adams Stockwell's favorite hymn," the minister requested. The mourners raised their voices in song to proclaim "'Tis a Gift to Be Simple."

It was followed by "Amazing Grace."

BOOK THREE

16

"BALANCE, YOU KNOW." There was humor in Mary Linstone Stockwell's sigh as she passed one of the envelopes across the pile of gold-embossed wedding reception invitations to her granddaughter Holly for sealing. "When I was younger I really believed that's how life worked. Good for evil, birth for death, joy for sorrow. Balance. But now..." Mary shrugged.

"Well, why wouldn't you think that?" Holly wiped a sponge over the lip of the envelope and ran her thumb over it with one motion, gluing it smoothly and firmly. "You came from one mercantile family, the Linstones, and you married into another, the Stockwells. Balance sheets have always defined your environment—profit-and-loss statements, financial and otherwise. And there is a kind of orderliness to the view."

"If there is one thing I've learned, it is that life isn't orderly. And while I can't speak for eternity, in the short run the balance—the profit-and-loss, if you will—is more often than not askew. Good does not balance off evil any more than wealth redresses poverty. There is more rain than sunshine in most lives. And while it's true the birthrate may exceed deaths, the prospect that raises is surely more ominous than reassuring."

"Still, there is progress," Holly said. "We're out of the caves. We live twice as long as we did five hundred years ago. For a great many people in the world life is easier, more rewarding."

"You know what the hardest thing about growing old is?" Mary asked her granddaughter abruptly, as if changing the subject, but actually doing no such thing.

"No. What?"

"Having to listen to the optimism of youth." She put a check mark beside a name on the invitation list at her elbow and reached for another envelope.

"I'm sorry, Grandma." Holly laughed. "But why is it necessary to equate maturity with pessimism and cynicism?"

"Not maturity. Old age. And I'll tell you why. Because a sour view of life makes the prospect of leaving it more palatable. That's why." The look of concern this brought to Holly's eyes made Mary immediately regret her words.

"Are you—" Holly started to ask.

"I'm fine." Mary reassured her.

"Your pills? The nitro?"

"Right here in my pocket, dear. It was only a joke, not a signal I'm about to have another heart attack." Mary was touched by Holly's concern, but it made her impatient, too. Dying was bad enough without people anticipating the event for you before you actually had to face it. She had managed to live with her heart condition for some time, and would go on living with it until she died. "A joke," she repeated. "Gallows humor. A mark of dotage." She took a deep breath. "Anyway, I sidetracked myself. My mentioning balance was only to point out that just when one doubts it most, along comes a wedding—only two months later—to balance off Matthew's funeral."

"And a June wedding at that." Holly nodded. "Yes, there is a sort of symbolic symmetry to it."

"A June wedding." Mary smiled. "For Alfred and Lizzie Tyler, a December couple. Life is full of surprises, isn't it?" Her penmanship small and neat, she addressed another envelope.

"Grandpa would have approved. He liked happy occasions better than sad ones."

"Matthew would neither have approved nor disapproved. He would probably not have paid the slightest attention. He walked through ceremonies—weddings, funerals, christenings, anniversary parties—in a sort of unseeing haze, his mind on the larger issues, the affairs of state, whatever. He had the common touch, he said all the right things, but actually he looked straight through all commonplace events and the people involved in them."

Holly looked at her grandmother curiously. It wasn't like her to speak negatively of the Governor. It wasn't like her to be bitter.

Mary interpreted the look correctly. "I'm furious with him for dying," she said. "It spills out inappropriately."

"That's natural." Holly inserted another of the gold-embossed invitations into the square envelope her grandmother now handed her.

"I'm angrier with him than at any time since our divorce. Just look at the mess he's left me."

"You mean Buffy's suit to break the will?"

"Yes. And everything that entails. The living arrangements here at Riverview, for instance. They're ridiculous!"

"Is that why you won't live here?" Holly asked.

"I prefer my own place. It's smaller and more manageable. And I like the fact that my cottage stands on Linstone property, not Stockwell. It makes it purely mine, without complications." Mary took another envelope from the pile, then put it back, remembering to first check off another name on the invitation list.

"But the properties are merged," Holly reminded her.

"I know. But even so, there are too many memories here at Riverview. And I am, after all, very close by."

"And very comfortably removed from the strain of those living arrangements you mentioned. You're lucky." Holly sighed, tucking a wisp of golden hair behind her ear.

"Well, you're sort of removed, too. All the way over in the north tower of the west wing."

"Not removed enough," Holly told her. "Big as Riverview is, none of us can seem to keep out of each other's way. The other day I was having breakfast when Uncle James and Buffy came into the dining room at the same time. The footman's hands shook with the chill coming off

135

the two of them when he had to walk the length of the table to serve them their kippers and eggs."

"Serves them both right. Kippers indeed! How pretentious and European. Whose idea was that?"

"Buffy's. A long time ago. But I must say neither Grandpa nor Uncle James objected. They just wolfed them down." Holly picked up a batch of envelopes and tamped them on the table, evening the stack as if arranging a deck of cards before starting to deal. "Uncle James still does."

"My son, my son." Mary deliberately exaggerated the betrayal. "Un-American." As mistress of Riverview she had never even thought of serving kippers.

"Riverview is yours now," Holly reminded her. "You could tell the cook to serve grits for breakfast."

"It would be fitting. Buffy was educated in the South, you know. One of those magnolia finishing schools specializing in poise, eyelash-fluttering, undulation, and coquetry. When I first knew her, she even had the remnants of a plantation accent. Once I actually heard her say Fiddle-dee dee."

"It's nice you bear her no ill will." Sealing another envelope, Holly was amused.

"I really don't, you know. My malice is really just annoyance. I have no real hatred—not anymore, anyway—toward Buffy. It's just that her hanging on at Riverview makes things . . . well, quite messy."

"You could make her leave if you wanted to," Holly reminded her grandmother. "Riverview is yours. There's no reason to let her stay while she's trying to get it away from you."

"That's exactly what James said. But I can't do that, Holly. Riverview has been Buffy's home for fifteen years. I can't just throw her out."

"You're too nice." Holly's thumb was heavy sealing the envelope, emphasizing her point.

"You don't understand. It's not for Buffy's sake, but for my own. I have a concept of who I am, and that dictates how I behave. At my age I don't want to change that concept."

Holly frowned. "It's not just Buffy. There's some sort of friction between Uncle James and Uncle Jonathan, too. They don't ride into the city together anymore. They take separate cars and drivers."

"Oh, dear." It distressed Mary when her sons didn't get along. James had always been so careful, so protective, of Jonathan's shortcomings. Mary herself had recognized them, of course. But then one does not love one's children for their business acumen or intellectual capabilities, nor cease loving them because of its lack. "I know Jonathan was distressed when James brought that Brewster woman to the memorial service—perhaps even more than Buffy herself. Jonathan is so Victorian when it comes to keeping the family name free of scandal. He is, of course, in the wrong family for that attitude." Mary made another check mark. "Still," she added, "I would have thought Jonathan would have forgiven James for that by now."

"I don't think he has. He referred to it sarcastically at dinner just the other night, and Uncle James seemed quite put out. Still, perhaps it's something else entirely. Perhaps it has to do with this business with Peter."

Her grandson Peter, as Mary knew, was pressing hard for increased control over a larger portion of the estate. He claimed to be acting for his father, that it was Jonathan's right, that equality of control with James and David Lewis had always been denied him. Peter's mother backed him strongly.

"Not that I don't love all my children and grandchildren," she told Holly, "but you're not convincing me that dinner with the family at Riverview is a nightly event I should regret missing."

"It's hard for me to believe that Peter and I have the same blood," Holly commented, almost as if she'd shared her grandmother's thoughts.

"You don't like him?"

"No."

"Why not?"

"Lots of reasons. But most of all, I think, because of how he treats Nicholas. He completely ignores him, just as if he wasn't there at all. And if Nicholas draws someone else's attention, then Peter is annoyed and doesn't bother to hide it. He reminds me of Christopher."

"Perhaps he just doesn't like children."

"Of course he doesn't." Holly sealed the next envelope with her fist. "Neither does Christopher."

"Well, people have a right not to like children."

"Oh, yes." Holly's smile was grim. "And people have a right not to like people who don't like children."

"How is Michael with Nicholas?" Mary inquired.

"Marvelous. You know Michael. Always a politician. If Nicholas could vote, Michael would win by a landslide."

"He is a lot like Matthew," Mary said.

"His brother?" Holly was surprised.

"Oh, no. I meant my Matthew, his grandfather. Michael's older brother may have the name, but Michael has the Governor's charm and ambition. A natural at politics, and with women too, from what I hear. Just like the Governor."

"He is good-looking," Holly agreed. "And he does seem to have a fatal attraction for the ladies." Holly positioned the roll of postage stamps and sponge to stamp the envelopes. "Do you think he'll succeed? Do you think he'll get the party nomination to Congress from this district?"

"Now how would I know a thing like that, Holly?"

"You've been around politicians all your life, Grandma. Don't be coy. The Governor used to say you could smell if he had a chance before he even thought of tossing his hat in the ring."

"Ah, shall I never be rid of my evil reputation? Well, then—yes, Holly, I think Michael's chances are excellent. He has the Stockwell name. He has the Stockwell money behind him. He's young, personable, and he looks wonderful on television. I'd say he's a shoo-in. Barring scandal, of course. The one thing I never thought to warn the Governor about," Mary added dryly.

"Given Michael's romantic track record, I'd say he should bear that in mind."

"Well, he's single as well as young, and these are liberated times." Mary grimaced, disapproving even as she granted the fact. "As long as it isn't something that people will laugh at, I'd say he didn't have anything to worry about. But being laughed at—that costs elections. People don't elect politicians to office whom they don't take seriously." Mary's pen slid over another envelope with perfect control. "In any case, he's got his father to keep him on the straight and narrow."

Holly said nothing. She felt she'd already upset her

grandmother enough by discussing the tensions at Riverview. She saw no reason to mention the recent strain she'd noticed between Michael and his father. Poor Uncle James. His youngest daughter Lisa had skittered back to Paris without a word of regret for the parting. His son Matt would always be a disappointment to him. And now there was this strange friction with Michael. Of Uncle James's four children, that left only Patrice to assuage his filial needs, and Patrice had confessed to Holly that she felt her father could never really appreciate her the way he should.

"Yes," Holly agreed when the silence brought her grandmother's eyes up from the envelopes with a look of inquisitiveness. "Michael has his father."

They addressed and sealed and stamped the envelopes without further conversation for a while. Finally Holly spoke. "It really is nice of you to go to all this trouble, Grandma," she remarked. "The caterers... arranging for the chapel at Gotham Memorial... making Riverview available... even seeing to the wedding invitations. I mean you and the Governor were divorced. It's not even your family."

"When you divorce you don't sever all ties with the family of the man you divorced," Mary told her. "Besides, I've always been fond of Matthew's sister's children. When John and Alfred and I were children we played together. With his sister gone, Matthew always regarded his nephews as his responsibility. I sort of feel I owe it to him to carry that on."

"Particularly since Buffy isn't likely to," Holly observed dryly.

"That, as the young people say, is for sure."

"Do you suppose she'll be here for the reception?"

"Buffy lives at Riverview. Unless she has something better to do, she'll be here." Mary laid down the pen and opened and closed her hand, uncramping the fingers. "I do wish it all wasn't so frenetic," she complained. "I mean, after all, Alfred and Lizzie have dragged their feet for three years since Alfred's wife died. Marrying her brother's twin shouldn't be any great change for Lizzie. He and Alfred looked exactly alike. So what is the big hurry?"

"Perhaps they want a June wedding."

"I suppose so. And at their age—our age—there aren't all that many Junes left."

"Or," Holly suggested straight-faced, "maybe Alfred got Lizzie in trouble. Maybe they have to get married."

"Holly!" Mary was scandalized. "Alfred is sixty-seven years old, and Lizzie is sixty-six. How—" And then, despite herself, a giggle bottled up in her throat since adolescence suddenly escaped. "In trouble! Geriatric Alfred and Varicose Lizzie. Well now. That does give me hope!"

"Why, Grandma!" Now it was Holly's turn to act shocked. "Underneath it all, I do believe you may truly be a dirty old woman."

"Well, I'm not," Mary assured her. "But there are times," she admitted, her gaze straying out the window to the newly summer-clad woodlands and rolling hills of the family estate, "when I would like to be."

17

GREEN, IN ALL its varied shades, predominated in June, spreading its lushness over Riverview. The pines stood out darkly against the brighter leafiness of oak, maple, sumac and elm. Summer soils, renewed by April rains, were mossed over, their brownness patined with a tenuous, delicate, spreading carpet of lime-velvet verdancy.

The sun replied by sponsoring a rainbowed attack against the forest green, an infiltration of the grasses by uncamouflaged wildflowers: brazen buttercups of pollen-polished gold, violet heather turning woodland to moor, bluebonnets mirroring the cloudless sky, Queen Anne's lace pure and white with filigreed virtue. The invasion thickened approaching the gardens of Riverview. The outrageous profusion of color, defying order, was finally halted by the manmade wall of stone setting off the domain of Riverview's formal gardens from the anarchy of the wildlands making up the rest of the estate.

On the other side of the stone wall, the land and its flowerings were the realm of Gustav Ulbricht, Riverview's head gardener, and his five assistants. Ulbricht had been hired away from the Roosevelts' Hyde Park estate by the Governor more than thirty years ago, and he'd known no home save Riverview since. Now, as on the day of the Governor's death, he was standing beside the stables long since reconverted into garages. They looked out over his domain as he conversed with Kevin O'Lunney, once the Governor's chauffeur and now the chauffeur of the new head of the family, James. On this occasion the pair had been joined by Berkley, Riverview's butler, to form a trio of the Stockwell's most senior servants.

"It's an insult." Gustav Ulbricht's nose was out of joint. "I designed these gardens, kept them up all these years with no word but satisfaction, and now they bring in these—these—landscape gardeners." His tone defined the last two words as beyond profanity.

"Sure and it's only for the wedding." Kevin O'Lunney tried to calm the older man. "Flower sculptures and such to make the occasion more festive. They'll be taken away the day following, and you'll not be remembering they were even here."

"Flower sculptures!" Ulbricht snorted. "If the good Lord had meant flowers to be sculpted, he would have made garden tools chisels and hatchets instead of shears and hoes."

"You don't understand, Gustav," the butler Berkley told him. "I heard Miss Holly discussing it with the first Mrs. Stockwell this morning. 'Thematic,' she said. It's all part of a theme, you understand, for the wedding. And it requires a certain expertise that's more artistic than just plain gardening."

"Oleander bushes shaped like swans!" the gardener snorted. "Cupids in the hollyhocks! And those damnable fountains everywhere, oversoaking the loam."

"You don't understand," Berkley repeated. "And I must say that your being discombobulated is nothing to what's going on inside the house."

"Inside is it?" Kevin O'Lunney was surprised. "Sure and I thought the reception was to be outdoors, it being June and all."

"That's right." Ulbricht would not be mollified. "Six hundred guests up from the city trampling all over my zinnias and catching their finery on my rose bushes. Over a hundred wrought-iron tables digging up my lawn. And there's a real doubt, you know, if it will be possible to re-sod this late in the season." This time he spit on the ground to show his contempt for the outside breed.

"It is supposed to be outdoors," Berkley answered Kevin. "But preparations must be made to move everything indoors in case it rains. A bandstand had to be set up in the ballroom as well as on the patio. Serving tables have to be prepared, the silver polished, indoor crystal made ready. A thousand details. But worst of all is the kitchen. Indoors or out, it will be chaos. I will have to contend with refereeing between our cook and the one on loan from the Four Seasons. Outside stewards tramping through our wine cellars and screaming arguments over appropriate vintages of champagne, and half my kitchen staff threatening to resign because they're insulted while the other half stands around bad-mouthing the intruders. Everything—everything!—will be a subject of conflict; the ripeness of peaches, how much basil in the sauces, the proper temperature for crème fraîche! Believe me, Gustav, you have my sympathy, but it is my authority with the household staff, which will be the first casualty of this wedding."

"Sure and you fellers are really downtrodden, you are," Kevin twitted them.

"It's easy for you to make jokes," Berkley responded. "This wedding business is no strain on you. All you have to do is get Mr. James home from the city, and your part is over."

"A piece of cake then, is it?" Kevin's eyes narrowed; his voice turned sardonic. "Well, let me tell you, it's no routine matter getting James Stockwell home to Riverview any night, let alone on time for a wedding reception."

"Why not?" Berkley wanted to know. "Why shouldn't you bring him straight from the church to Riverview, the same as all the other guests?"

"Because it's good reason he might have to not be wanting to come direct. A chip-off-the-old block's reason, you might say. The same reason as has me cooling my heels into the wee hours many a night of late, waiting for him to leave a certain apartment in the east Greenwich Village section of the city."

"The East Village?" Berkley's eyebrows shot up. "Mr. James? That is out of character. Ever since his wife died he's always seemed quite content to be . . . well, a middle-aged bachelor, and to stay home nights and attend to business days."

"Mid-life crisis." The gardener nodded his head knowingly.

"Sure, and don't I know that?" Kevin ignored Ulbricht's diagnosis and responded to the butler. "Didn't I calculate how the gonads must have skipped a generation from the Governor to Michael, with Mr. James content by the fireside? Only of late I've been proved wrong."

"Such an unsavory part of the city, the East Village." Berkley shook his head disapprovingly. "What could he see in a creature who would live there?"

"The same charms as caught the eye of the Governor." Kevin O'Lunney put the icing on the cake with quiet, backstairs satisfaction. "Sure and the lady fanning the flame of Mr. James's naughtiness is the very same one as did in his father."

"Do you mean . . . ?" It was Berkley who spoke as both he and Gustav Ulbricht stared from under shock-raised brows at James's chauffeur.

"Ah, well . . ." Kevin was pleased at their reaction. "As the feller said to the Orangeman after splitting his head with the shillelagh, that got your attention, didn't it now?"

"I can't believe it!" Berkley shook his head against a swarm of bees.

"Oh, you heard me right. It's the very same lady. Sure, and it's a taste for mature Stockwells she has, does Miss Vanessa ever-loving Brewster."

That same afternoon Vanessa Brewster was also the subject of a discussion between Jonathan Stockwell and his older brother James. It took place in James's mahogany-paneled office on the top floor of the Stockwell Building. The picture window of the office looked out over New York harbor, a sweeping panorama from the Brooklyn Bridge to the Statue of Liberty.

143

James was standing with his back to his agitated younger brother, facing the view but not really focusing on it. He might just as well have been looking out the window of Jonathan's office across the hall at the ugliness of the twin towers of the World Trade Center. His concentration was on restraining himself.

"You are jeopardizing not just your own reputation, but the good name of the Stockwell family as well," Jonathan was persisting. "For God's sake, James, this is the same woman that was *en flagrante* with the Governor—with our father!—when he died of his own lust. The newspapers—"

"Will not learn of it," James interrupted, speaking through clenched lips without turning around. "I am discreet. Furthermore, my private life is no business of the family's, and no business of yours, Jonathan."

"Isn't it bad enough that Father was notorious for his lechery? Do you have to follow in his footsteps as if it were a family trait?"

"Jonathan." Turning from the window and facing him, James's icy tone camouflaged his reluctance to utter the words he now spoke. "The foundation of your own house is glass. Don't throw stones."

"What?" Jonathan looked at him in confusion. "What did you say?"

"Father and I are not the only Stockwells to succumb to our desires."

Jonathan reddened slowly. "I was young," he protested. "I made a mistake. I've paid for it." He bit his lip visibly. "I didn't mean that the way it sounded. Actually, Ellen and I have been quite happy together, even if we were pushed into marriage by her pregnancy. The way Peter has turned out is proof of that, isn't it?"

"Of course." James sighed. "It was a cheap shot. I'm sorry."

In the wake of the apology the atmosphere was slightly warmer, more brotherly. Jonathan was reluctant to disturb it. But there was one more point he felt he had to make. "What about your son, James?" he said. "What about Michael? Have you considered the effect on his campaign for the congressional nomination? The tawdry circumstances of his grandfather's death were bad enough. If it comes

144

out that his father is involved with the same woman, Michael will be a laughingstock in every political back room in the state."

"You don't have to speak for Michael." Feeling harassed, James flared up. "My son can speak to me for himself." And he will, James thought to himself miserably, already dreading the inevitable confrontation. Michael knew about Vanessa Brewster; it was in Michael's eyes every time his son looked at him lately.

"What I don't understand is how you ever let yourself get involved with this Brewster woman." Jonathan sighed, temporarily out of umbrage and steam. "That's what I don't understand."

That's what you don't understand? James smiled to himself, not speaking his thoughts aloud. But it's so simple, Jonathan. It all happened so naturally. . . .

It had begun with the service at Gotham Memorial Church. James had not actually met Vanessa Brewster before the service. He'd entrusted the arrangements to a discreet senior executive who had been with Stockwell Enterprises for twenty years. The functionary had delivered her to James's limousine a few blocks from the church.

James had thanked her for coming. "You're quite welcome," Vanessa Brewster replied. Other than that, they hadn't exchanged words during the short ride to the church. Nor had they spoken as they disembarked and made their dramatic entrance.

After the service, maintaining the "friend of the family" fiction, James had escorted her back to the waiting limousine. The sharp interest of the scandal-oriented media had prodded him into the rear of the vehicle with her. Despite the fact that Vanessa Brewster had carried herself with a dignity and aplomb that both surprised and gratified James, the media's attentions were unrestrained.

Once the side-window shades had been drawn and the limousine was gliding away, James had acted out of an ingrained politeness. "Shall we take you home?" he inquired. "Or is there some other place you would like to go?"

"Home, please." She removed her eyeglasses and carefully polished the lenses. There was not a trace of nervousness in the act. Instead, it seemed a necessary efficiency in keeping with her utilitarian mourning dress and self-composed demeanor. "Tompkins Square. That's Tenth Street between avenues A and B."

James took the intercom speaker from its holder in the armrest beside the cigarette lighter and ashtray, pushed the button activating it, and relayed the address to his chauffeur.

Although this ride was longer by far than the first one they had taken together, again they did not speak. Vanessa Brewster took the silence in her stride, unruffled by it. She sat relaxed, her hands folded and half lost from view in the loose folds of her dark gray skirt. James, for his part, had no desire to make conversation with a young woman whose erotic behavior with his father might well have hastened his death.

As Kevin pulled the sleek black limousine up in front of Vanessa's residence, he sharply and nervously eyed the multishaded scattering of kids spilling over from the stoop of the library beside Vanessa Brewster's building and onto the sidewalk and street. The chatter of Spanish and the stacatto of Black English increased his wariness as he got out of the car and walked around to the other side to hold the door for Vanessa. Nor did the handful of adult addicts nodding out on the benches across the street in Tompkins Square Park reassure him. The sooner they got out of here, Kevin thought, the better chance they stood of making their escape with all four hubcaps and their chrome intact.

A hasty retreat, however, was not in the cards. Vanessa Brewster had other plans. "Come up for a drink," she said to James, not moving to get out, though Kevin was standing with the door open.

James was about to decline, but recognizing her tone, he aborted the refusal. Her words had been more command than invitation.

Of course, he thought to himself with distaste. Her cooperation at the memorial service has a price. Well, just as well to settle it now as later. Get it over with.

They exited the limousine. "I'll be down shortly, Kevin," James told the chauffeur.

"Yes, Mr. James." Kevin's hand touched his cap, a disapproving acknowledgment of the order to wait. As his employer vanished into the old-fashioned, shabby, although well-kept building, the chauffeur felt like he'd been left all alone to man a sentry post in hostile territory.

Vanessa's third-floor walkup apartment turned out to be clean but not neat, simple and yet cluttered. Evidences of her world travels were everywhere. Three books, laid down open to mark their places, demarcated the seating area of the room. A screen she'd brought back from Bali—a detour on her way from New Guinea to the Mosquito Coast—concealed the kitchen. Her bed, neatly made but without a spread, was in the shadowy, windowless area behind the rattan couch, the armchairs, and end tables which made up the living room furniture.

"They call it a studio apartment." She defined her quarters for James. "Scotch all right?"

"Fine, thank you."

He wandered around, picked up and scanned the books he saw as she poured the drinks over ice. All three were anthropology texts, obscure and with small print. When she handed him the drink and nodded toward the couch, he sat down. She took the armchair across from him.

James was a shrewd and experienced negotiator. He knew the importance of seizing the initiative. He did so now, tactfully, smoothly, but nevertheless directly.

"We have taken up your time and inconvenienced you," he told Vanessa. He took his checkbook from the inside pocket of his custom-made, faintly pin-striped suit jacket. "It's only right that you should be recompensed."

She looked at him, her expression inscrutable. "Why, I suppose so," she said finally, without inflection.

"It's difficult for me to know exactly how much . . . ." James appeared flustered but was really not. He wanted her to name the figure. If it was insignificant, he would write a check immediately. If it was high, he would bargain politely.

"Yes. I imagine it is." Vanessa did not relieve his calculated dilemma.

"Perhaps you have a figure in mind?"

"No. No, I don't have a figure in mind."

"But surely you must have some idea of what would be fair." James's tone remained pleasant, revealing nothing of his increasing distaste for the situation.

"Afraid not. You see, the idea of being paid hadn't occurred to me until you mentioned it."

"Oh." James thought a moment. "I see." He put his checkbook away. "Well, if I've offended you, I do apologize."

"No need. Why should I be offended? You were only offering to pay for my time and, ah . . . services."

"Well, in any case . . ." James got to his feet and set his glass down on the end table.

"You're not going, are you? Without paying me, I mean?"

"But I thought you didn't want money." Now James was genuinely confused.

"Oh, I never said that. I only said it hadn't occurred to me that you would pay me. I never said I wouldn't take the money."

"I see." James sat back down on the couch. Concealing his irritation with this cat-and-mouse business, he took out his checkbook again. "Shall we say a thousand dollars, then?" He started writing, eager to get it over with and leave.

"Only a thousand?" Vanessa's unique green eyes regarded him questioningly through the lenses of her heavy-framed glasses. "Why not two thousand?"

"Very well." James tore out the check he'd been writing and started to write another. "Two thousand."

"Why not four thousand?"

"Now see here!"

"Oh, I'm sorry. Is that too much? You see, I haven't had very much experience with this sort of thing."

"I'm sure you haven't." James's tone assured her that he believed precisely the opposite.

"I really haven't." Suddenly and unexpectedly, her tone was quite sharp. "And I do not lie about such inconsequential matters."

"If it's inconsequential, then why bother?"

"The process of barter fascinates me."

"What?" James felt as if he'd fallen through the looking glass and was being badgered by the dormouse.

"Barter. It's an ingrained part of many cultures, you know. Tribal African. New Guinea aborigine. Arabic. American Indian. The similarities are fascinating. And I've always suspected they extend to Wall Street."

"I see." James leaned back on the couch and thought about it. "Then my efforts to give you money are really only providing an opportunity for you to pursue your anthropological studies regarding the culture which I represent." He wasn't sure whether he felt miffed or amused. "So how do we stack up, we Wall Street traders, against the street peddlers of the medinas?"

"You have a lot to learn about haggling."

"Oh? How so?"

"It's not enough to make a move to walk away from the argument over the amount. You have to really walk. Your body language has to convince the other person that you really are willing to give up the deal. When you started to leave before, you should have kept going out the door."

"And then what?"

"I would have stopped you."

"Suppose I didn't let you? I wouldn't have been the loser, you would have. As a matter of fact, I have nothing at all to lose by letting this entire deal fall through. I'm giving. You're taking. If it comes apart, I gain, you lose."

"Oh," she said softly, standing up and stretching as luxuriously as a tabby in a pool of sunlight, "that's where you're wrong." The movement shifted the loose, undistinguished dress so that certain roundnesses and curves were provocatively revealed. "You would lose, too." She sat back down on the edge of the armchair, revealing somewhat more leg than she had before.

James felt a stirring in his loins. "You really aren't interested in the money," he concluded.

"Well, I'm not immune to money. But you're right. That isn't my primary interest. It's not why I asked you to come up."

"Why did you invite me up? And why did you agree to come to the memorial?" James asked, truly puzzled as to why she'd exposed herself to the discomfort of being ogled by the media and his family at the service for his father.

"The same reason everybody else came." Vanessa an-

149

swered his second question first. "To pay my respects to the man who died."

James thought about that a moment. "That was nice of you," he decided. "It was thoughtful."

"Your father and I had a relationship. Not of long duration perhaps, but a relationship nevertheless. Going to his memorial service seemed the right thing to do, the decent thing."

"Still, you could have just sneaked in quietly. You didn't have to agree to make an entrance with me."

"In the first place, I couldn't have sneaked in. I never would have gotten near the place. And in the second place, I had caused your family some embarrassment. I was—am—sorry for that. If my marching in with you could alleviate that embarrassment, then it seemed a small enough thing to do."

"Why did you get involved with my father?" James blurted the question out as it sprang into his mind, without consideration.

"I was attracted to him." Vanessa answered with absolute honesty.

"But he was so much older than you."

"I noticed." She smiled, her lips red and full, the dying April sunlight striating her suddenly sensual face through the half-shut venetian blinds. "Still, I was attracted to him. Perhaps that's why. His maturity, I mean."

"You like older men?"

"Oh, yes."

"But that much older?" James was trying to understand. "I mean, how old are you?"

"Thirty-four."

"Really? I would have thought much younger. Mid-twenties or so."

"Thank you." Vanessa took off her eyeglasses, folded the side frames carefully, put them in a leather case, and laid the case on one of the end tables. She opened the top buttons of her dress, as if discomforted by the heat from the radiator, though it wasn't at that moment working. She crossed her legs and smiled at James. "I really was attracted to your father," she said. "And I really am attracted to you." It was the answer to the other question he'd asked: Why had she invited him up for a drink?

The stirring in James's loins this time was more pronounced. He had not been chaste since the death of his wife five years earlier, but neither had he been overly active sexually. It had actually been some months since he'd been with a woman. Perhaps it was some trick of the light, but Vanessa looked much more appealing to him now than she had in the car or the church.

It was absurd, of course. How could he even think of making love to a woman in whose arms his father had died? It was obscene. He shifted uncomfortably.

"It doesn't matter." Vanessa spoke as if reading his mind. "What was between your father and me doesn't matter. It's what we feel that counts. You and I. What we're feeling right now." And her thighs, magically relieved of the weight of the skirt, were flushed and inviting.

"I don't think—"

"Don't think. That's right, James. Don't think. Feel." She was beside him on the couch now, cupping his face in hands that were soft and warm and promising. "Don't think." Her kiss was tender. And then, lips parting, tongue probing, it was urgent. "I do believe," she said when the kiss was over, "that you would be more comfortable if you took off your necktie." When he reached for it, her fingers slid under his and started unbuttoning his shirt.

Very excited now, James abandoned caution. As his hands discovered the heat of naked breasts and rising nipples inside the shapeless gray dress, he asked, "Are you sure that I'm mature enough for you?"

"We'll see," Vanessa murmured, rising, her dress and undergarments falling away, her shining, voluptuous, nude body leading him to the neat bed in the shadows. "We'll see."

That had been the first time. It hadn't been the last. Now, two months later, harassed by his brother Jonathan's censure, James was nonetheless glad it had not been the last. Indeed, these halcyon June days were matched by an unquenchable inner sunshine just because the last of his affair with Vanessa Brewster was nowhere in sight.

Still, although James had not admitted it to Jonathan,

151

his brother's barbs regarding Michael had sunk deep. Freewheeling as his own life might be, Michael would be devastatingly judgmental when it came to his father. And, although she adored him, so, too, would Patrice. Strange. The two children who most fulfilled his aspirations for them would be the least understanding of his behavior. And the two who disappointed him—Matt and Lisa— well, they simply wouldn't care one way or the other.

Lisa and Matt. Thinking of them brought a frown to James's face. Lisa back in Paris again, alienation her life-style, moving through a bogus world of pseudo poets in a pointless fog of her own making. And Matt...? James sighed. He wasn't sure. Did he reject all of his father's values just because they were his father's? Did he despise his father so much? Or was there truly some commitment there to which James had blinded himself? Ah, Matt...

Was it only the contrast of his own happiness with Vanessa, James wondered, that made Matt seem so terribly unhappy to him lately?

18

IT WAS NOT an illusion. Matt Stockwell really was feeling wretched that June. Without knowing the reason behind it, his father had judged Matt's state correctly. The probability that he was the father of a five-year-old child weighed heavily on Matt's conscience.

Before the afternoon he'd run into Wendy MacTavish in the Albany diner, Matt had been able to push thoughts of the child he thought he might have sired to the back of his mind. Years ago, in the confusion of Canada, when she'd left him, fatherhood had not been a reality for him. He'd never actually thought of Wendy giving birth. Time had helped him bury deep both guilt and responsibility. But seeing Wendy had opened a floodgate, and with the maturity Matt had gained in the intervening years, the recognition that he was almost surely a father had laid bare his emotions.

Hurting, he had sought out Kathleen and found solace in her arms. On this particular night his concerns had been blotted out by a mounting passion. Then, unexpectedly, it was thwarted.

"Please, no!" Kathleen's protest hung in the balmy night air between them as Matt reluctantly removed his hand from the sudden vise of clenched flesh blocking it from moving higher up between her thighs.

"I'm sorry," he said. "I thought you wanted me to—"

"Well, I did," she said, smoothing down her light cotton summer skirt over her still pale, strong and shapely legs. "But then I didn't."

Matt sighed and then shrugged. "Would you like a beer?" he asked.

"Lovely."

He stood up from the swing they'd been sharing on the porch of his ramshackle house, and opened the screen door. Kathleen stood, too. She wanted to go inside with him. Her grimace explained why, encompassing the wrinkled disarray of her clothing left by his hands. She went into the bathroom to freshen up.

When she came out, her blouse was tucked in and buttoned, her face washed, and her bright red hair neatly recombed and restored to its original ponytail. She accepted the beer Matt had poured for her, and they sat down facing each other in the living room.

With enough space between them to show that he wasn't pressuring her, Matt asked, "Why did you stop me?"

"More than one reason." She was evasive. Then she was specific: "You're not happy."

"You don't want to make love because I'm not happy?"

"That's right. What's the matter? Don't you think that's a good reason not to make love? I mean, it's supposed to be a joyous act. And if one person is miserable . . ."

Matt thought a moment. "As a matter of fact, I agree. It's probably one of the best reasons there is not to make love."

"Well, it's certainly not an unimportant reason. Your

unhappiness ... well now, isn't that more important than us doing it or not doing it?"

"Oh, yeah. Only right now I could wish you were more randy and less sensitive." Matt grinned wryly.

"Oh, I'm randy enough. You'll be finding that out." Lapsing into her Irish lilt gave Kathleen's words added weight. "About your unhappiness ..." She pinpointed her concern abruptly. "Have you heard anything from Canada?"

"No real confirmation, but there has been contact."

"Contact? You've heard from—what was her name?— Wendy?"

"Not directly. She wrote to Reverend Cabot at Gotham Memorial. She said that if he was in touch with me, he should let me know she was willing to meet with me, but only to talk. She said he was to tell me that Vermont seemed a reasonable distance for both of us to travel. She suggested Middlebury."

"Why didn't she write to you directly?"

"She doesn't have my address."

"Then why didn't she write you a letter in care of Reverend Cabot?"

"I'm not sure. I thought about that. The answer hurt. I think it's because it was more impersonal this way."

"The answer hurt?" Kathleen's green eyes were gravely questioning. "Are you still in love with her, then?"

"No. I don't think I am."

"You don't *think* ... ?"

"I'm sure I'm not," Matt amended. "But we were together for three years. We had feelings for each other. I'd be lying if I said I wasn't hurt by her structuring·things as impersonally as she can."

"I see." Kathleen's tongue was resentful, poking out her freckled cheek. "How did she know to contact you through Reverend Cabot?" she asked finally.

"Oh, I talked about him a lot when I was in Canada. He was a big influence on my decision to go there, and he wrote me encouraging letters all the time I was away. He kept me informed, reaffirmed that what I'd done was a valid act of conscience. Wendy knew how I felt about him. It was natural she'd figure that we'd still be in contact."

"Are you going to Middlebury to meet with her?"

154

"Yes. Reverend Cabot wrote back that I was willing, and he just heard from her again today confirming a time and place. Wendy has some friend who's a grad student at the college there. She's meeting me at her place."

"And will the friend be there?"

"I don't know."

"Cozy."

"Jealous?" Matt was pleased.

"Of course. You two shared a bed for three years. Naturally I'm not delighted you're traveling this great distance to be alone with her. Still, I know you have to do it."

"Ah, but you're right to be jealous, you know. I need all the protection I can get from my baser impulses. However, the solution's simple. Come to Middlebury with me."

Kathleen looked pleased at his suggestion. Then she shook her head. "I think not," she said.

"Why not?"

"Because if I went to Middlebury with you, you'd expect us to sleep together."

"Would that be so terrible?

"No. But I'm not ready for it. I don't think I'll be ready until you've reconciled your feelings for Wendy. Until I'm satisfied you've reconciled them, that is," Kathleen added hastily, cutting off his protest before he could voice it.

"Look," Matt said after thinking a moment. "I'm not suggesting that sex should be taken lightly. But still, don't you think you're making too big a deal about this? I mean, we have feelings for each other—physical, emotional— why put obstacles in the way of our pleasure?"

"I just want it to be right with us when we do it."

"Right, yes. But not perfect, Kathleen. It's never perfect."

"I don't think I want to hear that." She covered her ears.

"You've really got me mystified," Matt told her when she'd removed her hands.

"It should be perfect the first time. I really believe that," she told him. "And my first time is going to be as perfect as I can make it, or I'd just as soon not do it."

"Your first time?" He stared at her.

"Yes." She stared back, defiant.

"Kathleen, are you telling me you're still a virgin?"

"Yes."

Matt continued to stare at her, surprised. She was twenty years old. It had never occurred to him that there were still twenty-year-old girls around in 1980 who had never slept with a man.

"It's not a crime, you know." She was both embarrassed and angry.

"No. Of course not." Now he was embarrassed. He hadn't meant to put her down. He hadn't meant to be so all-fired cynical. "Is it because you're Catholic?" he asked. Immediately he regretted the stereotyping the question implied.

Kathleen was not offended. "Well, the sisters in boarding school did make their impression," she granted. "So my being Catholic is not entirely unrelated. But sure and it's because I'm a liberated woman as well as a Catholic one."

"Because you're a liberated woman?" Matt blinked.

"Oh, yes. In these times, who else but a woman who believes in her own liberation and right to make sexual choices could decide to remain a virgin?" Kathleen's eyes were twinkling, but Matt could see that she was serious, too.

"Kathleen O'Lunney, you are a pistol," he said. He was suddenly curious. "Do you intend to stay a virgin until you marry?" he asked.

"Is it panicking you are, now?"

"No. I don't think so." Matt laughed.

"Well, then, the answer is not necessarily. Marriage isn't the price I'm demanding for my virtue."

"Then it's only my unhappiness that stands between us and carnal ecstasy?"

"That and your still being involved with another woman."

"But I'm really not involved with Wendy anymore," Matt objected.

"Well, we'll know better about that when you return from Middlebury, won't we, now?" Kathleen looked at her wristwatch. "If I don't get home soon," she told Matt, "me chastity is all will stand between you and me faither's shotgun."

"Ach, the Irish!" Matt rolled his eyes at her deliberate

156

brogue. "Virginal and violent." He stood up and put his arm around her to walk her out to her car.

"When exactly are you going to Middlebury?" she asked.

He told her.

"You'll miss the big wedding."

"Can't be helped."

"Don't you mind?"

"Not really. The Tylers are cousins, and I like them well enough, but the truth is I don't really know the bride and groom very well."

"Still, it will be a very splashy affair. Everybody who's anybody at all will be there."

"Best reason I know to miss it. Weddings should be small, intimate ceremonies. When I get married, that's how it will be."

"Ah, now, is that a firm offer?" Kathleen teased him.

Teasing back, Matt repeated what she'd said to him before. "We'll know that when I get back from Middlebury."

"Well, now, that will give me something to think of while I peek in on the reception for the bride and groom." Kathleen paused beside her car and turned to him.

"Tell me," Matt wanted to know, "is it permitted to kiss a liberated Irish-American virgin good night?"

"Well, now," she answered, leaning into him, her hand sliding down between them. "I think we can do a bit better than just a simple kiss."

19

THE WEDDING HAD taken on a symbolic importance to Jack Houston. He wanted to attend it with Buffy. He wanted her to acknowledge, at a family function, the importance of his role in her life. He not only wanted to go public with their relationship, he wanted to do it in such a way that the Stockwells would have to take notice. He saw their attendance together as a public abdication of Buffy's position as a lordly Stockwell, and a public—as well as a private—affirmation that she loved him.

Determination lent urgency to Jack's voice as he pressed his case. Holding the telephone receiver to her ear and listening to him, Buffy recognized this. Nevertheless, her response when he stopped talking was not encouraging.

"Oof!" Buffy said. "Aarrgh!"

"What?" Jack was taken aback. "What's that supposed to mean?"

"Sorry, darling. I wasn't talking to you. That was for Kirsten."

"Who's Kirsten?"

"My rolfer."

"Your what?"

"My rolfer. The woman who rolfs me. You know." Buffy was impatient. "Whoo—ooh!" Again she reacted.

"No, I don't know. What's a rolfer? How does she rolf you?" Jack wanted to know.

"Violently!" Buffy expelled the word in a whoosh of air from her midsection. "Too violently. Take it easy, Kirsten. You are not kneading bratwurst, you know."

"The discomfort is the therapy." Used to such complaints, the massive Kirsten zeroed in on a knotted muscle and leaned hard on it with the heel of her hand.

"Oh, God!"

"Is it some kind of massage?" Jack asked on the other end of the phone.

"It's torture!"

"You sound like she's beating you up."

"She is."

"Send her away. If that's what you're into, I'll be right over."

"Thank you, but no thank you." Buffy was firm.

"I want to go to that wedding reception at Riverview with you," Jack repeated.

"Aren't you afraid it might be embarrassing?" With a peremptory gesture, Buffy signaled Kirsten to leave off pounding her for a moment. "Patrice will be there, you know."

"You're not still mad at me about that."

"Perhaps I am, just a little."

158

"It was meaningless, and you know it. I was angry. Patrice didn't mean anything to me then, and certainly doesn't now. You're the woman I love. You know that."

"Just a young man's slip of the—um—but then you will always be seventeen years younger than me, darling. Is that sort of thing what I have to look forward to?"

"Buffy, you're only using this as a red herring to avoid dealing with me about the wedding."

"I can't talk about it now."

"Why not?" Jack demanded.

"I'm expecting my lawyer. The new one from California."

"Your lawyer? I thought you were getting a massage."

"A rolfing," she corrected him. "And I can see my lawyer while I'm being rolfed. If necessary, I can even chew gum and talk foreign policy at the same time. I'm not Gerald Ford, you know."

"Your husband's dead. Stop quoting his nasty little political prejudices." Jack's tone changed to one of concern. "How is it going with the will business? Does it look like you'll be able to break it?"

"I hope so. I'll have a better idea after I talk to this new man."

"I'm rooting for you, Buffy."

"Of course you are, darling." A note of cynicism crept into Buffy's voice.

"Not because I want anything, damn it! Because I love you! And that's why I want us to go to that wedding together. Because I love you and you love me, even if you don't know how much."

"I can't discuss it now, Jack. He'll be here any minute."

"Well, when will he be leaving? I'll call back."

Buffy told him, and reluctantly Jack hung up. She smiled to herself. She would let him dangle for now, but actually it might be very pleasant to make her entrance at the reception on the arm of handsome, young Jack Houston. That should shake up the Stockwells. When Jack called back, she decided, she would let herself be persuaded to accede to his request.

Just as Kirsten resumed beating a tattoo on the backs of Buffy's bare thighs, the phone rang again. It was Berkley, the butler, announcing that the lawyer from California had arrived. Buffy instructed him to bring the gentleman to her in the solarium.

Hanging up the phone, Buffy readjusted the oversized bath towel around her otherwise nude body and resettled herself on the massage table. "Be a little careful, Kirsten. I don't want to distract this gentleman by the spilling over of forbidden flesh due to your overly enthusiastic exertions."

"He's from California," Kirsten replied, digging a thumb like a crowbar into a vertebra. "He won't even notice."

"Oh, dear God!" Tears of agony sprang to Buffy's eyes.

They were still there, lurking in the corners, when Berkley ushered in the guest and silently departed. The attorney's name was Halsey De Vilbiss. He was nattily dressed in a navy blazer with the ubiquitous gold buttons, lightweight slate-gray cashmere slacks, a slim, costly tie of subdued Ivy League striping that nevertheless screamed sincerity, and he was impeccably groomed, with just enough ear left showing by the blow dryer to attest that while he had both feet planted firmly in the now generation, he would never defy tradition. The aroma of his after-shave lotion was expensive, but he had used just a dab too much of it. His tan said he could afford leisure, and his velvety black moustache turned his thin-lipped mouth into a display case for unflawed dental pearls.

"Rolfing." De Vilbiss immediately identified Buffy's torment. "It was all the rage in California a couple of years back."

Buffy resented the implication that she had come late to the rolfing fad. She disliked Halsey De Vilbiss's California persona on sight. Nevertheless, it had been his California background, along with his reputation as a top gun in the field of estate litigation, which had made her retain him in the first place.

New York City was filled with brilliant, effective attorneys well versed in corporation law. Many had advantageous old school ties and clubby judicial connections. A few of these would gladly have taken on Buffy's cause in the hopes of being rewarded with the management accounts of some of the more lucrative trusts of the Stockwell estate. These counselors were quite on a par with the

160

wealth of legal talent available to the designated "troika," as Buffy had dubbed James Linstone Stockwell, David Lewis, and Peter Stockwell.

Despite all these factors Buffy had deliberately sought out a relatively young "new breed" California lawyer. The inbreeding of interests among top Wall Street attorneys had made her question the commitment one might bring to a case involving the Stockwells. The family's interests were so vast, so varied, that virtually every top law firm of the financial district had at one time handled some aspect of Stockwell business. She felt that even the possibility of conflicting loyalties would not be to her advantage.

Furthermore, like many others, she believed that the very old-school-tie connectedness of the legal in-group—Groton and Andover, Harvard and Yale, with an occasional southern prep school background or Columbia University diploma tolerated—made them gentle with each other in litigation procedures. Gentleness was not what Buffy wanted. She wanted a bare-knuckled champion true only to her—and ruthless to the opposition.

Halsey De Vilbiss had a reputation as a scrapper who didn't hesitate to skirt the ethical edge in pursuit of large settlements for his clients. Indeed, his tactics were even looked at askance in Southern California, where he was considered to be, despite his relative youth, Greater Los Angeles's most successful attorney in the field of corporate law. Buffy had gone to great lengths to investigate his qualifications before deciding to hire him over the three other attorneys she'd been considering.

"Sit down." Groaning under the continued beating of her flesh, Buffy indicated a bridge table set up in anticipation of De Vilbiss's arrival. "Have you gone over the papers?"

"On the plane."

"What do you think?"

"I think that I will not accept a fee of less than one million dollars against a thirty-percent contingency arrangement."

"Oof! Damn it, Kirsten, you are not pounding mortar. That is flesh you're sinking your hoofs into. . . . The thirty percent is out of the question," she told De Vilbiss. "There will be no contingency arrangement. Only a flat fee."

161

"In that case, five million dollars plus expenses."

"That seems very high."

"It is."

"Why is it so high, Mr. De Vilbiss?"

"Two reasons. First, because I'm worth it. Second, because the case is worth it."

"Then you do think I have a case?"

"Yes." He nodded. His mouth flashed pearls in what was meant to be a winning smile.

With Buffy it lost. "All right," she said. "I accept your terms."

"Win or lose. That's five million plus expenses, win or lose."

"I understand that."

"I'll have an agreement drawn up and delivered to you by hand first thing tomorrow morning." De Vilbiss unscrewed the cap of his fountain pen, took a lined yellow pad from his briefcase, made the first of many notes, and drew a line underneath it. "Now," he said, "let us talk about the Stockwells."

The "talk" involved a series of staccato questions not unlike a cross-examination. Punctuated by the slaps, crunches, and groans of rolfing, Buffy supplied De Vilbiss with far-ranging scraps of data, gossip, and family lore regarding each of the Governor's heirs. The California attorney was interested in everything—no matter how seemingly remote—relating to the Governor's naming his divorced first wife, Mary, the primary heir, while relegating Buffy to the position of a minor beneficiary. He also was seeking ammunition to challenge the competency of the troika to manage an estate to the satisfaction of so many disparate family members.

These family members would be the key to the strategy he would pursue. Thus De Vilbiss wanted to hear about quirks of character, old and new scandals, personal and political vagaries and posturings, any and all situations pertaining to individuals who might be persuaded to cooperate in breaking the will. His pen raced quickly and neatly over the legal pad, making notes of the buffeted Buffy's responses.

Between grunts she described to De Vilbiss the scene at Gotham Memorial, where James had presented Vanessa

Brewster as "an old family friend" to the world. Might not the will be broken on the grounds of collusion between the family and Vanessa Brewster to exert her erotic influence on the Governor to draft it to Buffy's disadvantage? After all, had not Vanessa Brewster's sexual behavior caused the strain that killed the Governor? Couldn't they insinuate, without making an outright accusation, that this was deliberate? James had provided them with a connection between the Brewster woman and the family. Why not use it?

The California attorney was not impressed with Buffy's reasoning. "If the family really does have her tied up as an 'old friend,'" he told her, "bringing in Vanessa Brewster could really backfire on us. If there was more to it, of course—something that could really lock James Stockwell or any of the Stockwells into collusion with Vanessa Brewster—that would be a different matter. But I gather you don't really have any hard evidence of anything like that."

"Ouch!" as Kirsten brutally rolfed a ligament at the back of her leg, Buffy admitted that she indeed did not have any hard evidence linking James or the Stockwells with Vanessa Brewster.

They moved along. Buffy told De Vilbiss about the battle already shaping up as Peter Stockwell—backed by his mother, who had no real power, but not in any effective way by his father, who did—brought pressure for greater control over more Stockwell interests against James and David Lewis. "Peter is very ambitious," Buffy summarized, "and his mother Ellen more than cancels out his father when it comes to influencing him."

De Vilbiss's nod was meaningful. He underlined the notes he'd just made in his concise script. "Ambition is always, ah . . . approachable. If not directly, then perhaps through the vehicle of mother-love." He inquired about the third member of the troika, David Lewis, the husband of James's sister, Alice.

Buffy replied that while James's brother-in-law David Lewis would probably stick by James as he always had, he didn't really like playing second fiddle to him. The Governor had often remarked on that. De Vilbiss took note. Even if David Lewis wouldn't switch sides, his resentment was a weakness that might be exploited. Yes, David Lewis might be a pressure point.

De Vilbiss flipped to a new, clean, lined yellow page. "Tell me about the offspring," he suggested. "We've discussed Peter Stockwell, but what about James's children? What about the offspring of David and Alice Lewis?"

"The Lewises have only one child left. They had a son, Mark, but he was killed in Vietnam. The surviving daughter is named Michelle."

"Tell me about her."

As Buffy complied, De Vilbiss jotted down the vital statistics. He made more detailed notes as Buffy told him about Michelle Carter's ambitions as publisher of *Elite*. He was particularly interested to hear that Michelle and her husband were buying up stock in the magazine, obviously seeking a controlling interest. "So she wants to call the shots when it comes to policy," De Vilbiss mused. "And her husband is an investment banker with financial know-how. What are her relations with her parents? Any conflict there?"

"I don't really know."

"Well, we shall see. Her desire to control *Elite* means we have inducements to offer her to support us against her uncle, James. She is very young. The new breed of woman." His smile now would have enraged a more committed feminist than Buffy; it merely annoyed her. "All too willing to match the ruthlessness of businessmen."

Buffy pointed out that Michelle—even considering her children's inheritance—did not have a large enough share of the estate to exercise a major voice in its management. Neither, she added, did any of the others among the Governor's grandchildren. De Vilbiss replied that all of these small voices could add up. Together, they might have an influence in their favor. Nor did it necessarily have to be a majority influence in order to sway a probate judge.

The point made, De Vilbiss went on to query Buffy about James's children. He noted her belief that Patrice, the eldest, would unwaveringly support her father. He was interested in Matt's having evaded the draft. Perhaps there was some vulnerability there that might be turned to advantage. When Buffy told him she didn't know of any, the lawyer nevertheless put an asterisk beside Matt's name. Where there had been youthful political commitment, there was no telling what might turn up. Particularly since, as Buffy related, there was some unresolved strain between Matt and his father.

De Vilbiss's smile was broad when he heard that Matt's younger brother Michael was seeking the Democratic nomination for Congress in the Riverview district. Michael might presently side with his father, James, but pragmatism always left politicians open to proposition. And by definition a politician's weaknesses outweighed his loyalties.

About Lisa Stockwell Buffy could tell De Vilbiss very little. The youngest of James's children was back in Paris, somewhat estranged from her family and her father, a would-be poet with her head in the clouds. Buffy doubted that Lisa had given much thought to her inheritance one way or the other.

They discussed Susan Gray's notorious past and her life in Hollywood. It could be useful. "What about her son, the baseball player?"

"I don't really know anything at all about Deke. Perhaps because of the way his mother was ostracized, he's always kept aloof from the family. He does seem on good terms with Susan, though. I imagine he'll go whatever route she goes."

De Vilbiss remembered seeing a rumor in one of the sports columns that Deke Wells had a shoulder injury that might keep him out all season. Could this mean he would need money? Could he be approached? The lawyer made a note to follow through on Deke Wells. Then he ran his finger down the list he'd made and brought up another name.

"Holly," Buffy responded. "She was the Governor's favorite among all his grandchildren."

"Well, that explains her preferential treatment in the will."

"She'll stand by Mary. She's very fond of her. That means she'll stand by James, too, of course. But even apart from Mary, Holly and her Uncle James get along well."

"Then the stock she votes for herself and her son can definitely be counted against us."

"Not necessarily," Buffy remembered. "There's Holly's

165

husband, Christopher. They're separated, but not divorced. Doesn't that give him a say in how their son's stock is voted?"

"Oh, yes." De Vilbiss questioned Buffy closely about the situation between Holly and Christopher Millwood. The picture that emerged was of a fortune hunter with some strange hold over his estranged wife. Christopher Millwood's support would be available for a price.

"*Yow!*" Buffy screamed. "Kirsten, you've gone too far! That really hurt."

"A parting shot to tide you over, Mrs. Stockwell." Kirsten was unperturbed. "That's all for today." She gathered up her lotions. "See you next Tuesday."

"Not if I see you first," Buffy muttered to Kirsten's departing back. The words weren't loud enough for the rolfer to hear, but Halsey De Vilbiss smiled at them.

"We're almost finished, too," he told Buffy. "I just want you to fill me in on the Tylers."

"I don't really know too much about them except that they're the descendants of the Governor's older sister—much older—Sarah Stockwell Tyler."

"This sister is dead?"

"Well..." Buffy thought. "I've always presumed so. Nobody ever talks about her. There's some sort of mystery or scandal or something. The Governor would never discuss it."

"A secret scandal might work to our advantage."

"Whatever it was, happened a very long time ago. Almost seventy years. The Governor himself was only an infant. How could that help us?"

"Well, for one thing, if the sister did happen to still be alive, then she would have a major claim to the Stockwell estate."

"Oh, she couldn't be."

"Probably not. Still... What about her children?" De Vilbiss wanted to know.

"Just two. Twins. One died. The other is Alfred Tyler."

"He's the one who's getting married next week?"

"Yes. To Lizzie Tyler, his brother's widow. They're both in their sixties."

"And where would they stand in the scheme of things?" De Vilbiss wondered.

166

It was Buffy's opinion that Alfred and Lizzie had always been grateful to the Governor for seeing to it that they were included as members of the Stockwell family, and that their gratitude would transfer naturally to Mary and James. That would also apply, she thought, to Paul Tyler, the heart surgeon son of John and Lizzie Tyler, and to his wife, Margaret. However, Alfred's children by his first wife, Suzanne, and the Tyler grandchildren, were another story entirely.

"There's a strong family resemblance among them." Buffy didn't know if that was important, but she mentioned it anyway. "All the Tylers have this lovely hair—sort of a burnished lemon-crimson color like a sunset. And they all have these really unique slanty hazel eyes."

De Vilbiss paid close attention as Buffy related the behavior of the other Tylers at the will reading. Obviously Max Tyler was already rebelling against the troika, and it sounded as if his sister Diana would go along with him. The other sister, Louise Papatestus, who hadn't been at the reading, was probably too wealthy to involve herself, and in any case lived in Greece. But Max and Diana might prove helpful since they had already announced their opposition to the status quo. Manipulating them shouldn't be difficult, De Vilbiss concluded.

There were also the twin daughters of Paul Tyler to be considered. Beth's outbursts and the threats she'd made against Peter Stockwell at the will reading indicated that she would be easy to co-opt. "What about the other twin?" De Vilbiss wanted to know.

"Carrie." Buffy smiled slightly. "She's wild. Likes the boys. Indiscriminate. She'd like to pull her money out so it wouldn't be under anybody's control but hers. Then she thinks she could squander it on pleasure, which as far as Carrie is concerned is the real purpose of life. Oh!" Buffy's sudden distress was genuine. "One more thing. Carrie's a cocaine addict."

"You mean she uses cocaine?"

"I mean she's addicted to it. Has to have it."

De Vilbiss nodded. An addict was always buyable. "But then the father has guardianship over their bequests," he remembered. "And if he'll stick by James for himself, he probably will for them, too."

"Well, yes, but don't underestimate the twins' ability to manipulate their father," Buffy told him. "They've always been able to twist him around their little fingers."

"Too bad. There are a lot of possibilities there." The lawyer shrugged.

"Then why is it too bad?"

"Because all the Tyler holdings together don't amount to enough to be any real help to us."

"Before you said these small shares could add up," Buffy reminded him.

"I did. And I meant it, too. But the Tyler holdings are really very, very small. Now, if they had shares equal to those of the Stockwell heirs, we could really go to work on them, sway them to our side and have this whole business settled in no time. Then they would be one hell of a weight against James Linstone Stockwell and his mother."

"But even so," Buffy reminded him, "the Tylers could be of value standing with us in opposing the troika setup."

Yes, De Vilbiss granted. But they would have to be very careful regarding the troika. Destroying the three-way arrangement could work against them. Backing Peter Stockwell or David Lewis against James in the troika could backfire because his mother had the power to discharge them from the trusteeship of the estate. The will was quite clear on that point. If that happened, James would have even more power. Unless... was there any chance of Mary siding with one of the others against James?

"No." Buffy was positive. James would act first and foremost in his mother's interest. And Mary, recognizing that, would surely back him up in any controversy that might develop with the other two trustees. "They are, after all, mother and son."

"Ah." De Vilbiss's lips parted to reveal their pearly treasure. "The mothers and sons who have betrayed that cherished ideal in courtroom situations are legion."

Buffy shrugged. Much as she might like to, she told him, she did not believe that would ever be the case with James and Mary.

"We shall see." De Vilbiss summed up: "This is how I line up the players. Firmly against us and siding with Mary Linstone Stockwell and her son James are his brother Jonathan, his sister Alice and her husband David

Lewis, his daughter Patrice, his niece Holly Stockwell Millwood, and Alfred, Lizzie, Paul and Margaret Tyler.

"Opposed to them, and surely strong probabilities as allies for us, are Peter Stockwell and his mother Ellen, Michelle Lewis Carter and her husband Andrew, Christopher Millwood—possibly acting for his son Nicholas—Max and Diana Tyler, and the twins, Beth and Carrie Tyler.

"Questionable, or downright neutral, are James Linstone Stockwell's children Matthew, Michael and Lisa, his sister Susan Gray and her son Deke Wells, and Louise Papatestus."

"That sounds right," Buffy granted. "But what does it really all add up to?"

"Those opposed to Mary Linstone Stockwell and her son James have to be persuaded that their best interest lies in throwing in with us. Those who are neutral, or questionable, have to be given good reason to be more actively opposed. The final lineup will have more than legal weight. It will have psychological and moral weight. These people are all related, after all. It's hard to stand up against a son, a sister, the weight of a large part of one's family. Still, I'd really like to study these Stockwells firsthand. Is there any way that could be arranged?"

"There's going to be a wedding reception here at Riverview. They'll all be here."

"Can you wangle me an invitation?"

"Not likely." Buffy smiled without humor. "Mary's taken charge of sending out the invitations." She thought a moment. She sighed. "You could come as my escort," she said finally and not without reluctance. Buffy definitely did not like the image of herself making an entrance on the too slickly Southern Californian arm of shysterish Halsey De Vilbiss.

"My pleasure." He gave her no chance to reconsider. "Until then." De Vilbiss stood up. The consultation was over. Smoothly, he told Buffy good-bye. His thin, dapper body made a movement halfway between a nod and a bow, and he made his exit.

As Buffy watched him go, the telephone beside the massage table rang. She picked it up. Jack Houston was calling back, as he'd said he would.

Buffy felt guilty, and that made her short with him.

169

"Your coming to the wedding with me is out of the question," she told Jack firmly. "My lawyer says I have to be very circumspect until this thing is settled."

Jack protested, but to no avail. Buffy cut him short. She really did need to think things over in a jacuzzi after her strenuous rolfing. She gave him no more chance to object to her decision. Pursing her lips in an automatic kiss that crackled in Jack's ear over the telephone, she hung up on him.

His anger building, Jack held the receiver for a long moment after Buffy disconnected. Finally, slowly, he hung up the phone. He stared at it for another long moment. Then he picked it up again. The dial tone buzzed in his ear. Slowly, reluctantly, not proud of himself, he pushed the buttons to dial another number.

20

PATRICE O'KEEFE'S BUBBLING voice on the telephone was drowned out by the happy noises around Holly. It bounced off the walls of her north tower studio. Three incorrigible sounds contributed to it; the shrill tooting of a mechanical train grinding over the hardwood floors and reversing direction each time it came up against an obstacle; Nicholas's delighted shrieks as he chased after the toy; and the joyous laughter of his great-grandmother, her face flushed and gray hair uncharacteristically askew as she breathlessly tried to keep up with the little boy.

"I'm sorry, Patrice, I can't hear myself think." Holly retreated to a corner of the room and cupped a hand to shield the phone from the hoopla. "There. That's better. Now, what did you say?"

"Prince Charming," Patrice repeated. "Two months and not a word. I really figured I was being let down easy. A one-night stand and nothing more. Then out of the blue he called."

"You're talking about the man I met with you at the Algonquin? Jack Houston?"

"Well, of course, silly. Who else would I be talking about?"

"He's asked you out again?" Holly covered the mouthpiece. "Could you two desperados hold it down to a dull roar?"

"Gram Mary making noise," Nicholas responded.

"Why you little devil! I am not!"

"You are definitely worse than he is!" Holly told Mary.

"Yes." Patrice's voice was exultant in her ear. "He said he really was tied up with business, but he'd been thinking of me. Isn't that delicious? Thinking of me. And he asked me to go sailing with him on Sunday."

"But that's the day of the wedding."

"I know. It was a problem. But I solved it, Holly. I asked him if he'd be my escort for the wedding, and he said he'd be delighted. Delighted! Isn't that delightful?"

"Delightful." Holly echoed her cousin, smiling at her enthusiasm.

"He didn't seem to mind having to spend the day at a family wedding at all."

"I'm happy for you, Patrice. But I really have to get off the phone before my two children wreck my studio."

"Two children?"

"Grandma's here. I made the mistake of giving her permission to play with Nicholas."

"And *she's* misbehaving?" Patrice laughed.

"Yes. And my son is following her bad example."

"Poor Holly. One child is bad enough. But two hellions..." Still laughing, Patrice told Holly good-bye and hung up.

Holly clapped her hands for attention. "Nap time."

The announcement was greeted with twin pouts and stalling, but finally Holly was able to coax Nicholas down the winding mahogany staircase and then to his room. His nursemaid was waiting, and Nicholas brightened up when he saw her. He loved to have her read him stories before his afternoon nap, even though he invariably fell asleep before the endings.

Holly returned to her octagonal studio to find her grandmother collapsed in an overstuffed Ethan Allen armchair, an original with knotty-pine arms. "He wore me out," she greeted Holly.

"It's your own fault. You make him wild."

"A grandmother's prerogative."

"You're his great-grandmother. Great-grandmothers are supposed to have more restraint."

"Nonsense. Permissiveness increases geometrically with each generation."

"Then Lord help Nicholas's wife when he marries and has children." Holly began picking up the debris left in the wake of her son's playtime.

"I doubt I'll still be around." Mary was realistic. "Besides, just now I'd settle for having your marital status settled without worrying about Nicholas marrying."

"It is settled. My marriage is over."

"Then why aren't you pressing forward with your divorce?"

"It's moving along." Holly was evasive.

"Really?" Mary was sarcastic, a trait she had acquired in old age. "Have you found it necessary to go outside the family for a lawyer, then?"

"Of course not."

"Then how is it that your Uncle James knows nothing of any divorce action having been filed?"

"One was filed in England. Christopher avoided service of the papers."

"Don't avoid the question, Holly. You know very well what I mean. Why haven't you brought an action here, in New York State? Christopher has been very much in evidence since the Governor died. There wouldn't be any real problem serving him, and if he avoided service, I daresay your Uncle James would know how to proceed with the divorce anyway. It's obvious that's not the problem. You're the one who's stalling, Holly. Why?"

"It's a long story, Grandma. Trust me. There are reasons why I have to proceed cautiously."

"My dear, as near as I can tell, you're not proceeding at all. If there are problems, talk to James about them. He is very discreet. He will not breach any client-lawyer confidentiality. Get off the dime, Holly, as the Governor used to say. You owe it to yourself, and you owe it to your son. Promise me you'll talk to James."

"I don't know if I can talk to Uncle James, Grandma." Holly was honest.

Mary looked at her for a long moment. She sighed. "That bad. All right, then, my dear. If you won't confide in me and you can't talk to James, then promise me this—promise me you'll talk it over with someone, a friend, a confidant. You're not seeing things clearly, Holly. You badly need another viewpoint, advice perhaps from someone who isn't directly involved. Promise me you'll at least do that."

"Very well, Grandma. I promise."

"Good. It will relieve my mind." Mary fell silent. She looked around the eight-sided studio at the abstract pictures painted by her daughter, Holly's mother. They triggered a memory. "I used to come up here often," she remembered.

"When my mother was alive?" Holly asked.

"Yes. When you were a little girl. Before the cancer took my precious Terry. So suddenly . . . so quickly . . ."

"What was she like, my mother? I mean, I know how she was with me. But you were her mother. How did you see her?"

"Like her father." Mary didn't hesitate. "Like the Governor. She was stubborn, determined, headstrong, and full of life. Oh, yes, she and Matthew were so alike. Now James and Jonathan and Alice, they always had more Linstone qualities. To some degree they all take after me. But Terry and Susan and my poor Tommy, they were real Stockwells, just like the Governor."

"Tommy?"

"Our second son, a year younger than James. He drowned when he was twelve years old." Mary's expression said that even now, talking about her dead little boy was painful for her. She moved her head sharply, shaking off the cobwebs of tragic memory. "But you were asking about your mother, Terry."

"Yes. Was she really like Susan? Flamboyant the way she is, I mean? I don't remember her that way at all."

"Oh, no. I've misled you. She and Susan were very different. Susan was five years younger. Terry was quiet, what today the young people would call laid back. I only meant they were similar in the way they stood up to the

173

Governor. But Susan has always flaunted her rebellion. Your mother just went her own way and did what she wanted to do quietly, without confrontation if she could avoid it, but with a will of iron. In that way she was much more like the Governor than Susan ever was. Quietly determined just as he was."

"Is that why they didn't get along? Because they were so much alike?"

"Well, it was one reason. Then, too, in fairness to the Governor, from his point of view once childhood was behind her, Terry seemed to go out of her way to oppose him, to flaunt his authority. When she finished at the Academy, she refused to go on to one of the better colleges, as her peers did. She wanted to paint, and she insisted on moving down to Greenwich Village. When the Governor threatened to withdraw his support, she took a job as a waitress and sent back the weekly check he sent to her. She had little money for clothes, and she would show up here at family gatherings wearing pants and a shirt—her usual outfit in the Village."

"That doesn't sound so awful." Holly gestured at the jeans and blouse she was wearing. "I don't understand. A lot of kids leave home—even then. Why did that make Grandpa so mad? None of this ever made any sense to me. I mean, such a fuss over clothes. Really!"

"These were the fifties, my dear. The very early 1950s. Girls in our circle might wear slacks on occasion, but they did not walk around the way Terry did. Her clothes, her behavior, the milieu in which she immersed herself—all of this distressed the Governor greatly. Nevertheless, as you know, he tried to patch up the situation with Terry. He had this studio built for her over the library. He went to a lot of trouble, but still he was very afraid she would reject it."

"But she didn't."

"No. She didn't. You see, your mother was not simply a dilettante playing at Bohemianism. She genuinely wanted to paint. She had talent, and she had determination. She fell in love with the studio. When she left the Village and moved back to Riverview, she even accepted an allowance from the Governor. She plunged into her work. And for a while things were much better between them."

"For a while? But then what happened? I mean I know so much, but then there are these gaps."

"What happened? Why, you did, my dear."

"You mean my mother became pregnant?"

"Yes."

"My father...?" The two words were the best Holly could do to frame the question that had haunted her all her life. She had asked the question before, of course. It was never answered, and she didn't really expect it to be answered now.

"I'm sorry, Holly. I simply don't know. Terry wouldn't confide in me, I suppose because she was afraid I'd tell the Governor. She was right to be afraid. In those days Matthew was always able to wangle things out of me that I didn't really want to divulge."

"But why was she so stubborn about keeping my father's identity from her father? That's what I've never understood."

"She knew the Governor, Holly. She knew that if he knew the man's name, he would have taken action."

"Action? What sort of action?"

"At the least he would have forced the man to marry Terry. If that wasn't possible, if the man was already married, say, the Governor would have taken punitive steps."

"Punitive steps?" Holly was outraged and amused.

"Yes. He would have found a way to punish the man. Ruin him in business, perhaps. Inform his wife of his adultery. I don't know. The Governor was vindictive, and he had many resources at his command. In such a situation he would not have hesitated to use his power to the fullest."

"No one ever told me. It makes sense now. But he was vindictive toward my mother, too," Holly remembered.

"He was furious with her for not revealing who the man was. Then he wanted to arrange a marriage just so you would have a name—a marriage which by agreement would have ended in divorce after your birth. Terry just laughed at him. That really pushed his anger over the brink. That and..."

"And?"

"Well, you're old enough to understand, I suppose. The Governor thought Terry should have an abortion. There were places in Switzerland—very high-priced, and quite safe. More than one young lady of your mother's class availed herself of their services. But she refused. From just about the time she began to show, the Governor and she were hopelessly alienated. That was the situation for years, right up until she came down with the cancer, and then it was too late."

"I'm surprised he didn't alienate himself from me, too."

"Oh, no. The Governor adored you from the day you were born, Holly."

"I know. I adored him, too. But then I was only a child and didn't know—" Suddenly Holly remembered something. "But that's why he never came up to this studio until after Mom died. And that's why Mom was never at dinner with us. It would be us and Uncle James and Uncle Jonathan, and other members of the family sometimes, but never Mom."

"It was hard for him, too." Mary felt called on to defend the Governor. "After your mother died—"

"But you and my mother weren't alienated."

"No, of course not. Terry was my daughter, too. There were very few instances in which I stood against the Governor, but my relationship with Terry was one of them."

"It's like something out of Galsworthy, or one of the Brontës. I can't believe Grandpa was like that. He was so different with me. How could he have been so harsh with his own daughter? All she did was have sex. I was an accident. Why couldn't I have just been supportive?"

"The Governor and I came out of a different time, Holly. I know how hard that is for you to understand. But the morality we grew up with, the morality ingrained in the Governor, was much more harsh. And in his case there was even more reason to adhere to it than in mine."

"Why?"

"His sister—" Mary stopped short.

"His sister?" Holly was puzzled. "You mean the one who died? The mother of the bridegroom?"

"Yes." Mary allowed herself a small smile at the designation. "Alfred's mother."

"But what did she have to do with Grandpa's attitude toward my mother?"

"Matthew's sister Sarah is the skeleton in the Stockwell family closet. The scandal she caused when the Governor was a boy was very traumatic for him."

"Not so traumatic," Holly pointed out, "that it kept him from causing a major scandal of his own." Her mother's shame, which she had always known about, had been kept within the family, Holly thought to herself. She had not before today known it was related to another family skeleton, which had also evidently been a well-guarded family secret, the Governor's sister. But neither woman had brought public disgrace to the Stockwell family in the way the Governor himself had. Even now, with all of it well in the past, the hypocrisy made Holly angry. "A public embarrassment," she stressed.

"You mean Buffy." Mary nodded. "Yes, that's true. But the Governor would not have looked at it that way. Scandalous behavior on the part of a man was more or less expected in society in our time. Divorce, of course, was not so easily forgivable, but even there I suspect Buffy bore the brunt of the shame, not the Governor."

"That's chauvinist, and awful."

"Oh, yes," Mary agreed. "And in his later years the Governor came to see that, too. But not at the time of your mother's pregnancy. He was a chauvinist then. It would not have occurred to him to be anything else."

"But he changed so drastically," Holly realized. She was thinking of the note the Governor had left with his bequest to her. Be wicked, Holly, he had written. Do not turn up your nose at carnal pleasures. It was hard to believe that the man who had written that could have been so stern and moralistic toward his daughter.

"Oh, yes. Drastically. People do, you know. It gives me no pleasure to say this, Holly, but I think Buffy had a lot to do with that change. I think that the Governor learned from Buffy that women have a right to behave every bit as uninhibitedly as men." Mary sighed. "It was a lesson I could never have taught him. I was brought up to be much too prim and proper. Only after his marriage to Buffy did the Governor start viewing women as human beings and not as some separate exotic species meant to exist on some higher moral plane."

177

"Buffy raised his consciousness?" Holly asked.

"I don't think either of them thought in such terms, but it's true. Too late for Terry, though. Anyway, at that time, in the Governor's mind, I think our daughter Terry was all mixed up with his older sister Sarah and her disgrace."

"But what was Sarah's disgrace?"

"She became pregnant by one man, married another, and then deserted him for a third."

"Really?" Holly could not restrain herself. "Well, good for her. At least she was one Stockwell who outwitted the chauvinists."

"It wasn't that simple, my dear. This was the 1900s. These events took place in 1912 and 1913. People had never heard of chauvinism in those days. A woman—a lady—was expected to adhere to certain standards of behavior, particularly if she was a Stockwell. For a little boy —and that's what the Governor was then—to be caught up in the maelstrom she created had to affect his later attitudes and behavior."

"I'm sorry, Grandma. I just don't think it's so terrible for a woman to have sex before marriage, or for her to leave her husband."

"That's too easy, Holly. What Sarah did was very hard for a lot of people who cared for her. First she became pregnant and refused to name the man responsible."

"Just like my mother."

"Exactly. And I'm sure that's why the Governor was so hard on Terry."

"It's no excuse," Holly said emphatically, her eyes narrowing. "But go on with your story. Sarah became pregnant and wouldn't tell anyone who she had slept with. Then what?"

"To save the family embarrassment, a marriage was arranged with another man, a landowner in need of money named Averill Tyler."

"He knew his bride was pregnant by another man?"

"The Governor was a young boy at the time so he has never been sure if Averill Tyler knew, or didn't know, or only suspected, or even if his suspicions only came later, after Sarah left him. Clearly, he knew by then. In any case, Jonathan and Amanda Stockwell provided a handsome dowry for their daughter and he married her. Seven months later Sarah gave birth to the twins, Alfred—the bridegroom, as you put it—and John. Then, when the twins were just over a year old, Sarah ran off with another man."

"Not the twin's father?"

"From all accounts, no. This was a man new to the valley. As a matter of fact, he was new to the country. He would still have been in Ireland when Sarah became pregnant."

"He was Irish?"

"Yes, he was Irish, and"—Mary couldn't help but pause dramatically—"he was her husband's coachman. You can't imagine the scandal that caused. The Stockwells were a very proper family, and the embarrassment they felt was considerable."

"What about Sarah's children?"

"She left them behind. At this point her outraged husband publicly denied his paternity of them and threatened to turn them over to the local orphanage. Amanda, Matthew's mother, couldn't have that, of course, so she took them in. But Amanda and Jonathan were quite prudish—and frankly, not very loving—and they never really got over the disgrace. They raised the Governor very strictly after that, and they never quite treated the twins as you would expect them to treat their grandchildren. As you know, when Jonathan died he left his entire estate to Matthew, with really only a small stipend to the twins. So the Governor has always felt a sort of responsibility to his nephews."

"And Sarah? Grandpa's sister? What happened to her?"

"She was never heard of again."

"Do you suppose she could still be alive?" Holly wondered.

"It's possible, I suppose. But she would be a very old lady. Eighty-five, if I calculate correctly."

"It's a fascinating story. I wish I had heard it before. Maybe it would have helped me to understand why Grandpa was so hard on my mother." Holly sighed. "Riverview certainly has more than its share of fascinating stories," she added thoughtfully. "George Cortlandt Stockwell saw that as far back as the 1820s."

"George Stockwell? He was Matthew's great-uncle. He's the one you told me about who wrote the satiric novel and died saving it from the fire?"

"Yes," Holly confirmed her grandmother's recollection. "In 1838. But it wasn't just ironic fiction. It was the truth. My research has shown me that just about everything he set down is solidly borne out by fact."

"You've actually found documentation."

"Oh, yes. Quite a lot of it. There are all sorts of family records for the van Bronckels, for instance."

"The original settlers of Riverview?"

"Yes, Dirk van Bronckel built a house on this very site in the 1640s."

"What happened to them?" Mary was curious. "Matthew and I both thought this land had always belonged to the Stockwells; just as the adjacent property belonged to my family, the Linstones."

"What happened to them?" Holly smiled. "The American Revolution, that's what. All through the eighteenth century, from the time of Dirk van Bronckel's death in 1690, his descendants prospered. By the early 1770s his great-grandchildren owned as much of the valley as the Stockwells and Linstones combined ever did. They were patroons—a Dutch word for landed aristocracy. Like most Americans who came after them, they had come a long, long way from their very humble beginnings. They had land. They had wealth. They had power. And they had— according to George Cortlandt Stockwell's account—the most beautiful daughter of any of the Dutch and Tory English families in the Hudson River Valley." Holly sighed.

"If she was so lovely, why does she make you sad?"

"Because," Holly explained, "she was doomed. She met a man. They fell in love. But they were star-crossed lovers."

"Romeo and Juliet." Mary smiled. "And what was her name, this Juliet?"

"Ursula," replied Holly. "Her name was Ursula van Bronckel."

21

I T WAS THE unseasonably warm March of 1775 and Ursula van Bronckel's sixteenth birthday had just passed.
She'd looked forward to it so eagerly, now it was gone and
nothing in her life had really changed. She was beautiful,
and her family was rich, and one day soon her father
would arrange a suitable match for her with a son of one
of the neighboring patroons.

The peaceful existence so valued by her parents bored
her. The rolling hills, the gentle farmlands and verdant
forests, even the Hudson which could sometimes be tur-
bulent—this wealth of scenery bored her. Moving through
its dew-drenched splendor sparkling in early morning
sunlight, Ursula dreamed vague dreams of far-off, more
romantic vistas.

She took advantage of her woodland solitude to push
down the square-cut, painfully boned bodice of her Jouy
print morning gown, revealing the rising half-moons of
her breasts in what Ursula conceived to be the wicked
French fashion. Her feeling of delicious liberation more
than compensated for the rash of goose pimples spread by
the cool early morning air.

Ursula came to a brook formed by a trickle of stream
bottled up on its way to emptying into the Hudson by an
eighty foot high configuration of three weather-joined and
rain-smoothed boulders known locally as Hanging Rock.

It had been called Hanging Rock ever since the days
when the early patroons executed Mohawk poachers
there. An Indian deer hunter who had trespassed their
estates would be hung from the huge oak tree overlooking
the rock—a rope tied around the neck and the poacher
pushed off Hanging Rock's topmost ledge. Bodies were
left dangling in the wind as an example to other savages
that civilization demanded the honoring of property

181

rights, and that trespassers would not be tolerated regardless of either tribal precedent or the need for winter meat.

The brook was on the river side of the landmark. Here Ursula removed her spangled, satin, high-heeled shoes—ridiculous footwear for walking in the woods, but easier to remove than her riding boots would have been—and her clock-embroidered worsted stockings. Ursula raised her skirt and petticoats and tucked them unevenly into the lacing of her stomacher. Shapely bare legs gleaming in the early morning sunlight, she waded up to her knees in the brook behind Hanging Rock.

Ursula half-danced gracefully across the slippery rocks of the brook, drops of silver water spattering her thighs. Suddenly there was a tread of boots, a snapping of twigs, and the rustle of leaves. Hearing this, and a murmur of voices fading into the early morning mist, Ursula darted quickly from the brook and crept silently around to the other side of the rock to investigate.

There were two small groups of men on either side of the expanse of wild, early spring grasses. From their powdered wigs, the style of their finery, and their frequent recourse to bejeweled snuff boxes, Ursula identified one party as aristocratic young patroons. The other group wore the blue-and-white officers' uniforms and tricorner hats of the Colonial Massachusetts Militia.

Ursula had heard rumors of an armed force of uniformed renegades from New England in the valley. Now she regarded them curiously. Would these men really dare to rebel against what her loyalist Dutch patroon father had recently referred to as "the superbly disciplined regulars of King George the Third's British Army?"

One man strode back and forth between the two groups, finalizing arrangements. Another stood to one side, opened a surgeon's satchel, spread a cloth on the still dewy grass, and laid out an assortment of probes and scalpels and medicinal fluids.

After a while two of the Colonial officers crossed to the other side bearing a large box of carved mahogany with an inlaid pearl top. Formal bows were exchanged, and the case was opened with a flourish. Ursula had a clear view of two long-barreled silver dueling pistols, the grips of which were also inlaid with pearl.

There was some discussion regarding the pistols. Finally the young Dutchman to whom the selection had been offered shrugged impatiently and picked one at random. The uniformed men who had brought them bowed again, turned and rejoined their group. Here, one of the Colonial officers took the remaining pistol from the box and hefted it.

Simultaneously the young Dutchman removed his fawn-colored cutaway jacket and his powdered wig. His hair was a fashionable cascade of dark curls. Handsome in white shirt-sleeves, he pushed his loose lace cuffs up from his wrists so that they would not snag the dueling pistol as he took it in hand. Graceful as he was, however, his grip on the gun was awkward.

By contrast his opponent handled his weapon with easy familiarity. The Yankee officer cocked it and sighted down the barrel. He put a bit of spittle on his thumb and ran it over the sight. He set his jaw with confident satisfaction.

From her place of concealment Ursula studied the two men. The young patroon wasn't personally known to her, but she knew his breed well. Even now, facing death, his air was lackadaisical, uncaring, slightly bored. When he yawned, covering his mouth with the back of his hand, it was a graceful gesture that seemed to say that this matter at hand, this duel, was of little moment, and that loss of life—even his own—was really of no great importance.

Ursula empathized with his ennui and admired his aplomb. She hoped he would win.

His opponent did not strike her fancy. Also bareheaded now, he had flaxen hair, straight and fine as silk. To Ursula it seemed peasant hair. Nor was the Colonial fine-featured. The bones of his face were prominent, his jaw craggy, and his nose slightly tilted from some long forgotten brawl. In Ursula's opinion, his lips were too full, his mouth too earthy, and his moustache scraggly and the color of bleached river sand. The only sensitivity was in his eyes, which were deep and gray with a soft, greenish cast.

Now Ursula watched him tilt his pistol and pour a measure of powder into the barrel. The young patroon did likewise, but his powder immediately dribbled out again. The Massachusetts militiaman inserted a large iron pellet.

One of the Dutchmen's friends took the weapon from him and loaded it. The Yankee poured in a bit more powder and then took the loading rod and expertly tamped powder and shot into firm position. The Dutchman's friend handed the loaded dueling pistol back to him.

"Your places, gentlemen!" The referee summoned the two combatants to the center of the clearing. "Once again I must ask you if this matter may not be settled in some less drastic manner."

"Yes," the young Colonial officer offered.

"No." Once again the patroon yawned.

"An apology perhaps?"

"I apologize," the blond militiaman said quickly.

"Unacceptable." The young Dutchman spoke without inflection.

"Very well, then, gentlemen." The referee sighed. "We will proceed." He positioned them back to back. "When I start counting, you will each take one step for each number up to ten. You will then be twenty paces apart. You will turn and face each other. When I say 'Ready,' you will cock your revolvers. When I say 'Aim,' you will raise them at arm's length and sight. When I say 'Fire,' you will pull the triggers. Is that clear?"

"Yes," said the patroon.

"Yes," echoed the Yankee officer.

"Very well." The referee started counting. "One . . . two . . . three . . ."

Ursula held her breath.

". . . eight . . . nine . . . ten." The referee finished counting and strode quickly to the sideline as the duelists turned and faced each other.

"Ready . . ."

There was the sound of a loud click as the Yankee officer cocked the hammer of his pistol. He waited patiently as the patroon struggled to pull his hammer into position. Finally there was a second click.

"Aim . . ."

The officer's arm rose steadily. The pistol in his grasp stayed firm and straight and still. One of his gray eyes narrowed and sighted down the barrel.

Ursula saw the patroon's arm start to shake, at first slightly, then more noticeably. His grip on the dueling pis-

184

tol had been casual at first; now it seemed tenuous. Squinting down the barrel, he adjusted his gaze three times, as if unsureness was blurring his vision.

"Fire!"

The patroon fired first. His shot went wide of the target. The Massachusetts officer smiled ambiguously. Ursula was not sure whether the expression was one of relief or menace.

Now the patroon struck a casual pose as he waited for his opponent to fire. Ursula realized that it was meant to show lack of concern, but it came off as foppish and insulting. If she had been the other duelist, she would have found it infuriating.

This did indeed seem to be the effect. The militiaman reaimed with a steadiness that seemed to ensure that his bullet would go straight to the patroon's heart. Then, to the shock of Ursula and all the others watching, two things occurred in the same split second. The Yankee officer's arm dropped suddenly in a straight line, a downward swoop, and he fired into what should have been the dust at the patroon's feet. Simultaneously the patroon's nonchalance deserted him along with his courage, and he flung himself into the dirt to avoid the bullet he was sure was about to be fired straight for his heart.

His sudden terror was his undoing. Had the Dutchman remained standing, the bullet would not have touched him. Diving to avoid it, he met it head-on. It pierced his chest and flung him over on his back. He lay quite still.

The surgeon moved swiftly to kneel and examine him. "Straight through the heart," he said, a note of astonishment in his voice. He closed the surprised blue eyes with his fingers and drew his cape over the handsome Dutch face, covering the curly black hair.

Like a blow from a hammer, Ursula realized that the young patroon was actually dead.

His friends tied their jackets into a rough litter, placed his body on it, and carried it solemnly off through the woods. The doctor packed up his instruments and likewise left, accompanied by the referee. The other Yankee officers gathered to one side, casting glances at their victorious comrade, obviously waiting for him to join them so they, too, could depart.

He was standing by himself, his back to the killing ground and his friends and to the hidden Ursula as well. Finally he spoke without turning around. His voice was loud and clear and unemotional. "You go on ahead," he said. "I'll catch up later."

There was a mixed murmur urging him to come along with them now.

"No!" The retort was as sharp as the pistol shot that he'd fired such a short time before. "I'll see you back at bivouac. Leave now!" The last two words were a command, and although his militia insignia was only that of a lieutenant and he could not possibly have outranked the other officers, it was obeyed.

When he was alone, the young Yankee turned and walked slowly back to the spot where the man he'd killed had fallen. He looked down at the grass, still bent to the contours of his victim's body; at the dirt, still clotted with the patroon's blood. He raised his rough-hewn face to the sun, now well up in the cloudless, azure sky. A sound like that Ursula had once heard a small animal make when its leg was caught in a trap escaped the lieutenant's full lips. Following the grooves etched by his squint against the sun, twin rivulets of tears ran down his cheeks.

Ursula felt stabbed by the sudden, unexpected, naked emotion. Spying on him now seemed unconscionable. She turned to flee the scene, intending to put the barrier of Hanging Rock between herself and his remorse. But her desire to leave was too forceful, her movements too hurried, her flight too unconsidered. Plunging back into the underbrush, her bare foot caught in a tree root. As her ankle was wrenched and she was pulled to the ground in a tangle of bare thighs and tucked up petticoats, she unthinkingly cried out.

The Colonial officer heard. Parting the undergrowth to investigate the cry, he discovered her. Blinking with astonishment, he automatically extended a hand and helped her to her feet.

"Thank you," she stammered. "I'm sorry," she blurted out. She untucked her petticoats and skirts from her stomacher and smoothed it down to cover her legs. Her face, she knew, must be flame red. "I'm sorry," she repeated.

186

"Sorry?" Realization dawned on him. "You saw the duel."

"Yes." Ursula voiced her curiosity. "What was it about?"

"What you'd expect in one of your local taverns. Bloody George's thieving taxes."

Ursula gasped. She had never heard the English king referred to with such disrespect before. To her loyalist father the monarch was "Good King George the Third," protector of the Tory status quo. If anything, the Dutch patroons of the Hudson River Valley were even more loyal to the English king than the Westchester Tories sworn to carry his standard into battle against the ragtail rebels if necessary. "If you spoke that way to our local gentlemen," she told the militiaman, "I don't wonder there was a duel."

"It was a barroom discussion, a political argument, for God's sake. Nothing to shed blood over. That poor hothead I killed couldn't justify the British colonial policy, and so he called me out."

She stared at him curiously. His words would have placed him beyond the pale to her family. Her father would never have allowed him to cross the threshold of their home. Indeed, it was not inconceivable that he might have called this Yankee rebel out himself. "Was it that?" she wondered. "Or was it a matter of honor?"

"Honor?" A scowl further creased his young, leathery face. "There are things worth dying for, but I don't know that honor is one of them."

Ursula gasped again.

"Except," he amended, "in the Hudson River Valley. That's obvious. The poor damn fool. Such a futile death! To die in war is one thing, but a duel—"

"Will you rebels make a war?" Ursula blurted.

"Oh, no. But Crazy George will. And when he does, we'll be ready."

"Will it come soon, do you think?"

"Yes. Soon. That's why we have marched here from Massachusetts to join forces with Ethan Allen of Connecticut. To make sure the battle is fought on Tory territory when the time comes."

"Well, if that's so, then the man slain by you today will

187

surely not be your only victim." Ursula had a sudden insight. "But he was the first you ever killed, wasn't he?"

"Yes." Suddenly his face, which had been defiant when he was talking about rebellion against the king, crumpled. "The first." His large hands, callused as if from farm work, came up to shield his visage from her view. His shoulders shook silently. Turning away, he sank down to his haunches and swayed back and forth on his heels.

"Oh, no!" Compassion welled up inside Ursula. "Don't." She leaned over and patted his shoulders. "Please don't."

Suddenly his arms went around behind Ursula, encircling the hidden panniers at her hips. He buried his face against her body. His tears dampened her bodice.

She was forced to clutch at him to keep from being toppled over. Then, holding him in his anguish, Ursula rocked him as she might have rocked a sobbing infant. "There, there," she heard herself saying. "There, there. It's all right. Cry it out."

A maelstrom of emotions swept through her. Never had she felt so tender toward another human being, and never before had she felt such a strong stirring of desire toward one particular man. She held his sobbing face tight against her breast. They remained thus for a long, stirring, bittersweet, unmeasurable time.

Still holding Ursula, he got to his feet. Her face turned up toward him as a flower reaches for the sun. His long neck craned downward. And then, moving together, without words, they kissed.

"My name is Roger Stockwell," he said when the kiss was over. "Lieutenant Roger Stockwell of the Massachusetts Volunteer Militia."

"I'm Ursula van Bronckel." Her words came as from a daze, a deliciously pleasant daze.

They kissed again.

"I would like to call on you at your home."

"My father would never allow it."

"I don't go around kissing every girl I meet, you know," Lieutenant Stockwell assured her. "I'm really quite respectable. My commanding officer will vouch for my good character. In Massachusetts he is himself known as a man of sterling integrity. I will ask him to call on your father

and plead my case. His name is Arnold. Captain Benedict
Arnold."

"My father is loyal to the Crown. To him, you and your
Captain Benedict Arnold are rebel traitors." Ursula sighed.
"I must go now. I will be missed." She allowed Roger
Stockwell a farewell kiss.

And she promised to meet Benedict Arnold's young
lieutenant again the following day at the same place, beside the brook behind Hanging Rock.

22

THE MOTORCYCLE OFFICER staked out behind Hanging
Rock was dressed like a New York State trooper but
was actually employed by Riverview Heights. His name
was Sergeant Rudolph Dammler, and he was the junior
member of the village's six-man constabulary. His assign-
ment was to apprehend speeders within the extensively
defined town limits. These included a six-mile stretch of
underutilized rural highway running alongside the Stockwell estate. Hanging Rock was off to one side, at the
northern end of this strip.

Most of what traffic there was went south to north.
Usually it consisted of nonresident drivers trying to avoid
the jam-ups on the Thruway and the Taconic Parkway on
their way to the upstate resorts. The fines collected, a welcome addition to the township budget, rarely came from
local people.

An abrupt drop in the speed limit from fifty-five to
thirty-five defined the speed trap. Few of those ticketed
were going more than fifty or so. On this particular early
evening in June, however, the restored Spyder Coupe
Porsche whipping past Hanging Rock was clocked by Sergeant Dammler at eighty-plus.

He was still whistling low in his throat as he gunned
his motor and gave chase. His siren drowned out the last

of the whistle. The Porsche showed no sign of slowing down.

Perhaps the driver hadn't realized the shriek of the siren was directed at the Porsche. The cycle was still pretty far behind it. Sometimes people had the radio on, or they were just wool-gathering and didn't connect the blare with themselves. In his three years on the job, Sergeant Dammler had never had a car actually try to outrun him.

The officer came down hard on the gas. His speedometer climbed past eighty, and the distance closed between him and the taillight of the Porsche. He sounded the siren again, a long, steady, demanding wail—an unmistakable command to pull over and deal with the law.

Instead, the Porsche speeded up. There could be no mistake now. It was trying to get away from him. Sergeant Dammler hunched low and gave chase. He was too intent on not losing the sports car to check his speedometer now, but he knew instinctively that both he and his prey were up around the big C. Sticking like glue, not gaining ground but not losing any, either, the officer bounced over the crests of hills, plunged tail up down the grades, burned screeching rubber on the curves, and pushed to the limit on the straightaways. They'd done six or seven miles since the chase started, and Dammler realized the Porsche was playing chicken with him.

Now the officer's heart sank. Up ahead was a stretch that had caught a summer shower earlier that day. Just a sprinkle, a sun shower, but enough to leave the pavement wet. Dammler prayed the driver would see it and have sense enough to slow down, but the Porsche maintained speed. It hit the slick hard and the spray flew from the designer-spoked wheels.

A moment later Dammler himself plowed into the first puddle. The spray came up over the front of the bike like a waterfall in reverse. He was just coming out of the wet, with the Porsche about an eighth of a mile ahead, when he heard the pop. It was like a firecracker, loud enough to be heard over the high-speed grind of the bike. "Jesus!" He anticipated the skid even as the Porsche careened into it. The coupe had blown a Michelin, left rear.

It swerved crazily, mounting the embankment and coming off it, miraculously, without turning over. Out of control, it narrowly missed a tree and screeched into a U-turn. The motorcycle was forced onto the shoulder to keep from being hit as it zigzagged past. Finally it bucked to a halt.

Sergeant Dammler climbed off his bike and took his gun from its holster as he started for the Porsche. Smoke was coming off the hood in back from the overheated rear-mounted engine. There was a long groove in the road where the wheel that had taken the blowout had gouged out its path. The damn fool had been braking all the way through the end of the skid. The acrid smell of burning rubber filled the evening air. As yet nobody had gotten out of the car.

Still holding his gun at the ready, Dammler shined his flashlight through the window. The beam caught the female driver full in the face. She was young, scarcely out of adolescence, and he couldn't help noticing, sexy as well as beautiful. Her hair was a wild swirl, its color striking, a red gold, like ripe apricots. Her hazel eyes gazed back at the officer, reflecting none of the fear he'd expected to see in them. On the contrary, they were suspiciously blank.

He peered closer. Oh, yes. She was zonked all right. Out of her gourd. He sniffed. No smell of liquor. Drugs was his guess, and not just Mary Jane, or even hash. This scrumptious cookie was high on something that packed a wallop. Dammler turned off the Porsche ignition and removed the keys.

She stared into the light, her eyes still not focusing, showing no reaction to its glare. Nor was she intimidated by the pistol leveled at her. After a moment she giggled, without humor.

"You behind the popgun," she said in a calculatedly sultry voice, "you like what you see? You dig the bod?" She clasped her hands behind her neck and undulated. Her uptilting breasts were outlined clearly by the skimpy tank top she wore, especially the prominent tips.

"Get out of the car." Dammler opened the door for her.

She complied, stumbling. He caught her. The slanted hazel eyes looked up at his face, focusing for the first time. They registered the fact that he was young, attractive.

"I clocked you from eighty up to a hundred," he told

her. "You're lucky you're alive. Let's see your driver's license."

"Glove compartment, Brown Eyes." She started to reach back into the car and stumbled again.

"I'll get it. You wait over there." He pointed to a small boulder beside the road and waited until she sat down there before he turned back to the car.

The glove compartment was locked. Dammler opened it with one of the keys on the ring he'd taken from the ignition. The driver's license and registration were in a small leather wallet jammed under a letter-size white envelope. The envelope was torn partly open. White powder was spilling out of it.

Wetting his finger, the officer picked up a few grains of the powder on the tip. He tasted it. Cocaine, all right. High-grade stuff. Uncut. Pure. Expensive.

Carefully, he left the envelope where it was. He fished out the wallet under it and looked at the documents. The name on the driver's license was Caroline Tyler. The Porsche was registered to Dr. Paul Tyler. The same address appeared on both documents: Eighteen East Sixty-third Street, New York City.

"What's your relationship to the owner, Dr. Paul Tyler?" Sergeant Dammler asked the girl.

"Daddy, dear old daddy." Carrie half sang the answer.

"You have his permission to drive his car?"

"Sure. And you know why? Because I'm twins, that's why."

"Come over here." When she obeyed, he pointed through the car window at the envelope spilling cocaine. "Is that yours?" he asked.

"Well, it surely isn't dear old daddy's, Brown Eyes."

"Do you know what it is?"

"Talcum Powder." She giggled again. "Talcum powder for Baby Carrie."

"It's cocaine."

"No kidding." Her red lips twisted sarcastically.

"I'm going to have to take you in, Miss Tyler. You're under arrest for possession of a controlled substance in excess of three ounces." Sergeant Dammler fished a small booklet out of his shirt pocket and shined his flashlight on it and the heading on the cover: Miranda Rights. "You have the right to remain silent . . ." he began.

"Whoa, Brown Eyes. Can't we discuss this?" Carrie put both hands on Dammler's shoulders and moved very close against him.

"Don't make things worse for yourself."

"I'm trying to make them better for you." She stroked his cheek, gently urging his face down toward hers.

"I wouldn't want to have to add attempted bribery to the charge, Miss Tyler."

"Attempted bribery?" Carrie's voice was a purr now. "Why, no such thing, Brown Eyes." Her fingertips danced over the lobe of his ear. "Seduction, maybe, but certainly not attempted bribery."

"Whatever it is, I'm not interested." Resisting his reaction—she was sexy, dammit!—Sergeant Dammler brushed Carrie's hand aside and stepped back from her.

"You really are arresting me?" Carrie stared at him with disbelief. "But that's silly. Nobody's going to press charges against me up here, not in Riverview Heights."

"Why not?"

"I'm a Stockwell, that's why not."

"The name on your driver's license is Tyler. Caroline Tyler."

"The Stockwells are my cousins. If you don't believe me, just ask them. They'll tell you I'm one of them. They'll vouch for me."

Dammler stared at her. She was too zonked to lie so glibly. If she really was a Stockwell . . .

The officer's mind raced. He had never thought of himself as corrupt. Still, he lived and worked in Riverview Heights. He knew the score. It was owned lock, stock, and barrel by the mighty Stockwells. If he nailed this kid for possession, he could be kissing off his career.

"You got a jack?" he asked the girl.

"In the trunk in front." Carrie showed him how to open it. She watched him position the jack in the custom-fit slot. "Are you taking my car somewhere?" she asked him.

"Your car, and you."

"Where?"

"Riverview manor," Dammler told her, jacking up the rear axle. "We're going to Riverview."

At Holly's urging, Mary had stayed to dinner at Riverview. Buffy was staying overnight in Manhattan. Now the two of them, along with James and his youngest son Michael, as well as Jonathan, Ellen, and Peter, were in the library having coffee.

Mary had been recapping for the others what Holly had told her about the origins of Riverview. "And so the Tory patroon maiden learns that the rebel officer who has been kissing her—the Stockwell—serves under Benedict Arnold," she concluded. "Now, doesn't that tell you how much Riverview is steeped in history? Benedict Arnold!"

"What happened then?" James asked his mother.

"I don't know, my dear. You'll have to ask Holly. That's where she left me hanging when we went to freshen up for dinner."

James was prevented from pursuing the topic with Holly when Berkley materialized in the oak-framed doorway to the library and cleared his throat discreetly. "There is a member of the Riverview Heights constabulary at the door asking to speak with a member of the family," the butler informed them.

Puzzled glances were exchanged.

James shrugged. "Show him in," he told Berkley. As the butler went to fetch the officer, James remarked to the others that it was probably a solicitation for the Riverview Heights Constabulary Benevolent Fund or something like that.

"Well, I certainly hope so," Jonathan harrumphed. "We certainly don't want any police notoriety to draw attention to the family. We've had enough scandal lately." His look at James was pointed.

"I'll second that," James's son Michael echoed quietly.

Ellen's eyes met those of her son Peter. He smiled. There were some kinds of notoriety that could only work out to his advantage.

Berkley reentered, preceded by a uniformed officer. "Sergeant Dammler." The butler identified him for the group and then left.

"What can we do for you, Sergeant?" James was courtly, as always.

Sergeant Dammler came straight to the point. "You can

tell me, Mr. Stockwell, if a Miss Caroline Tyler is related to your family."

"She is my niece." It was Mary who answered, concerned. "My great-niece," she amended.

"Our cousin," James told the officer.

"Yes, sir. I see." Sergeant Dammler drew a deep breath. He related the circumstances that had brought him there. "Miss Tyler is outside in the car," he concluded.

"Those turnip-headed Tylers!" Jonathan was the first to respond. "One way or another, they all cause trouble."

"That's not true, Jonathan!" Mary shook her head. "Paul has always been a decent, upstanding physician. And Beth is as sweet as can be."

"Perhaps. But Max is a deviate, and Diana is an overage hippie, Mother. And now we've got all this fuss with a wedding between two Tylers old enough to know better. Slanty eyes, squash-colored hair, and trouble, trouble, trouble—that's the Tylers."

Sergeant Dammler cleared his throat, and James spoke at the same time. "You're sure about the cocaine?" he asked.

"Yes, sir."

"Then we are most gravely concerned," James told him.

"I thought you would be, sir. That's why I brought her here instead of—"

"To jail." James frowned. He was torn. Carrie was a member of his family, and as such he was obliged to extend to her what protection lay within his power. On the other hand, he was not comfortable with circumventing the law—particularly where drugs were concerned. It crossed his mind that saving her from jail could conceivably cost Carrie her life.

Then, too, there was the matter of the police officer. What did he want? Did he expect to be bribed? That was something James could not bring himself to do. He'd always balked at the obligatory bottle of Scotch to have a parking ticket fixed. How could he countenance paying whatever price was expected to sweep this matter under the rug?

James regarded Sergeant Dammler coldly. "Just why have you brought her here instead of booking her, Sergeant?" he asked.

The officer was disturbed by James's tone. "Consideration for the family, sir," was the best he could come up with by way of a reply.

"Are you this considerate of all the families in Riverside Heights?"

"Dad—" Michael interrupted quickly. He knew his father, and he sensed where the discussion was going.

"Are you, Sergeant?"

"James—" Mary's only concern was for Carrie Tyler.

"Uncle James has a point." Unexpectedly, Peter piped up. "We can't go around bribing policemen every time some relative or other gets in trouble."

His mother smiled. The words had been spoken, the situation spelled out. Whichever way James moved now, it would be his responsibility, and that responsibility bore the seeds of a ricochet. If James pushed the police into booking Carrie, all of the Tylers would be bitter and Mary would be disappointed in him. Such a scenario could work to Peter's advantage. On the other hand, if James suborned bribery, that would be a weapon for Peter to use against him when the time was right.

"Well, Sergeant?" James would not let it go.

Dammler stared at him. The rich! The goddamn rich! Who the hell was with this guy anyway? Did he expect him to come right out and say he wanted to be bought off? Well, he didn't. He wasn't looking for a payoff. All he was trying to do was protect his ass so he didn't have Stockwells shafting him for the rest of his life. Only now his leniency with their cokehead cousin was backfiring, and he was being treated like some rogue cop on the pad.

"Just exactly what is it you want, Sergeant?" James persisted, his voice heavy with disapproval.

"All right, Dad. That's enough." Michael interceded swiftly and effectively. "My father's upset," he explained to Dammler. "Why don't you let me handle this, Dad?" His tone made the request a demand. "We're talking about the future of an eighteen-year-old girl, after all."

"Please, James." Mary's eyes begged her son to let Michael do what he could to protect Carrie.

"All right." James grimaced with self-disgust. His son would take him off the hook; his principles would be unsullied save by disinvolvement. It was, as they said, a cop-out. "All right."

"Let's you and I go into the other room and discuss this privately," Michael suggested to the officer. His tone was conciliatory, his look reassuring.

Relieved, Sergeant Dammler followed Michael from the library.

There was a brief silence. Peter broke it. "Another crisis dealt with by the tact and diplomacy of the natural-born politician," he remarked. "Grandpa would be proud."

James's face darkened. He was about to answer his nephew hotly, then stopped himself. There was truth in what Peter said. Michael was a politician, and he was naturally concerned about the effect a drug scandal might have on his career. Still, that didn't mean he wasn't concerned for Carrie as well.

The telephone rang in the hallway just outside the library. A moment later Berkley appeared in the doorway. "For you, Miss Holly. It's Dr. Meyerling." Berkley used the title by which Meyerling was identified in the media and at the Stockwell Institute.

"Thank you, Berkley." Holly went out to the hall to take the call.

"I'm calling about the wedding invitation." Meyerling's voice in her ear was warm and precise.

"You already RSVP'd," she recalled. "We're looking forward to seeing you."

"That's why I'm calling. After I sent my acceptance—just today as a matter of fact—something came up. I have to fly to Washington the day of the wedding. Regretfully, I can't attend. But I did want you to pass along my best wishes to the bride and groom."

"I will. And I am sorry you won't be there."

"I, too, am sorry. I was looking forward to the occasion. And," Meyerling added, "I was very much looking forward to seeing you again."

"Thank you." Holly was flattered.

"You're welcome." He paused. "Has your active life calmed down enough for us to perhaps have dinner?" he asked carefully. "You will remember that we did have a rain check."

"I remember." Holly took a long breath and then answered. "Why, yes," she said. "I think dinner would be very nice."

Why not? Zelig Meyerling was charming, cultured, well informed, amusing, and she'd really enjoyed herself the night she'd been his dinner partner. Regardless of its official status, her marriage was over. Seeing Christopher again had brought that home to her. So why shouldn't she go out with a man who—if the gossip columns were to be believed—had his pick of the most beautiful and fashionable young women in Washington and New York? Why shouldn't she relax over a pleasant dinner and fine wine with a notable escort?

"As I mentioned, I will shortly be flying back to Washington," Meyerling was saying in her ear. "Would I seem adolescently impetuous if I suggested tomorrow night?"

"Not at all. Just as long as you understand that I never kiss a boy on the first date."

He chuckled. "That will be most disappointing. But I promise to restrain myself." He suggested Le Veau D'Or, a particularly intimate French restaurant enjoying a vogue among New York's new elite. They agreed to meet there at eight o'clock, and Holly hung up.

Back in the library she was met with inquiring glances. "Zelig Meyerling," she explained. "He called to say he won't be able to make the wedding and to apologize."

"What a shame," Mary responded. "Zelig is always such an asset to any festive occasion. He's that rarest of all birds these days, a public figure who is also an entertaining conversationalist."

Holly noticed that Michael had come back into the room. The policeman, presumably, had departed. "Carrie?" she inquired.

"Upstairs sleeping it off." Michael's tone said that he didn't want to discuss the details of whatever arrangement had been arrived at.

James frowned.

Mary spoke quickly, deftly deflecting his disapproval. "Carrie has always been a difficult child," she said. "As long as I can remember, her father has had problems with her. She's headstrong, just like her great-grandmother Sarah. Poor Paul."

"Well," Holly said. "He's got Beth to compensate."

"Yes," Mary agreed. "They may be twins, but Beth is as different from Carrie as day from night. Paul and Margaret have had many a sleepless night over Carrie, but never over Beth. She won't ever give them any trouble. Not Beth."

Holly nodded silent agreement.

23

"YOU HAVE NO conscience!" Beth Tyler wasn't screaming, but her mouth was twisted into an uncharacteristic snarl as she hissed the words. "I'm ashamed that you're my father!"

"How dare you talk to your father that way?" Her mother was furious.

"She doesn't really mean it, Maggie," Dr. Paul Tyler said, trying to soothe his wife.

"Oh, yes, I do!" Beth's hazel eyes were angrily curved slits. "I really used to worship you—my father the doctor, healer of humanity, the dedicated surgeon snatching cardiac cases from the jaws of death! But now I even wonder about that. For all I know, all you've ever been is just a money-hungry quack."

"You're getting hysterical, Bethie." The surgeon was infuriatingly calm, his own almond-shaped eyes, so similar to those of his twin daughters, pleading for reason. "You're just venting your anger. You're not even remotely sticking to the point of what we were discussing."

"You're right." Beth ran her fingers distractedly through her hair, disturbing its smoothly combed sheen. "Why bother? You took care of that point first crack out of the box, because you've got the power and I don't."

"That's not fair, Bethie."

"It's true. It's my money, but you control it. Therefore, what I want doesn't count."

"I don't control it. I told you that before. James Stockwell controls it. He and his brother-in-law and nephew."

"Only because you agree to let them."

"I agree because I know the Governor—and it was he who left you the money in the first place, Bethie—would have wanted the administration of your inheritance left in their hands. Besides, I really can't hurt Great-Aunt Mary by taking the funds out."

"What nonsense! She has millions. She'd never even feel it. Why should she care?"

"Her feelings would be hurt."

"You're only saying that because you're too chicken to stand up against the almighty troika."

"She sounds like Buffy," Margaret Tyler murmured, disgusted with her usually well-behaved daughter.

"It's my inheritance, and I want it, dammit!" Beth brushed angry tears from her eyes. "I don't want my money paying for the pollution that little kids are choking on! How can you call yourself a doctor," she demanded of her father, "and not take steps to stop that when you have the means?"

Her father maintained his tranquillity. "This is pointless, Bethie," he said. "We're going around in circles."

"You're right. I'm leaving." Beth strode toward the door.

"What time will you be home?" her mother demanded.

"I don't know."

"Where are you going?"

"Out of here!"

"Come on, Bethie, where are you going?" Dr. Tyler's tone was more reasonable. Scenes with Beth were rare, tantrums unheard of. Always the screaming sessions had been with Carrie. He was willing to overlook a lot where his usually more amiable twin daughter was concerned. "Don't leave us to worry."

"Why not?" Beth actually bared her small, even teeth. "It will be a change for you. Worrying about me instead of Carrie!"

The door slamming behind her shook every bit of crystal in her family's fashionable Upper East Side apartment.

Getting out of the taxicab in front of the restaurant on East Sixtieth Street, Holly was concentrating on holding the hemline of her Suzana Monacella original somewhere within decorous distance of the silken knees below it. The new black cocktail dress was perfectly designed to show off her tall, willowy figure, and contrasted stylishly with her sleekly coiffured short hair. But it was definitely not meant for disembarking from cabs with decency, let alone dignity. Walking erect, Holly was the epitome of chic: stooped and wriggling and groping for the helping hand of the doorman as she was now, the strapless chiffon gown turned her into an exhibitionistic kooch dancer.

She was so intent on keeping her balance that she didn't see the woman hurrying down the street until she collided with her. "I'm so sorry!" Holly gasped. Then, focusing on the face, she recognized it. "Hello, Carrie," she said, sure from the sullen expression which twin it was.

"I'm not Carrie, dammit! I'm Beth!"

"Oops! My mistake."

"You've known me all my life, Holly. Don't you think it's about time you made the effort to tell me from my sister?"

"Listen, I really am sorry." Holly had always liked Beth. She was flabbergasted at her uncharacteristic behavior.

"Well, all right." Beth subsided a little, but her ill-humored expression remained.

"Where are you going in such a hurry?"

"SoHo. Diana's." Up until the moment Holly asked her, Beth hadn't been sure where she was going. She'd just been walking off her anger. Now, thinking of it, she realized that Diana's was the only place to go, the only refuge from her family and all the Stockwells and Tylers who suffocated her.

"Well, give her my regards." Holly gave Beth a peck on her angrily flushed cheek and started through the door the doorman had been patiently holding open for her.

Zelig Meyerling was already seated at a corner table. As soon as he saw Holly he stood up, then walked across the plush carpet to meet her halfway. "You look lovely," he greeted her.

"You should have seen me before I fell into the clutches of the New York City taxicab industry. But thanks anyway."

"You had cab trouble?" He waved away the headwaiter and seated Holly at the banquette himself.

"Like getting out of a sardine can. And then I bumped smack into my cousin Beth Tyler and insulted her by calling her by her sister's name."

"She is the young lady with the Magyar eyes and the lioness hair?" Remembering, Meyerling suppressed a shudder. "But I didn't know she had a sister."

"Oh, yes. A twin sister—Carrie. Beth and she couldn't be more different kinds of people, but they look exactly alike. That's why I got Beth mixed up with her."

"Twins." The sudden clarity that came to Meyerling made him feel like a cartoon character with a light bulb lighting up over its head. "Twins," he repeated. "Ah, yes, but different kinds of people. Very different."

Forty minutes later Beth sprawled in an overstuffed chair across from Diana in her cousin's SoHo loft. She sipped the glass of Chablis Diana had given her, wrinkled her nose at the cloud wafting her way from Diana's cigarette, and overlooked Diana's uncaring artistic frumpiness. What did it matter if Diana was ten years past the age where her apricot ponytail suited her? Or if the man's shirt hanging around her too-ample hips was caked with plaster? To Beth she was still a symbol of conscience, compassion, and commitment.

". . . and so I told my father exactly what I thought of him and left." Beth finished her account of the ruckus that had propelled her there. "This was the only place I could think to come. Will you put me up, Diana? Just until I sort things out, I mean."

Diana ran her finger around the inside rim of her wineglass. She didn't answer immediately. Having Beth around would surely interfere with the smooth schedule of her love-life. Still, Diana couldn't forget what it was like to be young and idealistic and all fired up to do battle for personal independence and global justice at the same time. "All right," she told Beth. "You can stay here for a while."

"Thanks. I knew I could count on you, Diana. You're not like everybody else in our family."

"That's for sure." Diana smiled. "Once a hippie, always a hippie. The sixties marked me for life."

"At least you took a stand. That's all I'm trying to do. I

just want to put a stop to what the Stockwells are doing with *my* money."

"Sure," Diana said, still believing it after all these years. "Passivity in the face of evil is complicity. . . ."

"Complicity," Meyerling was telling Holly over the delicately brandy-and-orange-sauced Homard Des Mandarins, "is a historical judgment pronounced after the fact. Active or passive, it doesn't matter." Neither his tone, nor the interest in his hooded eyes as they regarded Holly, were as didactic as his words. "Your Dutch Tories chose the losing side, and so in terms of the American myth, they are traitors. But if George the Third had prevailed, they would have been the true patriots and the founding fathers looked at as wild-eyed radicals defeated by the forces of law and order."

"And we would be closing the banks on Benedict Arnold's birthday instead of George Washington's." Holly laughed. Meyerling's interest in her historical research both flattered and warmed her. "But the trouble with that view is it implies that the two sides were ethically equal when they really weren't. The colonists' cause was just because it embodied freedom, independence, self-determination—all our corny, trite-but-true patriotic concepts."

"Good triumphs over evil," Meyerling capsulized, his glance now paying brief homage to the chiffon curve of her bosom. "Well, yes. But only if leaders use their power to make it come out that way."

"And if they use it to come out the other way?" Holly shifted her position in response to the tribute in his eyes.

"Why, then *sic semper tyrannis*." Meyerling spread his hands. "The tyrants must be overthrown. Only . . ."

"Only?" Holly folded her arms around herself, an unconsciously protective gesture.

Meyerling frowned. "Only great care must be exercised to discriminate the true tyrant from the false tyrant, and the true reformer from the mountebank."

"And how do you do that?" Holly asked.

"Ah," he said, self-satisfaction erasing the frown. "That is why we have experts. . . ."

"The experts were the first casualties of the sixties," Diana remembered. Beth had asked her what the era was really like, and now her brow was furrowed with the effort to explain. "Our leaders. Our statesmen. Our pundits. We stopped believing in them. The media called it the credibility gap. It translated into 'Never trust anybody over thirty.' Of course," Diana laughed, "we never stopped to think how soon we'd be over thirty ourselves, and then who would we trust?"

"But they still had the power, whether you trusted them or not."

"Oh, yes. They had the power." Diana smiled. "But we had compelling new voices, and they were heard. Martin Luther King, Betty Friedan, Marcuse, Fanon." Diana laughed, eyes shining with the memory. "Abbie Hoffman and Jerry Rubin, Jane Fonda and John Lennon, Bob Dylan and Joan Baez. The voices and the music. We were indestructible; we could not be moved; we had the music!"

"Seriously, Diana—"

"I am serious." Diana stopped laughing. "Our causes were just. Civil rights. Peace. Conservation. Gay rights. Equality for women. We were on the side of the angels always, and there is no high like the righteous high. Our juices never stopped running."

"You make it sound so . . . so . . . well, like it was one big Woodstock."

"Oh, there was more to it than Woodstock, all right. It would be a lie to deny the role that pot and sex played in the movement, but they certainly didn't define it. Today they try to present the sixties like that, but it's not true. Not the whole truth, anyway. Not the important truth."

"How would you define your generation, then?" Beth wondered.

"Why, we were the children of the dream. We were going to make it work."

"Dream?" Beth was puzzled. "What dream?"

"The American dream, of course. What else? Counterculture or not, we were strictly made in the USA. The American dream . . ."

* * *

"The American dream is valid. Every hypothesis must start with a given, and that is mine," Meyerling told Holly as waiters so silent as to be invisible removed the silverplate on which the entrée had been served. "It is, I confess without shame, a typically immigrant conviction."

Holly did not miss the erotic component in Meyerling's declaration of love for his adopted country. Looking into his golden-brown eyes, she couldn't doubt his sincerity. But this was not the Zelig Meyerling of media image. That Meyerling—and it was the one thing upon which both his admirers and detractors agreed—was no idealist. He was a hardball master of realpolitik, unsentimental and pragmatic. That Meyerling also had the reputation of a Casanova, and just now Holly had the decided feeling that she'd been marked for conquest.

"Everything I have done as a public servant," he continued, "has been done in the interests of that conviction. And I have no regrets."

"The Vietnam War," Holly said hesitantly. Meyerling had never wavered in his support of the war. Through all the changes in administration, he had remained a leading hawk.

"No regrets," he repeated. He reached across the table and took Holly's hand in his as if to stress his earnestness. But his touch was electric and conveyed more than politics. "The domino theory was valid. Not in its particulars, perhaps, but as a metaphor. We cannot afford to surrender the world through attrition. By definition the communist way of life stands opposed to our way of life. Their victory in Vietnam was our defeat."

"The cost in human life—"

"The American dream has never come cheap. Each generation has to pay the price anew. Nor is it just the dream that must be guarded. It is the reality as well." He squeezed her hand.

"Some people believe that the Vietnam War warped that reality." Taking issue with him, Holly nevertheless squeezed back.

"And they're right," Meyerling granted. "But it was necessary. It is a vulnerable reality, and an imperfect real-

205

ity, too. But it is what we have, and in the end the world will become democratic or it will fall to totalitarianism." He raised her hand and in a gesture that managed to be continental, formal, and yet intimate as well, brushed Holly's knuckles with his lips.

Holly was flustered, but not unpleased at the contact. "Some would say that your perception of danger is paranoid," she pointed out, her soft smile robbing the words of any insult.

"I know." Meyerling sighed. "And to that I can only say that there are none so blind as those who will not see. Which is why we can never chance idealists dictating policy. Impracticality could cost us the world, and idealists are by definition impractical. . . ."

"They called us impractical, but we were really the practical ones and they were the ones with their heads in the sand," Diana reflected. "We said that a guerilla war was unwinnable, and we were right. We pointed out that the Vietnamese had been fighting occupying forces on their soil for a thousand years. They had driven out Chinese invaders, Japanese invaders and French invaders, and they would drive out American invaders, too."

"I was brought up to believe it was Democracy versus Communism," Beth recalled.

"That was the hawks' mistake. To them it was Democracy versus Communism. To the Vietnamese it was natives against foreigners. That was the true pragmatic reality about Vietnam."

"The Vietnam War has been over for five years," Beth said with the impatience of the young toward history. "You'd think America would resolve it."

"The issue isn't just Vietnam. It's a matter of who decides how what's practical gets defined. *They* say the arms race is practical. We say it's suicidal and that a nuclear freeze is practical. *They* say you have to be pragmatic and balance ecology against economy. We say if you don't put ecology first, there won't be any people to have an economy. *They* say nuclear energy is necessary so we don't have to pollute the atmosphere by burning fossil fuels or be at the mercy of the Arab oil cartel. We say there are alternative technologies—solar, wind—and that our energy output can be cut fairly drastically without real hardship; we say that Three Mile Island and the other hundreds of accidents small and large at nuclear plants add up to no nukes."

"But *they're* still calling the shots," Beth pointed out.

"That can change. If there's one thing I've learned, it's that people *can* change things. If enough Quixotes tilt at the windmill, they topple it over. It starts with two or three visionaries walking around with placards and shouting into the wind. Maybe they're ignored, laughed at, but then a couple of other idealists join them. Now there are half a dozen of them, and that's a demonstration. A demonstration can create a groundswell. That's how a grass roots movement starts; that's how change begins."

"Like Sandburg? The People Yes?"

"Well, not quite." Diana laughed. "Most people probably get involved for all the wrong reasons—their needs, their power drives, their ambitions. But that doesn't really matter. More than Sandburg, it's what the founding fathers had in mind when they wrote the Constitution."

Beth was surprised at the allusion.

Diana explained. "Those old Colonial rebels knew what they were doing when they guaranteed the right of the people to peaceable assemblage in order to seek a redress of their grievances."

"In the end," Meyerling said, "those who truly had leadership potential among the anti-Establishment protestors are willingly co-opted by the American dream. It's ironic. They recognize the value of the system that created the climate that makes it possible for them to dissent. They accept it and eventually they rejoin it."

Holly was silent for a moment. It seemed as if she was mulling over what he'd said, and while in one sense she was, in another she was caught up in much more than the surface import of his discourse. He uses words to make love, she realized. All this talk is really aimed at getting me into bed. Does he do this with other women? Is that how he got his reputation as a Casanova? Am I simply sitting here, foolishly falling for the famous Meyerling technique?

The idea disturbed her. It made her voice sharp as she responded to him now. "That's simplistic," she said.

Meyerling registered surprise at her tone.

"Well, it is." Holly looked directly into his eyes. "And condescending, too. And smug. What you're saying is that there's no room for improvement, and that those who want to improve things will see the light and recognize how good they've got it."

He looked at her shrewdly. He understood that Holly was rejecting more than just his ideas. Somehow she had been offended by the overtures behind his words. But why? he wondered. She'd seemed so receptive before. "Well, don't they have it good?" he said carefully, continuing to ponder the change in her attitude.

"Some do, some don't. The homeless person sleeping on a grating in New York certainly doesn't have it so good. The migrant worker sprayed with insecticide doesn't have it so good. The farmer, the coal miner—"

Meyerling held up his hand placatingly. "I never said America was Utopia." He'd realized why her attitude had changed. She doubted his sincerity because at some level she was unsure of herself—and of him—and thought he was toying with her. But his interest was genuine. True, he desired her physically, but he was intrigued by her as a person as well. He knew he would have to make her understand that. He would have to move very slowly. "Only that it is an ideal in the making," he continued, "and the best possible ideal, considering man's basically animal nature."

"Darwin?" Holly grimaced. Animal nature indeed! That really was too obvious!

"And why not Darwin? If we concede evolution, how can we deny that we are animals?" His eyes looked into hers intensely. "There is more to animals, you know," he told her softly, "than breeding. They, too, know emotion. Even love."

Holly toyed with her profiterole. In the carpeted hush of the softly lit French restaurant, her head was whirling and her eyes sparkling with the vintage wine she'd consumed with dinner. Meyerling spun out ideas like a Fourth of July sparkler. Somehow he'd turned her around again. Not his words, but his intensity had convinced her that he was not just playing games, as he might with any attractive woman. His interest in her was genuine.

But was she interested in him? Holly asked herself. She wasn't sure; it had been so long since she'd allowed her emotions to be stirred, that she was no longer certain how to interpret their stirrings. Now, however, she forced herself to be honest. She admitted she found him attractive, that he was magnetic, intelligent, and very charming. And he was sexy; his reputation as a ladies man was not unfounded. His erotic intellectual talk and gently insistent dedication to his beliefs had undoubtedly been a great turn-on for many women. Yes, she was interested in him —and very attracted, both physically and intellectually.

She sighed. But that doesn't mean you have to sleep with him tonight, Holly reasoned with herself as she fought back the fierce desire to do just that. She was not ready for things to move too swiftly; of that she was sure. She looked at Meyerling across the table and smiled.

"Human beings are innately competitive, if not basically combative," Meyerling said, recognizing the latest change in Holly. Progress might be slow, he thought, but it would be worth it. "Humans are driven by animal urges to reproduce their species and to dominate other species. . . ."

"The world is a jungle and America has to hang tough." Diana snorted her disapproval. "That was the bottom line of the Establishment in the sixties, and it's still the bottom line today. It's the power brokers' universal rationale. The territorial imperative justifies everything. Those who don't dominate are dominated."

"It's a hard argument to answer," Beth suggested.

"No, it's not. Not when you see how it's ultimately used, where it leads. For instance, when the doves tried to redress their grievances like the Constitution says, the first thing they got hit with was that they were unpatriotic. It's as if this so-called 'basic' American right of dissent was only valid so long as it wasn't used. But aside from that, there was the fact that the Vietnam War was never declared. Actually, our generals were fighting it illegally. But they obscured the illegality with their universal justification. Man is innately aggressive, they said. He's an animal."

"Well, Darwin, after all—" Beth used the argument on Diana that had been so frequently directed at her.

"Darwin, my— Listen, if man is an animal, then why doesn't he behave like one? Other animals don't make wholesale attempts to destroy their own species. Besides, Darwin's just a way of justifying humanity's aggressive impulses. What about our philanthropic impulses? What about people helping people? It does happen, you know. Just as often as people killing people. No, the truth is that it's only a jungle out there if we agree to let it be a jungle. And with all those H-bombs floating around, that's a luxury we can't afford."

"Wow! You must have been dynamite in the sixties," Beth told Diana with a grin.

Diana laughed. "Oh, yeah. And would I do it all again? Just ask me. I do dearly love the sound of my own pronunciamentos. That and making love." She laughed again. "'Make love, not war!' When all's said and done, that may be the most important thing that came out of the sixties. The people's right to ball."

Beth winced.

"Does that offend you?"

"You sounded like my sister Carrie. Cheap sex. Any time. Any place. Any body. I hate that attitude. It's sleazy."

"You think sex is sacred or something?"

"No. But I don't think it should be like eating lunch either. I think it should have some special meaning. I don't think casual promiscuity is admirable."

Diana thought of her two lovers, George and Ernie. Oh, yes, it was going to be a problem having Beth around. It was definitely going to put a crimp in her love-life.

"But of course the urge to reproduce has political relevance." Meyerling answered Holly's skepticism as he added the tip to the check and signed it. His searching eyes, however, once again conveyed that there was more to such an urge than politics—and that the urge was pressing, if not urgent.

"What a convenient rationale for macho-man," Holly

210

retorted. More intellectual flirting, she realized. But now she welcomed it.

"Do I look like a macho-man?" Meyerling spread his well-manicured, slightly pudgy hands and blinked in a way that made his features seem even more owlish than usual. "I don't think so." He smiled. "Nevertheless, sex is a power drive as well as a reward for the exercise of power. And since this applies to women as well as men, it cannot be categorized as merely macho."

"Suppose it's true?" Holly stood as the headwaiter pulled the table out from the banquette for them. "What then?" The warmth suffusing her flesh was an echo. Indeed, what then?

"Why, it must be exercised." Adjusting Holly's light summer wrap around her smooth, porcelain-pale shoulders, Meyerling inhaled her perfume and nodded frank approval. "Power must always be exercised, or progress is left to chance—a toss of the coin. That's what really moves humankind forward, the exercise of power." His touch on her skin was firm and lingering.

"Well, considering how much sexual power *is* exercised," Holly laughed, aware that the conversation was proceeding—but not too quickly, thank goodness—from flirting to the inevitability of more tangible lovemaking, "it does seem as if the species should be a lot further along than it is."

"I was hoping *we* were further along," Meyerling murmured as he signaled to the doorman to whistle them a cab from the hack line waiting down the block.

"We?" Holly was again acutely aware of his lingering touch as he helped her into the back of the taxi. "The human race?"

"No." He settled beside her and turned so they were face to face. "We. You and I. Us."

And then, despite their banter the previous evening about not kissing on the first date, their lips willingly met and they kissed.

24

"WHAT HAPPENED AFTER the kiss?" Patrice wanted to know.

"After the kiss?" Holly squinted at her cousin across the oversized and streamlined modern teakwood desk. She couldn't see her clearly. The noontime sunlight pouring in the picture window of Patrice O'Keefe's executive office at Bartleby & Hatch blurred her face. "Zelig took me to Grand Central. He kissed me again, only this time it was good night, and he put me on the train. That was all."

"He didn't try to seduce you?" Patrice toyed with the frilly bow hanging out of her tailored jacket and thought of Jack Houston. "Dr. Zelig Meyerling, the stud of foreign policy, didn't even invite you up to his apartment?"

"You make me feel like I've failed some kind of test. Am I the only woman that Zelig ever went out with whom he didn't try to take to bed? My God! Did I have asparagus between my teeth? Should I check my deodrant?" Holly first giggled, then frowned.

"Sorry, cuz. It's your business. Only if it was me . . ."

"What, Patrice?" Holly wanted to know. "If it was you, what?"

Patrice searched her cousin's face for a moment. "I would not sentence myself to being a prisoner of chastity just because my marriage went kaput." The desk, the office, the skyline background—they all confirmed Patrice's executive authority. "I don't mean I'd turn into the queen of debauchery, but as the Governor would have put it, I would damn well sow a few of the wilder oats."

"That's not the way I am." Even as she said it, Holly knew it was a lie. There were nights when she burned with hunger for a man, any man. Her fantasies could be self-serving rather than loving, passionately immoral, and have little to do with tenderness or love. The truth was that at times her sexual hunger was so strong, she was

212

afraid if she gave in to it she'd lose control completely and not be able to stop. And that way lay a life-style Holly was certain she didn't want for herself. "Besides," she added, "I am still married to Christopher. I wouldn't want to give him any more ammunition to use against me in a divorce action."

"More ammunition? Then he does have some, doesn't he, Holly? And you haven't followed through on filing for divorce. Dad would have told me if you had." Patrice walked around from behind her desk and took both Holly's hands in hers. "I've been thinking about this a lot since the day we had lunch at the Algonquin," she said. "And there's only one conclusion I could reach. Christopher is holding something over you. He's blackmailing you. That's it, Holly, isn't it?"

Holly recalled her recent conversation with her grandmother. She'd promised Mary she would confide in someone. Patrice genuinely cared about her. Holly knew that. Patrice would understand in a way that Mary might not. Yes, if there was one person she could open up to about this, it was Patrice.

Slowly, Holly nodded in response to Patrice's surmise. "Yes." It was the first time she'd admitted it to anyone except her solicitor back in London. "Christopher is blackmailing me."

"I thought so. But you're not alone, Holly. You're a Stockwell. The family will back you up. Christopher can be made to realize what a powerful weight the Stockwell name is on your side. But you're going to have to trust us. Otherwise you'll be trapped in this marriage to Christopher for the rest of your life. And I don't think you want that."

Holly was silent for a long moment. Her hands, which Patrice had taken in hers, were holding on tightly now. Their responsive clutch was a plea, and also a sign of how fiercely she was working at summoning up the courage to speak. Finally, she did.

"Christopher has a letter," Holly said, looking directly into Patrice's eyes.

"A letter?"

"Yes." Holly let go of Patrice's hands. Her gesture sent Patrice back around her desk to her upholstered executive swivel chair. "From a girl—a young woman—named Winifred Fitzsimmons..."

The ancestral estate of Lord and Lady Fitzsimmons was adjacent to Millwood Manor in Sussex. After his marriage, Christopher had used Holly's money to restore his family property, and every autumn he had brought a group of friends up from London for the pheasant hunting.

Christopher and his friends called it "sport," but Holly didn't see how anything so one-sided as a barrage of gunfire against a flock of unarmed birds on the wing could be considered sporting. And so, when they left for what she thought of as the slaughter, Holly had a horse saddled up for herself and rode as far in the other direction as she could go. This particular day she had crossed the boundary line between the Millwood land and the Fitzsimmons estate without realizing it.

She'd ridden hard, and her horse was lathered, so she dismounted to walk him until he was rested. Leading the chestnut by the bridle, Holly heard the sound of a rippling stream, and mingled with it, the sounds of sobbing. A moment later she spied a young woman crumpled on the riverbank.

"Are you all right?" Holly said, thinking the girl might have fallen and hurt herself.

The woman sat up quickly, startled. "What? Oh! Yes, I—I—" Whatever she was going to say was lost in a fresh flood of tears. Her long mane of ribboned mahogany-colored hair was in wild disarray from the gouging of her frenzied fingers. It contrasted with the whitest skin and bluest eyes Holly had ever seen. Along with the slenderness of the girl's body, this contrast gave her an air that went beyond ethereal; she appeared otherworldly, her fragility and vulnerability wraithlike.

Holly went to her and put her arms around the sobbing girl. There seemed nothing else to do. Then, fiercely, the girl was grasping her as a drowning person grasps at a rescuer. Her fingers dug into Holly's arms and her face burrowed into Holly's breast so desperately that she later discovered one of her ribs had been bruised.

"Easy now," Holly said, unable to free herself from the girl's hysterical grip. "It will be all right."

214

Finally, after what seemed a long time, the girl's sobs transformed themselves into words. "Brett," she said. "Brett doesn't . . . said so . . . doesn't love me . . . Brett . . ."

"I realized she must have had a quarrel with a lover," Holly told Patrice. "Naturally I thought the lover—Brett— was a man."

"It wasn't a man?" Patrice looked carefully down at her fingers smoothing the bow out over her pinstriped lapels.

"No. Brett was a woman. Winifred—finally, she told me her name—was sobbing her heart out because she'd been rejected by her lover, a woman."

"But you're so young!" Inanely, that had been Holly's initial reaction when she realized what Winifred was telling her between her sobs.

"She said she loved me . . . that if I would . . . we'd always . . . But now she's gone with—I don't know her name—a cow with flaxen hair and big . . . you know."

"Well, perhaps you're well rid of her." Holly couldn't think of anything else to say.

"I want to die! I just want to die without Brett!"

"You'll meet someone else. A boy perhaps. A man. A handsome young man."

"A man?" Winifred released Holly and sat back and stared at her. "You really don't understand, do you? I don't want a man!"

"I only thought—"

"I can see what you thought—what you think. That I'm a freak, that's what. Unnatural." The laugh was harsh, a bray, out of keeping with Winifred's delicate pathos. "Don't you understand? I'm a lesbian, and I'm not ashamed. I'm tired of hiding it. I don't give a damn who knows!" The girl clenched her fists.

"Perhaps you'd better think that through," Holly suggested. "You're still very young."

"I know what I am, damn it! How I feel! Oh, damn!" She started crying again. "Of course you don't understand. The only one who ever understood is Brett, and now she's gone."

"I didn't mean to offend you," Holly said. "I only meant that your family is very prominent around here.

And this is Sussex, not London. People aren't very so-phisticated. If you start shouting out that you're a lesbian, they're probably not going to applaud. They will probably make you suffer, and make your family suffer, too."

"Well, I guess that's right enough," Winifred agreed sullenly. "So I'm right back where I was before Brett. No one to talk to but myself."

"You can talk to me," Holly told her. "If you like, you can talk to me."

"And that was the start of it," Holly told Patrice. "I became Winifred's friend, her confidante. She had nobody else. She was so young, so vulnerable. My heart really went out to her."

"Your heart went out to her?" Patrice's voice was care-fully nonjudgmental. "Do you mean you fell in love with her?"

"I did love her," Holly said. "But not the way you mean. Not the way Winifred would have liked me to, ei-ther. There was never anything physical between us. I wasn't drawn to that."

"You don't have to defend yourself. Everybody has those kinds of feelings."

"That's what Winifred said." Holly smiled. "But I guess I'm just too repressed. If I had them, I didn't know it. I was her friend. I cared about her. I loved her. But I didn't desire her, and I didn't want her sexually."

"But she wanted you?"

"Not at first. But later . . . well, yes."

"You must have driven her crazy."

"That's what she said." Holly sighed. "That's what she said just before she ran away from Sussex and went to London. . . ."

"Letter for you, love." Christopher had handed it to her.

Holly recognized Winifred's scent on the envelope. Christopher's eyes were on her. "Excuse me," she said. She went to her room and shut the door behind her. Then she opened the envelope and read:

Dear Holly,

When you receive this, I will be gone. But I will never forget you, my sweet, sweet Holly. At the time we met, I thought my life was over. You have made it worth living again. The tenderness of your touch, our long, lazy afternoons together in the woods, our woman-to-woman closeness—how much it has all meant to me.

Always I will dream of your loveliness—the warmth of your naked flesh in the sunlight as we bathed together in the stream, the gracefulness of your neck, your lovely limbs, the tenderness of your touch absolving me of blame for feelings which cannot be helped, the feelings that no one—not even Brett—brought out as strongly as did you, my own Holly.

I leave you with a kiss, and with the knowledge that when life is cold to me, I shall always warm myself with the fire of the memory of what we had together. Was it as meaningful to you, my sweet Holly, as it was to me? Or was I only "that silly Fitzsimmons girl" with whom you wiled away some lazy summer hours?

Ah, why do I torment myself with the question? My heart knows the answer. And so my love, I go. A part of you goes with me; a part of me remains behind. Treasure this truth as I do. It is a gift that only women who love one another truly know.

Always,
Winifred

"A love letter," Patrice summed up.

"Yes."

"From a woman."

"Yes." Holly shook her head sadly. "It was very compromising. The way it was written, it made it sound like there actually had been a physical relationship between us. Winifred had fits of deep depression, and I'd held her and rocked her as you would a child. On a couple of occasions in the summer we had taken off our clothes and swum in the stream together the way friends do—without it meaning anything. We'd kiss on the cheek when we met and when we parted—like you and I do, Patrice. I never gave any of that a second thought while it was happening. Only at the end, when I realized in Winifred's mind—"

"It all took on quite a different meaning," Patrice said, and nodded. "Yes, I can see how it would have. I mean, after all, you knew from the start that she was a lesbian."

"Well, yes. But that didn't make me treat her any differently. She was a kid in a lot of trouble, and she needed me. And I needed a friend, too. I liked her. I knew that she liked me, too, of course, but it never occurred to me that she would fall in love with me—not until right before she left."

"What did you do when she told you how she felt?"

"I tried to be gentle, but I was firm. I really was, Patrice. I told her it was impossible, that I couldn't have those feelings. She cried, and tried to convince me to just try making love with her once. But I wouldn't do it, and so she left."

"And then what happened?" Patrice wanted to know.

"About a week later Christopher confronted me with the letter. He'd taken it out of my bureau drawer and read it. I know it sounds stupid, but even though I knew his true character pretty well by that time—just how little regard he had for anybody's privacy but his own—it never occurred to me that he would do that."

"But he did."

"Yes. And he jumped to the conclusion that Winifred and I had been lovers."

"Well, you can't blame him for that."

"I blame him for not believing me when I denied it." Holly was bitter. "Christopher had always lied to me about his affairs, and now he assumed that I was lying to him. But that wasn't the worst of it."

"What was the worst?"

Holly started to answer, then broke off, shaking her head. Her face tightened, became harsh with humiliating memory.

"Holly!"

She took several deep breaths and expelled them. Finally she made herself speak the words. "He wanted me to arrange for him to sleep with Winifred and me together."

"Oh, Holly!" Her cousin was not so much shocked as indignant at the humiliation.

"He said he'd never been in the middle of a—a—a 'lesbian sandwich' before, but he'd always wanted to try it." Holly sat huddled now, her arms crossed over her breasts, clasping herself, her limbs turned into a fortress against the memory of degradation.

"The bastard!"

"I was numb. I couldn't believe he would make a demand like that. When he persisted, I finally had to believe it. That's when I told him I wanted a divorce."

"What was his reaction to that?"

"He didn't think I meant it until I actually filed. When I did that, and he realized I was serious, he told me he would never let me divorce him. He told me right out that the Stockwell name—the prestige and the money—were too important to him to give up."

"But how could he stop you?"

"He'd kept that letter from Winifred. He threatened to use it in the English divorce court. They're very prudish about such matters in England, you know. He could really have hurt me with it, and he also had outside testimony to corroborate that Winifred and I had had a lesbian relationship."

"Corroborating testimony?" Patrice was dismayed. "By who?"

"A stable boy at our house. Christopher had an affidavit from him saying he'd seen us embracing and kissing and that our clothes were opened and our breasts exposed."

"Was it true?"

"Partly." Holly was trembling from the memory. She composed herself. "One day we went swimming, and our blouses might not have been buttoned yet, although I'm sure that the bit about exposed breasts was an exaggeration. This was toward the very end of our friendship. She did hold me tight, trying to make it into more than I had ever meant for it to be. I pulled back, but at the same time I was trying not to hurt her feelings. I can see how that might have looked to someone who stumbled on us."

219

"You saw this stable boy then?" Patrice asked. "When he saw you, I mean."

"Yes. Briefly. He was there, and then he wasn't there. I shrugged it off at the time. I never dreamed anyone would turn it into anything more important than it was."

"But Christopher did."

"Well, he threatened to. Just as he threatened to use the letter from Winifred against me in divorce court. But I stood up to him. I'd already been to see my solicitor, you see, and he'd explained certain things to me."

"What sort of things?"

"That if Winifred testified in court as to the true meaning of what she'd written, her sworn statement would carry more weight than any inferences the other side might try to draw from the letter. If she testified under oath that there had never been anything between us, no affair, then neither the letter nor the stable boy's affidavit could stand up against that."

"And would she testify for you in court?"

"I was sure she would. And Christopher was sure she would, too. That's why instead of carrying through on his threat, he simply took off and avoided service of the divorce papers. He was convinced he'd lose, and so he simply disappeared."

"But now he's back. What's stopping you from filing for divorce here in New York now? He's here. You're here. Service wouldn't be any problem. From what you say, you'd be sure to win. What's changed?"

"Winifred's vanished." Holly raised her slender hands to her temples. "That's what's changed. Christopher has her letter and the stable boy's affidavit, and he's threatening to use them—to make them public if I try to divorce him. He says he'll file a countersuit for custody of Nicholas. And if he uses that letter and that affidavit, and I can't produce Winifred to testify to the true innocence of our relationship, then I could lose my son." A single tear followed the classical line of Holly's high cheekbone.

Briskly efficient, Patrice opened the left-hand drawer of her desk, took out a box of Kleenex, and handed Holly one. "Then what your problem boils down to," she said, her executive mind reducing the matter to its essentials, "is locating this Winifred Fitzsimmons. If she can be found and prevailed upon to testify, Christopher's case collapses and his threat to take Nicholas from you is meaningless."

"Yes. But I've tried to find her and failed. Just after the Governor died I wired my British solicitor, and he hired a private detective, but there haven't been any results."

"I'll talk to my father. He'll know what contacts the Stockwells have in London and put them to work on it. Scotland Yard maybe. I don't know. But Daddy will. And if that doesn't work . . . well, there is still one other possibility, Holly."

"What's that?"

"Christopher can be bought off."

"Yes," Holly sighed. "That's probably true. But it would take a lot of money, and he wants more than that. He wants to be able to throw his weight around as a member of the Stockwell family. I'm afraid that may be more important to him than any settlement."

"Well, we'll see. First we'll try to find Winifred Fitzsimmons." Abruptly, Patrice changed the subject. "Are you hungry?"

"Why, yes." How strange, Holly thought. She really was hungry. Telling Patrice about Winifred had been cathartic. "I'm starving."

"Then let's eat." Coming out from behind her desk, Patrice drew Holly to her feet, linked arms with her, and ushered her from the office and through the op-art reception room of Bartleby & Hatch. She paused at the reception desk to leave word where she could be reached for the next hour or so. Then she pushed the button for the elevator.

When it came, they went to lunch.

25

Aᴛᴛᴇʀ ʟᴜɴᴄʜ Pᴀᴛʀɪᴄᴇ parted from Holly and went back to her office. It was a pressure tank. Patrice was neck and neck with four male rivals for the vice presidency of Bartleby & Hatch in a race that had already been going on for three months. There was an office pool to pick the winner and the specific issue of *Advertising Age* in which the announcement would be made. The smart money in the office had just moved Patrice up from third to second place.

The fierce competition dictated that Patrice should have zeroed in on business to the exclusion of all else. The reason she hadn't was Jack Houston.

After the night they had slept together, she'd spent several weeks waiting hopefully for his call. When it didn't come, she sank into a deep depression. Then, when he finally did call, the anticipation had made Patrice too elated to concentrate on business. For the first time since her divorce from Miles O'Keefe, she considered whether her career really was the be-all and end-all of her life.

It wasn't that she wanted marriage and a family. Patrice had turned her back on that a long time ago, when she had divorced Miles. But wasn't there a middle ground? she wondered. Wasn't it possible to have a career and establish a stable relationship with one person? The most consuming career ought to leave room for that. A lot of women did it. Her cousin Michelle Carter, for instance, managed a husband and two kids along with her job as publisher of *Elite* magazine.

Yes, some kind of commitment to another person, and not just to the Bartleby and Hatch Advertising Agency. To Jack Houston? Patrice smiled at herself. My God, what was happening to her? One night with a man and she was already planning for their old age together. She ought to know better than that. Even in school she had not been one of those giggling girls who envisioned marriage after the third date. Jack's agreeing to escort her to the wedding reception hardly constituted a declaration of unending love. You've got it bad and that ain't good, girl, Patrice told herself. You'll scare him off, and he'll be right to run. Nothing's as much of a turn-off to a man as premature devotion. You're old enough to know better than that, and if you don't, you should. Despite her stern advice to herself, the possibility hovered in her mind, along with the twitch of a smile it brought to the corner of Patrice's lips.

"Laugh and the ratings go up." The smile was noticed as she passed the art director on her way to her private office.

"Tragedy tomorrow, comedy tonight." Patrice allowed her dimples free range. "What's up, Donny?"

"We got good news and we got bad news. State your order of preference, Little Bow Veep." The nickname paid tribute to both Patrice's sartorial trademark and the excellence of her chance for promotion.

"Don't call me that. You'll jinx me."

"You want the scuttlebutt, or not?"

"Scuttlebutt, no. Hard news, yes."

"Horse's mouth. The Dragon Lady herself." It was what the executive staff called Miss Plummer, private secretary to Stewart Bartleby, majority stockholder and president of the board of Bartleby & Hatch.

"Good news first, then," Patrice decided.

"Hazlett is out of the running."

"How come?" Patrice was pleased. Hazlett had been second choice to her third place, and had stayed a close third when she moved up to second.

"Mrs. Hazlett. Bartleby recognized her in a *Newsday* shot of a pro-choice picket line."

"That's a really lousy reason to scuttle him." Patrice's sense of fair play was often at war with her ambition. "What his wife does is her business. It had nothing to do with how fit Hazlett is to be an ad agency veep."

"Except when the ad agency handles a breakfast-food account for a company owned lock, stock, and barrel by the guy who finances the campaigns of every antiabortion congressional candidate in upstate New York."

"So it's down to four." Advertising was a dirty busi-

223

ness; so what else was new? Patrice accepted her good fortune, sure that she rated high above two of the four. "What's the bad news?" she asked Donny.

"Bartleby invited Panella to lunch at Lutèce tomorrow. Just the two of them."

"Ouch." Patrice whistled low in her throat. Panella was the one in the lead. Lunch with the boss just might cinch it for him. "Well, thanks, Donny. See you later." Patrice continued toward her office.

"With your shield, or on it?" Donny inquired of Patrice's retreating back.

Not on it. That was Patrice's undelivered answer when she sat down at her desk, found a message from her secretary to call Miss Plummer, and responded to it. Mr. Bartleby wanted to have lunch with her at Lutèce the day after tomorrow. Patrice's stomach unknotted. She was still in the running.

For the next hour she blotted out all thoughts of promotion, Holly's problems, and even Jack Houston. She focused totally on the ad campaign that Bartleby & Hatch would be submitting to Chase Manhattan. What would David Rockefeller think, Patrice wondered to herself toward the end of the hour, when he was told that a Stockwell—a grandchild of the Governor who had been a lifelong political rival of his brother Nelson—had conceived the campaign? Irrelevant, Patrice decided. She continued going over the execution of the concept with the fine-tooth comb of her mind.

Patrice was almost finished with her review when her secretary buzzed her to announce that Mr. Tyler was here to see her. Damn! Patrice had forgotten that she'd given Max Tyler an appointment today. She had agreed to it reluctantly, and now she was just as reluctant to keep it. Still—Patrice thought of her father—family is family. "Show him in," she told her secretary.

"I'm a little strapped for time today, Max," she greeted him, unwittingly putting him on the defensive.

"Then I'll come right to the point. I want you to create the ad campaign for my insurance company."

Patrice stared at him. "Your insurance company," she repeated. And then she remembered Max's declaration of his intention to start a firm that would provide insurance

224

at fair rates to the gay community. "Then you're really going ahead with your plans," she said.

"Oh, yes. I've already filed for incorporation. In Delaware, on my lawyer's advice."

"And now you're ready to be listed on the big board." Patrice was being ironic.

"Not quite." The look his new—moon—like hazel eyes deliberately bestowed on Patrice was the one that frequently made women think he hated their gender, although he really didn't. "My sister Diana and I are the only stockholders, and we'll keep it that way for a while."

"Then the two of you have financed this project all by yourselves?"

"Oh, yes."

"And against my father's advice and wishes."

"I'm afraid so. Still, James didn't put any obstacles in our way. He was really very decent."

"My father is very decent," Patrice said with emphasis.

"I never doubted it for a moment." Max smiled placidly.

"But since my father *is* against this, and since I agree with him, why come to me to do your ad campaign?"

"Two reasons. You have a very good reputation in the banking, financial, and insurance communities. And since Bartleby and Hatch isn't quite up there with the top ten agencies, we should be able to afford you."

"I see." Patrice thought a moment. "You know, with this battle over the estate shaping up, I'm not sure—" She broke off and then said carefully, "Where do you and your sister Diana stand?"

"Nowhere really." Max shrugged. "There's no reason to take sides."

"Does that apply to all the Tylers?" Her father, Patrice knew, would be interested in Max's answer.

"I don't really know. I would assume it does, though."

"Their support—the twins and their father, you and Diana, even Louise in Greece, and Alfred and Lizzie—it could add up. It could really help against Buffy."

"I suppose." Max was purposely noncommittal. "I can't speak for the other Tylers," he said, "but as far as Diana and I are concerned, we're only interested in our own welfare. We don't plan to take sides. But if there were

225

some advantage to be had..." The hazel eyes regarded Patrice blandly. "Is there?"

"There usually is some advantage to declaring yourself in such matters," Patrice told him cryptically. Perhaps taking this account would keep Max and Diana on their side. "Now, about this campaign of yours—"

"Then you'll take it on?"

"I don't know. Let's talk cost."

Patrice fired off a series of pertinent questions. Max answered them without hesitation, the information obviously at his fingertips. Impressed with his businesslike responses, Patrice made notes and jotted down figures. Finally she looked up at him and gave him a cost estimate. "Of course you'd have to figure a ten percent overrun," she added.

"That's too much. Can you shave it?"

"Sure. A campaign can always be shaved. But you give up market penetration."

"My potential market is concentrated, geographically and sociologically. We don't need penetration over a wide spread." Inside, Max was smiling at his choice of words. "Targeted penetration will do. Shouldn't that be cheaper?"

"If you really can identify your market that narrowly, yes."

"We can. That's the whole idea."

"All right, then." Patrice quickly reworked her figures. She told him the bottom line.

"In the ballpark." Max nodded, but reserved the right to shave a bit more here and there when they got down to particulars. "Now what do we get for that?"

"The first thing you get is a new name for your company. Gay Life Benefits and Mutual Fire is just plain too flip. Insurance is a serious matter involving serious decisions. Gay or straight, people don't want plays on words, or gimmicks. They want to know they're giving their business to a company that takes the responsibility seriously, not to one that's into innuendo and wordplay."

"I take your point." Max nodded slowly. "What do we call it then?"

"I don't know yet. We run a small survey—nothing big or expensive, just a select questionnaire confined to the gay community where we try out certain insurance code words. The ones that get the most positive results will determine the name of the company. The survey will also point the direction our campaign should take. We hold off on formulation until that's done."

Patrice looked pointedly at her Rolex. They'd gone as far as they could go for the time being. It was a polite hint for Max to leave.

He took it. He got to his feet. "Do you want a retainer?" he inquired.

"Not yet. First I have to clear our taking the account with Mr. Bartleby. It's a new area for us, after all."

"Insurance?" Max was deliberately dense.

"No. The gay market." Patrice countered with bluntness. "I'm not sure Bartleby and Hatch will want to be identified with it. There's our image on the Street to be considered, after all."

"On Madison Avenue? You've got to be kidding!"

Patrice's afternoon went by quickly after Max Tyler left. At five-thirty she put the Chase Manhattan campaign-proposal material away and shut up shop for the day. She left the office and walked east on Fifty-third Street to Maria's Cin-Cin, "the home of the purple martini," where she was meeting her cousin Michelle Carter for a cocktail.

The two had gotten into the habit of having an after-hours drink together on a casual once-a-week basis about a year ago. The origin of their meetings had been a family gathering where Patrice and Michelle had discovered that as the only two career woman executives of the Stockwell clan, they had a lot in common. They weren't close friends—they had never been that and probably never would be—but they had a genuine understanding of each other's problems as women on the fast track of what was still basically a man's world.

In contrast to her cousin, Michelle looked like her mother Alice, and indeed like many of the other young wealthy women of privileged Hudson Valley families. Her ash-blond hair had just a little too much curl and was a tad too long to be truly stylish, and her tall figure had a little too much weight to carry off the Perry Ellis's, Calvin Klein's, and Ralph Lauren's she habitually wore. With her long, full face and a small straight nose, Michelle was just shy of being pretty. An attractive smile, a little less makeup, a sparkling personality would have gone a long way to compensate, but Michelle was just too busy and too harassed to accommodate the prerequsites of beauty. Despite Patrice's innate conservatism, she outshone her cousin, partly because Patrice's personality was more dynamic, her personal life more placid, and her looks better endowed by nature.

Together they felt free to drop their facades of crispness and efficiency, and they did so now, both wincing at the waitress's suggestion that they try the purple martini. They ordered vodka gimlets instead, and when the drinks came they both quaffed them deeply, grinning at their mutual unwinding.

"How are Andrew and the kids?" Patrice paid lip service to home and hearth.

"Robin's teething," Michelle replied, referring to her year-old daughter. "I was up half the night with her."

"Did Andrew get up?"

"Are you kidding? You and I may have come a long way, baby, but not investment bankers. At Goldman, Sachs they're not into house husbanding—or child care." Michelle drained off the rest of her gimlet and signaled the waitress for another round. "I'm lucky he condescends to drop off Danny at pre-K," she added, referring to their four-year-old.

"Comes the revolution . . ." Patrice sympathized.

"It won't make any difference. Marriage sucks. You were smart to get out of yours."

"Funny you should say that. Lately I've been wondering." Reacting to Michelle's raised eyebrows, Patrice added, "Oh, I'm not thinking of getting married again or anything like that, but it would be nice to have a serious relationship."

"All relationships with men are foreign entanglements. Beware them."

Given Michelle's present attitude, Patrice decided against confiding about her fantasies concerning Jack Houston. She changed the subject. "How's the situation at the office?" she asked.

"On a par with home." She scowled. "Sorry. I'm in a foul mood." She put a considerable dent in the second gimlet. "What's happening at your shop? How's the veep contest going?"

Patrice told her about Hazlett being eliminated and both she and Panella being asked separately to lunch at Lutece by the head of the agency. "What's the score up at *Elite?*" she asked in return.

"Accounting one hundred, publisher zero." It was the reason for Michelle's bitterness. "We don't have an editorial policy anymore. All we have is a balance sheet. Publisher Michelle Lewis Carter." She snorted. "Strictly a paper title."

"Well, it's a magazine, but it is a business, too. Profits are relevant."

"Relevant, sure. And of course it's a business. I'm just not so sure *Elite* is a magazine any more. Your father's CPA's are turning it into a strictly monkey-see, monkey-do publication. They compare profit-and-loss statements with *Good Housekeeping* and decide we should run apple pie recipes. Apple pie, for God's sake! Or they find out *People* sales are up and begin chopping all our in-depth articles down to three paragraphs. It drives the editors crazy, and it drives the decent writers away. Believe me, if *Playboy* picks up two percentage points, they'll demand I fire the art department and start running foldout centerspreads of porn queens."

Patrice responded indirectly to the reference to James's accountants. "Have the sales gone up with their recommendations?" she asked.

"Of course not. And they won't either. They're floundering. What they don't understand is that a magazine has to have a firm identity and build on it. First you establish what you are, then you create readership loyalty step by step. It takes originality, and it takes time. If I had control . . ."

Patrice looked at Michelle shrewdly. "The rumor is that you're moving in that direction. You and Andrew. You've been picking up stock options for *Elite*, haven't you?"

"Suppose we have? What's wrong with that?" Michelle was defensive.

"You know what's wrong with that." Patrice regarded her cousin with impatience. "Computer transactions, that's what's wrong. If the stock goes below a certain point, the options are automatically activated and you've bought in heavy—maybe even heavy enough to throw your weight around. What's wrong is that the magazine sales have to go down for the stock to get to that point. You're the publisher. You should be working to increase sales. I'd say that was a conflict of interest."

"Did you meet me to make accusations?"

"Sorry. I didn't mean to come on quite so strong. I just thought you should know that the conflict of interest has not gone unnoticed by the powers that be."

"Meaning your father?"

"Yes. And Peter. And your father, too. Have you thought about that, Michelle? If you keep it up, you're going to be opposing your father at a time when he needs all the support he can get."

"Is it my father you're worried about, Patrice? Or your father and his holy troika?"

"It's you I'm concerned about, believe it or not. You might try to keep in mind that your father is one of the three members of that troika. Damn! I hate that word of Buffy's!"

"My father?" Michelle's smile was not pleasant. "Let me tell you something about my father, Patrice. He doesn't give a damn about his children. And he sure as hell doesn't act in their best interest. That's why I have no intention of worrying about *his* best interest."

"What do you mean?"

"My brother Mark. That's what I mean. If it hadn't been for my father, he would never have gone to Vietnam. He'd be alive today!"

"Oh, Michelle, you can't blame your father—"

"The hell I can't! I can and I do! And I can assure you, Patrice, that it's not his interests I'm concerned about, it's mine up at *Elite*. If that affects your father in the fight that's shaping up with Buffy, I'm sorry."

"You're only talking this way because your upset," Patrice's tone was meant to calm Michelle, not patronize.

It didn't succeed. Michelle jumped to her feet. She fumbled in her handbag, pushing her credit card aside and looking for money. "If my father and yours don't like my going for control with options, then tell them to make me publisher in more than name only," she snarled.

"Never mind the check. I'll get it."

Michelle ignored the offer. Her fumbling became agitated. "Because if they don't, I'm going to lay hands on a lot more stock than they ever dreamed I would."

"What do you mean? Where would you get that kind of money?"

"Where do you think?"

Patrice stared at her cousin. "Buffy," she realized. "But you wouldn't, Michelle. You wouldn't sell Grandma and the family down the river that way."

Michelle found some bills and flung them down on the table. She smiled bitterly. "It's a tough world, Patrice. That's what being a Stockwell's taught me. When it comes to blood versus money, it's always a toss-up."

"I know you've got good reason to be teed off, Michelle, but don't do this. You'll regret it," Patrice pleaded.

"I haven't done anything yet. But if things don't change at *Elite* soon..." Michelle held up a fist. Then she bent, kissed Patrice quickly and unexpectedly on the cheek, and started to leave.

"Listen, Michelle, don't go like this. Let's talk. You can't seriously be thinking about selling out to Buffy."

"Maybe I am," Michelle said over her shoulder, ignoring Patrice's plea to say, "and maybe I'm not." She vanished into the dimness of Maria's Cin-Cin. Her voice came back out of it just before she exited. "See you at the wedding, Patrice."

26

SOMEWHERE IN THE cosmos that June wedding day there may have been a cloud, but not above Riverview. Here the sky was cerulean, lit by a glorious sun that was balmy, not blazing. Its pale golden light lent additional splendor to afternoon frocks from the most exclusive designer salons of Paris, Milan, and New York.

Interspersed amongst the Matisse-like prints, puffed silk

sleeves, and layered tiers of chiffon, were well-groomed men in lightweight made-to-order suits and blazers accented by four-in-hand cravats and pocket handkerchiefs from Tripplers, or subtly patterned shirts from Pierre Cardin and Miguel Cruz. They snared goblets of champagne confidently from gleaming sterling silver trays of the liveried waiters who moved among them. As became people of breeding, their discourse was cultured, their voices muted.

Suddenly, for a split second, even the muted voices were silenced. Then, just as abruptly, almost as if the silence itself had been a breach of etiquette, they resumed. Well-bred homage had been paid to an eye-catching entrance.

The entrance had been made by Buffy Stockwell on the arm of attorney Halsey De Vilbiss. Though his was the first yachting jacket to arrive on the scene—a double-breasted sky-blue affair with gold officer trim set off by a white silk ascot—he was barely noticed. As blatantly Southern Californian as his attire was, it stood no chance of stealing Buffy's thunder.

Stepping into the sunlight at the top of the wide stone steps leading down to the terrace, Buffy's Bill Blass gown —an original crafted exclusively for the occasion—was one-shouldered with a large starched ruffle on the one long sleeve. The emerald-blue gown clung to her tall body with its full bosom, voluptuous hips, and rounded derriere, ending above trim ankles strapped into high heels. Provocative attire for a garden wedding, she was nonetheless admired by the fashion-conscious women and figure-appraising men.

Not bad for knocking fifty, De Vilbiss thought to himself. Even close up, Buffy's complexion was tawny smooth, her mane of wavy blue-black hair softening her aquiline features, and her classic visage worthy of immortalization on a Greek coin. Better than not bad. Nearing the half-century mark or not, the lady could compel even the most critical eye.

Holly, herself demure in a matching mauve blouse and skirt of Irish handkerchief linen with a white pierrot collar piped in mauve, was reminded of a remark the Governor had once made. "She's a force of nature," he'd murmured, observing Buffy make a similarly late entrance at a banquet he was hosting. "You can't take issue with an earthquake for its timing; you can only stand in awe of it and try to steer clear of the aftershock."

Holly was standing with the bride and groom in front of a massive Henry Moore sculpture which appeared to float in the Riverview lily pond. Behind her she could hear Riverview's head gardener, Gustav Ulbricht, muttering darkly about the effect of casually spilled champagne on the water blossoms he had so carefully cultivated.

"I didn't notice Buffy at the church," Lizzie Tyler, looking regal in an ecru silk gown, remarked to her new husband. Standing side by side, sipping champagne from antique crystal toasting goblets, they radiated a happiness that belied their age.

"Then she must not have been there." Being a surviving twin, Alfred had discovered late in life some of the dry humor that had once been the province of his brother—Lizzie's first husband—John. "If she were there, you can be sure Buffy would have been noticed."

"By you?" Lizzie made a mock moue, then laughed good-naturedly. "On our wedding day?" She reached up and tapped his cheek with her fingers, a play slap just under his faded red-gold sideburns. "Shame on you."

"Be glad I notice, sweetling." Alfred winked one hazel eye and adjusted his vest. "It bodes well for the honeymoon."

"Sixty-seven years old and he's still got a one-track mind," Lizzie sighed happily to Holly. "That's why I married him. Before I die, I want to be surprised."

"Astonished is what she'll be!"

"Give him two tranquilizers and call me in the morning." Holly laughed with Lizzie. "Excuse me."

She'd noticed that Buffy had left her escort standing all alone. The man obviously didn't know anybody. A conscientious hostess, Holly brought him a glass of champagne and introduced herself.

Halsey de Vilbiss told her his name in return. "Buffy said she'd be right back, but somehow I don't think..." He let the sentence trail off with a casual gesture.

Following it with her eyes, Holly saw Buffy standing beside a small, white wrought-iron garden table where Patrice was seated across from Jack Houston. Fanning herself with her hand, Buffy was leaning into the shade provided by the awning over the table as if trying to escape the heat of the sun. It wasn't that hot, Holly realized. At first she was amused by the blatant intrusion. Then, as Buffy bent low with her semiexposed bosom to say something obviously arch, Holly felt annoyed for Patrice.

Jack Houston got to his feet. Patrice's smile was bright, her nod forced. Of course she didn't mind. Holly could almost hear the tone in which she spoke the words. Buffy led Jack to the dance platform at the south end of the patio. The twelve-piece orchestra was playing an old-fashioned fox trot. Immediately Buffy and Jack were dancing as if their bodies had been fused.

Holly looked back at Patrice. Alone at the table, her petite form looked forlorn. Her fingers twirled a chestnut curl as if to punish her coiffure for having let her down. She took a pair of prescription sunglasses from her small purse and put them on as she returned her gaze to the dance floor. Her clenched hand squeezed the white bow tie attached to the blouse on top of her navy blue-and-white polka-dot dress. Holly couldn't help but notice that Patrice's attire—although eminently suitable for a wedding—looked schoolgirlish compared to Buffy's clinging gown. Suddenly, abruptly, Patrice stood and strode purposefully toward the dance floor.

Startled, Holly looked back toward the pavilion. Buffy and Jack were no longer there. Shifting her gaze, Holly was just in time to see them slipping into the east parlor of the mansion through the open French doors. Patrice was moving after them.

"Excuse me."

Holly had been neglecting Halsey De Vilbiss. Before she could apologize, however, she realized that his "Excuse me" had signaled his leave-taking. It was followed by a slight bow, and then he was walking away. Watching him, Holly got the decided impression he was following Patrice as she followed Buffy and Jack.

As it happened, that was exactly what Halsey De Vilbiss was doing. The look on Patrice's face as she followed the couple had interested him. Patrice Stockwell O'Keefe was one of those who would be aligned against them in the battle over the Governor's estate. They couldn't afford to alienate her more. She was obviously distraught at her escort being shanghaied by Buffy. And so, casually, he followed in Patrice's wake.

Also trying to appear casual, Patrice went through the French doors and wandered from the parlor into the hallway of the east wing. Although it was daylight, the hallway, where the Governor had ensconced his early purchases of post-impressionist paintings, was illuminated by hidden track lighting. As she moved from Duchamps, Picasso, and Dali to Kandinsky and Franz Klein, their color splashed Patrice's eyes.

She heard voices. The door to a sitting room was ajar. Standing in the shadow without being seen, Patrice observed Buffy and Jack.

Buffy's hands were clenching Jack's upper arms and shaking him slightly. His head was lowered, truculent. Their posture, Patrice realized, betrayed an intimacy that could not have been new.

"Yes," Jack was saying in a low, defiant voice, "I used her. I had no choice."

"And did you have to go to bed with her again to persuade her to invite you here today?" Buffy's tone was accusing.

"No, I didn't."

"You think I believe that?"

"You should. I don't lie to you. I never have, Buffy. I told you when I made love to Patrice. And now I'm telling you I didn't make love to her a second time."

"The day is young." Buffy was cynical.

"Please. As it is, I'm ashamed of myself for leading Patrice on. She's really very nice. Believe me, I wouldn't take further advantage of her."

"If you're so ashamed, my sweet, why did you do it?"

"To be here at Riverview with you. To see for myself what it is that's so much more important to you than what we've got."

"What we've got, angel, has a name. 'Sex.'"

"It's more than that, Buffy, and you know it." Jack was earnest. He also had suspicions of his own. Now he voiced them. "You said you didn't want me here today

235

because it would compromise your widow's status. Then you make your entrance with that joker in the tinseltown threads? Who is he anyway? What's he to you?"

"Jealousy?" Buffy was amused. "You really are such a boy sometimes, Jack. For a man whose been the places you've been and done the things you've done, you behave like some infatuated teenager."

"Answer my question! Who the hell is he?"

"He's Halsey De Vilbiss, my lawyer." Buffy looked up into Jack's eyes with more than a little genuine affection. "He wanted to size up the family opposition for himself. This seemed like the perfect opportunity."

"Your lawyer." Jack was abashed. "Well, what does he think your chances are?"

"He's quite hopeful, darling. Just like you." Buffy's cynicism reasserted herself. "All that delicious money. Dear Jack. You practically lick your chops when the subject comes up."

"Damn it, Buffy! That's not fair! You know I don't give a damn about the money! It's you I love! You!" He seized her firmly and crushed her mouth with his. As soon as the brutal kiss was over, he kissed her a second time, slowly, deeply, lingeringly. "You."

"If you love me, darling, then help me," Buffy murmured, nestling in his arms. "Patrice is infatuated with you, and she's very close to her father. He confides things to her about business. Perhaps you could find out—"

"Never!" Jack moved apart from Buffy as he protested hotly.

"It doesn't matter. I'm afraid that wouldn't work anyway."

The male voice interrupting their heated tête-à-tête took them both by surprise. It was Buffy who finally answered the interloper. "Why not?" she asked.

"Because," De Vilbiss told them, "Patrice is on to you. I met her coming down the hall only a moment ago. She was—and I think it is an accurate description—crying a river."

"She heard us." Jack was appalled.

"Just about everything, I should think. You were just ending your first kiss and starting your second one when I came on the scene. My impression is that she bolted with the initial pucker."

"The poor kid!" Jack sounded really ashamed.

"Go easy on the *mea culpa*, my darling," Buffy told him. "After all, your relationship was casual. Carnal but casual," she amended. "You didn't break her heart, you only bruised her ego."

"I'm not so sure." De Vilbiss said. "Anyway, speaking as your lawyer now, I want you two lovebirds to cool it. A widow is an object of sympathy, but a grass widow definitely isn't. Do I make myself clear?"

"Too damn clear!" Jack's fists were clenched. He didn't like this Hollywood hotshot. Not one little bit.

Buffy's hand on Jack's arm calmed him.

"Good." De Vilbiss smiled slightly at the efficacy of her gesture. He turned on his heel and left them.

Back in the garden, De Vilbiss ran into Holly. "Would you like to dance?" he asked her.

"All right."

As they moved onto the pavilion and started dancing, another couple glided smoothly past them. "That's Susan Gray the actress, isn't it?" De Vilbiss said to Holly.

"Yes."

"She sure does like them young."

"That's her son," Holly told him coldly. She was liking Halsey De Vilbiss, with his outré Hollywood yachtsman's outfit and slick gangster moustache, less and less.

"Oh. I thought— Well, on the coast the papers were full of her and this young actor."

"I know."

"And I knew his predecessor—the attorney who tried to rearrange his nose in the nightclub."

"The way I heard it, it was the lawyer who got the worst of it," Holly remembered.

"That's true."

"Justice," Holly decided.

"Why do you say that?"

"When a Hollywood lawyer gets thrashed, it's bound to be justice."

"I'm sort of a Hollywood lawyer myself."

"Are you?" Holly murmured. Suddenly Buffy's relationship with this overdressed, overslick outsider she'd chosen to escort her to the reception came into focus. "Are you indeed?"

They finished dancing in silence.

When the music ended, Susan Gray and her son preceded Holly and De Vilbiss from the dance pavilion. Just to the right of them on the terrace, an angry female voice was raised, filling the void left by the orchestra. In the silence it was particularly loud and jarring.

". . . even care that you're killing people!" Beth Tyler, hazel eyes blazing, was furious.

"Your righteousness doesn't entitle you to scream at me like a banshee." Peter Stockwell's reply was muted, reasonable, and supercilious.

"Am I embarrassing you, Peter? Well, good!"

"You're embarrassing the entire family."

"Not that! Not the mighty Stockwell clan! It's all right to poison the rivers and poison the air, but it's not good form for a Stockwell—not even a Stockwell thrice removed like me—to raise her voice in protest. Oh, no! That embarrasses the family!"

Peter's dark eyes narrowed as he spoke, "Do you know how ridiculous you are, Beth?"

"Ridiculous!" Beth quivered, the strands of her red-gold hair blurring in the sunlight.

"Bethie." Diana Tyler was coming up fast to try to control her cousin, but not fast enough.

"Ridiculous!" Beth flung her full goblet of champagne in Peter's face.

His response was instinctive. But as his burly hand came up to slap Beth, it was stayed by a viselike athlete's grip from behind which robbed it of its momentum.

"You don't really want to do that, cousin." Deke Wells's voice was soft and reasonable.

Peter didn't fight it. Instead, with his other hand he reached into his pocket for a handkerchief to wipe the champagne from his face.

Deke stepped between him and Beth, facing her. Unconsciously her fist was around the stem of the empty champagne glass and she was wielding it like a deliberately smashed beer bottle in a barroom brawl. Now Deke pried it free of her hand.

"Why don't we get you another glass of champagne, and maybe one for me, too." Deke's face with its infield tan beamed down on her.

Beth moved her head vigorously from side to side as if shaking off a daze. Her sleek, neatly combed apricot hair swirled over the pinstriped white-and-green organdy sundress she was wearing. "All right," she agreed finally, expelling the words with a deep, trembly breath.

"And you can tell me what you've been up to for the last twelve years." Deke guided her away from the onlookers. "Except for the Governor's funeral, that's as long as it's been, hasn't it? You were about six years old, and now you're . . . eighteen, is it?"

"Eighteen. Yes."

"Well, you're certainly grown up. And you twins still look exactly alike." Deke snagged two goblets of champagne from a passing tray as deftly as if he were fielding a pop-up. "Now don't be angry, but just which one are you?"

"Beth. I'm Beth."

"Beth. And Carrie is your sister." He handed her one of the crystal glasses. "Well, what have you been up to for the past twelve years, Beth?"

"I start college in the autumn." What a silly answer, Beth thought to herself even as she spoke the words. "Bryn Mawr. Unless I change my mind," she added, and then felt that was even sillier. "What have you been up to?"

"Oh, playing a little baseball." Deke grinned self-deprecatingly. "For the Boston Red Sox . . ."

Cute! Observing Deke Wells with her twin, interest stirred in Carrie. Good chest and shoulders, and from the way he'd grabbed Peter before, his muscles must be hard. He'd be wasted on Beth, of course. She wouldn't know a stud from a dud in a men's shower room.

Beth looked interested in him, and that was reason enough for Carrie to be interested, too. Competition was a rule of twindom. Funny, Carrie thought, how she'd been born knowing that while Beth had not yet really come to terms with it.

"You've recovered, I see."

Carrie turned to find Michael Stockwell at her elbow. "Yes." She had to tilt her head to look up at him. He was tall, like his father. At twenty-five he was already blessed with the image all politicians covet: distinguished and trustworthy. "I've recovered." She grinned up at him.

From her early teens Carrie had been intrigued by Michael. There were always innuendos floating around family gatherings regarding Michael and girls. When she was twelve and Michael was nineteen or so, he'd been sent down from Harvard because of a scandal involving some Radcliffe girl. Stockwell influence got him reinstated so he could go on to law school there. After his graduation Carrie had kept up with his mildly scandalous involvements via the gossip columns.

Then, quite suddenly, about a year before the Governor died, Michael had apparently reformed. Seemingly overnight he turned into the soul of discretion. His name no longer appeared in the scandal sheets, and his romantic exploits faded from the public consciousness. Once Michael had decided to go into politics, his new image was spanky clean.

Carrie rather preferred the former Michael. Now she looked up at him speculatively. "I've been wanting to thank you for rescuing me from the clutches of the Riverview Heights narcs," she told him.

"Self-interest," Michael admitted freely. "The primary's next week, and I don't want drugs associated with the Stockwell name."

"Sounds wise," Carrie granted. "How does the primary look?"

"I'll win it."

"And the election? Will you be going to Congress?"

"That depends. If Reagan wins big, I might just slide in on his coattails. And he should win big with the Ayatollah on our side. The Iranian hostage situation has made Jimmy Carter a very unpopular incumbent."

"Can you run on the same platform with Reagan? I mean, the Stockwell family has always been known as the backbone of liberal Republicanism." Carrie, who unlike Beth wasn't really interested in politics, was quoting her father.

240

"Strange bedfellows." Michael shrugged.

"My favorite kind." Carrie's almond-shaped hazel eyes looking up at him were suddenly quite bold.

"And from what I hear, you don't find any shortage. You know, Carrie, you're pretty young to be doing what you're doing. Lord knows I have no claim to being a moralist, but I'm really worried about you. Cocaine. No one wants to see you snort your life away."

"A lecture?" Carrie swiveled her head. "This is hardly the place, Michael." She took his hand. "Come with me."

"Where are we going?" Michael was taken by surprise, but he accepted her lead docilely enough and walked alongside her down the winding garden path leading into the woods.

"The gazebo. You can reform me there to your heart's content without going public."

"Hey!" Michael protested. "This really isn't a role that comes naturally to me."

"You'll get the hang of it." A few moments later they reached the gazebo. Carrie seated him on a wrought-iron bench inside the tree-shielded structure and stepped back. "Now, you were saying?"

"Just that I've done my share of partying, but cocaine's something else, Carrie. You could really hurt— Hey!" Michael half rose from the bench. "What are you doing?"

Carrie's two hands were up under her full tangerine-colored taffeta skirt. "Just cooperating with being reformed, Michael." She wriggled briefly. Her panties dropped out from under the billowing skirt to her slim ankles. "You were saying about your experiences?" She kicked her panties aside. "And about your concern over me." She straddled Michael's lap, facing him. "I'm really touched by your concern." She pulled down the top of her strapless bodice and took out one firm, pear-shaped naked breast. "And I promise to be a good girl, Michael." She held the nipple, taut, red, and very long, to his lips. "And when I'm good," she crooned, reaching between her thighs to unzip his fly and release his thick, hard, throbbing penis, "I am very, very good." Holding it in her eager hand, Carrie rose up and then came down slowly, savoring the moment of penetration to the hilt. "And when I'm bad," she panted, "I am torrid."

"Jesus!" Michael began to move grindingly.

"Very torrid!" Carrie moved hungrily with him, gently squeezing the swollen sac containing his testicles with her hand as she did. "Now let's fuck!"

The sounds were unmistakable. Kathleen O'Lunney heard them coming from behind the curtain of leaves shielding the gazebo. Of course, she did not intrude.

She had cut through the woods from the servants' quarters to have a look at the festivities. She wasn't planning on crashing the party. She was simply curious to see the end product of all the preparations.

Now, veering away from the gazebo, Kathleen spied a moustached man wearing a yachtsman's jacket emerging from the underbrush. He must have been investigating the sounds of lovemaking. He hadn't been so dedicated a voyeur, however, as to wait around for the conclusion. The sounds were still audible as he moved away and passed from Kathleen's view without having seen her. Kathleen didn't recognize him and thought there was something furtive in his manner.

Her bright red hair and freckles made Kathleen easily visible as she continued to move briskly through the woods toward the garden party. James Stockwell, seeking relief from the chatter of the crowd, immediately recognized his chauffeur's daughter coming toward him on the path. "Just what the party needs," he greeted her. "A really pretty young lady." Vanessa Brewster had been a liberating influence on him. James had always been shy with attractive young women, and could now deliver a compliment without strain.

"But I've not been invited, Mr. Stockwell." Kathleen returned his smile, and looking down at the wrinkled cotton skirt of her white sundress, added, "And I'm not properly dressed."

"Nonsense. I'm inviting you right now." He linked her arm in his and turned back toward the terraced gardens. "And beauty sets its own style." With his newfound charm, he propelled Kathleen to the dance pavilion and led her into, of all things, a waltz.

"A waltz!" Buffy was remarking to Halsey De Vilbiss, who had just rejoined her. "Bride and groom or not, that is the sort of corny request that should have been resisted."

"They seem to be enjoying it." De Vilbiss nodded toward Alfred and Lizzie Tyler twirling blissfully to the strains of Johann Strauss. His eyes moved beyond them to James Stockwell waltzing with a redheaded girl. "Who's that with the troika czar?" he asked Buffy.

She smiled at the label. "The chauffeur's daughter," she told him. "Kathleen O'Lunney. Backstairs rumor hath it that she's involved with James's son Matt."

"The draft dodger?"

"Yes." Buffy flashed him a look of irritation.

"An upstairs-downstairs romance." De Vilbiss thought about it. "And what's Daddy's attitude toward that?" he wondered.

"Quite positive, I should say. Just look at him."

De Vilbiss looked. Buffy was right. James was beaming at Kathleen. "Mmm." He filed away the Matt Stockwell-Kathleen O'Lunney romance in the archives of his brain along with all the other juicy tidbits he was picking up at the Riverview wedding reception.

Unaware of being observed by the man he might one day have to face in court, James Stockwell had been thinking of his eldest son Matthew as he danced with Kathleen O'Lunney. Now he spoke his thoughts aloud. "My son is a lucky man," he said to her as they circled to the easy rhythms.

Kathleen blushed. "Thank you," she said.

James liked that. No false coyness. No pretending not to understand the compliment. "But he's a damn fool," he added. "Why isn't he here with you? What's he doing in Vermont anyway?"

He sounded genuinely concerned. That impressed Kathleen. From her father's gossip, she knew about the affair between James and Vanessa Brewster. It had given her a negative opinion of James, which she realized now was probably unfair. And Matt, in discussing his father, had always made him seem cold and unconcerned. But it didn't seem to Kathleen that James was either an aging roué grasping at forbidden erotic straws or the emotionally sterile father Matt had hinted he was. On the contrary, he seemed like a very nice man indeed.

"He went there to meet with someone he used to know in Canada," Kathleen said, answering James's question.

"Political." James's face darkened.

"No. That's not it." Kathleen stopped dancing and looked into his eyes. "It's not political. I promise you."

"Then what is it?"

"Personal. Very personal."

James's brow furrowed the way it did when he was gauging a return in tennis. "Is the family involved?" he asked slowly.

"Possibly." Kathleen held up a hand. "I'll say only one thing more," she declared. "It's just this. Talk to Matt. I think perhaps he could use a friend—a father—right about now."

"I'm grateful to you for telling me." James finished out the dance with her in silence.

As they left the floor his eye caught that of his niece Holly. She smiled. James realized that there was more in the smile than just an acknowledgment of eye contact. It said that she approved of Kathleen, of the role she was assuming in Matt's life, and of James's making his own endorsement known to the gathering at large by dancing with his chauffeur's daughter. Faintly but firmly, James returned Holly's smile.

Holly's eyes followed them toward the buffet table. Her train of thought was interrupted by a discreet voice at her side. "Miss Holly."

"Yes, Berkley?" She swiveled toward the butler.

He did not answer, but his eyes moved.

Following the butler's glance, Holly saw Christopher standing above him on the wide veranda staircase. She bit her lip. "All right, Berkley," she told him. "I'll take care of it."

"Very well, Miss Holly." He faded away in the direction of the caterer's maitre d' to discuss matters of protocol. If the discussion proved as fruitless as it had up to now, Berkley decided, he would spear the culinary interloper with a silver toothpick and eat him alive like one of his too garlicky snails.

"What are you doing here, Christopher?" Holly demanded.

"Family party, love. Only right I should pay my compliments to the bride and groom."

"They don't want your compliments, and I don't want you here. Please leave."

Christopher detected a new resolution in Holly's tone. "Has something changed since our last chat, love?" he inquired.

"Yes." Holly took a deep breath. "I've decided to go ahead with the divorce—regardless of the consequences."

"Most unwise, Holly. Don't forget the *billet doux*. Bad business for the Stockwell image, you know."

"I don't care. Do what you want. I'm divorcing you. Now just get out of here before I tell Berkley to fetch the security guards and have you thrown out."

Christopher's eyes narrowed. "You can't have me thrown out, Holly. We're still married. I'm still the father of our son."

"I'm warning you, Christopher—"

"I want to see my son!" He raised his voice. "Where is Nicholas?"

Heads turned. There was nothing Holly abhorred more than screaming matches in public between husbands and wives. She gave in. "All right," she told Christopher in a low tone. "You can see Nicholas—not that you ever showed any interest in him before. He's upstairs in the third-floor nursery with the nursemaid and Danny Carter."

"Who's Danny Carter?"

"Michelle's son. He's a year older than Nicholas. His little sister Robin is up there, too. She's one."

"How old is the nursemaid, love?" Christopher leered.

"Damn you, Christopher!"

"A joke, Holly." He held up his hands placatingly and backed away. "Only a joke." He turned and went into the house, ostensibly to visit his son.

Halsey De Vilbiss had not missed the brief scene between Holly and Christopher. Where there was marital discord, he knew from experience, there was always profit for lawyers. He did not, however, speak this thought aloud to Mary Linstone Stockwell.

She had been telling him about the frequency of twins in the Tyler family. Privately, she was somewhat surprised at the overdressed young man's interest in the subject. Mary wondered just who he was. He'd told her his name, but it hadn't rung a bell. He seemed out of place at Riverview. Still, she'd seen him with Holly before. Perhaps he was a friend of hers, she thought. If he was, then he must certainly be all right.

"Albert and John," she enumerated. "Beth and Carrie. And Diana and her twin, who unfortunately was born dead. Three sets in all. Still, I imagine that does constitute a genetic trait."

"And they're all descendants of Sarah Stockwell Tyler," De Vilbiss remarked casually. He was following up on what Buffy had told him about the Governor's older sister and some long-forgotten, mysterious scandal.

"Why, yes." Mary looked at him in surprise. "How did you know that?"

"Somebody mentioned it to me at the wedding," De Vilbiss replied glibly. "I don't remember who. I think they were wondering if Sarah Tyler was there."

"Oh, no!" Mary blurted out the words. "She wouldn't be there."

"I guess she's estranged from the family," De Vilbiss said easily.

Mary's lips compressed tightly. "No. She's dead, I assume."

"But she *was* estranged? In the past, I mean?"

"Well, yes," Mary answered reluctantly. She had never lied easily, and it was such a long, long time ago.

"Now I wonder why that was?" De Vilbiss persisted.

But he'd gone too far. Mary had no intention of dredging up the scandal of Sarah Stockwell Tyler and her two illicit love affairs for the benefit of this stranger. "I wouldn't know," she answered him curtly.

"You said before that you supposed she was dead?"

"She was born in 1895. And no one's heard from her in over sixty years. It seems likely."

"But you're not sure?"

"No." Mary obviously wanted to get off the subject. "I'm not sure."

Skillfully, De Vilbiss backed off, but not altogether. "I was only wondering if the twin strain was a Stockwell strain," he explained. "Was Sarah a twin?"

"No. The hair and the eyes come to the Tylers through the Stockwells. The Governor's mother and Sarah both had them. But not the propensity toward twins." Of course, Mary thought, but did not say aloud, the real father of John and Alfred—not Averill Tyler, but Sarah's first illicit lover, whoever he was—undoubtedly accounts for the twins.

Holly had been noticing her grandmother talking to Halsey De Vilbiss. She didn't like the lawyer. He came on too strong. She was relieved when Mary excused herself and left De Vilbiss. A moment later he drifted over to Holly's cousin, Michelle.

"Lookee, lookee. Con-man-spi-ra-cy!"

Patrice had silently come up behind Holly to also focus on Michelle and the lawyer. She was swaying on her heels, an empty champagne glass in her hand and what looked like the contents on her dress. Her hair was disheveled and her smile lopsided.

"Oh, Patrice." Holly gasped. "I think we'd better get you some coffee."

"More bubbly, you mean."

"What happened, Patrice? Where's your date? Where's Jack?"

"Buffied."

Just then James Stockwell joined his daughter and Holly. "Who is that fellow with Michelle?" he inquired. "I've been wondering all day."

"I think he's Buffy's lawyer." It was Holly who answered him.

"Oh." James watched De Vilbiss deep in conversation with Michelle Carter. She was listening intently. Then she nodded in a way that managed to seem both reluctant and defiant at the same time. "Oh!"

"Daddy!" Patrice claimed her father's attention. "Daddy, I think I'm going to be sick."

"Oh, Patrice!" Holly was dismayed. "You should lie down."

"She's drunk." James was surprised. He had never seen his daughter Patrice drunk before, not even mildly tipsy. "Help me get her into the house," he said to Holly.

"All right. We'll take her upstairs to one of the bedrooms, where she can lie down and sleep it off," Holly suggested, then they each took an arm and supported Patrice toward the stairs.

"What happened, honey?" James asked his daughter, concerned.

"Buffied," was the answer as they guided her into the mansion. "I've been Buffied!"

About a half hour later James emerged from the upstairs bedroom in the east wing where he'd left Patrice with an icebag on her head, muttering to Holly that never again was she going to be some man's patsy. From now on it was going to be strictly business for her. Tired, he stepped into one of the bathrooms, intending to splash cold water on his face. As he entered, his youngest son, Michael, was just finishing cleaning up and combing his hair after his interlude with Carrie Tyler.

"Hello, Dad."

"Michael." James turned on the faucet and adjusted the flow.

Michael watched his father splash water on his face. He started to say something, stopped, then blurted out what he wanted to say. "Dad, I'd like you to stop seeing the Brewster woman until after the election."

"Not just the primary?" James inquired dryly. "The general election in November? Five months from now?"

"Yes."

"You don't feel hypocritical asking me to do this, Michael?"

"Yes, I do. But I'm not making the request on moral grounds. We both know my own past performance rules that out. I'm speaking strictly pragmatically. The talk about you and the lady is spreading. It could cost me in the northern townships where I should be strongest."

"Talk? What talk?"

"I personally overheard a remark in the locker room of the New York Athletic Club last Thursday. And then at lunch at the Harvard Club on Monday, R.R. hinted tactfully."

In the mirror James raised his eyebrows. R.R. was the second-ranking Republican in the New York State party. "What did he say?"

"He was oblique. General. But he finished up with a non sequitur about the state of your health."

"The bastard!" James was not given to casual profanity.

"Will you drop her, Father?" Michael was direct.

"No." James took a deep breath, and a note of pleading crept into his voice. "It's not casual, Michael. However it may have started out, it's not casual now."

Michael stared at his father. "Marriage?" he asked disbelievingly.

"I would. But not Vanessa. She says it's not her style. She's right. It's not." James wiped his face with a Porthault hand towel. "Look, Michael," he said finally. "I'm fifty-two years old, and I'm a widower. How can anybody fault me for sleeping with a woman I care about? And even if they can, how could they fault you?"

"Politics isn't fair, Dad. Vanessa Brewster was with the Governor when he died. The papers were filled with innuendo. Now, if the same woman turns up as the girlfriend of the Governor's son, my father, the Democratic media will have a field day. The Stockwell name will be identified with sleazy sex, and even in these liberated times the people don't vote sleazy sex into Congress. Not in the Hudson River Valley anyway."

"All right." James—wincing at the words sleazy sex—rubbed his face more briskly than was necessary. "I'll be more circumspect."

"Will you stop seeing her?"

"No. But I will take every precaution. I promise you that, Michael."

"Then I'll have to be satisfied with that." Michael

249

turned on his heel, obviously not satisfied at all, and left the bathroom.

Downstairs he encountered his uncle Jonathan, his aunt Ellen, and his cousin Peter. "Have you had a chance to speak to your father?" Jonathan asked Michael in a discreet tone.

"Yes. Just now. He says he'll be more circumspect."

"He won't break it off, then?"

"No."

Jonathan shook his head disapprovingly.

Ellen exchanged glances with Peter. They viewed James's affair as an Achilles heel to be exploited.

"Excuse me." Christopher Millwood materialized before them. "Have you seen my wife?"

"She was showing Diana the new hedge maze in the west garden," Ellen told him.

"Thank you, Aunt Ellen." Christopher made a point of acknowledging all the relationships to which his marriage into the Stockwell family entitled him. After a casual bow he moved off in the direction of the hedge maze.

Emerging from the maze, Holly and Diana came upon Paul Tyler and his wife Margaret. "Could we talk to you for a moment, Diana?" the heart surgeon asked his cousin. "We're concerned about Beth."

"I don't think you have to be," Diana replied. "She's a really good kid, Paul. I know she's been giving you a hard time lately, but really, you should be proud of yourselves for the way she's turning out."

"Margaret and I feel she should be living at home."

"Listen, I'm not that crazy about having her with me. My place isn't that big. Still, I think the smartest thing would be to give it a week or two. Let her simmer down."

"Excuse me." Holly felt as if she were intruding. "I'm going to get myself something cold to drink. I'll see you later, Diana." She left them squinting into the bloodred Hudson Valley sunset which was taking shape.

"A vision of loveliness." Christopher, blurry in the dying light, appeared in front of her.

"Why are you still here? You were supposed to leave after you saw Nicholas."

250

"I thought that we might have a talk, love."

"We have nothing to say to each other."

"Don't be unreasonable." He took Holly firmly by the elbow and guided her to a stylized stone bench in the antiquarian courtyard of the sculpture garden.

Here they were surrounded by the Byzantine, Greek, and Roman treasures the Governor and his forebears had collected. Pale white nymphs and satyrs cavorting with flutes and lutes took on rosy life in the twilight. Elongated felines, temple bulls, and unicorns found motion in the deepening shadows. Cherubs and gargoyles, Olympian gods and Roman goddesses, ravishers and revelers all combined with classic libidinous artistry to greet the falling night. Alone with Christopher in this unreal setting, Holly's recent resolution to stand firm waned in spite of herself.

Holly shivered. Was it the chill of dusk? The eeriness of the stone figures surrounding her? Or was it Christopher's touch on her arm, gentle but firm, still holding her there with him?

Her husband's touch. Once it had been more important to her than all the words that passed between them. Her physical reaction to Christopher had always been pronounced. Indeed, it had overcome each betrayal of her trust in him up until the final one involving Winifred Fitzsimmons. And even now, against her will, her flesh responded to it.

Christopher recognized the reaction. Immediately he moved to capitalize on it. "It's wrong for us to be apart, love," he murmured, his voice intimate, his hand caressing her arm. "The attraction between us is too strong."

"It's dead, Christopher. It's over." She started to get to her feet.

Gently he restrained her. "Our bodies say differently, Holly." His caress became more pronounced, more intimate on the bare skin of her arm. His other arm slid around her shoulders. His mouth moved toward hers.

"No." It was a moan. At that moment Holly hated herself even more than she did him. It had been so long. So long! Her legs felt weak, and she was immobilized with a torpor born of the memory of passion. It had not all been a lie, what they'd had. Not all of it! There had been long,

251

lazy nights of lovemaking that she could never exorcise from her mind. "Don't. Please don't do this."

"Why not, love?" Christopher made a subtle miscalculation. "You want it even more than I do." His hand slid down her dress and cupped her breast. His thumb traced the aureole around Holly's trembling nipple. "You know you do. You always have."

He'd been too sure of himself, and his arrogance broke the spell. Holly's revulsion turned away from herself and toward him. It gave her strength to resist him. As she turned from his kiss, she pushed him away with a strength he hadn't anticipated. "No, Christopher!" There was no ambivalence in her voice now. Her weakness replaced by determination, she got to her feet. "It won't work anymore!"

"Ah, don't fight it, pet." He rose and forcibly embraced her.

"No!" She struggled.

"You know fighting just makes you more randy." His hands were all over her body now, crumpling the sheer linen of her dress.

"Damn it, let me go!" Holly moved her head back and forth violently, managing to avoid his kiss.

"Ah, Holly . . ." His hand moved possessively between her thighs; his muscles turned into steel bands imprisoning her in his embrace.

"The lady said no." The masculine voice was deep, authoritative. "Let her go."

"She's my wife. This is between us." Christopher did not relinquish his hold. "Mind your own bloody business."

"I said let her go." The speaker stepped from the shadows into the dying light. Holly recognized him. It was Jack Houston.

"Or what, chappie?" There was a feral anticipation in Christopher's voice.

The tone was familiar to Holly. During their years together she had heard it on several occasions. Always it had been the prelude—the challenge and the snare—to violence. It had not taken long for her to discover that few things gave Christopher more pleasure than entrapping another man into a fight.

He savored such occasions because he knew he had an edge. Christopher looked aristocratic and slightly effete. Although he was quite tall, there was nothing macho or tough in his appearance.

It was a deception. Christopher had won amateur honors in boxing at Eton, and later he'd been heavyweight champion of his regiment for two years. In both environments he'd also gained a reputation as a brawler outside the ring.

During his marriage to Holly, her elegant beauty had always drawn attention from men. Christopher enjoyed escalating their interest into confrontation. It had happened several times. He would start out by chastising her for flirting with someone. Almost always the man would intercede in her behalf, saying—truthfully—that she had done no such thing.

This provided the pretext Christopher sought. He would immediately and viciously turn his wrath on the hapless intruder. More often than not it would end in a fight with Christopher slowly and expertly chopping up the man with his fists until the victim's face resembled raw meat.

Following such occasions, Christopher would be particularly passionate. Holly had come to expect it. Like some jungle animal, when Christopher's blood was up his lust became unbridled. His lovemaking on such occasions had elements of violence.

At first this had frightened Holly. Later—and she never got over feeling ashamed of her reaction—when his violence was directed at other people it disgusted her, but when it was channeled into physical passion, she forgot the events that inspired it, and was aroused by and enjoyed the heated lovemaking.

"If you don't let her go," Jack said to Christopher now, "you and I are going to tangle, chappie."

"What cheek! Coming between a man and his wife!" Christopher's voice rose calculatedly to an almost feminine shriek. "Why are you interfering? What's your relationship with her?"

"Relationship?" Jack was taken aback. "There's no relationship. We've met exactly once."

"And where was that, old boy?" Christopher sneered. "In your bed?"

"Don't be silly. You're insulting your wife and you're making a fool of yourself." Jack strode to them, put his hands on Christopher's wrists, and pried them loose from Holly.

They came easily, too easily. "Be careful!" Holly exclaimed, trying to warn him, aware of what was coming.

As Christopher let her go without resistance and fell back, his left fist shot up in a short, powerful jab and caught Jack on the cheekbone. The raised Greek letters on the Eton ring Christopher always wore opened the skin. A trickle of blood oozed out.

Jack stepped back, shaken. "Well, all right then," he said, almost to himself. "All right."

"Don't," Holly moaned. "He's not what he looks like. He knows what he's doing. He's fought in the ring."

Christopher struck an awkward pose with his arms curled like those of an old-fashioned pugilist. He threw a roundhouse right at Jack's chin, deliberately telegraphing it. Jack ducked the blow easily, but he didn't anticipate the instantaneous swing back. Christopher's elbow caught him on the side of the jaw and sent him reeling.

He gave Jack no chance to recover. No longer awkward, he swarmed all over him with a powerful tattoo of lefts and rights to the body. Jack dropped his hands to protect himself, and Christopher hit him in the eye, grinding his thumb in with the blow.

Jack clinched. He held onto Christopher tightly, struggling to get his breath and his bearings. Christopher broke the clinch with a punch well below the belt. He followed it up with a short chop that started Jack's nose bleeding.

"Stop!" Holly was sobbing. "Please stop! It's not fair. Let him go!"

"Listen to her pleading for her lover." There wasn't a mark on Christopher. He wasn't even breathing hard. "Are you really worthy of such devotion?" He loosed a classic one-two and Jack sank to his knees. Christopher bent to deliver what he judged would be a final uppercut.

He judged wrong. His maneuver had put him slightly off balance. Jack's hand, like the blade of a hatchet, caught him right behind his left knee, and Christopher missed the punch and stumbled. Jack butted him in the groin with his head.

"Fight fair!" It hurt, and Christopher was furious.

"Not a chance." Jack snarled.

Christopher backed off, waiting for Jack to stand up so he could knock him down again. This time he meant to really hurt him. Then he would finish him off. And then he would drag Holly off to bed.

Jack got to his feet. Christopher moved in for the kill. He feinted low. Jack dropped his guard. Christopher loosed a vicious uppercut.

To Holly's surprise it missed Jack by a hair. He hardly seemed to move at all, but he avoided it. He was ready this time when the elbow swung back. He met it with a karate chop that left Christopher's right arm dangling at a very odd angle.

With a roar of rage Christopher swung his left. Jack ducked low, came up under it, grabbed Christopher's forearm and used the momentum to smash the fist into a tree. Then, with the flat of his hand, he struck Christopher on his neck just under the back of his head. A whoosh of air went out of Christopher and he sat down hard. He looked up at Holly and Jack glassy-eyed, not focusing.

"Will he be all right?" Despite herself, Holly was concerned.

"He won't be picking any more fights for a while, but he'll live. I think his elbow's broken, though."

"Where did you learn to box like that?" Holly was impressed. Nobody had ever been able to thrash Christopher before.

"Box?" Jack managed to laugh behind the handkerchief he was using to staunch the flow of blood from his nose. "I couldn't box my way out of a paper bag. I don't know the first thing about boxing. I only know how to survive."

Holly looked down at Christopher. The Looney Tunes expression was still on his face. "You did more than survive," she said.

"Commando stuff." Jack shrugged. "Dirty tricks for dirty—" He broke off abruptly.

"You were a commando?"

"More like a guerilla, really. In Angola for a little while.

Not long, though. I quit when I realized I was getting paid so well because I was on the wrong side."

"Safari guide . . ." Holly remembered what Patrice had told her about Jack. "Algonquin bellhop, soldier of fortune . . . is there anything you haven't done?"

"Yeah. I haven't learned how to stop a nosebleed."

"Ice," Holly told him. "Come on back to the house, and we'll pack it with ice."

En route they encountered Gustav Ulbricht. "Mr. Millwood has had an accident," Holly informed the gardener. "He's in the sculpture garden. Would you please go and help him."

"Yes, ma'am."

Holly and Jack continued on their way. She took him to an upstairs bedroom in the east wing. Then she went and got him an ice pack. "Rest clots blood," he told her. "Just leave me here awhile, if that's okay." And so Holly left Jack Houston lying in the early evening light, with his head hanging down backward over the side of the bed and the ice pack pressed to his upper lip.

Coming down the steps, she became aware of a commotion. The younger women were congregating at the foot of the broad, sweeping, circular stairway. As Holly reached bottom, there was a sort of group sigh of anticipation. Heads were craning upward. She looked, too.

Lizzie Tyler, the mature bride, was standing at the head of the stairs in a gray crepe traveling suit beside her new husband. In her hands she held her bridal bouquet. As everybody watched and waited expectantly, she raised it high over her head and flung it to the group below.

End over end, it toppled straight for Holly. Instinctively she reached up and caught it. The import of the flowers in her hands did not dawn on her until she heard the sighs of disappointment from some of the younger women.

"But she's married!" one complained.

"There's more to dinner, dear, than the first course," was the cynical reply.

Not everybody, however, was resentful of Holly's having caught the bridal bouquet. "I'm happy for her," Mary told Halsey De Vilbiss, who had sought her out in the entrance hallway to resume their chat.

"I can see that you are." His smile was approving. He returned to the subject under discussion. "We were talking about twins," he prodded her. "About how they occur in the Tyler family, but not the Stockwell."

"That's right. Twins run in my family, too." Mary remembered. "But I'm a Linstone."

"Are you a twin yourself, then?" De Vilbiss asked.

"No. But my father was. So were two of my great-aunts."

"But none of your brothers or sisters?"

"I only had one brother. Ellis. He wasn't a twin." A shadow crossed Mary's face. "He died in 1913."

"That's a very long time ago."

"Yes." She sighed. "It is indeed."

"Your brother Ellis must have been very young when he died," De Vilbiss realized.

"He was only eighteen."

"You must have been just a child yourself."

"I was five." Mary shuddered.

"Was it an accident?"

There was a long pause before Mary responded. She was staring off into space—a space long past, a space filled with anguish. "My brother Ellis committed suicide," she said finally. "He hanged himself." Mary suddenly felt the weight of her years, and she realized she was very tired. It had been a long and exhausting day. She said as much to Halsey De Vilbiss and excused herself.

He watched her petite figure as she started up the stairs to her room. Her slow movements revealed how much she wanted to lie down, to rest. Halfway up the flight of stairs she had to lean heavily on the oak banister and pause to get her breath.

Yes, Mary thought as she looked down at the family milling about in the entrance hall below. It had indeed been a long, exhausting day. And despite the fact that weddings should be happy occasions, it had been far from a joyous one. In her quiet, unobtrusive way, Mary had observed much of the friction, the backbiting, the turmoil that had marked the garden wedding reception at Riverview.

It made her weary; it made her sad. Unbidden, a phrase popped into her mind which summed up her feelings. The phrase was from a book Mary had read when she was a very young woman, *Anna Karenina* by Leo Tolstoy: "Happy families are all alike; every unhappy family is unhappy in its own way."

It might have been written about the Stockwell family: Most certainly it was "unhappy in its own way."

BOOK FOUR

27

OCTOBER PAINTED THE Hudson River Valley with a Van Gogh vibrancy. Changing from day to day, the fall colors spread over Riverview with a shimmering intensity that brought back to Holly's mind the woodland wanderings of her childhood. Once again she felt the crackling carpet of leaves underfoot as in autumns past, when her grandfather led her by the hand down paths lined with fall foliage of burnt sienna and flaming vermilion, brilliant topaz and lustrous tangerine, dusky violet and passionate coral.

With the Governor gone now, the season was both nostalgic and painful. The Taconic pine trees in particular brought a lump to Holly's throat. There they stood, greenly stubborn and unaltered amidst the constantly changing finery of oak, elm, and cedar. The tall, green-needled pines were as dependable in this mercurial season as the Governor had always been. How irretrievable was his loss!

But she knew the Governor would not have approved her mourning, so one early October day Holly turned her back on the multicolored glories of the Stockwell estates and went into Manhattan to continue work on her project —the early history of Riverview. Her destination was the

259

central library on Fifth Avenue and Forty-second Street, known as "The Lions" because of the unique life-size stone sculptures guarding its main entrance.

Holly did not intend any in-depth research today. If she had, she would either have gone to the Charles Stockwell Research Foundation, with its wealth of private papers available to her, or she would have availed herself of the private cubicle in the library's Frederick Lewis Allen Room and access to the rare books collection she'd waited over a year to secure. All she was after this particular day, however, was easily accessible background information, and so she went to the third-floor Reading Room, a facility open to the general public.

Having obtained the books she needed, Holly settled herself at one of the long tables in the north half of the Reading Room. After poring over them for two hours and jotting down notes until her fingers hurt, she took a break, gazing at the interior of one of the world's great libraries.

Art had been the Governor's passion, and he'd taught Holly to view it with the eye of a connoisseur. The pleasure this gave Holly was served well in the north half of the Lions Reading Room where priceless details of wood sculpture unnoticed by many of the library's users captured her attention. She looked up fifty-two feet to the rectangular ceiling canvasses of sky and clouds painted by James Wall Finn. She smiled at the winged cherubs and the satyr's mask where the wall arched into the ceiling, and she lost herself in the cornucopia of ornamentation surrounding the businesslike reading tables of the North Reading Room.

"As breathtaking as the Pitti Palace."

Holly looked up to find Jack Houston grinning down at her. "It's too beautiful," she agreed. "My attention always strays."

"Well, since it's strayed anyway, could I tempt you to take a break and have a cup of coffee with me?"

"No." Holly smiled. "But you could tempt me with some hot cocoa."

"Autumn nectar." He helped her gather up her books, and waited while Holly went to the desk and had the librarian put them on hold. Then they went down the wide marble stairs and exited The Lions.

They bought cocoa and Danish at a takeout counter and carried the steaming Styrofoam containers back to one of the stone benches outside the library. "What were you doing in the research room?" Holly asked him, blowing on her cocoa.

"I was looking something up in the *African Quarterly.* I'm putting together a brochure on Kenyan camera safaris for a travel agency."

"You write?" Holly was surprised.

"Oh, yeah. I read, too. And I can do simple addition."

"Don't be defensive. I wasn't pigeonholing you."

"Well, all right, then. Writing travel brochures is one of the ways I support myself in New York. When I'm in Africa I go in for more active employment."

Holly sipped her cocoa and felt the warmth spread through her. "I never really did thank you properly for your help at the wedding reception," she said.

"You're welcome." Jack's next words were delicately chosen. "Is that situation straightening itself out?"

"My marriage to Christopher?" Holly sighed. "Not really. I've filed for divorce. Or, rather, Uncle James has filed in my behalf. But—" Holly cut herself off and then decided to plunge on, "Christopher has filed a countersuit demanding half of my inheritance and sole custody of our son Nicholas."

"No court will give him that. He'd have to prove you were morally unfit or something."

"That's what he's trying to do. We're fighting him." Holly sighed, but did not go into detail.

Over three months had elapsed since the renewed search to locate Winifred Fitzsimmons had been launched. They'd engaged private detectives and used Stockwell influence to secure the unofficial cooperation of Scotland Yard, all to no avail. Winifred had vanished from England. She'd been traced as far as Paris, and then her trail had petered out in a dead end.

Breaking the silence, Jack asked how Patrice was.

Holly was surprised and offended. "Do you really care?" she replied. "You treated her so badly."

"I know. I feel lousy about that. I liked Patrice. I still like her. That's why I'd like to know she's okay now."

"She's still hurting, but she'll get over it, I guess."

Holly's voice was noncommittal; her eyes gazed in the distance.

"You really think I'm a heel." Jack nodded. "Well, I can't blame you."

"Patrice is my friend. I don't like to see her hurt. Still," Holly said, "I'm not your judge. I guess you had some reason for what you did." Holly's tone implied that she doubted any reason would be good enough.

"Oh, yeah." Jack was rueful. "No secret about my reason."

"Buffy?" Holly guessed.

"Yes. Buffy."

"I'll never understand that!" Holly blurted out. "The attraction I mean."

"You don't like Buffy. Most women don't."

"Well . . . she's much older than you are."

"Seventeen years. Yeah. I know." Jack eyed Holly shrewdly. "The rumor around town is that you've been dating Zelig Meyerling pretty regularly," he said. "How much older than you is he?"

"Fourteen years or so." Holly sipped her cocoa and thought a moment. "Touché," she decided finally.

"When it's the other way around, nobody thinks it's unusual." Jack drove his point home.

"That's true." Holly was embarrassed. She'd been wondering if some sort of mother fixation might account for Jack's infatuation with Buffy. Now she realized how simplistic that was. While her desire for the father she never had might enter into the attraction she felt for Meyerling, so did many other factors. Meyerling's effect on her was an amalgam of maturity, urbanity, experience, wit, and knowledge. In fairness, an equally complex mixture would explain Buffy's allure for Jack.

"Are you in love with him?" Jack asked bluntly.

"I don't know." Holly answered honestly. "Are you in love with Buffy?"

"Oh, yeah. Completely."

"I guess there's more to her than I see."

"Is that what you guess?" Jack was mildly sarcastic. "You mean like maybe there's more to you than a svelte, well-groomed blonde who looks like she stepped out of *Vogue*?"

262

"Do I really appear as plastic as that?" Holly was hurt.

"No. You don't. That was a cheap shot." Jack was rueful. "It's just that you've known Buffy—what? most of your life?—and all you see is the surface."

"That's all she lets anybody see," Holly pointed out.

"Yeah." He sighed. "I know. That's how she is. Beautiful and brittle by design. But damn it, Holly, you don't have to be a psychiatrist to see that's a facade she sets up because she's really so vulnerable."

"Vulnerable? Buffy?" Holly was skeptical.

"Yes, damn it! She's a marshmallow underneath. Comes on like gangbusters, fights tooth and nail, but if you touch her—a nerve, her sympathies, whatever—all that toughness collapses. Take our relationship, hers and mine. Except for sex, she won't let herself feel anything for me. You know why? Because she's terrified of getting older and seeing that aging reflected in my eyes. If she doesn't accept me, then I'll never be able to reject her. And if that isn't vulnerable, I don't know what is!"

"Oh, Jack!" Holly, sensing the depth of his feelings, took his hand in hers and held it. "You really do care for her, don't you?"

"Of course I do. But she's less threatened if all we have is sex. If I push for closeness, I push her away. I love the woman, damn it! But it's a no-win situation!"

"Still, I don't know," Holly said. "She always acted so la-di-da. And her promiscuity—" Holly broke off abruptly. Oh, God! she thought. I wish I hadn't said that!

"Well, why not?" Jack dealt with the characterization head-on. "Why shouldn't she have had men? The Governor was no monk. And neither," he admitted, "am I."

"I'm sorry."

"About what? It's true. Buffy has been promiscuous. For all I know, she still is. The other person's promiscuity hurts, but it never stopped anybody from loving anybody."

"That's true." Holly thought of Christopher.

"I wasn't exactly being faithful myself where Patrice was concerned."

"Why did you do that? I mean, if you're so much in love with Buffy—"

"Buffy and I had a fight. I was furious with her. I wanted to get even."

"Poor Patrice. That's not very easy on her. Weren't you attracted to her at all?"

"That night at the Algonquin?" Jack smiled slightly. "Maybe a little, but the truth is I was much more attracted to you."

"I suppose I was attracted to you, too," Holly recalled honestly.

"Oh, yeah? Then why did you leave?"

There was a look in Jack's eyes that she didn't want to see. Interest? she wondered. Maybe. "I knew Patrice was interested in you, and I didn't want to get in her way," Holly said, and took another sip of cocoa. "I'm glad I didn't go to bed with you," she added bluntly.

"Why?"

"You're too macho. That's what kept me married to Christopher for years. Oh, I know he doesn't look it, but he is. And it turned me on. I admit it. You would have turned me on that way, too. But that's not what I want. I want something different from a man now."

"Zelig Meyerling?"

"Well, yes. I don't really know where our relationship is going. But Zelig is the kind of man I think I need. It's what I've been groping with: the need to choose civilization over violence, humanity over machismo. I want to be with a man who's as different from Christopher as possible." Holly was surprised by how easy it was to talk to Jack.

The little cocoa left in the Styrofoam container was cold now. Holly walked over to a wire trash basket and got rid of the container. "You know what I wondered about that first night?" she said to Jack when she returned to their bench. "I wondered how you came to be a bellhop at the Algonquin."

"Simple. My family lost their money when I was a little kid. My parents died when I was young. So when the time came, I had to go to work instead of college."

"How did they lose their money?"

"The Korean War," Jack replied tersely.

"Oh?"

"It's a long story."

"Oh. Sure." Holly perceived his reluctance. She

glanced at her watch. "I have to catch a train back to Riverview Heights anyway."

"I'll walk you over to Grand Central."

He waited in the station with her until her train was announced. "You know," Holly said, "I'm really glad we met and talked." She looked Jack directly in the eyes. "I'm glad we didn't get involved that night at the Algonquin. It would have been a shame if we became lovers, because then we never could have become friends."

Jack grinned. "We are friends, aren't we?"

"Why so surprised?"

"Well, I've known a lot of women in my life. I've had a lot of different kinds of relationships with them. But you know something? You're the first woman friend I've ever had."

Holly filled with a sudden happiness. "It is special, isn't it?" she said. "Friendship, I mean."

"Oh, yeah," Jack said. "And it sure is a helluva lot less complicated than love."

28

THE FRAIL, sickly man propped in a sitting position in the cranked-up hospital bed looked even older than he sounded. He was in his eighties at least. His blue eyes were dull and rheumy, but they narrowed and became sharp when he saw who his visitor was.

Jack Houston, sitting in a chair next to his grandfather's bed, listened with patience as the old man recited a familiar litany of complaints, interrupted often by the old man's wandering train of thought. His grandfather's intermittent vagueness didn't bother Jack half so much as his entrenched meanness. Grandpa was living proof that adversity didn't ennoble people. The gas his aging engine ran on was pure vitriol. Age had narrowed his focus to revenge.

"It was the 1950s, the Korean War, and I had this shipyard," Jack's grandfather was saying. "I made ships for the Navy. Battleships. Cruisers. Carriers. Even a couple of subs. Had my picture on *Time* magazine. The story inside compared me to Henry Knudsen. I was the biggest ship-builder in the country until—"

"I know, Grandpa. You've told me all this before." How many times? From when he was just a kid, how many times had the story been drummed into him? "You don't have to tell me again."

But the old man was not to be deterred. "Navy contracts. Pull the strings. Grease the skids. Make sure the right initials appear at the right time on the cost over-runs."

"Grandpa—"

"Subcontract to the right people. Interesting list, boy. Same names turned up years later as major contributors to the first gubernatorial campaign of Matthew Adams Stockwell. Interesting coincidence."

Jack looked at his watch. He sighed. The visiting hour still had a ways to go.

"Coincidence. Never direct. And there were innocents. Harry Truman . . . to him I was the patriotic businessman who handed Bess the bottle of champagne to christen the battleship. He didn't know beans about vicuna coats. He didn't know beans about the pipeline from my shipyard to the Navy Department procurement bureau via Matthew Adams Stockwell's office. You know how come that snobby Hudson Valley sonofabitch hooked into a shirt-sleeve junkman turned shipbuilder like me, boy?"

"The war, Grandpa." Jack automatically supplied the answer the old man wanted. "The Korean War."

"The Korean War. That's how come. After World War Two Stockwell Industries retooled its own shipyards. Peacetime production. Pleasure craft. Everything from canoes to sailboats to yachts to luxury liners—which even back then was a dying proposition. Korea caught Stockwell with its pants down." The old man wheezed a laugh. "But me, I was all tooled up. I had this nothing Navy contract—PT boats, obsolete coming off the skids—for under a million dollars. But I was ready to go. So Stockwell sent his man to me. Wouldn't come himself, the patrician snob; wouldn't dirty his hands. Stockwell

Industries would underwrite my expansion and see to it I was awarded this Navy Department contract for fifty million dollars—fifty million dollars!—and that was just for openers. Now how could I say no, boy?"

"You couldn't say no, Grandpa."

"Damn right, boy. And what if it meant taking on a new partner, a silent partner, name of Matthew Adams Stockwell? Hell, boy, he still had the Navy Department contacts from World War Two. He delivered the contracts. I made the subcontracting deals Stockwell wanted, and I delivered the ships. Never had actual contact with my silent partner, of course. Only saw the go-between. But it was sweet. We were raking it in hand over . . . hand over . . . hand over—"

"Fist."

The old man was blank for several moments. Then he spoke again. "The Korean War was winding down." To Jack it was a welcome skip forward. "Ike had been elected on his pledge to make peace. That would be it for us war contractors. We all figured there's no profit in peace. But Stockwell's man paid me a visit. He said Stockwell was privy to a different scenario, one geared to American business. It wasn't going to be peace and recession versus war and bloodshed, the way it had always been. It was going to be defense. That was a new word back then—defense. It meant we could keep on turning out battleships, guns, bombs, whatever, and have peace, too."

"Defense." Jack looked at his watch again. Good. The visiting hour was almost over.

"The Governor was hand in glove with the people who cooked up the idea of defense. Stockwell Industries was in on the ground floor. Yessir, defense. But first there was a little matter of the stock market. Now, the stock market . . . the stock market . . . the stock market . . ."

Damn! The light in the window was out again. The old man was dangling from an uncompleted synapse.

"Insider trading," Jack prompted him. "Stock manipulation."

"Red Hook." Grandpa grabbed hold of memory at a different spot. "Floating distance of the old Navy yard. Stockwell's man sat in this little seafood bar with me, the two of us with our mouths on fire eating clams right off

267

the half shell smothered in hot sauce, and he says the Governor—Governor-to-be, you know, Jackson—he says the Governor has it timed to the dime. His exact words. 'Timed to the dime.' And that meant..." The old man paused and looked at Jack.

"Carefully scheduled."

"Meticulously, boy. Meticulously scheduled." The old man started counting points off on his gnarled, veined fingers. "One—the Navy Department announces plans for mothballing. Two—the procurement office announces a rollback. Three—Stockwell's man on Wall Street leaks the rumor that my latest forty-million-dollar contract is going to be canceled. Four—their broker begins unloading huge blocks of my company's stock, pushing the price down. Five—I start unloading my own stock through my broker. Six—the value of the stock plummets. Seven—when it hits bottom, a dummy brokerage house set up by Stockwell buys every share of stock it can lay hands on. Eight—the Navy Department procurement office announces that not only will my forty-million-dollar contract *not* be canceled, but that the national defense requires upping the fleet, and I am in line for a new batch of contracts. Nine—the stock in my company soars back up again, way past where it was before. Ten—Stockwell's broker and my broker start selling again and reap a huge profit. Except that ten never happened. What happened instead was the Securities and Exchange Commission came down on me like a ton of bricks."

"I know, Grandpa."

"Stockwell double-crossed me. Set me up for a whistle-blower. The SEC stopped all trading in my company's stock. They froze me out. I was caught on the margin. I couldn't exercise my stock options. I lost everything. And who do you think I lost everything to?"

"Matthew Adams Stockwell, Grandpa," Jack replied wearily.

"Matthew Adams Stockwell." The fury was as fresh in the old man's eyes now as if it had all happened that very morning. "I was prosecuted. 'Insider trading.' Oh, yes. 'Stock manipulation.' Oh, yes. Federal Court in Foley Square, and the chief witness against me, the man they gave immunity to in exchange for his testimony, was

Stockwell's man, who brought me into the scheme in the first place. He testified that Stockwell was one of those I'd victimized."

"Yes, Grandpa. I know."

"He got off scot-free for helping them nail me. I went to jail. Eight years in the federal penitentiary with time off for good behavior. It was almost six before they let me out. Matthew Adams Stockwell was Governor of New York State by then. Of course, Stockwell Industries had swallowed up my shipbuilding company. Not right away, but slowly, over the time I was in the penitentiary. Well, when I got out I went to see the Governor. I figured he owed me. And you know what? The sonofabitch wouldn't see me!" The old man was pounding his fist on the bed now, very red in the face.

Jack took his hand and held it, trying to calm him. "It was a long time ago, Grandpa. It's over now. He's dead. The Governor is dead."

"He pushed me hard, fast, set me up to cut corners with too-sharp edges." The old man panted. "Rich, richer, richest. I was his patsy." The old man's eyes started to go vacant again, then suddenly refocused sharply on Jack. "Not over." His tone was savage, insistent. "Over for me, boy, but not for you. The widow, Jackson. The way to a man's fortunes is his widow. You get that money back. You get even. I raised you. You do it, boy! You promise me!"

A bell sounded from the corridor outside the room. Visiting hours were over. Relieved, Jack stood up. He bent over and kissed his grandfather's creased and stubbly cheek. "I have to leave now, Grandpa."

"You promise me, boy!"

"I promise, Grandpa," Jack Houston said as he started for the door.

"You promise me. You get even."

Jack closed the door on his grandfather's words, and with a grim expression strode down the hallway.

29

ON A BEAUTIFUL autumn afternoon the complexities of love pushed Matt Stockwell to follow the rainbow of fall foliage down Route 684 from his horse ranch on the perimeter of Riverview to the State University college at Purchase. Here he'd wandered from the registrar's office to the chemistry lab building to the dormitory, where he'd finally caught up with Kathleen O'Lunney.

"What are you doing here?" She did not hide her distress at seeing him.

"Mountain coming to Mohammed. You haven't been home weekends since school started. You're avoiding me. Why?"

"Your life's too complicated. I don't want to complicate it any more." There was a quiver along with the lilt in Kathleen's voice.

It made a few of the other students in the dormitory lounge look up curiously. Matt noticed. "Is there some place we can talk alone?" he asked.

"My roommate's studying."

"Will you take a walk with me?"

"All right, then." Distractedly running her fingers through her bright red hair, Kathleen led him from the dorm. She struck out on the trail leading to the fence separating the campus from Westchester Airport. It was a dead-end path, not much used. "It's no good, Matt," she said after they'd walked a few moments in silence. "You're not a sharing man."

"I think I am."

"Not with your pain you're not. You're a miser, you are, with troubles."

"You're upset." His smile was wry.

"That I am." Kathleen took a deep breath. "How many times have you been to Vermont or Canada in the last couple months, Matt?" she asked.

"That's not important." He evaded the question.

"Isn't it, now? You travel a great distance to spend weekends with a woman you lived with for three years, and I'm supposed to agree that it's not important. Ah, Matthew Sykes Stockwell, it's the Governor's grandson you are."

"It's not what you think."

"And what should I think? After the first trip you were a clam when you came back from Vermont. Well, he'll talk when he's ready, I thought to myself. Don't push. Ask no questions and you'll get no lies. So for months I've asked no questions and I've got no answers at all."

"What do you want to know?"

"Why won't you talk about your son? Why do you keep going up to Vermont? Why haven't you told your family?"

Matt looked down at the leaf-carpeted ground for a long moment. When he finally spoke, his voice was very low. "I told you his name is Bruce. She gave him her own last name. Bruce MacTavish. He's five years old."

"Yes, you told me that. But why haven't you told me anything else?"

"There were things I had to work out."

"About your son? Or about his mother?"

"All right, then! At first it was a question of sorting out my feelings about Wendy."

"At first. I see. And now?"

"It's over with Wendy and me."

"And the cozy weekends you've been spending in the north country?"

"I go up there to see my son, Kathleen. I want to get to know him. He's really a terrific little boy." Enthusiasm crept into Matt's tone. "Honestly, Kathleen, you should see him."

"I'd like that," she said softly. "Will you take me up there with you the next time you go?"

There was a long, painful pause.

"I can't do that," Matt said finally.

"Why not?" Kathleen asked quietly. "You wanted me to go with you that first time. What's changed?"

"Wendy wouldn't stand for it."

"Wendy wouldn't stand for it," Kathleen repeated. "I see." Her tone said plainly that she didn't see at all.

271

"It's not you, Kathleen. It's anybody with any connection at all to Riverview. It has to do with the past, during the war." Matt groped for the words to make her understand. "You see, back then it was them and us. You were either for peace or you weren't. If you weren't part of the solution, you were part of the problem."

"But that was then. This is now."

"Not for Wendy. Time hasn't changed things for her. After Bruce was born, she went back to her father's house. She stayed three months. All that time he never let up on her about her Yankee draft-dodger lover and her bastard kid. She had no money and no place to go. All the same, she picked herself up with Bruce and left and never went back. She's made her own way for the two of them ever since. Bruce is her life now. No family, very few friends, no involvement with a man."

"Except for you."

"Except for me. I won't deny it. In her bitter, resentful way, Wendy is still involved with me. She didn't see me for over five years, and during that time she was on one of those love-hate head trips that keep someone going at the same time it eats them up inside. But it's Wendy's head trip, Kathleen, not mine. As far as I'm concerned it's over between us. Except for Bruce, our son."

"And it's her head trip, is it, that says you can't bring me with you to visit your son?" Kathleen's gaze was direct. "Then just what is it you're asking of me?"

"To see me. To be with me. To be patient until I can work this out."

"To be what to you? Your lover, is it?"

"That would be nice." Matt allowed himself a wan smile. "If you're ready."

"Well, I'm not." Kathleen's scowl brought out her freckles.

Matt stopped and turned to Kathleen. Her gaze meeting his was still direct. It was full of resentment and resistance, but behind that there was another message entirely. It was this message to which Matt responded. He took Kathleen by the shoulders, pulled her to him and kissed her hard.

Kathleen stiffened, resisting. Then, slowly, the fight went out of her. Her muscles went slack. Her lips parted.

272

She returned his kiss. "Ah, well," she said when the kiss was over. "Ah, well, we'll have to be working it out together, then, won't we?"

"Yes." Matt bestowed a quick kiss on the little pulse at the lightly freckled base of Kathleen's neck.

"Would Wendy perhaps let you bring your son down here for a family visit, then?" Kathleen asked, snuggling in his arms against the late-afternoon autumn chill.

"I suggested that. She flatly refused. In Wendy's mind the Stockwells—my family—are the enemy. In her head nothing's changed since the Vietnam years. Riverview and Dow Chemical and Agent Orange are all one to her. My family cooperated with the Vietnam War effort, and that makes them responsible for the war."

"But the war is over."

"Not to Wendy. El Salvador, Chile—it's all the same war. She hates my family almost as much as she does her own father. And she doesn't want our son to be any part of it."

"But he is a Stockwell. She can't deny that."

"She does deny it. She won't let Bruce be a Stockwell. To her, Stockwell means much more than just a name."

"Well, she does have a point there." Kathleen smiled wanly at Matt. The smile was a recognition of a deeper truth.

The deeper truth was that there were indeed many ramifications to being a Stockwell.

30

"SHE'S A STOCKWELL? Are you sure?"

The words were lost to the outrageous decibels crowding out the smoke-blue air of Xenon's. From the overhanging floor above, the slender man to whom the words had been addressed cupped his ear to show he hadn't heard. In this setting he was a man who both blended in and was noticed—particularly by women. The slender man's nickname was Harmony.

Harmony's face was youngish—too young for the impeccably styled blue-gray hair razored precisely at the midpoint of his ear. His eyes were brown, limpid, empathetic. His shirt, bent back from its open vee, exposed a hairless, sinewy, vaguely serpentine chest down to the Greek coin which was Harmony's belt buckle. The ormolu intertwinings of the buckle's border matched the design of the gold chain around Harmony's graceful neck.

From his wheelchair the older, stouter man who had spoken crooked his finger. He was Harmony's employer. His name was Stone.

Harmony bent, holding the gold chain with one well-manicured hand to keep it from dangling in the disabled man's face. He put his ear close to Stone's lips.

"I asked if you're sure she's a Stockwell."

"All checked out." The manicured hand patted down the blue-gray wave. "She's a cousin. Name of Caroline Tyler. Left a bundle in Governor Stockwell's will. Up to her come-hither eyes in the battle that's shaping up over it."

"It's a name that sells," Harmony's employer mused. "A name with market value—Stockwell."

"Worth ten points at the newsstand, twelve if it hits same time as the brouhaha over the estate." Harmony's voice was gentle, sympathetic, understanding. It was an attitude that endeared him to Mr. Stone. "I'll see what I can do," he said, smiling sweetly. He straightened up and moved off toward the writhing bodies on the dance floor.

Stone watched Harmony go from eyes that were pale, washed out from the constant appraising of sales figures. Nevertheless a small glint appeared in them as he observed Harmony moving in on the young, voluptuously coltish figure with the red-gold hair aswirl in the strobe lights. "Stockwell." Even pronouncing the name silently brought Stone's tongue into satisfying contact with the roof of his mouth.

Harmony slid easily between his prey and the young man with whom she'd been dancing. Her eyes—slanty blue green—signaled interest. Harmony didn't meet the gaze. Instead he looked over her shoulder and danced. He let his body do the talking.

The message wasn't subtle. It drew Carrie Tyler's eyes from the gold chain down the exposed chest to the belt buckle and then farther down. They paused at the calculated movement of tight designer jeans. She quickly looked up at his face. This time Harmony returned her gaze.

His look surprised her. It was soft, trustworthy. She had anticipated a come-on-strong eye contact to match his lack of inhibition, but it wasn't there. Instead there was an open friendliness without pretension that, in Carrie's experience, was quite unusual in this milieu. She found herself smiling back.

They continued dancing. Carrie became more intrigued by the warmth and candor in Harmony's face, and found herself drawn to him.

"Take a break," he suggested finally, when the perspiration drenching them gleamed plainly in the flash of lights. Guiding her off the dance floor, he spoke intimately in her ear. "I have some pure Ivory," he said.

"What makes you think I do lines?"

"If I'm wrong—" Harmony began earnestly.

"My mother told me never to take candy from strangers."

"We could never be strangers." His eyes were lambent, calflike. "I want us to be friends." ·

"I can't do snow here." Carrie was practical. She'd learned something from her experience at Hanging Rock.

"My place isn't far." Harmony's tone was innocent, without a hint of innuendo.

"Somehow I knew it would be." Carrie's eyes dropped and then came up again. "All right," she said. She linked arms with him. "Let's go."

Harmony's TriBeCa loft apartment really was nearby. Its chrome-and-leather interior was much more impressive than the outside of the building had led Carrie to expect. Glittery and sharp-edged, his furnishings complemented his laid-back persona.

He sat Carrie down on a white kidskin divan and settled next to her. Pulling out a mirror, he set it on the coffee table in front of them. Tamping adeptly, he poured a

275

mound of cocaine from a small vial onto the mirror. Picking up a gold razor, he expertly laid out six lines and then excused himself and went into the kitchen. On his way he turned on the stereo. Harmony returned from the kitchen with two glass tooters and handed one to Carrie.

She snorted up the first line gratefully. He matched her, and they exhaled together, smiling. It was very potent. Then they danced slowly, close together to the Parker beat. Carrie felt herself starting to turn on.

They each snorted another line and kissed. His hands moved over her body and removed her silk blouse. Her mouth moved over the vee of his naked, hairless chest. He peeled Carrie's jeans from her legs like snakeskin. Then he stood up and removed his own clothes.

Both naked now, they snorted the last two lines. They caressed each other lazily, but with heightening passion. Then, unexpectedly, Harmony leaned back, away from her, and smiled. He stretched his arm over the smoked-glass coffee table and his hand came up with a fountain pen. He wrote something on a piece of paper and held it up for Carrie to see.

"They call me Harmony," he had written. "But my name is really Harlan P. Kentworth. What's yours?"

From beneath a pad on the coffee table Harmony pulled out a sheet of paper, pushed it toward Carrie, and indicated that she should write the answer there. Giggling, she complied. "Caroline Tyler," she wrote.

As soon as she finished, Harmony took the pen from her hand, laid it aside, and kissed her passionately. Very aroused, Carrie returned the kiss. Her head spinning from the cocaine, she felt him pick her up in his arms and carry her naked into the bedroom.

Not quite so dizzy after Harmony set her down on the bed, Carrie's eyes fluttered open. She looked down the length of her nude body between her flushed, hard-breathing breasts to where Harmony was stroking the sensitive inner surfaces of her thighs. Carrie squirmed. Her thighs clutched at his teasing hand, and then they parted widely.

She moaned and her hazel eyes turned murky with passion as Harmony's fingers invaded her. The touch of his fingertip on her straining clitoris vanquished the last of her restraint. Her bottom rose up from the bed and she engloved his fingers as deeply as she could. She reached for his erection with both hands. "Do it!" she said hoarsely. "Do it now!"

Harmony mounted her. His first thrust was sharp, piercing the afterhaze of the cocaine. Carrie's long nails dug deep into his naked buttocks, drawing blood, urging him to pound harder.

When he had finished making love to her, Harmony got out of bed. "Where you going?" Carrie asked sleepily.

"Bathroom."

"Oh."

But Harmony walked past the bathroom door into the living room. He walked straight to the coffee table and picked up the undersheet of paper Carrie had signed. He looked at the section that had been hidden by the pad on top of it. The heading read STANDARD PHOTOGRAPHER'S MODEL RELEASE FORM. It said that the model was over eighteen years of age and granted all rights to the pictures for which she was posing to the Sweetlife Magazine Corporation for publication or resale as they saw fit. It said she had been paid for her services, with a blank space to indicate the amount.

The space and the notary stamp would be filled in later. Harmony put the form in a desk drawer, locked the drawer, and put the key in another drawer in the kitchen. Then he really did go to the bathroom.

During this interlude there had been a certain amount of silent activity in the space above the loft bedroom where Carrie was waiting. A zoom-lens camera had been fitted into its braces and focused through a hole in the floor. The lens glittered in the ceiling over the bed on which Carrie was stretched out naked. The photographer made some adjustments and then stepped back from the camera.

The wheelchair glided silently over. Mr. Stone bent low. He peered through the viewfinder and nodded to the photographer. He pulled back with his wheelchair. The photographer stepped in, grateful that Stone—who could be very finicky—had not found fault with the lighting. He snapped the first picture.

Harmony came back into the bedroom. "You look yummy," he told Carrie.

She blushed, pleased. She knew that all men paid you compliments before. Not many paid them afterward.

"Very athletic," Harmony added. "Are you athletic?" He was standing directly over her now, naked.

The photographer refocused quickly, narrowing the range. The frame encompassed the lower half of Harmony's naked body, Carrie's smiling face, and one of her bare breasts. He lined up Harmony's lazily semierect penis with Carrie's pursed lips. He snapped the shot.

"I keep in shape," Carrie answered Harmony.

"I can see that you do. Still . . ."

"Yes?" Carrie looked at him questioningly.

Harmony grinned his soft-eyed grin. "I'll bet you can't touch all four bedposts at once," he said.

Carrie laughed. "Games," she said. "I like games." Carrie reached behind her and stretched to clasp the bedposts with her hands. Then she arched her naked body to its limit. Her breasts strained, nipples erect, quivering. The red-gold triangle at the base of her belly parted. The lips of her vagina separated. The rose petal interior, still dewy with lovemaking, was revealed. Finally she managed to touch the soles of her feet to both bedposts at the same time. Overhead the camera clicked rapidly.

"I feel a little guilty about this," the photographer blurted out as he narrowed the focus to the area between Carrie's legs.

"You can't afford to feel guilty." Mr. Stone was brusque. "If you want to work in magazines, you have to have a thick skin. *Sweetlife* magazine only gives the public what it wants, and what it wants is celebrities, skin, and scandal. That's what sells magazines. And when sales go up, circulation goes up, advertising revenue goes up, and that can mean that wages go up because profits are higher."

31

"THE BOTTOM LINE is profit!" Ellen Stockwell stood over the four men, her hands on her narrow hips, a pose demanding their attention.

"Damn it, Ellen! This is Sunday." A petulant whine robbed Jonathan's protest of force.

"What other day are the four of you all together at Riverview?"

"We are trying to watch the football game." David Lewis gestured toward the wall-size screen where the Jets were colliding with the Patriots as a rabbity quarterback backpedaled to avoid being sacked before he could unleash a long pass.

"Did you see that?" James was indignant. "If that wasn't pass interference, I don't know what is!"

"You're not listening to me!" Ellen strode over to the knotty-pine paneled wall of the west wing den and pushed the switch that plunged the giant-size television screen into darkness.

Her husband Jonathan was devastated. Throughout most of their twenty-five-year marriage Ellen had been docile, if dour. She had emanated disappointment with her life as a Stockwell but had not made waves. Lately, however, since Peter had become active in the Stockwell business—and particularly since the Governor's death had raised him to a position of power in the troika—Ellen had changed markedly. She'd become openly aggressive in her crusade to secure parity—superiority, if possible, Jonathan suspected—of power for their son. Jonathan wasn't happy with this change.

Ellen's aggressive behavior now startled even her son. "Mother," he said, "I don't think—"

"Hush, Peter." Ellen waved away her son's protests. "The fact is that you three"—she ignored Jonathan—"are supposed to be managing the estate equally. But that isn't what's really happening. Although, as I said, the bottom line is profit—and the new profits generated by Peter in the ERC market are more impressive than any other developmental area of the Stockwell enterprises—you, James, and you, David—are using your entrenched position to deny my son managerial equality."

"If we are entrenched, Ellen, it's by age." James tried to soothe her. "Peter shouldn't envy us that."

"How can we hand more power over to a boy whose mother has to plead his case?" Growling, David Lewis undid James's peace effort and raised the hostility level at the same time.

"My mother does not have to speak for me!" Peter's voice was low and cold as ice. "As a matter of fact, I wish she hadn't. But since she has, I should tell you that I agree with her. The two of you continue to treat me as a junior partner. And I am most emphatically not a junior partner!"

"But you are junior," David snapped back. "That is a simple matter of chronology. You are half our age. You have a fifth our experience."

"The Governor," Ellen retorted, "knew that when he wrote his will."

"The will," James pointed out, "said that Jonathan could designate Peter in place of himself. It did not mandate additional responsibility. But we're going to be fair, Ellen. We just think Peter needs a little more seasoning."

Again David Lewis undid James's peacemaking. "It said Jonathan could designate Peter, and that implies that Jonathan can undesignate Peter if he wants."

"Jonathan?"

"Damn it, Ellen, if you don't let us get back to our football game, I just might do that."

It was a joke, albeit an ill-timed one. The men, Peter included, recognized that. Ellen did not. "All right," she said through clenched teeth, flicking the switch back on. "Watch your damn football game. There's more than one way to skin a cat!"

"What do you suppose she meant by that?" Jonathan wondered as the screen flickered back into focus.

"Haven't the vaguest," Peter answered, lying. He knew exactly what Ellen meant because they'd discussed it. She meant the one obvious alternative direction by which he might pursue his business objectives—Buffy.

"What's this? What's this?" His father's exclamation interrupted Peter's thoughts as the television screen swam back into focus.

Thanks to Ellen they had missed the last play of the first half. Now it was halftime and there was a news update on the screen.

The lead coverage was of a demonstration at an upstate Stockwell utility plant. The demonstrators had manacled themselves to the gate of the chain-link fence surrounding the plant's nuclear generator. As the police tried to cut them loose, a second group of protesters mounted a nearby hillside and ignited a large bonfire. They proceeded to burn three straw-stuffed dummies. The crude effigies were of James Stockwell, David Lewis, and Peter Stockwell.

"You wanted equal responsibility, Peter," David Lewis commented dryly. "Well, now you've got it."

"Look! Look!" Jonathan was on his feet and pointing excitedly at the giant screen.

The camera was focusing on a demonstrator scrambling up the hillside with a fourth effigy to burn. This one, overstuffed insultingly in the belly, was of Zelig Meyerling.

"I don't understand." James was bewildered. "Zelig has nothing to do with that plant."

"The Institute." Peter recognized the connection. "It was his paper for the Institute that secured government approval for putting the nuclear reactors on-line."

"That's true." David Lewis smiled without humor. "Whether he likes it or not, Zelig Meyerling is going to hang on the Stockwell petard."

The camera zoomed in for a close-up of the young and attractive female demonstrator who was now dangling the effigy of Meyerling by its rope over the fire. There was a look of exaltation on her face, and her red-gold hair gleamed in the firelight. The network voice-over identified her as a cousin of the very same Stockwell family whose exercise of nuclear power was being protested.

Her name, the viewing audience was informed, was Elizabeth Tyler.

32

AFTER THE ANTINUKE demonstration, grubby and tired, but proud to have acted out her convictions, Beth rode the rented bus back to New York. She took the subway from where it dropped her down to SoHo. Diana was alone in the loft apartment.

"It was great," Beth exulted as she flopped down on the couch. "You should have been there."

"I have. Many times." Diana's voice betrayed tension.

"Is there something wrong?" Beth asked.

"George and Ernie," was the answer. "George hasn't showed up all week. And this is Sunday night, the weekend's over, and no Ernie."

"If you ask me, you're well rid of them," Beth told her cousin. "George is a smirky adulterer having his week-night cake and eating it, too, and Ernie is an over-the-hill, bed-hopping traveling salesman who uses your pad to rest up from his exertions during the week."

She's young; she's naive; she really is concerned for me, Diana reminded herself, and then exploded anyway. "George does not smirk!" Diana's large bosom rose and fell quickly with her agitation. "He has never smirked. Never! And Ernie is only forty-two years old—seven years older than me. If he's over-the-hill, then I must be over-the-hill, too." Diana had a sudden thought. "You saw George last, Beth," she remembered. "I was out grocery shopping. He was gone when I came home. Did something happen?"

"We talked. That's all." Beth's tone was conciliatory.

"What did you talk about?" Diana was suspicious.

"Well, his children, actually," Beth told her reluctantly.

"Oh, great!"

"Well, it was awkward alone here with George waiting for you to get home." Beth tried to explain, hoping to de-fuse Diana's mounting hostility. "I had to make conversation with him, didn't I? So I asked about his kids, and he showed me snapshots of his three daughters. One of them is the same age as me. That's the one that looks just like his wife."

"He showed you a picture of his wife?" Diana gritted her teeth.

"Well, actually, it was a family group shot. It was only later that he showed me this photographer's portrait shot of her. She's really kind of attractive." Weary, Beth blurted it out.

"Don't ever consider a career in the diplomatic corps," Diana told her cousin grimly.

"I'm really sorry." The sentiment was genuine, but then Beth thoughtlessly undermined it. "Anyway, that's when I realized how much their oldest daughter—the one who's the same age as me—resembled her."

"You didn't tell George that," Diana moaned.

Beth was silent.

"You did. Oh, Beth!" She really cares about me, Diana again reminded herself. She's just very young and—dammit!—very dumb. Forgive her, Dear Abby, she knows not what she did.

"Well, I didn't plan it out, Diana. I was just making casual conversation, the way you do when someone shows you pictures of their family." Beth's tone was apologetic. "I didn't expect it to have the effect it did."

"And what was that? The effect?"

"Well, George got sort of misty-eyed. I mean, he didn't exactly cry or anything, but you could tell he was feeling emotional."

"Emotional," Diana repeated dully.

"Yes. And then he picked himself up and said he had to go home. When you came in I told you he said he'd had to leave. You remember that . . ." The pleading note in Beth's voice was as much for understanding of her innocence as for recollection.

"I remember." Diana's jaw muscles were aching from grinding her teeth. "Ernie," she said. "What happened with Ernie?"

"Well, whatever you think about George, Diana, you should thank me for getting rid of Ernie for you." Beth stopped groping for tact and succumbed to righteousness.

283

"Thank you," Diana said dryly. "Now tell me what happened?"

"He actually came on to me. He came up here to sleep with you, and when he found me here alone, he made a pass at me."

"What kind of pass?"

"He said I was attractive. And then he asked if I liked older men. I didn't make any mistake, Diana. I know when a man is coming on." Beth's indignation was patently more on Diana's behalf than because she herself had been insulted.

"I believe you. Ernie is constitutionally unable *not* to come on to an attractive woman. It's his nature. I came to terms with it long ago."

"That's what he said," Beth remembered. "When I threatened him that I'd tell you, he said you knew he had other women and that it didn't bother you. He was so damn smug about it that I got mad. That's when I gave him a little sauce for the gander."

"Sauce for the gander?" Diana was apprehensive.

"Yes. I told him about George. I let him know that what was fair for him was fair for you, too, and so you had this other lover." Even in the face of Diana's chagrined reaction, Beth didn't quite realize the thoughtlessness of her actions.

Diana, reminding herself again that Beth had thought she was being protective of her, couldn't quite suppress her anger. "Does Deke Wells know you're such a tight-ass?" she asked nastily.

Beth cringed and blushed before saying softly, "I guess you have to get your hostility out."

You bet your Pampers I do, baby! Diana thought to herself. Immediately, though, she sighed. What's the point? Her fury would be useless in the face of such innocence. "Well, now it's all out." Diana lied. "The hell with it. Let's cook up some spaghetti and kill a bottle of wine. Manless as I am, I'm damned if I'll watch the calories tonight. Let the middle-age spread fall where it may."

"All right." Beth was relieved. "You do the pasta, and I'll make a salad to go with it."

They worked in silence for a while. Diana took her anger out on the yellow and red peppers she was chopping while Beth tried not to think about her cousin's angry reaction to her meddling.

"What *is* happening with you and your ball player?" Diana finally spoke up as she sauteed the peppers and the mushrooms.

"We're seeing each other. I like him. He likes me. We haven't slept together, if that's what you want to know. I like Deke, but I've got a lot of things on my mind right now."

"Such as?"

"The Stockwells and what they're doing to the environment with the money I inherited from the Governor—my money. Peter, buying and selling those ERC's as part of his real estate deals. The lack of concern of both Great-Aunt Mary and the troika." Beth began tossing arugula, cucumbers, and tomatoes into the salad bowl.

"Holly told me that her Uncle James is trying to stop Peter from dealing in ERC's," Diana informed Beth.

"If he is, it's only because he's concerned with the Stockwell image," Beth retorted. "The Stockwells are the Establishment, Diana. You taught me that. We have to stand firm against them. Even Carrie agrees."

"The two of you will be standing against your father, too," Diana warned.

"That can't be helped. And it won't be just the two of us. There's Matt Stockwell, for instance. He's always been a concerned, committed person."

"It's by no means sure to what extent Matt will stand against his family." Diana dropped the pasta into the boiling water.

"Well, anyway, there's Max and you. His insurance company is against the Stockwell interests. And you're in it with him, after all."

"My brother's struggle is my struggle," Diana conceded. Then she grinned. "Besides, I think he's right. I think we might eventually make a lot of money by investing in the gay community. Then *we'll* be the Establishment."

"It's going well, then? Max's insurance company?" Beth chopped radishes vigorously.

"Oh, yes. Max has even been approached by an outside investor who wants to put money into it. Of course,"

Diana laughed, "the fingerprints of that Halsey De Vilbiss are all over that offer."

"Buffy." Beth nodded. "Will Max accept?"

"Oh, yes. Max is a shrewd businessman. If Buffy wants to invest in his company, he'll let her." Diana began to set the table.

"Suppose the condition is siding with her in the battle over the will?" Beth wondered.

"We already oppose the Stockwells—Max and I both. Neither of us have anything against Buffy—yet."

"Neither do Carrie or I." It was an admission.

Now it was Diana's turn to regard Beth shrewdly. "You've been approached by De Vilbiss," she realized. "But doesn't he know that the money you and Carrie inherited is controlled by your father?"

"He thinks there's a chance that that can be upset in court."

"And you two are going along with him?"

"We want it upset. We want to control our own money. I certainly don't want it used to buy ERC's. We could never afford to mount a court challenge to Daddy's trusteeship on our own. If Buffy's willing to finance it . . ."

"You've come to the same decision that Max and I have," Diana realized slowly. "It takes power to stand up to power. And that means siding with Buffy. Still," she wondered, "how important can we Tylers really be to De Vilbiss? Even with you and me and Max and Carrie standing together against the Stockwells, it only adds up to a gnat annoying an elephant. Even if it was all the Tylers— which we four are not—we wouldn't be any match for them. The Tyler share of the Stockwell estate is just plain too small a piece of the pie."

"That's true." Beth finished mixing the salad dressing.

"Action, reaction," she sighed. "Money is turning all of us into connivers."

"That's true, too."

Diana poured the wine. She waited for Beth to stop tossing the salad, then handed her one of the glasses. "Well, then, so be it," Diana said.

They clinked glasses and drank to conniving.

33

CONNIVING HAD BECOME a modus operandi to Patrice O'Keefe at Bartleby & Hatch over the past three months. Her humiliation at the hands of Jack Houston had honed her determination to land the job as vice president of the advertising agency. That would be only the first step. From now on, she told herself, her career would be her life. Patrice had vowed bitterly to never again leave herself vulnerable to being hurt by any man.

There was a vice presidency up for grabs, and she was in the running along with three men. Three men! It was not, since Jack Houston, Patrice's favorite gender.

Analyzing the competition, Patrice judged all four of them—her three rivals and herself—equally competent. Consequently, it wasn't the pluses that would determine the outcome, but the minuses. Her strategy, then, was not to strive, but to undercut.

This required subtlety. Her rivals must not perceive the new starch to her ever-present bows. Her campaign was one of attrition chipping away at their chances.

One of the contenders, Scourby, had a habit of preening in the presence of attractive young women. Noticing that this irritated Bartleby—the head of the agency—Patrice pulled some strings with personnel. The most nubile and short-skirted member of the secretarial pool was assigned to take notes at the next staff conference. Throughout the meeting Scourby straightened his tie, fluffed up his pocket handkerchief, patted down his sideburns, and stroked his moustache. Finally his preenings brought a sharp request from Bartleby to "Please stop fidgeting, Scourby!" Patrice was content.

Gerberg, another of her rivals, had an Achilles heel in the person of his incompetent assistant, Wilson. For years, because he was by nature kind-hearted, Gerberg had covered up Wilson's snafus. Patrice bided her time until Gerberg was in Los Angeles making a presentation, and then she capitalized on Wilson's ineptitude.

In Gerberg's absence, Wilson was empowered to initial routine expenses. Patrice saw to it that an authorization for the questionable outlay of an additional five thousand dollars on a specific account was mixed in with the other vouchers. Wilson, who always signed what was shoved under his nose, okayed the expenditure. At the staff meeting following Gerberg's return, Bartleby chided Gerberg on the need for management executives to be responsible for subordinates, and to develop the toughness to rid themselves of incompetents.

When it came to Panella, the front-runner, Patrice was even more Machiavellian. One of his new accounts involved a female fashion executive who attended luncheons of a businesswomen's caucus to which Patrice belonged. The woman was an outspoken feminist.

Through a mutual acquaintance, Patrice made sure that the woman executive learned that Panella had once brainstormed a designer campaign with a bondage theme. Models in jeans and blouses, swimwear and evening gowns, had been shown in chains and warding off whips. The story Patrice floated did not mention how far in Panella's past this had occurred.

Soon after, a request was made to Bartleby—without explanation—that someone other than Panella be assigned to the new fashion account. Panella's stock at the agency nosedived. The odds in the office were now eight-to-five that the new veep would be Patrice O'Keefe.

Patrice thought her chances even better than that. If she couldn't have love, then she was damn well going to have success. The afternoon she was summoned to Bartleby's office, Patrice fully expected to be offered the vice presidency. The last thing she was prepared for was to find Halsey De Vilbiss there.

"I believe you two know each other." Bartleby was his usual smoothly affable self.

"Yes." Patrice shook hands with De Vilbiss. She smoothed her bow nervously and sat down in the chair indicated by Bartleby. What was this all about?

Bartleby supplied the answer. De Vilbiss, it seemed,

was representing Star-Agena, Inc., a new holding company with capital in excess of twenty million dollars. Star-Agena had diversified interests in many areas and recently acquired some major properties in the publishing field. An advertising agency was needed to devise campaigns to promote these properties, and Bartleby & Hatch had been highly recommended to Star-Agena. The account would initially be budgeted at three-quarter million dollars a year, and the growth potential was unlimited.

"Unlimited?" Patrice asked. "What does that mean?"

Halsey De Vilbiss spoke for the first time. "It means that growth will be determined by the resources at the command of the majority stockholder."

Bartleby's gaze locked into Patrice's. The message in his eyes was clear. The majority stockholder was Buffy, and if she succeeded in breaking the will, Bartleby & Hatch would gain. This account would put Bartleby & Hatch over the top. They would no longer be one of half-a-dozen up-and-coming agencies on Ad Row. This would put them right up there with the majors.

"If Star-Agena decides we're right for the account," Bartleby told Patrice, "it would, of course, have to be handled by an officer of our organization."

Patrice understood that he was saying she could be that officer; it meant the vice presidency for which she'd been competing. There was another, unspoken message, which she also understood. She responded to it now. "I could not act against my father," she said bluntly.

Bartleby winced. It was Halsey De Vilbiss who responded. "Of course not," he said with a warmth Patrice did not for one moment believe. "There was never any thought that you would."

"What would I be expected to do, then, to secure this account?"

"Do?" Halsey De Vilbiss spread his hands. "Why nothing." He spaced out his next three words carefully. "Just . . . do . . . nothing."

"Nothing at all," Bartleby echoed.

Patrice nodded. It was clear. The price of the Star-Agena account was for her to stay neutral in the battle over control of the Stockwell estate. She did not have to take any action against her father, but neither was she to take any action in behalf of him. She was to be neutral, as far as opposition to Buffy was concerned.

"I'd like to think about this," Patrice said carefully.

"The court hearing concerning the will has been set for early November," De Vilbiss remarked casually.

"I see." Patrice got to her feet.

"Nice seeing you again." De Vilbiss shook her hand. Bartleby put an arm around her shoulder and walked her to the door. It was a fatherly gesture, and it reminded her of James.

Patrice was still thinking of her father when she got back to her own office. It had, after all, begun with him. Because she was a girl, James had never really seriously considered her for a major role in the multifarious business concerns of the Stockwells. Always it had been her brother Matt, even when—time after time—Matt had frustrated his father's ambitions for him.

Damn it! Matt would have been so lousy in business! And she had such a natural aptitude, but even now her sex held Patrice back. She had to compensate. It was the only way. She had to seize the opportunity when it was offered to her, didn't she? Men always behaved according to self-interest, didn't they? In love or in business, it was always the same. They were always wheeling and dealing and looking out for themselves.

Maybe it was time for Patrice O'Keefe to put her own interests in front of her father's.

34

"YOUR ETCHINGS?" Holly stared at Zelig Meyerling with amused disbelief. "You're inviting me up to your apartment to see your etchings?"

"They are very special, my etchings." He was urbane and unflappable in the face of her reaction.

It turned out to be true. Meyerling had acquired, over the years, some forty or more of the earliest examples of the art of etching done in central Europe. These included limited edition prints by Daniel Hopfer and Urs Graf from, respectively, Germany and Switzerland. He had two examples of the half-dozen etchings done by Albrecht Dürer between 1515 and 1519, before the artist switched to engraving. And he also had dry point prints by such later masters as Rembrandt and Van Dyck.

Holly, who thanks to the Governor was steeped in the history of art, was impressed. "These really are something," she granted, circling the large livingroom of Meyerling's Riverside Drive apartment slowly and pausing frequently for a closer examination. "When you said etchings, you really did mean etchings."

"Were you expecting Hieronymous Bosch?" Meyerling was amused. "What would you like to drink?" he asked her.

"Would a martini be too much trouble?"

"No trouble at all." He left Holly studying a Lucas van Leyden as he went into the kitchen to mix a pitcher of martinis.

"How was Washington?" she called to him after a moment.

"The same as always. Paranoid."

"Then I suppose the reason for your trip is confidential."

"Not at all," he assured her. "The reason comes under the general heading of foreign policy input."

"Whose foreign policy? Carter's? Or Reagan's?"

"Both." Meyerling came in and handed her a martini with an olive in it. "I had lunch with the incumbent and dinner with his opponent."

"Fair enough. And just what was your foreign policy advice?"

"I told Carter to put his faith in Amy, and advised Reagan to let Nancy handle the summits."

"Really?" Holly laughed. "Nancy, eh. Somehow, I don't think that would have been Kissinger's advice."

"He won't be asked for advice. Henry is anathema to the Reagan people. He was, after all, the architect of détente."

"What did you really tell Reagan?"

"That the China card should be the centerpiece of his foreign policy."

"And President Carter?"

"To put on a yellow ribbon. The hostage crisis will not go away, and other than that, there is nothing to be done about it. Jimmy Carter will be the victim of his own decency."

"You're sure he'll lose the election, then?"

"Oh, yes. David Rockefeller and Henry told him that the United States had an obligation to the Shah, and from the moment Carter acted to meet that obligation, the Ayatollah had him by the unmentionables. History will record that the Chase Manhattan Bank cost Jimmy Carter his second term."

"You're awfully positive. The election isn't over yet." Holly was thinking of how much the Governor, a lifelong Republican, had been opposed to Ronald Reagan. Extremism in defense of the O.K. Corral, he had said, is poppycock!

"It is over. Believe me." Meyerling took Holly's half-filled martini glass from her hand. "Nothing will change during the few weeks between now and Election Day." He set her glass and his own down on the end table. "Ronald Reagan will be the next President of the United States." He stood up and held out his hands to Holly. "He will be elected by a landslide." When she took them, he drew her to her feet and kissed her.

They had kissed before, but even as their lips met, Holly knew that this time was different. Meyerling's mouth was demanding now. His hands on her body, while gentle as always, were purposeful. It was not his small, muscular tummy she felt pressing against her through their clothing now, but rather the firm ridge of his virility.

Holly was aroused. It had been so long. At the same time, she felt apprehensive, unsure of herself. "Zelig," she said breathlessly when the kiss was over. "I'm not sure that I—"

"I am sure." He kissed her again. His hands moved over her hips and the roundness of her buttocks. "Very sure." He pressed into her. "Very."

A surge of warmth and desire possessed Holly. And yet her trembling increased. Embarrassed by the contradictory signals her body was communicating, she tried to explain what she did not herself understand. "I . . . I'm not casual about—"

"Hush," Meyerling said. The tip of his tongue flicked a sensitive spot just inside her ear. "Ssh, now." Standing, facing her, he took her by her hips. His fingers curled around the wool of her dress. "Don't be afraid." Slowly, whispering to her, reassuring her, he raised her skirt. "It's all right."

His golden-brown eyes looked deeply into hers. Inch by inch he gathered the wool until her skirt was above her waist. Then he kissed her again, the material of his trousers rough against her thighs, his desire pulsing against her belly.

Holly clung to him. There was no decision left for her to make now. The floodgates had been opened, and she felt dizzy with desire and close to being overcome by the dizziness.

Meyerling touched her intimately and found her ready. He sank to his knees in front of her. He removed her stockings and her silk panties. "Beautiful!" His voice was hoarse, the precise lilt more pronounced than usual.

Cool lips moved over the burning flesh of Holly's quivering inner thighs. They moved higher, and warm breath ruffled the golden triangle of gossamer at the base of her belly. A velvety tongue moved over her, and from what seemed like far away, Holly heard an impatient moan and then realized that it was she who was moaning.

His tongue stabbed deep, stroking her clitoris. Holly sobbed, overwhelmed. Her fingers tangled in the tight curls on top of his head. She pressed down, grinding, and his probing kiss provided a passionate release. Holly's climax was quick and intense.

Meyerling stood. He removed all of Holly's clothing and then quickly undressed himself. He was breathing hard and fully aroused.

Holly's eyes widened at the unanticipated girth of his erect penis. He was a man of medium build with a noticeable bulge of tummy and the soft hands of an academic. Holly had always thought his roue reputation a figment of media exaggeration. Now she wondered.

He gave her no opportunity to dwell on his image. He

293

judged correctly that her orgasm had only stoked her libido. Holly's patrician features were contorted by a hunger for more sex. Heart pounding, she stared at his penis. They moved together, both anticipating their bodies coming together.

Later, in his bed, her wits more accessible, Holly dwelt at length—both with her mind and tactilely—on their subsequent lovemaking. It had been slow and exploratory, filled with the thrills of discovery and deeply satisfying. It lasted a very long time and when—this time together—their passion had crested, Holly had been filled with a sense of wonder at the intimacy of the experience.

They dozed off in each other's arms. When Holly woke, Meyerling's hooded eyes were already open and gazing at her fondly. Holly stretched luxuriously. She felt like purring. "What time is it?" she asked.

"About one A.M. Are you hungry?"

"Famished."

"Come on then." He handed her a robe, pulled on his pants, and led her into the kitchen. "You're in for a treat," he told her. "When my accomplishments as Secretary are long forgotten, the State Department will still be praising the Meyerling mushroom omelette."

"Now don't be modest, Zelig. We both know that your place in history is secure."

"Well, you're the historian." He cracked eggs expertly into a mixing bowl. "I bow to your expertise."

"Don't be sarcastic." Holly reacted to the humor lurking behind his hooded eyes.

"Sarcastic? Absolutely not. I have nothing but admiration for you historians." He kissed Holly on the cheek. "You make order out of the chaos wrought by would-be statesmen like me."

"Well, I certainly don't do that." Holly kissed him back before continuing to help him chop the mushrooms finely. "At best I'm an adequate researcher."

"And how goes the research lately?" He coated the bottom of the skillet he'd been heating with butter.

"It gets more and more fascinating."

"The further adventures of Ursula—what was her name?—van Bronckel. Ursula van Bronckel." Holly had already told him the story of how the Dutch Tory maiden had witnessed the duel with the Massachusetts Colonial rebel, Lieutenant Roger Stockwell, and subsequently agreed to a clandestine meeting with him. "I can hardly wait to hear them." Meyerling added milk and a bit of cheese and beat the eggs lightly.

"It is turning into quite a story," Holly granted.

He added the mushrooms and carefully transferred the mixture to the sizzling frying pan. "Tell me about it. Please." There was no doubting the sincerity of his interest.

"Well, all right," Holly agreed as the kitchen filled with the savory aroma of the mushroom omelette cooking.

32

ROMANTIC AS URSULA'S dreams had been, they paled beside the reality of the sixteen-year-old maiden's meetings with Roger Stockwell. For the next seven months after their first encounter, they met once or twice a week at Hanging Rock. The trysts were, of course, secret.

They embraced, kissed, and talked interminably—the sweet twaddle of lovers down through the ages. Flushed, overheated, breathing hard, they approached the brink of lovemaking. They did not cross the forbidden line; they did not make love.

One night in the unseasonably frosty autumn of 1775, Ursula returned home from one of these meetings, her cheeks crimson with cold and unrealized passion, to find her mother awaiting her. Mefrou van Bronckel had news for Ursula.

"Ah, *schattebouw!*" She hugged her daughter, her eyes teary. "I turn for an instant and you have grown to womanhood. And everyone notices save me, your mama."

"What has happened, Mama?" Ursula was apprehensive.

"Meinjeer Hoek has been to see your father."

"Oh." The apprehension increased.

"On behalf of his son. Hans wishes to marry you."

"To marry me." Ursula repeated the words numbly. Her apprehension was confirmed.

"Your father has agreed. My *schattebouw* is betrothed. Do you understand, Ursula? You are betrothed."

"I understand." Indeed, Ursula understood perfectly. She understood that it would do no good to protest to her mother, or to her father, either, for that matter. They would not care that she did not want to marry Hans Hoek. Most certainly she could not tell her parents about Roger Stockwell. There was only one person who could save her from her fate—Hans Hoek himself.

There was to be a dinner party that evening at a neighboring English Tory estate. It was being given to introduce a visiting young cousin from a prominent Philadelphia family to the local gentry. Although traveling alone save for the ineffectual female relative chaperoning her, she was only slightly older than Ursula. Her name was Margaret Shippen, but she was called Peggy. The van Bronckels were going to the dinner, as were Meinjeer Hoek and his son Hans.

All through dinner Ursula composed in her mind exactly what she would say to Hans as soon as she had the opportunity to be alone with him. The meal seemed interminable, and she sat through it in a fog. Nobody noticed. The focus of everyone's attention was Peggy Shippen.

She was not only beautiful—as was Ursula—but she was also a conversationalist and raconteur accomplished beyond her years. Not only had she lived in Philadelphia and New York with her family, but she'd been abroad as well. For one so young, Peggy Shippen was astonishingly sophisticated, and she dazzled the untraveled, burgherlike patroons of the valley and their equally stolid English Tory neighbors.

Powdered curls tossed on her bare pink shoulders as Peggy's bosom heaved with the trill of her laughter. Her blue eyes were mischievous and insinuating in a way that belied her youthfulness. Her flamboyance quite overshadowed Ursula. Despite her shiny raven hair and ivory skin,

Ursula's serious, quiet mood relegated her to a place in the Philadelphia damsel's shadow.

"Philadelphia and New York are both so deliciously exciting of late. The sitting rooms are filled with the most attractive young officers fresh from Mother England."

"I am devastated, Mistress Shippen," proclaimed an enchanted young Tory with cheeks as pink as Peggy's own. "Do these recent arrivals so outshine us, then?"

"Rest easy, sir." Peggy fluttered her fan coyly. "From what I have seen of the Loyalists of the Hudson River Valley, you need not flinch at an infusion of fresh British blood. I was only commenting on how gay the city has become for a young lady, with so many officers in attendance. Indeed, for a Tory patriot such as myself, their presence is most heartening as well."

"Then what we hear of dissidents in Philadelphia need not alarm us." Ursula's father beamed with self-satisfaction. "It is what I have said right along."

"Oh, there are dissidents, Meinjeer van Bronckel," Peggy told him. "But not among the people who count. The leading families of Philadelphia, I assure you, are staunchly Loyalist."

"What of the Philadelphia merchants?" a less easily reassured patroon inquired. "And the plantation owners from the Carolinas and Virginia? It is said they willingly lend support to this revolutionary nonsense spawned in Boston."

"They are not true aristocrats." Young Peggy's shrug capitalized on her décolletage. "They are no more than landed hoi polloi. Our young officers—true gentlemen and warriors—will hang a dozen or so of them when the need arises, and there will be no more talk of revolution. You may be sure of that."

"Are all the young ladies of Philadelphia so deliciously bloodthirsty?" The rosy-cheeked youth's attempt to flirt fell flat.

"I am loyal to the Crown, sir." Peggy drew herself up and looked down her pretty nose at him. "I do not consider hanging traitors bloodthirsty in the slightest. I consider it justified. There is nothing more base than a traitor."

Inside herself Ursula squirmed. Nothing more base than a traitor indeed! Why, there was nothing base at all about her beloved Roger. The aide to the recently promoted Major Benedict Arnold of the Massachusetts Colonial Militia was the furthest thing from base. Indeed, he was the most honorable of men. Was Ursula's intact virtue not proof of that?

"Is it not possible," Ursula asked in a very small voice which had not yet been heard that evening, "that these so-called traitors may have some just grievances? Would it not be wise to inquire into them before our English officers start hanging people?"

"It would be best, daughter, if you did not venture an opinion on matters of which you have so little knowledge," her father cautioned her.

"Just grievances?" Peggy Shippen was truly bewildered. "I surely never expected to hear such radical notions voiced in Loyalist company."

Hans Hoek looked at his intended bride with bewilderment and disapproval.

"I spoke unthinkingly." Discretion brought forth the words from Ursula's berry-red lips. Having caught Hans's attention, she dazzled him with a slightly pouting smile and let her eyes drift beyond the footmen to the archway of the anteroom. The message was clear. She wanted to speak with him alone.

Hans's cheeks puffed out like those of a pouter pigeon. It was a sign of his pleasure. He nodded discreetly, already looking forward to hearing Ursula's joy at their betrothal.

It made him impatient through brandy and pipe smoking, a ritual the gentlemen observed apart from the ladies. He was not, however, as impatient as Ursula, who sat quietly through the further rattlings of Peggy Shippen regarding the sacredness of the Tory cause and the superiority of Loyalist society.

Finally the men returned and the company mingled. Several young patroons and Tory bucks gathered around the vivacious Peggy. Ursula took advantage of the attention Peggy was attracting to draw Hans Hoek into the anteroom.

"It is too risky," he told her without preamble. "I know

how eager you are to seal our betrothal, dear Ursula, but we dare not kiss here."

"It's about the betrothal that I want to talk to you, Hans. You see, I really don't want to be betrothed to you."

"But your father told my father—"

"Two men on in years." Ursula looked into his eyes pleadingly. "What do they know of love?"

"Of what?" Hans Hoek was genuinely bewildered.

"Love."

"Love? But what has that to do with anything, Ursula?"

"You don't love me. I don't love you. Why should we be betrothed."

"Our family's lands are contiguous."

"We don't love each other!"

"That will come, Ursula." Hans Hoek was dense, but truly not unkind. "Love is a mature emotion."

"No it's not!"

"What? Are you contradicting me? We are promised, Ursula, and you really shouldn't do that. It isn't seemly. And I assure you that after we are married, I will not stand for it."

"I don't want to marry you!"

"Well, at this moment I, too, have doubts. Nevertheless, it's settled. My father and your father arranged all the details this afternoon. And there's an end to it."

"If I am forced to marry you, I will make you miserable, I promise you."

"Yes. Well, from what I have heard, that is not so very unusual among those who commit themselves to the institution of marriage."

"Please, Hans."

"There there, Ursula. It's only natural that the news of our betrothal should make you apprehensive. But I will try to be a gentle husband in all things. All things," he repeated meaningfully. "Come now." He enfolded her arm in his. "Let us rejoin the company before we are missed."

Her heart weighed down as by pewter, Ursula accompanied Hans back into the other room, where Peggy Shippen was holding forth on the need for Loyalists to stand together in defense of the God-given reign of England's King George the Third.

"Mad King George's mightiest fortress," Major Arnold informed his aide three days after the dinner party welcoming Peggy Shippen to the Hudson River Valley. "That will be our ultimate objective. We will break camp on the morrow to march to Montreal for a major assault."

His commander's decision filled Lieutenant Roger Stockwell with an increased sense of urgency as he went to meet Ursula that afternoon. Distraught, a prisoner of duty, he was not prepared for the even greater urgency Ursula brought to their tryst.

"Make love to me!" she greeted him fiercely.

He kissed her.

"Don't stop."

He kissed her again, and told her of his imminent departure for the fields of battle.

"Make love to me." Ursula opened the stays of her bodice.

"I do want you!" The lieutenant's hands reached hungrily for the warm, milk-white globes. "But I care for you too much to soil our love by taking advantage of you."

"Do not reject me!" Ursula was beside herself, tearing at ties, disposing of petticoats, ignoring the effect of the cold November air on the flesh she was baring.

"Don't, my love. Patience. We have but to wait. When the war is over I will come back, and we will be married."

"My father has betrothed me to another!" The words, torn from Ursula's lips, were seized by the wind and transformed into a howl of pain.

"No!" Roger was stunned. "Ursula, no!"

"If you don't make love to me, I will knot my stocking around my neck." Even as she spoke, Ursula was pulling off her stockings in a manner that tossed her one remaining chemise above her creamy thighs. "I will tie the other end to that very tree." She pointed with her right hand and disposed of her corset with the left. "I will leap from Hanging Rock." She stepped naked from the last of her clothing and came shivering into his arms. "If you do not make love to me," she told Roger, "I will kill myself."

Lieutenant Roger Stockwell could not let the woman he loved do that.

35

MATT STOCKWELL STROKED the neck of the chestnut Morgan horse he was riding and maintained his firm, easy grip on the reins.

Beside him his father rode comfortably astride another Morgan. The crest of the bluff along which they were riding paralleled the Hudson River. The ten-mile riding path was part of the Riverview estate. The horses, however, were stock from Matt's breeding farm.

They stopped talking and spurred their mounts to an easy canter. It was a perfect day for it. The October air was crisp, invigorating without being too cold. The sky was overcast, but the sun lit it up from behind so that the grayness shimmered like the swordplay of Toledo-tempered blades. In the wake of the riders there rose up a cloud of rainbowed dust, earth colors from the autumn leaves pulverized by the hooves of their steeds.

James was filled with a sense of well-being. The exercise was light, but his body tingled with it. Or perhaps, he reflected with an inner smile, it was tingling with the memory of the previous evening and Vanessa Brewster's bed.

Vanessa aside, though, it did feel good to be riding here beside his eldest son. There was a feeling of rare camaraderie. It was as if the years of strain over Matt's opposition to the Vietnam War and his decision to go to Canada were at last behind them.

The meeting was long overdue. It had been more than three months since Kathleen O'Lunney had advised James to talk to Matt, had confided in him that his son needed a father, a friend. He'd meant to act on that recommendation immediately. When James tried, however, Matt had not been available.

His son had been making a series of trips, first to Vermont, and then to Canada. When James inquired as to

301

their purpose, Matt had been evasive. James hadn't pressed his curiosity, and had accepted Matt's excuse that when he was home that he needed to catch up with the business of his horse farm.

Nor had James himself always been available. Between days spent preparing to fight Buffy's challenge to the Governor's will, his usual business duties, and the nights filled with the joyful reawakening of his manhood in Vanessa's arms, James had little free time. And so the months had slipped by until today, and this afternoon's horseback ride with Matt.

Coming to a straightaway where the bridle path broke from the banks and turned inland across an open field, they spurred their horses to a gallop. After a mile or so they pulled them up by tacit agreement, dismounted, and walked the overheated steeds.

Striding side by side, father and son, they seemed mismatched. James, in his highly polished riding boots and fawn-colored coat and breeches from Abercrombie & Fitch, would not have been out of place on a Virginia fox hunt. Matt, in work shoes, faded denim jeans, and an old jacket of peeling leather, looked anything but aristocratic.

The difference in dress was just one sign of the difference in their life-styles. Despite his unorthodox affair with Vanessa, James would always be an orthodox person, and Matt's convictions would always place him outside the Establishment.

Nevertheless, James was determined to hold on to the feeling of closeness the ride had promoted. "I like your young lady," he told Matt.

"Kathleen?" Matt grinned. "Well, so do I, Dad. She's really special."

"Is it serious, then?"

"For me it is. Very. For Kathleen . . . well, there are problems."

"Would these problems have anything to do with your mysterious weekend trips to Canada? Are you involved with another woman up there, Matt?" Sometimes James's shrewdness extended beyond business.

"In a way. But not the way you think. Not the way Kathleen is afraid I might be."

"Tell me about her," James suggested. "This Canadian woman."

"There really is nothing to tell. Not about her, anyway. It's all over between Wendy and me. It's really been all over for five years." Matt paused, then continued with obvious reluctance. "There is something you should know, though. You're going to have to sooner or later. I guess it's relevant to the Governor's estate, although that's the least important thing about it as far as I'm concerned."

"To the estate?" James was surprised. "What—"

"I have a son!" In the end, for all the advance thinking he'd done about breaking the news to his father, Matt blurted it out. "His name is Bruce. He's five years old."

"A five-year-old son?" James had trouble taking it in. "Were you and this—what's her name, anyway?"

"Wendy. Wendy MacTavish."

"Were you and this Wendy MacTavish married?"

"No. We lived together for three years. Back then, I mean."

For a long moment all James could think of was the joyful news that he had a grandson, but then practicality broke through. "That could be a problem when the will comes up for probate."

"I don't care about that."

"Well, Bruce might when he grows up. And I care that my grandson's holdings are protected."

"Your grandson." Matt was touched. "I like that."

They grinned at each other.

"He's five years old." James shook his head in wonder. "When do I get to see him?"

"That's a problem, Dad. And not just as far as you're concerned." Matt went on to explain to his father about Wendy's attitude regarding the Stockwells. "She thinks the family is evil incarnate," he summed up. "To her the Stockwells are the system. And you can't conceive of how deeply Wendy's hatred of the system goes."

"Deeper than yours?"

"Much." Matt smiled ruefully.

"Are you beginning to put all that nonsense behind you then, Matt?" he asked hopefully.

"Not at all. It's not nonsense to me." Matt sighed. He really didn't want to get into this with his father again. "I believe the way the Stockwells live is wrong. I think the way I live, my life, is the only way in the long run to make the world a better place."

"Then you're still nothing but a dropout. You still refuse to take up your family obligations, to assume your rightful place in the Stockwell organization."

Matt frowned. Why couldn't his father accept his life? "Business isn't for me, Dad. It never will be. That hasn't changed. Face it."

"But damn it, Matthew, can't you see—"

"I really don't want to fight about this again, Dad. We were having a really good day, the two of us. Don't spoil it."

"All right." James sighed in agreement. "I don't want to spoil it by arguing either."

They walked their horses in silence for a while. Then they remounted and started back. The sun, a dying ember, but glowing red, broke through the taupe clouds.

James spoke one more time, his words recementing the closeness between them. "A grandfather," he said. "I'm a grandfather!"

36

"A GRANDFATHER!" James repeated to Vanessa Brewster in her Tompkins Square walkup that night. "What do you think of that?"

"I think we should celebrate." Vanessa had been wearing a bathrobe. Now she took it off and revealed that she wasn't wearing anything underneath.

"You want to celebrate everything." James laughed. "When your toenails grow, you declare a celebration."

"What's wrong with that?" Unselfconsciously naked, Vanessa released her hair from its customary topknot and fanned it out with her fingers over her bare shoulders and large breasts.

"Absolutely nothing." James undressed quickly. He reached for her and drew her down to the bed.

Later, when they'd settled into the companionable ease that always followed their lovemaking, James told Vanessa in more detail about his day with Matt. "We were close," he said. "It really felt nice. It's not often I feel that close to any of my children. I've always had a problem with that."

"With your children?" Vanessa asked drowsily.

"Not just with them. With closeness generally. Sometimes I feel close to someone but I can't express it. It's always been like that. With my wife, my children. With my brothers and sisters. Until I met you, Vanessa, I'd never really been able to express emotion toward anybody since—" Abruptly James broke off.

"Since?"

"Nothing. Never mind."

Vanessa sat up straight against the pillows, struck by the sudden tension in the room. "I'm not just your lover, you know," she said to James gently. "I'm your friend, too. Tell me what you were about to say."

"It was all a very long time ago," James replied, looking away. "It's better forgotten."

"James?"

"All right, then." He took a deep, shaky breath. "I had a brother..."

"Jonathan?"

"No. Not Jonathan. Before Jonathan. I mean he was born before Jonathan. His name was Thomas. Tom. He was a little more than a year younger than I was." James's voice was very low. "He's dead. He's been dead almost forty years. Tom was twelve when he died. I was thirteen."

"How did he die?" Vanessa asked quietly.

"I killed him." James's voice was a whisper now, a whisper filled with despair and self-loathing.

"James?"

"It's true. I killed him. Tom looked up to me. I was older. I was responsible for him. He was timid. I was always daring him to do things he was afraid to do. When he wouldn't, I'd make fun of him. If I teased him long enough, Tom would always do them, no matter how scared he was."

"Kid stuff." Vanessa tried to soothe James. "All young boys do things like that. Older brothers always tease their siblings."

"I tell you I killed Tom."

"What happened?"

"I dared him to go sailing on the river with me. It was cloudy, and the Hudson was choppy, and Tom was scared. I made fun of him. He still hedged; he wanted to ask our mother for permission. But he knew she'd say no, and so did I. Anyway, I just kept at Tom, calling him a scaredy-cat and a mama's boy—things like that. I had him almost in tears. Finally he couldn't take my teasing anymore. He said all right. He'd do it. He'd go out on the sailboat with me . . ." James paused, unable to continue.

Vanessa waited for him to compose himself.

Finally he did. "We'd been out about twenty minutes," James resumed. "We were in mid channel, where the river is deepest. The storm came up sooner than I'd expected. It broke fast. Hard. We couldn't get the sails down fast enough. We capsized.

"I felt myself being sucked under. Down and down. I thought I'd never get to the surface again. Somehow, though, I fought my way back up. Tom was nowhere in sight. I held onto the capsized boat and looked everywhere. Nothing. The Hudson had swallowed him up. I've never been so frightened . . .

"It was two hours before they found me. I was frozen, and I was sick for a long time."

"Your brother?" Vanessa asked.

"Three days after the accident his body washed up downriver."

"You were a child yourself." Vanessa put her arms around James. "Only a child." She rocked him.

"No one said anything, but they all knew. My father, my mother—they knew how it was with Tom and me. They knew I was always teasing him and daring him to do things he was afraid to do."

"You felt guilty. You were projecting." She held him tight and kept on rocking him.

"No. For a long time the Governor could barely bring himself to talk to me. And then it was never the same between us. My mother would look at me and start to cry. She couldn't help it."

"Oh, James, James . . ." She rocked him in her arms. "It was a long time ago . . . such a long time ago."

"I killed Tom. I killed my brother."

"No. No. Hush." Vanessa held his face against her naked breast. "Hush, now." She kept on murmuring for a very long time. Slowly she felt the tension easing out of him. And finally she felt the warm wetness of tears on her bosom.

"You're the only one I've ever been able to bring myself to talk to about that." Finally James stopped crying.

"Your wife?"

"No. I loved Cecelia, but I could never bring myself to discuss Tom's death with her."

"Your children?"

"No. Patrice knows, but not from me. My mother told her, I think. Patrice once tried to discuss it with me, but I cut her off. It was too painful."

"It's no wonder closeness is so difficult for you," Vanessa realized. "All this time you've been consumed with guilt. Fear, too. At some level you believe that if you get really close to someone, you'll cause their death, too. But you've got to stop thinking that now, James. It's not rational. It's what keeps you from relating to your children. It's the wall between you and Matt."

"I know. But it really wasn't there as much as usual today. I think it's because of how you've opened me up, Vanessa."

"Nothing any hot-blooded lady anthropologist with a penchant for older men couldn't have done." Deliberately, Vanessa lightened the mood. "You must be very excited at the prospect of seeing your grandson for the first time," she said, changing to a happier topic.

"I would be if I were going to get to see him, but I'm not." James repeated to Vanessa what Matt had told him about the child's mother not wanting him to have any contact with the Stockwells.

"But you're not going to just let it go at that!" Vanessa was indignant.

"Well, what can I do?"

"Go up there and plead your own case. Don't leave it to Matt. Go and see her yourself."

"You mean demand to see my grandson?" James was dubious. "I don't think I'd get very far."

"No. Don't demand anything. Charm her."

"Charm her? Me?" James laughed.

"You can be very charming when you want to be. And if you don't go up there and do it, I'll be very disappointed in you, James."

"Charm her, eh? Well, all right, on one condition. You have to come with me."

"I thought you'd never ask." Vanessa smiled. "As a matter of fact, I've never been to Canada. I've always wanted to go."

"But where will I find the time?" James had second thoughts. "I really am up to my ears in this battle over the Governor's estate."

"You'll find the time." Vanessa was sure. "And we'll go." She waited for his nod of agreement, then asked James how his struggle to maintain the will was going.

"All right, I think." James sighed. "But in the end what it will come down to is a matter of people choosing up sides."

"Who's on your side?"

"Well, let's see—Mother, of course. She's the main beneficiary, and essentially it's the provision naming her primary legatee that the other side is trying to break. Alice and my brother-in-law David are with me, of course. And my brother Jonathan."

"But you said he isn't very active."

"That's true. His son Peter exercises Jonathan's power. With advice from Ellen, his mother," James added dryly. "They'll act strictly according to self-interest. My brother won't have too much effect on what they do."

"But surely they won't side with Buffy."

"I don't think so, but I can't be absolutely sure. Anyway, my niece Holly is on our side. And my cousin Paul Tyler—even though he's getting a rough time from both his twin daughters about not pulling their money—which he controls—out of the Stockwell portfolio. I think I can count on my sister Susan granting me power-of-attorney to go on handling her interests, too."

"And what about your own children?"

"Well, I'm sure of Patrice. Lisa, too, for that matter. She's too busy running around Europe to even take an interest in what's going on. As for Michael..." James sighed. "Probably he's all right. But with Michael politics comes first, so I can never really feel secure."

"And Matt?"

"Matt's an idealist." James smiled with both fondness and exasperation. "They're the most unpredictable of all."

"But you'll prevail." Vanessa kissed him. The kiss said she was ready to make love again.

"Oh, yes." James pressed against her, letting her know that he, too, was ready. "How can I not prevail against that two-bit California shyster Buffy has retained?"

37

HALSEY DE VILBISS was waiting patiently for a pause in the rain of blows falling on the flesh of his employer so that he might summarize the present status of the pending litigation.

"Kirsten," grunted Buffy, her teeth rattling under the latest impact, "was trained personally by the Marquis de Sade. Isn't that right?"

"Wrong." Kirsten chopped happily at a kidney. "It was Torquemada."

"In any case," Buffy groaned, "she won't stop until I'm reduced to dog meat. So just ignore her, Mr. De Vilbiss, and proceed."

"Very well. Star-Agena first. Our new company has offered a very attractive account to Bartleby and Hatch, and so Mr. Bartleby has spelled out the conditions of her future career to Patrice O'Keefe. I was present, and from her reaction, I think the possibility is strong that she's been neutralized."

"Can't ask for more than that." Buffy writhed under a new series of pokings by Kirsten. "Patrice would never actually act against her father."

"Star-Agena," De Vilbiss continued, "has also bought up enough stock in *Elite* magazine so that together with the shares owned by Michelle Carter and her husband Andrew, we, rather than the Stockwells, control the parent company. Michelle Carter will stand with us in our efforts to seize control over management of the estate from the troika."

"Go on." In vain Buffy twisted to escape the pressure of Kirsten's thumbs.

"Star-Agena has put up money to back Max Tyler's insurance company. It's understood that we can count on the support of him and his sister Diana."

"Does Diana understand that?"

"Her brother says he can deliver her support."

"Don't count on it. Diana has a mind of her own."

De Vilbiss shrugged. "In any case, just yesterday Star-Agena scored a much more important coup than all the Tylers put together."

"*Oww!*" Buffy blinked back the tears. "What coup?" she asked De Vilbiss.

"Michael Stockwell's campaign manager has accepted a sizable contribution from Star-Agena."

"I thought corporate contributions were limited by law."

"They are." De Vilbiss smiled, pleased with himself. "That's the beauty of it. We've broken it down into a list of individual proxy contributors. By going along with this, Michael's campaign manager has made him vulnerable. Either Michael votes with us regarding management of the estate, or we make public the financial manipulations of his campaign and cost him the election."

"Michael will never allow that to happen." Buffy smiled through her pain. "He's too much like the Governor."

"Moving right along," De Vilbiss said, "Star-Agena has arranged to provide free legal services for Beth and Carrie Tyler to challenge the stewardship of their father."

"A thorn in James's side." Buffy shrugged and winced. "Nothing more. All the Tylers together don't swing as much weight as, oh . . . say Matt Stockwell."

310

"I've given a lot of thought to Matt Stockwell," De Vilbiss told her. "He's an idealist. He wants to separate his inheritance from the Stockwell operations because they're involved with weapons production, pollution, apartheid, etcetera. In that respect he's not unlike Beth Tyler, except that he has control over his legacy—which is larger—and she and her sister are still trying to get theirs. Anyway, Matt Stockwell just needs a push in the right direction, and I think I know how to give it to him."

"I'm listening."

"He is committed to the movement against the Carter administration's involvement in El Salvador, and he's concerned that if Reagan is elected, U.S. interference will snowball and spread throughout the rest of the region. He would like to donate some of his inheritance to organizations opposed to that."

"Yes?" Buffy held up a hand to indicate to Kirsten that she'd had enough. "So?"

Kirsten ignored the hand and kept on pummeling.

"A matching fund," De Vilbiss told her. "We set up a fund to match, dollar for dollar, whatever money Matthew Stockwell pledges to divert from the family portfolio to the fight against U.S. intervention in Central America."

"That just might work," Buffy realized. "Have you approached him yet?"

"I've made overtures. He's not unwilling to discuss it."

"Good." Buffy sat up and glared at Kirsten. "Enough!" It was a command. "I've had enough for now!" She turned back to De Vilbiss. "What else?" she asked.

"Best for last." He ran his fingers over a stickpin that definitely did not belong east of the Rockies. "Ellen Stockwell has approached us on behalf of her son Peter. We have split the troika!"

"That is good news. What does Peter want?"

"Everything he can get." Halsey laughed. "He's a greedy young man. Or at least his mother is greedily opportunistic for him. It's hard to tell which of the two is more ambitious. Anyway, they want assurances that if he uses his influence as a member of the troika in our behalf, we will help him get the kind of control he now has to share with his two uncles."

"And did you give them those assurances?"

"Of course. I agreed to everything. People as manipulative as they are never think that anyone else might be manipulating them. He will keep James Stockwell and David Lewis very busy with his opposition, and that will divert their attention from us."

"Together with the others you've lined up," Buffy wondered, "will Peter's support put us over the top?"

"Not really," De Vilbiss admitted.

"Then what does it all add up to?"

"It gives us leverage. But it's not decisive."

"Do you have some plan that is decisive?"

"Yes," De Vilbiss assured her. "I think I'm on to something that will be very decisive indeed. I'll know better in a few days."

With a discreet cough from the doorway, Berkley informed them that there was a call for the lawyer. He plugged the phone in for him and left. De Vilbiss picked up the receiver.

"Hello." De Vilbiss listened. Then he covered the mouthpiece. "Ellen Stockwell," he told Buffy.

Buffy's eyebrows shot up and she waited.

"Thank you, Mrs. Stockwell," De Vilbiss said finally. "I'll be away on a business trip next week, but you can assure Peter I'll get in touch with him as soon as I return. Yes, well, good-bye for now, then." De Vilbiss hung up the phone.

"Well?" Buffy asked impatiently. "What did she have to say?"

"The lady thought I should know," De Vilbiss replied, savoring the information he was passing along, "that James Stockwell is having a love affair."

"So what?" Buffy was unimpressed. "James is a widower. He's entitled. I don't think anybody will care very much."

"The lady he's involved with is Vanessa Brewster, the 'friend of the family' who, as I'm sure you know, was with the Governor under highly compromising circumstances when he dropped dead." De Vilbiss pointed out the obvious: "There are implications here that can only work out to our advantage."

"Scandal always works out to someone's advantage." Perhaps remembering her own experience, Buffy grimaced. "That's the nature of scandal."

38

MEANWHILE, A DIFFERENT SCANDAL was breaking, and it broke first at *Elite*. A young makeup woman in the art department roomed with another young woman who had a similar job at *Sweetlife* magazine. When her roommate brought page proofs of an upcoming *Sweetlife* sixteen-page center section home with her to check one night, the *Elite* employee immediately recognized the subject of the centerspread. Her eye on the rungs leading up the corporate ladder, she made color Xeroxes of the entire sequence and brought them to her boss, publisher Michelle Carter, the next morning.

With some satisfaction, Michelle called her father. "Remember how you had your watchdog kill my Beth Tyler demonstration story because it might embarrass the family?" she reminded him. "Well, tell the Stockwells to fasten their seat belts, Daddy. Sister Carrie has gone Beth one better."

David immediately summoned James, Jonathan, and Peter to his office. Jonathan was the first to respond to the news that their cousin Carrie was featured "in the pink" in an upcoming issue of a top circulation skin magazine. "The Stockwell name is being dragged through the mud!" he wailed in genuine dismay.

Michael Stockwell, when he learned about it later in the day, reacted from more practical considerations. "Just how much will this hurt us?" he demanded of his campaign media consultant.

"If we were in an urban district, not at all," was the answer. "But here upstate . . ."

Upstate, at Riverview, Holly heard the news with dismay. There seemed no end to Carrie's downward spiral. She was so young. It was such a waste. But even though Holly thought it a lot more tragic than any embarrassment

313

to the Stockwell family, she decided to spare her grand-mother the news for the present.

Mary heard it anyway. Ellen Stockwell passed it along to her with some satisfaction. She was well aware of Mary's fondness for the Tyler twins and of how upset Mary would be by such sleazy publicity, but that didn't stop her. As far as Ellen was concerned, Mary would always be the linchpin of the power preventing her son from reaching his full potential. She was all too happy to upset her.

Patrice O'Keefe, raised in the sixties, was not nearly as upset as her grandmother. She was one of the few Stock-wells who actually saw the lascivious pictures before *Sweetlife* was out on the stands. Michelle had sent a copy of the lewd photo feature to her office. Patrice was more amazed than outraged at how clinical the shots of Carrie's private parts were. Describing the photos to her brother Matt, she opined that "they wouldn't be out of place in a primer for gynecologists."

Matt, however, like Holly, was concerned with the effect on his grandmother. His concern prompted him to call Holly to caution her not to tell Mary, only to learn that he was too late. His aunt Ellen had already spilled the beans. "And," Holly added, "I'm worried about what will happen when the damn magazine is published and Chris-topher sees it."

"Christopher?" Matt drew a breath. "How could this concern Christopher?"

"I'm afraid he'll drag it into the custody suit for Ni-cholas. He'll say Carrie is a member of the family and that her visits to Riverview make it an unsuitable environment for raising a child."

"But that's ridiculous."

"I hope so, Matt. I hope I'm just being paranoid. But believe me, if there's a way to add to the family's embar-rassment so they—and I—will settle with him on his terms, Christopher will find it."

Holly's reaction and that of the other Stockwells, al-though charged with emotion, was not as intense as that of Carrie's immediate family. Her father and mother were a lot more concerned with the visible evidence of their daughter's depravity than they were with the text linking her to the wealthy and politically powerful Stockwell clan. First there had been the cocaine incident, and now this. Not even the knowledge that the shame involved would hurt him professionally pained Paul as much as what the photographs said about the value his daughter Carrie placed on herself—her name, her future, her life. Margaret, like her husband, regarded the shocking photos as the visible evidence of their failure as parents. Both of them were at a loss as to how to deal with Carrie, whose defiance had gone beyond all limits. They couldn't talk to her, because she refused to listen. She hid behind a closed bedroom door at home and an unaffected pose wherever she went. None of her family, not even Beth, knew how much pain and shock she was really suffering.

Beth was furious, and more concerned with herself than her sister. She confided her feelings to Deke Wells, whom she had been seeing more of lately. "Suppose people think it's me? After all, we look exactly alike. There's bound to be some confusion. It's just not fair!" Beth wailed. "Damn Carrie anyway!"

Diana Tyler didn't follow the family's hard line. She thought Carrie had been foolish and indiscreet in posing for the pictures, but she didn't view it as a tragedy. "Naked and sexy." She shrugged it off to her brother Max. "Well, she's young and good to look at, even if the poses are more awkward than stimulating. I don't know what all the fuss is about. People just aren't focused on sex or nudity or the Stockwells as much as the family seems to think they are. After all, this is 1980."

In a way, this was the view echoed by Buffy when she learned of the soon-to-be-published nude centerfold of the most uninhibited young Stockwell cousin. "Two genetic traits mark the Stockwell strain," she remarked to Halsey De Vilbiss. "One is the appetite for scandal, and the other is the enjoyment of being shocked by it."

39

"ARE YOU SHOCKED?" That was the first question James Stockwell asked Buffy when she told him why she'd asked to speak with him privately after breakfast.

"Because you're having an affair with Vanessa Brewster?" Buffy laughed. "Amused, perhaps, but not shocked."

"Amused?"

"Yes, James. I am human. I do remember your attitude when the papers were having a field day with the Governor's affair with me."

"I'm not married, and your husband had been a classmate of mine. He was a friend, and I felt personally embarrassed. And I was concerned for my mother."

"You behaved like an insufferable prig. It hurt your father, and I hated you for it. But you're right. It was a long time ago. It's just that I can't help noting that now the shoe is on the other foot."

"Only as I just reminded you, I'm not married. I'm a widower, and no spouse will be hurt by my actions." James was formal.

"James, you know better. The whole world realizes that the Governor died making love to this woman. All the Stockwells will be a laughingstock when it comes out that she's your mistress."

"Next you'll be accusing her of causing the Governor's death and me of complicity because I'm her lover."

"I had thought of that," Buffy admitted.

"Except it won't hold up. I hadn't even met Vanessa when the Governor was alive."

"Strangely enough, I believe you. But will anybody else?" Buffy arched her brows.

"What's your purpose in telling me all this, Buffy?"

"I thought you should know that we know—and just

about everybody else, too, it seems—that you're compromising the family with this woman."

"The family? Are you trying to tell me that you're concerned about the family, Buffy?"

"I do think that in the wake of the Carrie Tyler pictures, another scandal might be a bit much for the family's good name. That's why I'm warning you that your secret is out, James."

"Warning me? Are you warning me, Buffy? Or are you threatening me?"

"Why don't *you* decide, darling?" Buffy bestowed upon James her most dazzling smile. "I have an appointment at the hairdresser. Ta-ta." And she was gone.

Passing through the Riverview main hall in her wake, James ran into Peter and David. "Uncle David and I were discussing your memo," Peter told James as the three of them continued out of the house.

They got into the limousine which would take them to their offices in the Stockwell Building in Manhattan. The Fleetwood glided toward the main gates of the Riverview estate before James asked, "What about my memo?"

"It isn't pragmatic, Uncle James," Peter told him.

"Not in the short run, perhaps." James disagreed. "But in the long run our corporate image will be a lot better off with us out of the Emission Reduction Credits business. In the long run the public is going to demand that the government come down hard on polluters."

"Which government?" David Lewis inquired softly. "The polls indicate that Reagan is a shoo-in. That means Watts will run Interior."

"Do you agree with Peter, then?" James looked hard at his brother-in-law.

David Lewis, who really did agree with Peter, sidestepped the question. "Not my area. You decide."

"There are three of us in charge of the estate," Peter reminded his uncles stiffly. "If two of us disagree, then the third should cast the deciding vote."

"Surely we don't have to be so formal." James knew that, as always, David would stand with him even if he disagreed. It was tacitly understood between them that Peter's voice should not be conclusive in the decision-making process until he had gained more experience and maturity. "After all, we are all three family."

"And Beth Tyler?" Peter asked sarcastically. "Does she count as family, too?"

"Why, yes. As a matter of fact, she does. The Governor always considered all of the Tylers a part of the Stockwell family. After all, they are the descendants of his sister."

"And so Beth Tyler is entitled to decide our policies involving real estate and investment and production according to her extremist and radical opinions concerning the environment?"

"Now I never said anything like that, Peter. You know that I believe that the concerns of the environment always have to balance out with the concerns of the economy."

"That's true." David, secretly convinced that any increase in Peter's managerial power would come at his own expense, not James's, sided with his brother-in-law. "Business always comes first with James."

"Really? Then you both should take a look at the latest quarterly report. Percentage-wise there's more profit growth in our ERC operations than in any other single aspect of our domestic operation."

"I don't deny it, Peter." James's tone was amiable, but he had no intention of backing down. "And all credit to you for having built the ERC operations up to such an extent. Nevertheless, when I get back from Canada I would like to see a schedule from you for phasing them out."

Peter bit his lip and said nothing.

"How long will you be in Canada?" David inquired.

"No more than a week," James told him. "A week should be more than enough time."

40

"IT'S A RELIEF that he's in Canada," Patrice remarked to Holly later in the week. "At least he isn't parading that Brewster woman around New York."

"Aren't you being unfair?"

"No, Holly, I'm not. This is the woman who was in the sack with the Governor when he died! She probably suffocated him to death with those big mammaries of hers. And now she's got her hooks into his son, my father."

"You really do think she's taking advantage of your father, don't you? But how? What do you think she's after? Marriage? What?"

"I don't know," Patrice admitted. "But I'm all too afraid that eventually I'll find out. And my father will find out, too." Her tone was severe. It didn't help matters that her father was all too obviously in love with this woman. Patrice had no patience for love at the moment.

Holly noticed Patrice's edginess. Not just her tone, but a tightness around the corners of her mouth attested that she was under considerable strain. Holly wondered whether it was just her concern over her father's affair. "How are things at the office?" she asked.

"The usual pressure. Nothing I'm not handling."

"The promotion?"

"On hold." Patrice bit the words off. It was obvious she didn't want to discuss the vice presidency. "How's your divorce coming?" She changed the subject.

"We're waiting for the court to set a date for a hearing."

"Has there been any progress finding that woman?"

"No." Holly sighed. "We think she's somewhere in southern Europe, but we haven't located her yet."

"That's really too bad." Patrice was genuinely sympathetic. "I was sure you'd have found her by now."

"I'm really terrified," Holly confessed. "Without Winifred's testimony to counter that letter, I don't know what will happen. I'm afraid the court will declare me an unfit mother and give him custody of Nicholas."

"That might not happen, Holly. People are more enlightened about homosexuality than they used to be. More and more lesbian mothers are being given custody of their children."

"But I'm not a lesbian mother." Holly sighed.

"I only meant that even if the court thought you were, the judge might still give you custody. It's at least a fifty-fifty chance."

"That's not good enough! This is my child we're talking about."

"I know. And you're a damn good mother. I really do believe that it will work out for you, Holly."

Despite her general edginess, the warmth Patrice communicated to Holly was genuine. Grateful, Holly took her cousin's hand and squeezed it. "Really, Patrice," she said, "how is your life going?"

"Work and sleep. Sleep and work. Not exactly *la dolce vita.*"

"Be patient. You're bound to meet someone."

"A man?" Patrice shuddered. "Ugh! That's the last thing I want."

"I know how you feel. I felt that way after I left Christopher. But I learned something, Patrice. Bitterness makes for loneliness. You're too young to be a recluse for the rest of your life."

"Reformed recluses are worse than reformed drunkards," Patrice observed. "And there's nothing as smugly insufferable as a woman in the middle of a love affair she's really enjoying."

"I confess," Holly smiled. "That old Meyerling magic has me in its spell."

"I guess I shouldn't be surprised." Patrice was cynical. "Rumor hath it that the irresistible Zelig is decidedly over-endowed in the equipment department?" She wagged her bow suggestively.

Holly's blush was a confirmation.

"Then it's true. And I always thought it was only a case of yet another government official running a rumor up the flagpole to see how many ladies would salute."

"The flagpole stands on its own without benefit of rumor." Holly burst out laughing, very red in the face now. "I do not believe this whole conversation," she said. "I sound like some jock bragging about his girlfriend's tits to the boys in the locker room."

"You're entitled. Women have locker rooms now, too."

"I know. But seriously, Zelig's not just a sex object. Equipment aside, he's a tender and considerate man."

"You're not telling me you're in love with him, I hope. That wouldn't be smart. There's a long list of ladies who will testify that Zelig Meyerling is definitely not a one-woman man."

Holly didn't reply. Inside, though, she smiled wanly at Patrice's concern. Her characterization of Meyerling was the exact opposite of her grandmother's. "After all his running around, I sense that Zelig Meyerling is ready to settle down," Mary had said when she learned that Holly was seeing him frequently. "He's ready for real love in his life. And when he finds it, he'll commit himself."

With a lifetime of experience behind her, Holly knew, Mary Linstone Stockwell was rarely wrong in her judgments of people.

41

MARY LINSTONE STOCKWELL had arrived at another judgment, one that had been much more difficult. It concerned her grandson, Peter. She summoned him to a Riverview sitting room to inform him of her decision.

"This is very painful for me, Peter," she began.

"Is there something the matter, Grandma?"

"Yes, Peter. You. You are the matter."

"I don't understand, Grandma."

"Don't you? Then I shall explain. Your uncle James, before he left for Toronto, made it clear to you that he wanted a schedule from you for the phasing out of Stockwell investments in Emission Reduction Credits. He has been back three days. Each day, he tells me, he has asked you for the schedule, and each day you have failed to comply with his request. It is James's opinion that you have no intention of complying."

Peter shrugged. "ERC's are highly profitable and becoming more so every day."

"James is aware of that. So am I. Profitability is not the main concern in this matter. James assures me that this was made clear to you."

"But Grandma—"

"It is not just *his* wish that Stockwell Enterprises have nothing further to do with this pollution business. It is mine as well."

"Pollution business? Grandma, you've been paying too much attention to these environmentalist nuts. That's the kind of talk I'd expect to hear from Beth Tyler."

"Well, you're hearing it from me!" Mary's voice quivered. "But I fear you're hearing it too late."

"Grandma?" Peter blinked.

"You are aware that we are engaged in a battle over the estate, are you not, Peter?"

"Buffy? Of course I'm aware."

"And whose side are you on in that battle, Peter?"

"Grandma, how can you—"

"How can I? With ease, Peter. You have been—and I know that it is a wartime phrase, but I do believe that it is nevertheless quite appropriate—consorting with the enemy. You and your mother have been meeting with that tricky lawyer De Vilbiss, and with Buffy as well. You have been making deals with them to oppose us. And your price has been an agreement that you be appointed sole manager of the estate."

"How did you know—"

"Do you think that a fortune the size of the Stockwell fortune could be handled by anyone who didn't make it their business to know?"

"Are you saying that Uncle James has been spying on me?"

Mary allowed herself a small, pained smile. "As a matter of fact, your Uncle James was in Canada. In his absence it was your Uncle David who safeguarded the family interests against you and your mother. Furthermore, ames was actually against the action I am about to take. But for just this once I am going to side with your Uncle David."

"What action?" Peter was both sullen and fearful.

"I am removing you as a member of the triad managing my estate."

"But I was appointed by the Governor! You can't do that."

"At my pleasure, Peter. The Governor specified that the three trustee-managers serve at my pleasure. And it is not my pleasure that you should be one of the three anymore. You are dismissed, Peter."

Peter stared at her for a long moment. His gaze was angry and resentful, but also contemptuous. It told Mary clearly that he thought she was old and would die soon and that then—somehow—he would fight his way back up to control of the estate. He was young, only twenty-ive. He would outlive them all—Mary, James, David, even Buffy. Peter turned on his heel and left.

Alone, Mary took her hands out from under the cashmere shawl over her lap. They were pale and shaking. She took a deep trembly breath, which ended in a sigh.

She hadn't had to take action so distasteful to her in many, many years, and it had extracted a great price. Reaching down into the knitting bag at the side of her chair, she removed a small phial. She took out a nitroglycerin pill and popped it under her tongue. Soon, Mary hoped, the viselike grip of the angina on her chest would ease.

42

"SHE ACTUALLY FIRED HIM." Buffy laughed as she passed the news along to Jack Houston. "I never thought that Mary had that kind of gumption."

"How come you're amused?" Jack wondered. "I mean,

since you already co-opted Peter Stockwell, wouldn't it have been better if he stayed one of the three managers?"

"I suppose so. On the other hand, he knows a lot about the Stockwell operation, and now he'll spill it all to us. Peter's mad. He wants to hurt back. That could turn out to be an even bigger asset than having him as one of the troika."

"Jesus!" He was dismayed. "You're beginning to talk just like De Vilbiss."

They were in Jack Houston's one bedroom apartment on Riverside Drive. Lately, Buffy came there rarely. Jack had been both surprised and gratified when she dropped in this particular noontime. Her next words, however, took the edge off his pleasure.

"If you're going to ball me, darling," she said, "you'd better hurry up. I have to be downtown exactly two hours from now."

"Damn it, Buffy, I'm not a sex machine!"

"No? Oh, dear. I must have gotten the address wrong."

"Very funny." Miffed, but aroused by Buffy as always, Jack followed her into the bedroom. "Why do you have to be downtown?" he asked as she turned her back for him to pull down the zipper of her dress.

"Business meeting at Star-Agena." Buffy sat down on the edge of the bed and kicked off her shoes.

"Well, at least it's not a hairdresser's appointment." Jack pulled his turtleneck off over his head. The well-developed muscles of his chest rippled in the early noon sunlight coming through the bedroom window.

"What does it matter what kind of appointment it is?" A thrill of desire flicked Buffy's nipples as she looked at Jack's chest. Such youth. Such ready energy. She peeled the stockings from her long, lightly muscled legs.

Jack looked at them appreciatively. It was a silly thing, but the red mark where Buffy crossed her thighs always excited him. He dropped to the floor beside her and kissed it. Then he answered her question. "It matters because Wham, bam, thank you, ma'am is insulting. I'll buy it for business reasons, but when you pull it because your dressmaker is waiting, you leave me feeling used—like a stud."

"But you are a stud, darling. A delicious stud. My very own marvelous stud." Buffy got to her feet and slipped off

324

her skirt. She stood before him in bra and panties. Reaching down, she squeezed his erection through his pants. "My ever-ready stud."

"Damn it, Buffy! I hate that!"

"Do you?" She squeezed again. "Wherever do you suppose I got the idea that you enjoyed it?"

"You know what I mean! I hate it when you treat me like a sex object and nothing else." But even as he spoke, Jack was aware of the throbbing in his pants where her hand encircled him.

"Why darling, you sound like a feminist." Buffy let him go. Straightening up, she removed her bra and panties and stood before him naked. "Why don't you take off your pants darling," she suggested, "so I can see your lovely cock."

Her body was magnificent. Looking at her, Jack never registered that she was almost fifty years old. He saw only flesh that was firm and glowing with desire, and that never failed to excite him. He pulled off his pants and his shorts.

Naked, they embraced and kissed. Still kissing, they settled to the bed. Her long fingernails traced the line of his back, scratching slightly. "Ooh!" Buffy writhed under his caresses. "That's it, darling. I love the way your hands feel on my breasts."

Jack's mouth followed his hands to her bosom. His tongue traced her aureoles. He sucked one and then the other of her long, red nipples.

Panting, Buffy stroked his bottom. She gently squeezed the swollen sac of his scrotum. Her fingertips danced over the ridge of passion building in his now fully erect organ. She took Jack's hand and guided it to her warm, squirming thighs.

His hands were strong, demanding, and yet gentle, too. Teasingly, his touch moved higher, and Buffy's body arched to meet it. She opened to him like a flower to the sun. "Now," Buffy whimpered, her face flushed, her dark eyes sparkling with desire. "Come into me now, darling."

Jack entered her slowly, savoring the moment, relishing her first, eager engloving of him, loving the sensation of possessing her. At this moment—and only at moments such as this—Jack felt that Buffy was truly his. Such moments were more than worth the humiliation she all too casually inflicted on him.

And then Buffy spoiled it.

"Oh!" she exclaimed with unfeigned enthusiasm. "You really are my very own lovely young stud!"

Jack pulled back. He looked down at her coldly. "Is that really what you want, Buffy?" he asked, his voice controlled, his eyes hard.

"Yes." Buffy wriggled and her voice was very close to being a squeal. "Ravish me!"

"I'm not playing games with you now, Buffy. I mean it, I want a straight answer." Jack's penis lay purple and erect across her thigh. "Do you just went me to screw you and nothing else?"

"Yes, damn you! Don't tease! Do it! Do it!"

"I'm not teasing. I just want to be sure what you want. With or without tenderness today, Buffy. What's your pleasure?"

"With! Without! What's the difference? Do it, dammit!"

"All right, then!" Jack surprised her by reaching down with both hands and grabbing her ankles. He bent her forcibly in two, her feet at her ears, her womanhood widely exposed. Then he rose up and stabbed deep into her as hard as he could.

"Oh!" Buffy wasn't hurt, but she was taken by surprise. The act was one of abasement, and she was not insensitive enough to miss it. At the same time, the demands of his anger were fiercely arousing.

Moving in and out of her with long, deep, penetrating, knowledgeable strokes, Jack wasn't violent. But he was thorough, and efficient, and detached in a way that made her body respond with a demand for something more, something intimate, something he withheld. He quickly brought Buffy to the brink of orgasm and then held her to him, grinding as she came.

When her climax was over, he remained embedded in her. He kissed her and caressed her breasts and her buttocks and began moving deep inside her again. Buffy thought that since he had not himself had an orgasm, that was what he wanted. But when he manipulated her to a second climax, he was once again not with her.

Immediately, without pause, he started over again.

Buffy stopped him. He looked at her from a face as devoid of expression as a domino mask. "Time to leave for your business meeting?" he inquired.

"No. Not yet. But you haven't...is there some problem, Jack?" Her passion for the moment satisfied, Buffy now discerned the depth of his remoteness from their lovemaking.

"No problem."

"Then why haven't you—"

"I'm a stud. I give pleasure. I don't necessarily take it."

"Oh, Jack, don't be silly." Her tone, more than her words, expressed concern.

He withdrew from her, still fully erect. "I'm not being silly," he told her. "I'm just giving you what you want."

"What I want is for us to enjoy ourselves together. Together," she stressed.

"Sorry. Togetherness isn't a stud talent."

"Well, if you're going to behave this way, then I will be leaving for my business appointment." Buffy hoped the threat might make him stop behaving so coldly.

It didn't. "All right." He lay back on the bed naked.

After a moment, not knowing what else to do, Buffy got up and began to dress.

He watched her. "This is the last time, Buffy," he told her as she was putting on her makeup.

"Oh, Jack, don't be a child." Her tone was deliberately light, but beneath it, her concern was growing.

"I mean it. I'm going to make arrangements this afternoon to leave for Africa just as soon as I can get a flight."

"Because we had this silly argument? Oh, Jack."

"No. Not the argument. Because I love you, Buffy. I'm leaving because I genuinely love you, and you do not love me."

"I adore you, darling." The lightness of her tone still disguised the depth of her feeling.

"Yes. I know." Jack smiled. "But do you love me?"

"Of course I do. There's no man in the world I'd rather—" Buffy stopped short. She looked at him. Her tone changed. "You're serious," she acknowledged.

"I'm serious."

"You really will leave?" Buffy felt as if she were tottering at the edge of an abyss. She hadn't faced the depth of

327

her feelings for Jack until this moment when there was every chance of losing him.

"Yes."

Buffy bit her lip. Her next words were not glib, and she spoke them with some difficulty. "What do I have to do to make you stay?"

"You have to love me...to really love me. Not just to say it. Not just the physical act. But to mean it. You have to be in love·with me, Buffy. If you're not, then there really isn't anything you can do to make me change my mind."

"I love you," she said. She was only just admitting it to herself, but nevertheless, her voice was rich with the sincerity of her declaration.

It jolted Jack. He looked at her narrowly. He pulled the sheet up over his nakedness. The gesture testified to how vulnerable she had made him feel. "Buffy—"

"I mean it. I love you." Oh, God! she prayed silently. Make him know it's true. "I really do love you."

"Then marry me."

Even as she rejoiced inwardly because he believed her. Buffy could not stop herself from being practical. "Oh, Jack, this is such a bad time. So much confusion. The law-suit—"

"The hell with the lawsuit. If you love me, marry me."

"I might lose it." Buffy attempted a small joke. "Then you'd be sorry."

"Get out!" There was real fury in Jack's voice. "Leave like you were going to. Get the hell out of my life!"

"It was a joke, darling. Only a joke." Buffy was frightened and contrite. "I was being funny."

"It wasn't the first time. But I'm telling you, Buffy, it better be the last! If you ever again insinuate anything about my marrying you for your money, I'm going to walk, and I won't look back." Jack cooled down slowly. Her wide eyes told him his message had gotten across. Finally he relented. "Now, how about Saturday?" he asked.

"Saturday?"

"For the wedding."

"My God, Jack! I can't—Oh, you're such a boy." The reminder was a knife stab to Buffy. "And you're still sev-

328

enteen years younger than I am. Oh, Jack, think what that will mean ten years from now!"

"It won't mean a goddamn thing."

"It will. It will. Oh, Jack, promise me that the first time you feel that, you'll tell me. Promise me we'll get divorced right away. I couldn't stand it sitting around watching you be considerate the way people are with old people."

"Stop it, Buffy! Just stop it! I love you. Can't you get that through your head? Age isn't important. It doesn't matter now and it never will. Now, how about Saturday?"

"All right. Saturday. But listen—don't get angry, Jack, we will get married Saturday—but can we keep it a secret until the trial is over? I know that's not very romantic, but it really is necessary, darling."

"All right. We'll keep our marriage a secret until the trial is over," Jack agreed. "But"—he nailed it down—"this Saturday we get married." When her gaze assured him of her commitment Jack dropped his eyes. They fell on his still fiercely erect penis. "Saturday," he sighed, "is a long, long way off."

Buffy looked at her wristwatch. "There's still time."

Jack moved quickly to undress her. He entered her quickly, deeply. She rose to meet him, her renewed passion filled with tenderness. More lovingly than they ever had before, they made love.

This time their climax was mutual.

43

"I NEVER DREAMED I could feel so close to another person." Beth Tyler turned on her side, leaned on her elbow, and looked down into Deke Wells's face. Abruptly she giggled.

"What?"

"I was just thinking of Diana. I understand now why she was so miffed at me. Sex really is enjoyable."

"Did you think it was supposed to be a chore?"

"Well, no. But up until tonight what experience I've had hasn't been so—" Beth took a deep, happy breath and let it out. "If it was my sister Carrie here with you instead of me," she said, "I'll bet she'd never be promiscuous again."

"You're crazy." Deke was embarrassed. "I'm not some great lover. I'm just an ordinary guy."

"No, you're not." On impulse, Beth tickled him. "You're my super lover. You're my All-Star Major League woo pitcher!"

"And that's all I'll be pitching from here on out." Beth's choice of words reminded Deke of what had happened that day, and now he was depressed again.

"Oh, I'm so sorry." Her red-gold hair cascading over their naked bodies, Beth hugged him to her breast. "That was a really dumb thing for me to say." She tried to comfort him.

Deke's despondence had been obvious earlier, when he'd arrived at the SoHo apartment to take Beth to the movies. Diana was out for the evening. When Beth asked him what was the matter, Deke told her he'd just been permanently dropped by the Red Sox. Her efforts to console him had propelled them into making love.

Now Deke sat up beside her in bed. "It's no good not facing it," he said. "I'm twenty-four years old and my career is over."

"Maybe not, Deke. Maybe after a long rest—"

"Nope. The doctor was very clear. The ligaments are permanently separated. They won't fuse by themselves, and they can't be sewed together in any way that would stand the strain of pitching. The Red Sox won't even send me back to the farm team. I'm washed up in baseball."

"You're still young, Deke. Your career as a Major League pitcher may be over, but your life isn't."

"So what do I do for the next forty or fifty years?"

"The first thing you do is stop feeling sorry for yourself." Beth kissed him to soften the briskness of her words. "Are you broke?" she inquired.

"Not really. I've got some money saved up, and there's my inheritance from the Governor."

"Then an immediate job isn't your problem?"

"Well, no. But there is the future to think about."

"Nukes. Polluting the environment. The button. Armageddon," Beth summarized. "Why worry about the future? There may not be any."

"Maybe you're right, but I can't live my life waiting for the end of the world."

"No. But you can live it to prevent that happening. I'm going to do that. As long as you're at loose ends, you might want to consider that."

"Consider what? What are you talking about?"

"I've decided not to go to Bryn Mawr. I'm joining Greenpeace instead," Beth told him. "That's what."

"That Save the Whales activist group?"

"It's more than saving the whales, Deke. It's saving our world. From itself," Beth added.

"And you're planning to join Greenpeace?"

"Yes. If I can get my hands on my inheritance money, I'll outfit a boat for Greenpeace. If I can't, as soon as the will is settled I'll join one of their crews anyway. They're mounting a new campaign against oceanic pollution and the shipment of nuclear arms in the Mediterranean."

"The Mediterranean?" Deke was trying to take it all in. "What kind of a boat?"

"The operation will be mostly in coastal waters. As large a sailboat as I can afford."

"Do you know anything about sailboats?"

"Do I?" Beth laughed. "My sister Carrie and I grew up yar. We've been sailing at Newport and on the Hudson since we were five years old. I can't count the regattas I've taken part in. And I was crew captain in three of them."

"And just exactly what will you do for Greenpeace with your boat, Captain?"

"Interfere." Beth grinned. "Police the shipping lanes. Get in the way of the tankers dumping their sludge. Block port entry to vessels carrying nukes. Any daredevil stunt that seems feasible to draw world attention to the munitions trade fueling the carnage in the Middle East."

"Sounds like fun."

"It's very serious, Deke. Greenpeace isn't just a bunch of crazies out to get their picture on the six o'clock news. It's a serious campaign to alert people to activities like the arms race which is bringing us closer and closer to destroying ourselves."

331

"Sure. I didn't mean to trivialize it. But all the same, it does sound like fun."

"Well, yes," Beth conceded. "But what's wrong with having fun for a good cause?"

"Nothing. Nothing at all."

"Then do you want to come along?"

"It intrigues me," Deke realized. "Has-been Major League ball player on the high seas. That even might have some publicity value for Greenpeace." Deke had a sudden suspicion. "Is that why you want me?" he asked Beth.

"No. I never even thought of it," she assured him. "This is why I want you along." Her hands slid slowly down his body.

"I see." Deke kissed her as his organ swelled into renewed tumescence. "You're just recruiting me out of principle, then."

"Mmm," Beth murmured, opening to him. "Principle."

44

"PRINCIPLE?" MR. BARTLEBY of Bartleby & Hatch stared disbelievingly at Patrice O'Keefe. "You're doing this out of principle?"

Patrice twisted her bow around her finger. "Believe me," she told him, "you can't be any more surprised at me than I am at myself."

It was true. For a long time Patrice's thinking had been conditioned by two factors. One of these was that her father was a chauvinist who'd never see in her the heir-apparent he so desperately wanted her brother Matt to be. She loved her father, but she always felt hurt by his inability to conceive of her in the starring role.

The second factor was her ambition. She thought of herself as relatively ruthless—in the time-honored manner of *men* of business—where her career was concerned. She'd always been sure that she would recognize opportunity and then grasp it.

These two factors had fused the day Halsey De Vilbiss made clear to her that if she just stayed aloof from the battle over the will, the vice presidency of Bartleby & Hatch would be hers. No one was asking her to actively betray her father. She would only be putting her interests ahead of his in the same way he'd always put Matt ahead of her. Indeed, it seemed only fair and just to Patrice that she should act in her own best interest.

Only she couldn't. Her love for her father wouldn't let her. When it came right down to it, Patrice found that this love dictated a strong loyalty toward her father which she hadn't known she possessed until it was put to the test. Whether she opposed him passively or actively, it didn't matter. She could not bring herself to abandon him.

And so principle she had not known she possessed had won out over ambition. This really did surprise Patrice. It didn't make her think better of herself; it only left her piqued with a softness she thought she'd overcome a long, long time ago.

"But what has principle to do with it?" Bartleby was asking. "You were never being asked to do anything against your father, only to remain neutral."

"That's where principle comes in. I can't stay neutral. Believe me, I've thought about it long and hard. My neutrality wouldn't be neutrality at all. It would be giving an edge to Buffy against my grandmother and my father."

"I thought you were ambitious, O'Keefe."

"Oh, I am Mr. Bartleby. Believe me, I am. Ambition took me right up to the brink, but everybody draws a line somewhere, Mr. Bartleby. This is where I draw mine."

"You know what this means?"

"I can guess. I'll start cleaning out my desk. I'm fired, right?" The price was high. Patrice would have been lying to herself if she didn't admit she resented it. Nevertheless, she was firm in her willingness to pay it.

"Wrong." Bartleby looked at her now with the distaste of the pragmatist for the moralist. "Oh, if it was up to me, I'd fire you in a minute. You're not being a team player, not acting in the best interests of the agency. That would be enough for me to scuttle you, O'Keefe. But that's not what Star-Agena wants. So you're not fired."

"Thank you." Patrice was surprised.

"Even so, you won't be handling the Star-Agena account."

"They want me here, but not working on their account." Cynically, Patrice realized that the pressure to make her change her mind was going to continue. Otherwise, they would have fired her. Well, she assured herself a bit grimly, I can take it. "All right," she told Bartleby.

"And I think you'd better turn the proposal for Chase Manhattan over to Scourby."

That hurt. "All right."

"And fill in Gerberg on the Penta-State ad campaign. He'll be handling it from now on."

"Yes, sir." Patrice tried hard to make her tone as respectful as her words, but she didn't quite succeed.

"As for the rest of your accounts, O'Keefe, they'll be supervised by Panella."

"I see." Patrice drew a deep, resentful breath. "What about my cousin Max Tyler's account?" she asked. "The insurance company?"

"All yours." Bartleby smiled expansively. "Nobody else in the agency would touch insurance for gays with a ten-foot pole."

"Well, if there's nothing else right now, Mr. Bartleby, I'll get back to work." Patrice did not trust herself to stay in the office with him one moment longer. She was—damn it!—one of his very top account executives. How could he cave in to outside pressure in this way? If she didn't leave right now, she thought, she'd brain Bartleby with the goddamn *Ad Age* award she'd nailed down for him.

"You do that, O'Keefe."

Patrice exited. Walking back to her office, her anger turned toward her father. He'd never appreciated her. He wouldn't appreciate this either. He'd just go on wishing one of his sons would take an interest in the family business. Patrice's anger waned, giving way to an old bitterness. Well, she hadn't really done it to score Brownie points. And a good thing, too, my girl, she told herself, because your father doesn't know from Brownies—only Boy Scouts.

"Hey there, Little Bow Veep." Donny, the Art Director greeted her.

"Misnomer, Donny." Patrice tucked her bow out of sight in her jacket.

"Bows going out of fashion?"

"Nope. Women veeps are."

Donny looked back toward the closed door of Bartleby's office. Then he looked at Patrice again. "You're kidding."

"Nope. Bet the bank account on Panella."

"How come?"

"Principle, Donny." Patrice continued on her way to her office. "Bartleby's making Panella veep on principle."

45

"I DON'T LIKE BEING made fun of this early in the morning." Holly snuggled into the pillows as she cast a sleepy glance at Meyerling, propped up in bed with his breakfast tray.

"Lovemaking makes you cynical." Meyerling smeared his toast liberally with Scottish plum preserves. "It makes *me* hungry." He bit off a piece of toast. "And I'm not making fun. I'm serious. I want to marry you."

Of course, she doubts that I mean it, Meyerling reflected. I've been a diplomat for too long. I don't know how to say what I feel anymore, and to say it directly. When I declare my love, it sounds like Henry playing Ping-Pong with the Chinese. He sighed. Loving Holly and convincing her that he loved her were evidently two quite different matters.

"Crumbs." Holly wrinkled her nose. "How can I marry a man who eats breakfast in bed?" She met his eyes. "You are serious," she realized after a moment. The knowledge confused her. She didn't know what her reaction was, couldn't sort out her feelings. She couldn't quite trust him either. He seemed to care, to love her. He seemed to be all she wanted in a man, but was he? "Why, Zelig?" She blurted it out. "Why marriage?"

"I love you." They were possibly the three most nakedly honest words he'd spoken since his departure from Harvard Graduate School many years before.

Holly blinked. Recognizing the sincerity of his declaration, she panicked. Was she in love with him? Only a few years ago she would have responded with an immediate and unqualified yes. But experience had not only made her wary, it made her doubt her judgment. Never again was she going to let sex and emotion sweep her off her feet as they had with Christopher. She realized, of course, that Zelig was a very different man than Christopher, but that did not necessarily make marriage to him right. Their lovemaking was wonderful; they had stimulating, intellectual conversations and a deep bond of understanding; and Holly sensed that he deeply and truly cared for her. And he was not one to make a marriage proposal lightly—or marry her for her name or fortune. All this should warrant a yes, she thought.

But was it really enough? She wanted to be married. She yearned for the intimacy and commitment of marriage, but was terribly afraid of being hurt again. Or of exposing Nicholas to further pain. Holly was determined to take better care of herself—and her son—this time around. And Meyerling had not spent much time with Nicholas; would he make a good father?

Feeling pressured, Holly sought refuge in flippancy. "I've never thought of you as the marrying kind."

"That wasn't the answer I was hoping for. I was hoping to hear that you loved me, too."

Again she was a long time answering. "I'm not sure I do," she said finally. It was at the same time both an honest answer and a repudiation of the strong attraction she felt for him, the attraction Holly refused to label "love."

He frowned, disappointed.

"I'm going through a very confusing time," Holly added truthfully. "There's a lot of pressure. The divorce. The custody battle with Christopher. The lawsuit over the will. I just can't complicate my life any more right now." But was it all that? she wondered to herself. Or was it really love itself that she couldn't handle?

"I see." Meyerling spread more jam on his toast and wolfed it down. He grimaced not at the taste, but at her rejection. He hadn't expected it and didn't quite know how to deal with it.

She felt his pain and reacted to it. "I'll think about marrying you. No, listen!" Holly responded to a second grimace. "I mean that. I'm too mixed up right now to know if what I feel for you is lust or love. I want to be with you, Zelig. I want to make love with you. I do feel very passionately toward you. And maybe I'm in love with you, but I'm just not sure. So I mean what I say. I will think about it." Holly was making a tremendous effort to be honest in a situation where she was still unable to sort out her feelings. "Will you give me a chance to do that, Zelig?"

"Of course." He shook the crumbs from the sheet. "Take your time." His years as a diplomat had trained him to push down disappointment. Deliberately, he distanced himself now from their situation. "I'll be in Washington quite a lot over the next few weeks. That should give you —what's the word they use these days?—space? Yes, plenty of space."

"You, too." Holly took refuge from the strain between them by teasing him. "Lots of space for your many ladies to convince you not to take yourself out of circulation."

"That is not why I am going to Washington."

"Why are you going?" She welcomed the chance to change the subject.

"The Russian back channel."

"I feel so naive when you talk governmentese."

"When the Russians wish to pass along a message through other than official channels, that is called a back channel."

"Sounds James Bondish."

"It is."

"Should you be telling me about it, then?" Holly wondered.

"Well, it is highly secret." Meyerling buried his disappointment deeper with banter. "But, then, you come from a long line of Republicans, so I know I can trust you not to reveal it to Jimmy Carter."

"Now let me get this straight. You are the back channel for a message from the Russians, and it has to be kept secret from the President of the United States? Is that right?"

"The lame-duck President of the United States," he corrected her. "That's what he will be after the upcoming election anyway. The message is for Reagan."

"But why," Holly wondered, "don't they just wait until after he's elected?"

"The world is in a very delicate balance, my dear. The Russians want to give assurances that as far as they're concerned, Reagan's election won't disturb that balance."

"That's very considerate of them."

"Consideration has nothing to do with it. They want similar assurances in return."

"But why through you?" Holly wondered. "You're not a Reagan Republican."

"Principle," he told her. "My country comes first, my anti-Reagan sentiments second. Even the Russians know that."

"You always sound ironic when you talk about being patriotic. I can never tell if you're serious."

"You don't believe I'm serious about marriage. You don't believe I'm serious about patriotism." The look in his hooded eyes pleaded with Holly to understand that he was completely serious about both. "What a scoundrel you must think I am."

She read the look correctly. "No, I don't." Holly took his hand in hers and held it tightly. "I really do think you're a man of principle. And," she added sincerely, "I am honored that you want to marry me."

Embarrassed by the compliment, even as he took pains to lighten up the conversation, Meyerling allowed hope to shine in his eyes. "Principle is the raison d'être of every scoundrel in history. Sometimes it's called statesmanship. He who succeeds is a statesman; he who fails is a scoundrel."

"That was Benedict Arnold's conclusion," Holly remembered. "He died believing that if the British had prevailed in the Revolution, he would have been acclaimed a true patriot."

"That's right. You did tell me Benedict Arnold was involved in the early history of Riverview, when that Dutch family still owned the estate. What happened to them anyway?" Meyerling asked. "The van Bronckels, I mean. Did Ursula run off with the Stockwell?"

"Oh, no. She couldn't," Holly replied. "There was no room for women on Arnold's forced march to Montreal. No, Ursula stayed behind and married Hans Hoek, the patroon to whom her father had betrothed her."

"Lucky patroon." He emitted a mock sigh. "Men didn't have to deal with rejection in those days."

"True. But I'm not rejecting you," Holly assured him once again. "Really. I just have to have time."

"And we are agreed that you shall have it." He pulled Holly to him and encircled her in his arms. He kissed her cheek and nuzzled her ear. "Now," he said, "tell me what did happen to the van Bronckels."

"Well, since you're so interested," Holly began as she snuggled next to him, glad to be able to relegate her ambivalence to the back of her mind, "I'll tell you. . . ."

46

DURING THE MONTHS between her betrothal and her wedding, Ursula did not sleep well nights. She lay awake burning with passion. The passion was not for her husband-to-be, Hans Hoek, but for her lover, Lieutenant Roger Stockwell.

Stockwell was far away, in the area between Montreal and Lake Champlain. Ursula heard of his activities only indirectly. What she heard was not reassuring.

On New Year's Eve of 1775 British soldiers came charging out of the fortress-city of Montreal and lifted the siege Arnold had imposed. He was forced to retreat to the south, the retreat turning into a rout with heavy casualties. Ursula could only pray that Roger was not among them, even as her father, her fiancé, and the other Loyalist patroons rejoiced.

For the next year the Colonial forces under Benedict Arnold were on the run from the redcoats. Despite this, Arnold was promoted to brigadier general. During this time, Ursula had no word from Roger Stockwell and heard no news about him.

He's dead, she told herself on the October night before her wedding to Hans Hoek. He must be dead. And far from anticipating the blissful lovemaking of her wedding night, Ursula wept into her pillow for the rapture she had known but once and now would doubtless never know again.

Much, much later Ursula learned of the battle that took place on Lake Champlain the day she was married. For months before, Arnold and his men had been secretly constructing a flotilla of warships off Valcour Island. On October 11, 1776, this flotilla attacked the British and inflicted severe losses. It was the first taste of victory for the Colonials, and because of it, the first and most renowned hero of the emerging American nation was Benedict Arnold.

To Ursula the day was as devastating as it was to the British. She could deal with her wedding only by shutting it out of her mind. She walked in a daze through the lavish ceremony at the Dutch manor house. Later she would remember nothing of the ceremony. Her only memory, a hazy one, would be of the dinner that followed, and of the chatter of Peggy Shippen, who was a guest. And Ursula would remember that only because of what happened later.

The center of attention as always, particularly male attention, Peggy held forth on the ongoing delights of the social scene in Philadelphia, the city that was her home. "The British officers assure us that the upstart Washington is finished," she assured her audience. "Victory is certain."

"There is danger in such overconfidence," one of the elder patroons harrumphed. "Philadelphia should take care lest the frivolities of citified society render it complacent in the face of real danger to the Crown."

"We Philadelphians are aware of our obligations, sir," Peggy replied stiffly.

"Obligations involve sacrifices. Wartime is not a social season."

"The gentleman does Philadelphia an injustice, and one I take quite personally." Peggy Shippen's eyes blazed with the fire of zealotry. "There is nothing I would not do to

340

preserve the monarchy in our colonies. Nothing! Nothing at all!" The intensity of her conviction impressed itself unforgettably on the company.

Ursula heard the echo of her words long after all memory of her wedding night had vanished.

The following year dragged by without hope. She and her new husband stayed in the van Bronckel mansion while the foundation for their own new home, a gift from Ursula's father, was being laid. But the war made it difficult to obtain building materials, and so construction was delayed again and again. They resigned themselves to living with Ursula's family until this bothersome rebellion was squelched.

In late September 1777 word reached the Hudson River Valley of the first Battle of Saratoga. General Horatio Gates, backed up by General Benedict Arnold, fought a superior British force commanded by "Gentleman Johnny" Burgoyne to a standoff. The patroons were concerned. A delegation was dispatched to Saratoga to consult with General Burgoyne regarding the extent of the threat to the Hudson River Valley.

While they were there, on October 7, 1777, Burgoyne attempted to flank the Colonial army and stage a surprise raid with fifteen hundred soldiers of his five-thousand-man army. The Americans, led by Benedict Arnold, staged a fierce counterattack. Burgoyne was severely defeated. Ten days later he surrendered his entire army to General Gates. It was the first major victory for the Colonials, marking the turning point of the Revolutionary War. Once again Benedict Arnold was confirmed as the foremost hero of the American cause.

Word of Arnold's exploits was brought back to the Hudson River Valley by the delegation that had witnessed the battle. With grudging admiration, they told how Arnold had galloped at the head of a badly outnumbered advance force, taking the British by surprise with his audacity. Under constant fire, he'd deployed his men brilliantly and decisively, seizing positions in the midst of the enemy and holding them until reinforcements could be brought up from the rear. As soon as one position was secured, he would lead the charge to establish the next. Finally, however, he took one chance too many and was unhorsed by a bullet which left him lying on the battlefield seriously wounded and in imminent danger of death.

Seated between her husband and her father, Ursula had only been half listening to the grisly account. Now, however, a name was mentioned that claimed Ursula's attention. It was the name of the Colonial officer—a captain now—who had carried General Arnold from the field of battle and saved his life: Roger Stockwell.

He lived! He was unharmed! Ursula's heart sang.

Nine more long months passed before Ursula once again had word of Stockwell. This time his name was mentioned incidentally in a letter from Peggy Shippen in Philadelphia.

Through the winter of 1777–78 the British General Sir William Howe had occupied Philadelphia. Among his officers Peggy Shippen had been one of the most popular Loyalist belles in the city. However, in the spring of 1778, in the wake of repeated attacks by the Colonial army under General Washington, the British had evacuated the city, leaving Philadelphia Tories at the mercy of rebel rule. In June 1778, because General Arnold's wounds at Saratoga had left him temporarily unfit for battlefield command, Commander-in-Chief Washington assigned him as military governor of Philadelphia.

Peggy Shippen was, of course, appalled at this turn of events. What greater insult to those Philadelphians loyal to the Crown than that the victor of Saratoga should be placed in charge of their city? Decent Tories would not speak to General Arnold unless forced to by circumstance, nor to any of his officers, particularly his aide Roger Stockwell—the captain who had carried him wounded from the field at Saratoga.

Again Ursula rejoiced. Surely Philadelphia was the safest of billets. For as long as he was there, Roger would not be risking his life in battle.

Although it had been two-and-a-half years since the one time they had made love, Ursula's ardor had not cooled. Roger was alive, the memory of his embraces immediate, her love for him the fuel that stoked her courage.

She wrote to him in Philadelphia. It was not at all difficult. Packets of civilian mail were passed through the lines by both sides regularly. A month later she had a reply as filled with vows of eternal love as her letter had been.

They carried on the correspondence for some eight months. During this time Ursula read Roger's letters over and over again. His declarations of devotion were a flame to loins icy to her husband's touch.

Meanwhile the war had left the Hudson River Valley relatively serene. Technically it was ruled by the Colonials, who had gained control of the area through the naval battle of Tappan Zee. Following this, the focus of the Revolution had shifted south. Thus the patroons had experienced little actual rule by the rebels in command of their region.

In early 1779, however, the Colonials were considering the Hudson River Valley as a staging area for an attack against the British in Canada. The fort at West Point could serve as Colonial headquarters for the drive north. It was thought likely that Washington would name General Benedict Arnold to command West Point. But before the campaign was finalized, various officers were dispatched to the Hudson River Valley to appraise the situation. One of those officers was Captain Roger Stockwell.

He wrote Ursula that he was coming, and on a warm afternoon in late April of 1779, they met at Hanging Rock. They had not seen each other for three-and-a-half years.

It did not matter. Their passion burst forth as fresh as if that one time they'd made love had been only yesterday. The fever of desire turned their words to gibberish. Garments seemed to melt away in the heat of their passion, and their flesh was joined without question—and fiercely.

Later, with the sun going down and plans for their next meeting already agreed upon, Roger admiringly described to Ursula the exploits of the man under whom he served —General Benedict Arnold. "The foremost hero of the American revolution," Roger pronounced. "Until just recently I would have sworn that he thought of nothing but the cause."

"And what has happened recently to change that opinion?"

Roger grinned. "On April eighth last, General Arnold took a lady of Philadelphia to wife. One Margaret Shippen by name, commonly called Peggy. And never have I seen a man so smitten with his new wife."

Ursula stared at her lover. "Peggy Shippen!" she exclaimed. "Married to Benedict Arnold! That is most unexpected!"

47

CERTAINLY IT WAS the unexpected that shaped events in the courtroom at Foley Square in early November 1980, when the Stockwells, the Lewises, the Tylers, and their lawyers gathered to settle the estate of Governor Matthew Adams Stockwell. Both sides had agreed to a change of venue, allowing briefs to be filed and motions heard in Probate Court in Manhattan rather than upstate New York.

Seeking sensation, the media was frustrated at first. Despite the inherent drama of prominent family members pitted against one another in a fight over one of the world's great fortunes, the early proceedings could not have been more tedious. Mostly they consisted of the filing of various papers by the lawyers involved.

First the Governor's last testament, along with affidavits from those who had witnessed it and the attorneys involved in drawing it up, was introduced by Ulysses Blandings. These affidavits attested to the soundness of the Governor's mind at the time the will was drawn. Next Blandings filed with the court a 247-page document listing the assets distributed in the will. The reporters groaned. This document would be the source of the value their stories would have to set on the Stockwell estate. Despite the documentation, media accounts arrived at widely different estimates.

Following Blandings, James Linstone Stockwell filed two affidavits by his mother. The first, referring back to the clause in the will that empowered her to do so, was an authorization for the Stockwell estate to be run by the troika. The second removed her grandson Peter Stockwell as a trustee, reducing the troika by one third.

To these James added sworn statements by himself, his brother Jonathan, his sister Alice, her husband David Lewis, his sister Susan Gray, his daughter Patrice, his daughter Lisa, his niece Holly, his cousins Alfred and Lizzie, Paul and Margaret Tyler, and Louise Papatestus. Each of these statements served a threefold purpose. They attested to personal knowledge of the Governor's sanity during the last years of his life, expressed satisfaction with the management of the estate by James Stockwell and David Lewis, and formally requested that the estate in which they shared to a considerable extent continue under that management.

The following day it was the turn of the other side to present its papers. Acting for Buffy, Halsey De Vilbiss filed a series of separate motions. The first, which was really a fallback position, cited community property precedents under New York State law entitling Buffy as the legal widow of the deceased to automatically inherit between one third and one half of the Governor's assets, depending on just which precedent the judge might choose to honor.

De Vilbiss followed this by filing a charge challenging the validity of the will as "a document executed under undue influence." Those named as having been in collusion to exercise that "undue influence" were Mary Linstone Stockwell, James Stockwell, David Lewis, and Ulysses Blandings. The elderly barrister turned red with rage; in his sixty years at the bar it was the first time his probity had ever been questioned.

As the afternoon session was drawing to a close, De Vilbiss requested the court to issue a subpoena for yet another person involved in the "undue influence" conspiracy—Vanessa Brewster. The heads of the reporters, which had been nodding under the weight of legalisms and paper, now jerked up. As the hearing was adjourned for the day, they mobbed De Vilbiss, shouting questions regarding the bombshell he'd dropped.

Was he going to accuse the woman who had been with

the Governor when he died of influencing him to cut Buffy out of the will? Was he charging that she used sex to accomplish this? Was he going to say she'd been acting in the interests of other members of the family, who had profited so greatly by the terms of the will? Just what was Vanessa Brewster's relationship with the Stockwell family?

"Ask James Stockwell." De Vilbiss's smile was a razor slash under his thin moustache. "Ask James Stockwell how involved Vanessa Brewster is with the Stockwells." And with the reporters still shouting questions at him, De Vilbiss climbed into Buffy's waiting limousine and was driven away.

The next day, giving the media a chance to dwell on the questions raised by Vanessa Brewster being subpoenaed, De Vilbiss presented to the court another pile of paper. It consisted of various affidavits from Stockwell heirs, charging that the estate was not being managed to their satisfaction by James Stockwell and David Lewis. The affidavits were from Buffy, Peter Stockwell, Christopher Millwood in behalf of his son Nicholas and his wife Holly—who contested his right to be a party to the dispute—Michelle and Andrew Carter, Max Tyler, and Diana Tyler.

In addition, De Vilbiss filed with the court a notice of the suit on behalf of Beth and Carrie Tyler to remove control of their legacy from their father's hands. This was accompanied by sworn statements from Beth and Carrie attesting to their dissatisfaction with the management of the Stockwell estate and with its portfolio of investments.

Separate statements from Matthew Stockwell, Michael Stockwell, and Deke Wells covered considerably narrower ground but were nonetheless damaging. They did not take issue with the overseer roles of James Stockwell and David Lewis, but they did serve notice of their intention to sever their legacies from the main estate, and respectfully asked the court to probate the will with deliberate speed so that they might do this.

At this point in the proceedings Holly and Patrice exchanged pained glances. Though Matt may have acted for reasons of principle, and Michael for political advantage, they knew that James would be deeply troubled by this action on the part of his sons.

Michael's action, Holly thought to herself, was a commentary on the perfidy of politicians. Four months ago, despite the talk caused by the circumstances surrounding the Governor's death, he had won the primary handily. Today, with the liberal Republican Anderson in the presidential race drawing off votes from Carter, all the polls had Reagan way ahead, and experts were predicting that the coattail effect would sweep a Republican majority into Congress. One of the races considered safe for the GOP was Michael's. Nevertheless, Michael had hedged his bets. What was the going rate these days, Holly wondered, for politicians' souls?

Neither Holly nor Michael's father ever dreamed that Michael had been squeezed by the threat to reveal the illegal contributions to his campaign so craftily engineered by De Vilbiss. Michael had actually had no personal knowledge of them at the time they were made. Nevertheless, if the threat was made good, it might not just have cost Michael the congressional seat, but could have resulted in his being prosecuted under the election laws as well. He could have gone to jail, and it certainly would have been the end of his fledgling political career.

Something else puzzled Holly. She leaned to whisper in Patrice's ear. "How come Deke Wells?" she wondered. "Susan, his mother, kept the faith."

"Beth Tyler," was the answer. "They're involved."

That afternoon the last of the papers were filed and then court was adjourned. The next day, television reporters promised their audiences, the battle over the Stockwell will would begin in earnest.

When the hearing was reconvened the following day, the judge summoned the lawyers for the two sides to his chambers. "I've decided to separate the two issues," he told them. "If there's no objection, we'll deal with the validity of the testament first, and then depending on whether probate is granted or not, we'll come to grips with the management of the estate."

Neither attorney had any objection.

"Very well, then. I believe that makes you the lead-off batter," the judge told Halsey De Vilbiss.

For his first witness Halsey called Buffy to the stand. Buffy, dressed plainly in a deep blue suit and wearing little makeup, testified that her husband, the Governor, had

347

been under the influence of his eldest son James and his ex-wife Mary, and that this influence had been a major factor in his estrangement from her. She made an excellent witness, regretfully recounting her husband's increasing absences and the pain this had caused her. She did not overdo it, and the pain seemed to come straight from the heart.

Under cross-examination, James established that Buffy could provide no evidence that the Governor was of anything but sound mind. "Then if he was influenced by myself or my mother," James summed up, "it was by his own choice and not because of any weakening of his faculties." Before Buffy could answer, James excused her from the witness stand, his point made.

Next Halsey summoned Ellen Stockwell to the stand. Peter's mother backed up Buffy's testimony and embellished it with details that James, sick at heart, knew were made up out of whole cloth. "Your witness," De Vilbiss declared finally.

James gazed at Ellen for a long moment. Then he looked at his brother Jonathan, sitting beside David Lewis at the counsel table. Jonathan's head was bowed, his face in his hands. James could not launch an attack against his brother's wife. And he could not rely on Ellen to admit the truth. He sighed. "No questions," he told the judge. "Witness excused."

Ellen was followed to the stand by her son Peter. He testified that his uncles, James and David, had taken advantage of the Governor's waning concentration to solidify their control over his estate. James immediately objected. The testimony at this time, he reminded the judge, was to be limited to the Governor's competency in drawing up his will, and the management of his estate was irrelevant.

The judge pondered a moment. "I will allow the testimony in the narrow sense of influence exerted by the trustees-to-be on the testator," he decided. "But," he cautioned Peter, "you will limit yourself to the effect on the state of mind of the Governor and not get into the management of the estate."

When De Vilbiss had finished with Peter, James rose to cross-examine him. "Did you ever witness a discussion between either the Governor and myself, or the Governor and David Lewis, regarding the drawing up of the Governor's will?" he asked.

"No."

"Then you cannot testify that you ever saw either one of us try to influence the terms of the will. Is that correct?"

"Yes," Peter replied reluctantly. "That is correct."

"And neither have you ever been present when your grandmother, Mary Linstone Stockwell, tried to influence the Governor regarding his final testament. That is also correct, is it not?"

"Yes. That is so."

"In short, Peter, your entire testimony is hearsay. Is that not also true?"

"Objection, Your Honor!" De Vilbiss was immediately on his feet.

"Withdraw the question." James didn't wait for the judge to rule against him. "No further questions of this witness, Your Honor."

The hearing was adjourned for the day. Things were warming up.

Double the usual number of reporters crowded into the room the next day. The word was out—De Vilbiss had leaked it—Vanessa Brewster was to testify.

"Won't she be a hostile witness?" Buffy worried.

"Oh, yes." De Vilbiss smoothed his tattersall vest. "Very hostile indeed, I would think."

When Vanessa, clad in her customary khakis, topknot, and glasses, was summoned from the antechamber back of the courtroom, James stepped out into the aisle and held out his hand to her. She smiled at him and took it. An audible gasp swept the courtroom.

He's going to brazen it out, Buffy realized. Well, good for him! was her grudging private verdict.

De Vilbiss elicited her name and address from Vanessa. "You were with Governor Matthew Adams Stockwell at the time of his death, were you not?" he asked.

"Yes."

"What were the circumstances?"

"I'm an anthropologist. He knew of my interest in Minoan artifacts. He was showing me the private collection he kept in his office."

"And he had a heart attack?"

"That's right."

"Isn't it a fact, Miss Brewster, that you were having sexual relations with the Governor just before he died?"

"Objection!" James was on his feet.

"No." Vanessa answered calmly, without waiting for the judge to rule. She had no qualms about lying. What she did in bed was her own business, and the hell with the perjury laws.

"No?" De Vilbiss repeated her answer in a tone ringing with disbelief.

"Objection!" James was shouting now. "The question is irrelevant and immaterial, and I move that both it and the answer be stricken."

The judge crooked his finger, summoning both attorneys to the bench for a private conference. "Is there some purpose to dragging this court through the mud, Counselor?" he asked De Vilbiss. "Or are you just playing to the six o'clock news?"

"We will show a connection between the witness and the family, Your Honor. If she had a sexual relationship with the Governor and was also tied in to the family, then a presumption of undue influence can be established."

"Sounds mighty tenuous to me." The judge was dubious.

"The connection is far from tenuous, Your Honor. It is"—De Vilbiss chose the word carefully, looking directly into James's eyes—"ongoing."

"Well, then, establish it first, Counselor," the judge decided. "Then we'll see about the sex stuff."

"Very well, Your Honor."

James went back to his table, and De Vilbiss resumed questioning the witness. "Aside from the Governor," he asked, "how well do you know the Stockwell family?"

"I've met some of them."

"Isn't it a fact that you were escorted to the Governor's funeral by James Stockwell?"

"Yes."

"And on that occasion didn't you and Mary Stockwell embrace and kiss?"

"Yes. We did."

"And didn't you sit with the family throughout the ceremony?"

350

"I did."

"Then you knew the family very well indeed?"

"I know them."

"And which member of the family do you know best, Miss Brewster? Would it be James Linstone Stockwell?"

"We are friends," Vanessa admitted.

"Only friends?" De Vilbiss was sarcastic. "Isn't it true that you are lovers as well?"

"Objection!" James bellowed. "Objection!"

De Vilbiss ignored him and kept talking over the objection. "Isn't it a fact that he is your lover, and that he put you up to becoming his father's lover, and that you then proceeded to influence—"

Several things happened at the same time then. Vanessa, realizing for the first time what he was accusing her of, began to shake. James let out a roar and charged toward De Vilbiss with raised fists. The judge pounded his gavel for order. The bailiffs were rushing to separate the two attorneys. The newspaper journalists were breaking for the telephones, and the television reporters were simultaneously charging the exit doors to alert their camera crews to be ready for interviews with the principals as they left the courtroom.

After a long time order was restored. By order of the judge the courtroom was cleared of spectators and media personnel as well. Then he ordered a fifteen-minute recess and retired to his chambers.

In one of the antechambers Buffy confronted her lawyer. "I want it stopped," she told him.

"You hired me because I'm tough," De Vilbiss reminded her. "Now you're not letting me be tough."

"We don't need it."

"It's insurance," he told her.

"You told me yourself long ago that it wouldn't hold up. It's overkill."

"I don't get it. I thought you wanted me to cream these people."

"I wanted you to get me my rightful inheritance. You're not long on sensitivity, Mr. De Vilbiss. This is family and when this trial is over I'm still going to have to live—one way or another—with the Stockwells. It's true, I will do anything to win. And I would certainly let you go ahead

351

with Ms. Brewster if that were the only thing that could ensure my winning. But it isn't. We both know that, and so when we go back, I want you to stop playing inquisitor with the Brewster woman."

"All the rolfing has pounded you into being a softie." De Vilbiss all but sneered.

"I'm a woman, De Vilbiss. I know how it feels when someone like you starts spray painting scarlet letters. If it was necessary, believe me I'd tough it out. But it's not necessary."

Court was reconvened, and Vanessa Brewster was reminded that she was still sworn to tell the truth. She watched apprehensively as De Vilbiss strode toward her in the witness box. She was totally unprepared for his words.

"I'm through with this witness," he said.

Slow to realize what had happened, James was also slow getting to his feet. He looked at Vanessa for a long moment, then smiled lovingly. "Witness excused," he said.

De Vilbiss asked for an adjournment. His next and final witness would not be available until the next day, he told the judge. The adjournment was granted. Vanessa, James, Buffy, and De Vilbiss all ran the gauntlet of television cameras and reporters as they exited.

The next day the scene was comparatively subdued. De Vilbiss's witness was elderly. She advanced slowly down the aisle with the help of an aluminum walker. A court attendant hovered behind her, concerned.

Her face was wrinkled. Her body thin and bent, was garishly clad in a peacock-blue dress. Her sparse hair should have been gray, but it wasn't. It was dyed a strange shade of apricot gold. And old as she was, her hazel eyes were bright and alert in their almond-shaped sockets.

"Tell the court your name, address, and age, please," De Vilbiss requested when the witness had been sworn in.

"Sherri Larouche. Juneau, Alaska. And I'm eighty-five years of age."

"Sherri Larouche. Is that your real name?" De Vilbiss asked.

"No. It's the name I go by, though. It was my professional name for years."

"Will you tell us your real name, please."

"Tyler. Sarah Tyler."

There was a collective gasp in the courtroom from the various family members present. Mary Stockwell half rose from her seat. Lizzie, Alfred Tyler's wife, glanced at her husband's pale face with alarm. His hazel eyes burned into the woman on the witness stand.

"And is that the name you were born with?"

"No. That's my married name."

Holly noticed that her grandmother Mary, at the counsel table next to James, had also gone quite white. James turned around, "Mother. . .?" he said.

"That's her." Mary nodded. "It's Sarah."

"And what was your name before you were married?" De Vilbiss asked the witness.

"It's Sarah. Matthew's sister," Mary gasped. "The one who ran away."

"Stockwell." The witness replied to the question. "I was born Sarah Stockwell."

48

"I UNDERSTAND WHY everybody's surprised, but why are Uncle James and Uncle David so upset?" Holly asked Patrice after court had adjourned for the day and they'd stopped for cocktails.

"When the Governor's father—a widower by then—died, he left everything he had to his surviving children. But his daughter Sarah was presumed to be dead, and so the Governor got it all. Now she turns up alive, and so she's entitled to half of her father's estate. And that means she's entitled to half of the Stockwell estate left by the Governor."

"But hasn't it increased greatly in value since her father died? I mean, she isn't entitled to half of what it is today, is she? Only half of what it was when her father died—isn't that right?"

"It's iffy. Sarah's money earned money. The funds were mingled, just like the Governor's and Grandma Mary's estates were mingled—which makes the situation more confusing. I'm not a lawyer, but my guess is she's entitled to her half of the earnings, and not just fifty percent of the original principle. Which means that the Tylers will one day end up with more than half the Stockwell money, since they'll probably eventually inherit from Sarah as well as the Governor."

"So what happens now?" Holly asked.

"Well, my father is trying to figure a way to separate Grandma's own funds from the rest of the estate. Even if she loses half of what the Governor left her, he wants to make sure that her Linstone money is protected."

"It's really complicated," Holly said.

"It sure is. If this old lady should pull her money out along with Buffy, for instance, then the whole Stockwell portfolio could come tumbling down like a stack of dominoes. There would be a run on the market like you wouldn't believe."

"Wouldn't that affect the economy?"

"Oh, yes. And not just our country's either. The ripple effect would go right 'round the world."

"That's awful."

"Well," Patrice told her, "I don't think it will actually happen. Dad and Uncle David will come to some accommodation with the other side before the dominoes fall. It wouldn't be to Buffy's advantage, or Sarah's, either, to pull the rug out from under the Stockwell estate."

"I just hope it doesn't all drag on too long." Holly frowned. "I'm concerned for Grandma. Did you see how she looked in court today?"

"Yes, for Grandma it must have been a ghost turning up from the past."

"I wish she wouldn't go to court tomorrow."

"She will." Patrice was sure. "You know Grandma."

Patrice was right. When court convened the next day, Mary was at her usual spot between James and David at the counsel table. Her eyes were riveted on Sarah Stockwell Tyler as the old lady with the dyed red-gold hair took her place once again in the witness box.

De Vilbiss's questions led her through her testimony. "You were born Sarah Stockwell and then you married Averill Tyler, is that right?" he began.

"Yes."

"What year were you married?"

"It was 1913 . . . sixty-seven years ago."

"And how old were you?"

"Eighteen."

"And Averill Tyler, the man you married? How old was he?"

"Forty something." Sarah Stockwell narrowed her hazel eyes, trying to remember. "Maybe fifty. I'm not surely exactly."

"But much older than you."

"Oh, yes. Much older."

"What was your marriage like?"

"Loveless." Sarah Stockwell Tyler summed it up in one word. "Loveless."

"And so you left him? Your husband?"

"I ran away. Yes. With Tyler's coachman. With Brian Mulrooney." Sarah Stockwell's corrugated lips crinkled cynically. "Out of the frying pan, you might say."

"You went to Alaska?"

"With Brian Mulrooney, yes. We parted company after a month in Nome." The hazel eyes flashed with some long-ago memory. "There's no place like Nome," she said, fully intending the pun. The sound she made was very like a cackle.

"And so you were on your own then?"

"Yes. On my own."

De Vilbiss consulted his notes. "Before you ran away with Mulrooney, you had borne two children. Is that correct?" he asked Sarah.

"Twins." Briefly, pain distorted her face. "Yes."

"And you left them behind with their father?"

"No."

"I beg your pardon?"

"I left my twin sons behind. . . ." She paused. "But not with their father."

"Did you not leave them with Averill Tyler?"

"I did. But Averill Tyler was not their father. I was pregnant when I married him. He didn't know it then, but he guessed later, after we were married, after the twins were born."

"They were conceived out of wedlock then?" De Vilbiss inquired.

Sarah Stockwell Tyler stared at the California lawyer for a long moment. Her hazel eyes gleamed with dislike. "It was sixty-seven years ago," she said finally. "Isn't there a statute of limitations or something on bastardy?"

"Please answer the question," the judge instructed her gently.

"Yes. They were conceived out of wedlock."

"And their real father?"

"He was dead. Suicide."

"And why did he kill himself?"

"I told him I was pregnant. The shame was too much for him. Times were very different back then, you see. His family—my family—we were people of substance, respectable people. What a sham! I saw through it, but he didn't. He was so young! He couldn't face the disgrace. Mostly, I think, he couldn't face my disgrace more than his own. So he hung himself."

"No!" Mary whispered at the counsel table. "It's not possible!"

"Now tell us if you will"—De Vilbiss paused for dramatic effect—"What was your lover's name?"

"His name was Linstone," the old woman replied. "His name was Ellis Linstone."

"Bingo!" Buffy whispered softly to herself and smiled. "Bingo!"

The murmur that swept over the courtroom indicated that many of the media people present had picked up on the import of the name as well. Holly, however, was slow in comprehending the legal aspects of this revelation. She looked questioningly at Patrice, sitting beside her.

"Ellis was Grandma's brother," Patrice whispered. "If he had lived, he would have inherited half of the Linstone estate. Since he's dead, the entire estate went to Grandma and was merged with the Stockwell estate after they married—after Grandma's parents died, that is. Don't you see? The Tylers inherit half the Stockwell estate via their mother, Sarah, and half the Linstone estate through their father, Grandma's brother. But since we have to share with Buffy, and the Governor left funds to the Tylers, we Stockwells are relegated to a backseat. If Sarah Tyler can prove she's telling the truth, that is."

"Do you have any proof that Ellis Linstone was the father of your twin sons?" De Vilbiss asked now, defusing the question before James might have a chance to ask it during cross-examination.

"Twins." Sarah smiled her corrugated smile again. "Lots of twins in the Linstone family."

De Vilbiss smiled, pleased with himself. The conversation about twins he'd had with Mary at the wedding reception had started him down this road in the first place. "Anything else?" he asked.

"This." Sarah removed a locket from her neck and opened it. Inside the locket was a faded picture. "It's Ellis." She identified it. "My lover, Ellis."

De Vilbiss took the locket from her. "I'd like to introduce this into evidence, Your Honor." The judge nodded approval. As was customary, De Vilbiss took the piece of evidence over to the opposing counsel's table to show it to him.

It was not James, however, but Mary who stood to take the locket from him. She recognized the locket and examined the picture. "Yes," she said. "It's my brother. It's Ellis." She handed the locket back to De Vilbiss.

He started to take it to the Clerk of the Court so that it could be marked into evidence.

Behind him, Mary sat back down. "James," she said quietly. "Would you hand me my bag from the floor?"

James handed it to her.

It slipped from her fingers. Mary tried to smile. "Would you give me the phial of nitro in the bag," she said.

"Of course, Mother." James started to hand her the phial and then took one look at her and opened it quickly instead. He took out a pill and held it to his mother's lips. When her lips parted, he put the nitroglycerin under her tongue.

In the back of the courtroom Holly realized with horror what was happening. "Grandma!" She was on her feet, then, hurrying down the aisle, not caring about the startled glances she drew. "Grandma!" She went through the swinging wooden gate and knelt beside Mary at the counsel table. "Please, Grandma!" she pleaded.

But it was too late.

BOOK FIVE

49

I T WAS ONE of those late March days at Riverview that anticipates both April and May. In the woods, the trees and the mossy ground were damp and muggy with the imminence of showers. At the same time, the paths were patched with warm islands of sunshine like promises of happy endings. The season, like the period of mourning from which Holly and her son were emerging, was both somber and full of the promise of more pleasant days.

Mary Linstone Stockwell's death had been a sudden and sharp blow to Holly, and only time was softening her grief to a dull ache. After her mother had died, it was her grandmother who had raised Holly and seen to her happiness. Her grandparents had given her a great deal of love and security, and now, just when Holly most needed Mary's advice and comforting presence, she was totally alone. She had Nicholas, but dealing with Nicholas's loss was difficult as well.

Holly's son had been closer to Mary than he'd ever been to the Governor. She had played with him often, and he'd adored her. When Holly had explained to Nicholas that Mary was dead, he protested in the stubborn way children have when they don't want to be forced to face reality, that Great-Grandma was only away "in the city" and was coming back "tomorrow" with "jellybeans for Nicholas." Even after Nicholas had accepted the finality of Mary's death, he would forget and blurt out that "tomorrow when Great-Grandma comes we're going to—" He would catch himself, break off, and a look of such pure inconsolable grief would spread over his little face that Holly would herself fill up afresh with sorrow.

Each morning—to a decreasing degree, but still declaring itself—the grief would be there. When winter broke, Holly had begun a routine of dressing Nicholas early, having a warm breakfast with him, then hiking the paths of Riverview to walk off their sadness. Returning from one such hike this last day of March 1981, and looking forward to hot cocoa and a light repast by a crackling fireplace in the east-wing breakfast room, Holly received an unexpected but not unwelcome greeting.

"What on earth are you doing here?" was her response to the grinning "Good morning" from Jack Houston, who was enjoying a hearty brunch of kippers and scrambled eggs all by himself in the breakfast room.

"I'm a leftover." He stood up and greeted Holly with a kiss on the cheek. "I stayed overnight with Buffy, and she didn't wake me when she left this morning."

It was a first, Holly realized, and Jack looked happy about it. Although he and Buffy had been married four months, and Buffy occasionally came home to Riverview, until today Jack had not come with her. Holly suspected that in Jack's eyes their spending the night together at Riverview was a confirmation on Buffy's part of the change in her status, demonstrating to her late husband's family the permanence of Jack's role in her life.

Holly realized that Jack and Nicholas had not met before. "This is my son, Nicholas. Nicholas, this is Mr. Houston."

"Jack," he corrected her as he took the little boy's hand. He shook it gravely, and when he spoke to Nicholas, it was without condescension. "Have you been hiking in the woods?" he asked.

"Yes. We go every day. Almost."

"Do you see interesting things there?"

"We saw a frog."

"No kidding. You know, Nicholas, when I was only a

360

little older than you, I once caught a frog and kept it as a pet."

"Was it hard to catch?"

"Well, yes, it was. But a friend of mine and I finally got it with a paper bag."

"I'd like to do that," Nicholas decided. "Only Mommy wouldn't let me keep it because she says they're icky."

"Frogs aren't icky," Jack told Holly firmly.

"That's what you say." She laughed. "If you're so fond of them, you can go out and help Nicholas catch one."

"Would you, Mister . . . Jack?" Nicholas's blue eyes were large with hope.

"Absolutely," Jack assured him. "How about after you've had lunch?"

"After his nap," Holly corrected Jack.

With that prospect before him, Nicholas raced through his lunch. Then, without his usual stalling, he went up to his room to take his nap, leaving Holly and Jack alone.

"Thanks a lot, pal," she told him. "If you get a call at three o'clock in the morning from a hysterical woman with a frog in her bed, don't be surprised."

"Nuts. I predict that you and Nicholas's frog will get to be great friends."

"I could never be friendly with any creature that hops around on legs apt to turn up sauteed in garlic sauce on my plate at Lutece."

"Are you afraid of lambs, too?" Jack inquired.

"If you're going to be logical, I'm going to change the subject." Holly regarded Jack closely. "You're looking very well," she told him. "Marriage must agree with you."

"It does. I'm very happy. Really very happy."

"I'm glad for you, Jack." Holly reached over and squeezed his hand. She may never have been fond of Buffy, but she knew how much Jack loved her.

"And I'm going to be a lot happier," Jack added with a laugh, "after today."

"That's right," Holly remembered with a frown. "This is the day they hammer out the rough agreement on the estate. No wonder Buffy left early for the city. Uncle James and Uncle David and Peter were all gone by the time Nicholas and I came down for breakfast at eight o'clock."

"Buffy was probably gone by then, too," Jack said.

"How come you didn't go with her?"

"The judge wants it to be a reconciliation meeting, and he specified that only the principals were to attend."

"Reconciliation or not," Holly observed with a sigh, "it looks like Buffy has pretty much won the battle." She let her coffee cup clank against the saucer.

"Not really." Jack frowned. "It's not that simple. Sure, Buffy is almost as happy to have the Stockwells lose as she would have been to pick up all the marbles, but the big winners are really the Tylers. Sarah Tyler's testimony at the hearing insured that."

"But she and Buffy are on the same side."

"Yes and no." Jack shrugged. "I'll tell you something none of the Stockwells know. De Vilbiss cut a deal with Sarah back in Alaska that gave her a chunk of money in exchange for coming to New York to testify. But the deal also tied her in as far as managing whatever she inherited was concerned. Buffy thought Sarah was locked in to her. Now it turns out that the one Sarah Tyler's really locked in to is De Vilbiss himself. When she took the money from him, she signed a paper appointing him guardian of her estate. So Buffy's only as secure as De Vilbiss's loyalty—which I'd guess has the consistency of ice cream melting in the California sun."

"Well, that should further complicate a complicated situation." Holly was recalling a conversation she'd had with Patrice a few days before.

Patrice had ticked off the intricacies the probate judge would have to unravel. They not only included the question of whether to uphold the Governor's will against Buffy's claim on the estate, but also deciding how much of the estate was not really the Governor's to leave, having actually belonged to his sister. Parceling out the Tyler shares of the Stockwell estate among Sarah Stockwell Tyler and all the other Tylers was a prime consideration as well. And if they really were descendants of Mary's brother Ellis Linstone, they had an even bigger claim over the Stockwell heirs. The proof was not absolute, and the Stockwells could fight the Linstone claim in court—but it would prove another lengthy battle. And breaking up the Stockwell-Linstone holdings would work to the detriment of all the heirs. Yet if they continued to be a single, multifaceted entity, it was impossible to continue the current management under James Stockwell and David Lewis alone. Creating some new system of management with either wider, or possibly even narrower participation, was the likely outcome, but would the heirs ever be able to come to agreement?

Each of these dilemmas, Patrice had pointed out to Holly, broke down into a collection of lesser issues which also had to be considered. It was quite possible that the entire probate process might disintegrate into a series of nit-picking arguments and lawsuits that could result in the case dragging on for years. It was to avoid this that the judge had summoned the principals to his chambers in an effort to arrive at a solution to which all—however grudgingly—might agree.

"You're a principal," Jack Houston remembered now. "How come you're not at the meeting, Holly?"

"Oh, I'm quite content to let Uncle James look out for my interests and those of Nicholas. And if my proxy gives him more clout, then it's all the better."

"Aren't you afraid your ex-husband will be there throwing around his weight on the basis of his son's share of the estate?" Jack wondered.

"Nope!" Holly's smile was free of tension. "Christopher will not be throwing his weight around anymore."

"I couldn't have hit him that hard." Jack looked at her quizzically.

"You were a knight in shining armor," Holly assured him, "but you're right. Having Christopher the albatross off my neck is not your doing."

"So who's doing is it? What's happened? Are you going to tell me, or do I have to guess?"

Holly told Jack Houston about her friendship with Winifred Fitzsimmons and the letter. "That's why I was so hesitant about divorcing Christopher," she concluded. "I didn't want to lose my son."

"But something changed."

"Yes. Winifred has been found. After all the failures of my solicitors in London, private detectives hired by Uncle James, and even Scotland Yard—just when I'd given up—by a sheer fluke Winifred turned up."

"What sort of fluke?"

"Well, it really is the most amazing coincidence," Holly told him. "Diana and Max Tyler have a younger sister, Louise. She lives on Crete with her husband—you must have heard of him—Spiro Papatestus. One day, on the beach, Louise bumped into Lisa Stockwell, Patrice's younger sister. Lisa was on holiday in Greece with another young woman and Louise wrote her sister Diana about meeting their cousin and casually mentioned that the woman Lisa was traveling with was Winifred Fitzsimmons. Then Diana called Patrice to say Louise had run into her sister, and she mentioned the name, too. Patrice recognized it."

"Patrice knew about your problem with the letter from this Winifred Fitzsimmons?"

"Yes. She and Uncle James were the only ones who knew until I told you today. And so, of course, Patrice called me right away."

Jack Houston thought a moment. "Is this Lisa—Patrice's younger sister—a lesbian?"

"Patrice is worried that Lisa has turned gay. Lisa's only twenty-three, and she's never been really close to anyone in the family, so Patrice is concerned."

"Would this Winifred, um, take advantage of her?" Jack wondered. "I mean, maybe because she's a Stockwell?"

"Oh, no. Winifred's not like that at all. She's very neurotic, obsessive even, but she's not calculating. It's emotion that counts with her, not wealth or prestige."

"Have you contacted her?"

"Yes. Uncle James drew up an affidavit, and Winifred signed it quite willingly and even had it notarized. And Winifred wrote me a separate note saying that if it was necessary for her to come to New York to testify in my behalf, she would. Uncle James showed both documents to Christopher and his lawyer, and they caved right in. Christopher took a lump-sum settlement for his nuisance value, and in exchange he signed papers relinquishing any claim for custody of our son. Then he left for England. So you see, he really is out of my life."

"And the divorce?"

"Uncle James is pushing it through just as fast as he can. It shouldn't take long at all."

"And what then, Holly?" Jack asked her.

"Well, Zelig Meyerling has asked me to marry him." Holly hadn't told anyone yet.

"No kidding!" Jack whistled. "The most eligible bachelor in Washington is willing to trade in his little black book for domesticity with you? By God, Holly, under that cool blond exterior of yours, what fires must rage!"

Holly blushed. "There's more to it than that."

"There always is." Jack's grin was back. "So you're going to marry Meyerling," he said.

"As a matter of fact I haven't really decided. When he asked me, everything was in such turmoil that I told him I needed time to decide. And we haven't seen each other since Winifred was located and my divorce from Christopher was settled. I mean, we talk on the phone, but it's the kind of thing you'd like to talk about face to face." Holly still felt confused, but the more she thought about it, the more certain she was of what her answer would be.

"He's in Washington?"

"Oh, yes. Very busy, too, from what Michael says."

"Michael?" Jack turned cynical. "Our congressman?"

"Yes." Holly had her own low opinion of Michael and didn't mind expressing it. "Kind of shakes your faith in democracy, doesn't it? I mean, Michael didn't just win. He won big."

"Reagan's coattails."

"I suppose. But Michael should have figured on that. It might have saved his relationship with his father."

"They're estranged?" Jack asked.

"Of course." Holly was bitter. "Nothing Buffy did in this battle over the will hurt quite as much as co-opting Michael."

Jack frowned. "What about the other son, Matt?"

"That hurt, too, but Uncle James understands it. Believe it or not, Uncle James has a lot of principle. He may not agree with Matt, but he knows he acted out of what he believes in, and I think he admires that. But Michael's a different story. He betrayed his father to get elected, and that hurt won't go away for a long time." Holly sighed. "Anyway, Michael did see Zelig in Washington. He's trying to cultivate him."

"Well, Zelig Meyerling is a very important man. A lot of people thought he'd get a post in the Reagan cabinet."

"Oh, no. He and Reagan are worlds apart on really basic views. He'll work with him, and Reagan will be glad to have him, but Reagan would never put Zelig in a position of real power." I'm beginning to sound like him, Holly thought to herself.

"Still, it is Reagan that Zelig's in Washington to see, isn't it? I saw that in one of the columns," Jack remembered.

"Yes. As a matter of fact I spoke to him on the phone last night, and he said he had a meeting with the President today at the Washington Hilton. Reagan's giving a speech or something there."

"But Zelig's been in Washington since the inauguration, hasn't he? That's been more than two months."

"Well, yes. He's been helping to orient some of the new—" Holly broke off as Berkley the butler came into the room. In contrast to his usually impervious expression, there was concern on his face. "Yes, Berkley?" Holly reacted. "Is something wrong?"

"I think I should turn on the television for you, Miss Holly." Berkley took a deep, shaky breath. "The President has just been shot."

"The President?" Holly looked at him uncomprehendingly. It was on the tip of her tongue to ask which president? The president of what?

"Yes, Miss Holly. President Reagan."

Jack got to the TV first. The network picture swam into focus on a scene of pandemonium. It was an instant replay of an event that had taken place only moments before. The screen showed Reagan, flanked by two secret servicemen in plainclothes and followed by his press secretary, James Brady, emerging from the Washington Hilton. Suddenly there was a popping sound like firecrackers being set off. The President, both secret service agents, and Press Secretary Brady sprawled to the ground. One of the secret servicemen rose immediately and pushed the President into the waiting limousine. The camera dollied wildly, searching for the assassin in the crowd.

Suddenly Holly saw Meyerling. He was in the front of the group right behind the first four men. There was more popping sounds and Holly watched in horror as he stumbled, shock on his face. The camera panned away from

366

him, and it was impossible for Holly to tell if he'd been hit or not.

With a sob Holly cried out. "Oh, God!" Was he hit? Was he hurt? Was he alive? As the reporters commented on the scene and repeated the videotape, Holly realized with the force of a vise closing around her heart just how much she really loved Zelig Meyerling.

50

HELD IN JUDGE'S CHAMBERS behind doors locked against the public and press alike, the meeting to settle the Stockwell estate was insulated from outside events. Those present did not learn of the assassination attempt until later. While the rest of the world was focused on Washington, they struggled to reach an accommodation over a vast fortune, splintered by greed and a complex legal history.

Aside from Ulysses Blandings, who was present out of a sense of duty, those in attendance were each committed to his or her own interests. James and David Lewis were as concerned with maintaining control of the estate as they were with guarding its assets against claims by Buffy and Sarah Stockwell Tyler.

Buffy wanted to break the will so that the bulk of the estate left to Mary by the Governor would go to her, and to share control on at least an equal footing with James Stockwell and David Lewis. Halsey De Vilbiss was out to parlay his roles as Buffy's attorney and Sarah Tyler's financial guardian into a permanent role of power in the Stockwell empire. Peter Stockwell and his mother were there to hold Buffy to her promise that in exchange for his help in breaking the Governor's will, Peter would have a decision-making position in the running of the Stockwell estate.

All of the Tylers—because the revelations of Sarah Tyler had opened the door to additional claims to the Stockwell estate, as well as to the Linstone estate—had merging and diverging goals in the negotiations. As Dr.

Paul Tyler and his wife saw it, Alfred Tyler, as one of the twin sons of Sarah and Ellis Linstone, and Lizzie Tyler, as the widow of the other twin, were jointly entitled to a full half-share of both the Stockwell and Linstone estates. Until her death, however, Sarah was the real winner. And Sarah Stockwell Tyler—who seemed not to care at all about her children, grandchildren or great-grandchildren — had gone back to Alaska and left it to Halsey De Vilbiss to look out for her interests.

Some members of the family were notably absent. Matt Stockwell continued to stay aloof from the battle. His decision to withdraw his money from the general Stockwell fund was on the record, but he'd told his father that no further undercutting was forthcoming.

Jonathan Stockwell, deeply depressed by the open confrontation with his wife and son, had at the last minute added his proxy to the others held by his brother James. However, he had not been able to bring himself to be there to oppose his wife and son in person.

From those who were present, the judge heard brief summations of the arguments, which nevertheless lasted until one in the afternoon. He then decreed a two-hour recess. At the end of that time the principals reconvened.

"These are my recommendations," the judge began. "As you know, they are not binding under law. They are an attempt to arrive at a series of compromises to which all will agree. If a general accord can be reached, there will still be countless hours spent, I am sure, in coming to an agreement on all of the details involved in the settlement and future management of an extremely complicated, multitudinously held estate."

He paused, referred to his notes, and resumed speaking. "The first claim challenging the validity of the Matthew Adams Stockwell testament was filed by Brenda Stockwell, his legal widow. Charges of 'failing mental faculties' and 'undue influence' were made. I find no substance to these charges. However, consistent with community-property precedent in New York State—admittedly not law, and admittedly not binding—I recommend that Brenda Stockwell be awarded fifty percent of that portion of the estate bequeathed by Governor Matthew Adams Stockwell to Mary Linstone Stockwell."

Buffy and Halsey De Vilbiss exchanged satisfied glances. Buffy refrained from smiling only by exerting the greatest willpower. If it held, the judge's recommendation made her a major shareholder of Stockwell Enterprises.

"However," the judge continued, "this fifty percent is exclusive of that half of the Stockwell estate which must revert to Sarah Stockwell Tyler. . . ."

Buffy's face fell. Instead of getting half, she was only getting half of half: a quarter. Halsey, realizing what this would mean to Sarah Tyler, whom he now effectively controlled, did not share Buffy's disappointment.

"Indeed, all allotments under the Matthew Adams Stockwell will must be made from that half of the assets that were legally his. None may be made from the half that has reverted to his sister. Since one half is far in excess of adequate, I would suggest that the original *cash* bequests be confirmed and disbursed from the testator's half of the estate." The Stockwell empire had just been cut in half, and was now being whittled away.

There had been large bequests to various charities and institutions, but nobody wanted to be in the position of publicly challenging them. As for the rest, for the most part the bequests consisted of relatively small gifts to servants and distant relatives. It was chicken feed. Nobody objected.

"I now turn to the estate of Mary Linstone Stockwell," the judge announced. "It can, of course, on demand be probated separately. Nevertheless, it is so intertwined with the Stockwell holdings that I am recommending that the two testaments be dealt with in tandem. Now bear in mind that there has already been considerable loss to this estate through the award of half the Matthew Adams Stockwell bequest to Brenda Stockwell."

Again the Judge adjusted his glasses. Again he referred to his notes. "I am recommending that the Mary Linstone Stockwell will be probated as written."

James Stockwell and David Lewis nodded their satisfaction. Dr. Paul Tyler shrugged. He was not by nature a greedy man. Nevertheless, he was disappointed that the Tylers—descendants of Mary's brother—would not participate in Mary's substantial bequest.

"An explanation is owing." The judge dealt with the

369

Tylers' exclusion. "Testimony as to the paternity of Ellis Linstone of the twin boys given birth to by Sarah Stockwell Tyler is unsubstantiated. Sixty-seven years have elapsed since that birth. Under such circumstances this court cannot lawfully declare Tylers to be Linstone progeny. During all that time the estate has been the property of Mary Linstone Stockwell, and therefore must now be probated as such."

Again the judge paused. This time the pause was extended. He wanted to give them all time to absorb the meaning and ramifications of his recommendations.

In effect they divided the joint Stockwell-Linstone-Tyler holdings into three roughly equal parts held by the Stockwells, Buffy, and the Tylers. There was, however, defection as well as solidarity among those controlling each part. It was a prescription—depending on how one looked at it—for either checks and balances, or for ganging up and double-cross dealings. In the future each individual might well regard him or herself as holding a balance of power by which to wrest concessions from other contending parties.

"I predict World War Three," was David Lewis's murmured comment to James Stockwell.

The judge cleared his throat. "I also have some recommendations as to the management of this joint estate."

James Stockwell and David Lewis exchanged worried looks. Obviously their advantageous status quo was about to have the rug pulled out from under it.

"I am recommending the establishment of a six-person board of trustees." The judge confirmed their fears. "This would include the two present trustees, James Stockwell and David Lewis. I am restoring Peter Stockwell to his former position as his father Jonathan Stockwell's proxy. This was the testator's wish, and it is likewise the recommendation of his widow, Mrs. Brenda Stockwell. Also, Mrs. Brenda Stockwell is entitled herself to a seat on this board. She may either exercise this prerogative personally or assign it to a subordinate of her choosing. That leaves two seats vacant. One of these is reserved to Sarah Stockwell Tyler, and she, too, may delegate it to a person of her choosing which, considering her age, she will undoubtedly do. The other is to be occupied by someone to be

370

jointly decided upon by members of the Tyler family—
hopefully before we adjourn for the day."

The Tylers looked at each other in dismay. They were
very far apart on so many issues. Nevertheless, at the
judge's suggestion they filed privately into an anteroom to
see if they might not resolve their dilemma.

Behind them Buffy was fairly content. She'd never expected to get the full estate. All along she had wanted to
share control even more than she'd wanted money. She
would have at least one ally—Peter Stockwell—and as
least as good a chance of enlisting the two others on her
side as James Stockwell and David Lewis had of enlisting
them on theirs.

Halsey De Vilbiss was also privately elated. He would
represent Sarah Tyler's considerable interests on the
board. The old lady had no choice. Her commitment to
him was in writing.

Ellen had drawn her son Peter off to one side to whisper to him. "Your uncles are furious," she exulted. "With
Buffy's backing, you can push them to the wall on ERC's
or anything else."

"Don't be too sure." Peter saw it clearly. "Buffy plans to
use me, not to be used. It's going to be hardball with all
the players, not just my uncles."

"You can handle her." All of Ellen's faith, so misplaced
in her husband, her marriage, and herself as well, was
now centered on her son.

"Yes." With Mary dead, Peter had regained his arrogance. "Buffy likes them young. In a pinch, she can be
handled."

The implication shocked Ellen. For a brief instant Ellen
saw her son clearly and ungilded by motherly love, and
for that instant she was truly appalled.

Meanwhile, in the other room the Tyler discussion was
deadlocked. The twins' price for cooperating in naming a
board member was freedom from their father's monetary
supervision. He was surprised at their solidarity. Carrie
was backing up Beth just as if she hadn't spent most of her
young life competing with her.

Finally Max Tyler made a suggestion. "Now you twins
have use for some of your money," he began, having
heard from Diana about Beth's desire to finance a sailboat

for Greenpeace. "But you don't need it all. You just don't want to leave any in the estate because it might be used for things you're against, like ERC's. Is that right?"

Although Carrie nodded with reservations, Beth was quick to agree. "Yes. That's what it's being used for. And now with Peter back—"

"Well, I have a suggestion. Paul, you let them take out the money they need, but no more. The rest stays there." Max turned to Beth. "It gives you a lever to influence Stockwell activities inside the setup. That's much more important than fighting it from outside."

"How would we be able to fight?" Beth asked. "Neither of us will be on the board."

"But you can put someone on who feels the same way you do and who will try to influence the other board members."

"You," Beth realized. "You're talking about yourself."

"Yes."

"I'd rather have Diana," Beth told him bluntly.

"So would I." Max grinned. "But she won't do it. She will, however, assure you that you can trust me to do what I say I'll do."

"You, Max?" Dr. Paul Tyler was disbelieving. "You want to be on the board?"

"I promise to keep a stiff wrist, Paul," Max told him dryly. "And I also promise to raise my level of hetero consciousness." He looked at Beth. "Well?" he asked. "What do you think?"

Beth looked at Carrie.

Carrie shrugged.

"Dad?" Beth looked inquiringly at her father.

"How long would you agree to leave the balance of your money in Stockwell Enterprises?" Paul wanted to nail it down.

"A year," Beth decided. "But then we reevaluate their policies in terms of pollution and apartheid and armaments production."

"Fight that battle when you come to it," Max interjected hastily. "Well, Paul, what do you say?"

"All right." Dr. Paul Tyler agreed. Max was a good businessman. He was too busy to assume the position himself, although he had at first assumed that was exactly what he'd have to do. Now, he'd be off the hook with his daughters. Ruefully, he realized he was abdicating authority in order to let Max take the heat.

Paul called his mother and stepfather, Lizzie and Alfred Tyler, and then Max called Diana. All were agreeable to Max representing them. It was settled.

They filed back into the other room and informed the others that Max Tyler would be acting for the Tylers' interests on the board of trustees. The other board members were nonplussed. Each had assumed that Paul Tyler would have taken over the responsibility, but David Lewis alone was outraged. He fairly sputtered with rage, and James realized that the split between David and Max would make it even more difficult to keep the Tylers' interests in line with those of the Stockwells.

Their business concluded for the time being, the judge adjourned the meeting. The cards had fallen and now it was up to the Stockwells, the Tylers, and Buffy to make it work.

As they were leaving, Carrie fell in beside her sister. "Bethie," she said, "can we talk?"

Beth looked at her, surprised. Carrie and she had never been confidantes. She was even more surprised by her twin's request than she had been by her unexpected support these past few weeks. "Sure," she said. "Let's go have coffee."

Watching them leave together arm in arm, their father and mother asked each other which was the more astonishing thing about parenthood: The unexpected joy of seeing your children become friends? Or the pain of having them view you, their parents, as the enemy?

51

LOOKING AT HER twin across the Formica tabletop in the coffee shop booth, Beth couldn't help noticing the signs of strain. Carrie's hazel eyes were bloodshot. There

373

was a small muscle pulsing in her jaw. Her hands twisted, the long fingers wringing out an invisible dishrag.

"My life's a mess!" Carrie blurted out.

Beth sighed. The nude shots in *Sweetlife*, the increasing reliance on cocaine, the promiscuity—how could she disagree? Carrie's life was indeed a mess.

"Can you imagine how I felt when I saw that magazine?"

"I didn't know you felt any particular way." Beth neither wanted to argue with her twin nor to add to her unhappiness, but she had no talent for dissembling. "You didn't show it."

"What would have been the point? I couldn't expect much sympathy. I was the victim, but the way everyone carried on, you'd think it was each and every one of them personally displayed naked with their private parts exposed."

"They didn't pose for the pictures," Beth was forced to point out. "You did."

"No, I didn't."

"What do you mean? They were of you, weren't they?"

"Of course." Carrie was defiant now, obviously not expecting her sister to believe her. "They were of me, but I didn't *pose* for them. I made love with this guy I met. I certainly didn't know anybody was taking pictures."

Beth was skeptical, just as Carrie had expected her to be. "If that's true, then you could put those people in jail for a very long time."

"If I could prove it, maybe. But I can't. I was high, and I signed a release without knowing what I was signing." Carrie's tone was sullen. "When I found out about the pictures, I went up to *Sweetlife* to try to stop them. I said I'd go to the district attorney. That's when they brought out this release with my signature on it. I started yelling it was a forgery, and so they brought in Harmony—this guy I'd slept with. He said he'd swear I signed voluntarily."

"Well, it's done." Beth had no solace to offer her sister, only the recognition that what had happened was behind her. "Maybe you'll learn from the experience."

"That's condescending. You're always so righteous, Beth." Then her tone changed. "But there's something to it, too," Carrie admitted. "It made me realize my life is going down the drain."

"Well, if you snort coke all the time and hop into bed with every man that comes along . . ." Beth's tone was gentle, and she held up a hand before Carrie could protest. "I don't want to dump on you," she said. "But that's what you've been doing, Carrie. It's not just that I'm more prudish than you. It has to catch up with you sooner or later."

"I know." The resentment seemed to go out of Carrie like air from a balloon. "I don't want that." She looked at her sister directly, pleadingly. "I need help. I've known that for a long time, but I couldn't think who to turn to. I kept coming back to you, Beth. You're my sister. You're the only one I can turn to. Will you help me?"

"Well . . . sure." Beth was taken aback by Carrie's frank plea. Twins though they were, throughout their lives they had always abraded, never been truly supportive of each other. It had been a competition of sorts, with each sister reacting against the other. Still, there was love between them, no matter how many layers of sisterly rivalry it was buried beneath. "Of course I'll help you, Sis." She reached across the table, separated Carrie's twisting hands, and took one of them between her own. "I'll do anything I can."

"Will you?" Carrie took a deep breath. "Will you take me with you?"

"What?"

"When you join Greenpeace. I want to join with you."

"But Carrie, you've never been interested in environmental protection, or the peace movement, or anything like that. Why, just last year you bought a sealskin coat."

"But I could be. I've got to do something . . . something that doesn't leave me time to think of myself."

"That doesn't sound like much of a commitment." Beth was doubtful.

"Maybe not. But would you believe me if I said I'd suddenly got the do-good religion? You'd know I was lying. But I do want to make a change. Beth, I can't do it alone."

"I don't know, Carrie. I really don't think Greenpeace is for you."

"I'd be willing to go fifty-fifty with you to buy the sailboat. And you know I'd be an asset on deck. I'm almost as good a sailor as you are."

It was that bit of tact that got to Beth finally. They were both good sailors, but they both knew that Carrie had more natural aptitude. Beth had always had to work to be yar; Carrie was born that way. "Well, all right." Beth grinned. "It will be the Tyler twins on the *Bounding Main* then, and God help those Aegean garbage dumpers."

"Oh, Beth, thanks. You won't be sorry. You'll see. The two of us will be a real team."

"Three. The three of us." Beth signaled the waitress for the check. "Remember, Deke Wells is coming, too."

"Yes. So are you two involved or what?"

"Well, yes."

"Are you sleeping together?" Carrie's natural mischievous grin appeared on her face.

Beth blushed. "As a matter of fact we are."

"Well, I'm glad you finally found someone." Carrie made the effort to sound sincere. "And you're right. We'll make a great threesome, you, me and Deke."

Despite the effort, there was a smoldering of interest in Carrie's almond eyes at the prospect of being in close sailboat proximity to Deke Wells. It should have been a warning signal to her twin. But it wasn't.

52

TOO LATE. It was too late to renege now, Patrice reflected when she was summoned to Bartleby's office. She had opted for filial loyalty, and the fact that the Stockwell estate had now been settled in a manner not particularly advantageous to her father didn't alter the fact that Patrice had aligned herself against Buffy.

The word was out that Star-Agena had acquired a controlling interest in Bartleby & Hatch. The climate-controlled air of the agency was heavy with the imminence of a shake-up. Patrice had been spared once before to perform Mickey Mouse chores. With Buffy's parent company in full control now, she did not expect to be spared again.

Her fear was made tangible when she entered Bartleby's office to find Buffy seated there. Mr. Bartleby was pouring coffee from a steaming silver carafe. He poured a cup for Buffy and one for himself. He did not offer Patrice a cup. Who, she wondered idly, would water the philodendron in her office after her departure?

"I believe you and Mrs. Houston know each other." Bartleby's tone was cold.

"Yes." Inwardly Patrice winced. Mrs. Houston! What a patsy she had been! How eagerly she'd let herself be used. "Hello, Buffy. How's Jack?" And if that reminded Buffy that Patrice had once been to bed with her husband, well, so much the better.

"Thriving," Buffy replied sweetly. "Marriage really agrees with him."

Patrice's fingers rearranging her bow mentally gouged out Buffy's eyes. Abruptly, she changed tactics; she had enough of cat-and-mouse—not just with Buffy, but with Bartleby as well. "Why am I here?" she asked bluntly.

"Mrs. Houston asked that I send for you, O'Keefe. As you've probably heard, Bartleby and Hatch is now under the Star-Agena umbrella. We are all of us now responsible to Star-Agena. That includes me. Mrs. Houston tells me that certain changes will be made in our modest operation. Star-Agena wishes to move Bartleby and Hatch up to the big time. Dead wood—a cruel phrase, perhaps, but an accurate one—will be removed."

"And so I'm being axed," Patrice saw no reason not to get it over with quickly.

Bartleby looked at Buffy. Obviously he believed Patrice had called it right. Nevertheless, the new situation—which had lined his pockets generously but removed his authority—called for deference.

"No." Buffy met his gaze. "You're not being fired, Patrice. You're being promoted."

Patrice and Bartleby were equally surprised. Bartleby found his voice first. "Well, of course, Patrice is one of our most effective account executives. Just recently she came within a hair of a vice presidency of the agency. And as a matter of fact, the way Bartleby and Hatch will be expanding under Star-Agena, I see no reason why we shouldn't have another vice president."

Patrice? Not O'Keefe? Vice president? Who would do the paste-ups she'd been reduced to doing for herself these past months? Patrice wondered. And then she was struck by another thought. What could Buffy be up to?

"Vice president wasn't what I had in mind," Buffy responded to Bartleby. "I thought perhaps something higher up the ladder."

"Higher up the ladder?" Bartleby was puzzled. "But there is nothing higher up the ladder."

"Oh, but there is. Think, Mr. Bartleby."

"But the only thing higher is—"

Oh, my God! Patrice was a beat ahead of him in grasping Buffy's meaning. The dead wood was being cleared out all right. And what deader timber at Bartleby & Hatch than Mr. Bartleby himself?

"I see." Bartleby had gone quite white. "I do think you might have told me privately," he said stiffly to Buffy. He lurched out the door, heading for the men's room.

"I thought breaking the news with you present would get us off to a better start," Buffy told Patrice. "You deserved to see him reap the harvest of his treatment of you."

"I almost felt sorry for him." Patrice looked at Buffy in amazement. Her knees were shaking and she desperately wanted to sit down, but she remained standing. "What he did to me he did because your man De Vilbiss put him up to it," she recalled. "I hardly see how you're justified in being moralistic toward him."

"Now we are not getting off to a good start," Buffy observed dryly. "I don't understand you, Patrice. I'd always heard from the Governor how ambitious you were. The word on Madison Avenue confirms that. What's your problem? Don't you want to be in charge of Bartleby and Hatch?"

"That depends. Why are you doing this?" Patrice couldn't believe that the offer was genuine. "You don't like me. I don't like you. And we've both got good reason. So why should you go out of your way to advance my career?"

"Like?" Buffy shrugged. "I never let my likes and dislikes interfere with business. You shouldn't either, Patrice. And I have good reason. I think you can build this agency into a Madison Avenue leader. I think you can make Star-Agena a lot of money."

"Why me? Why not Bartleby? He was doing all right."

"Because 'all right' isn't good enough. I want growth. Half the growth of this agency over the last five years has been from campaigns you've handled. That's what our survey of Bartleby and Hatch showed. With additional financing and managerial control, I think you can push Bartleby and Hatch right to the top. And if I'm wrong, you'll be out on your too-cute little bottom just like that."

"Strictly business, then?"

"That's right. What do you say?"

"I want a raise."

"All right. My people at Star-Agena will negotiate one with you."

"And complete authority."

"Of course. How else can you make a success for me?"

"And stock options, Buffy. I want stock options."

"All right. But limited. Limited stock options."

"How limited?"

"My people will negotiate."

"Well, all right, then. Contingent on the negotiations, I accept."

"Congratulations." Buffy got to her feet and surprised Patrice by holding out her hand.

Hesitantly, Patrice took it.

"I wish you luck as the new head of Bartleby and Hatch." For the first time since Patrice had entered the office, Buffy smiled. It was not a friendly smile. It was businesslike, but it was something else as well. It was... wicked.

"Thank you." Patrice recognized the kind of smile it was, and for one wild moment she thought of changing her mind and walking out of Bartleby & Hatch forever. But the moment passed, and Buffy passed out of Mr. Bartleby's office with it.

Patrice exited behind her, turning away from the elevators and back toward her own office. En route she encountered Donny, the art director. Perceiving that she had

379

just left Bartleby's office, he greeted her with a quizzical and worried look. "Has the defecation struck the whirling blades?" he asked her.

"Relax, Donny. Your job is safe."

"And yours, Lady of the Bows?"

"Call me Ms., Donny."

"Huh?"

"Or sir. Yes I definitely prefer sir. With a capital S. Call me Sir."

"Why do I have the feeling that you're trying to tell me something."

"I am, Donny." Patrice decided it was all right to laugh. "I'm your new boss." She turned away from his wordless open-mouthed astonishment, went into her own office and closed the door behind her. She looked at the philodendron and smiled. "And your future's safe, too," she said out loud.

But the euphoria didn't last. She had finally got what she wanted. Her career was really off the ground now. But there was no one to share it with. Jack Houston had married Buffy and there was no other man in Patrice's life.

Except, of course, if you counted James, her father.

53

"YOUR FATHER, ISN'T IT, went to the trouble to make things right?" Kathleen O'Lunney demanded of Matt. Hands on hips, the springtime sunlight lending sparkle to her freckles, she was the picture of indignation. "So the thanks he gets is you stand on your high-and-mighty principle and back off when he needs your support most!"

They were in Matt's horse barn. Earlier that morning Matt had noticed that one of his yearlings had developed a limp. Now he was crouched beside the colt with his back to Kathleen.

"Last fall," Matt responded, "when I did what I had to

do, I didn't know Dad had gone to see Wendy." Glad not to have to face Kathleen's green-eyed anger, Matt held the stallion's fetlock in large hands, which were both firm and gentle, and examined it. "And the stand I took then wasn't to set myself up against Dad. It was to insure that the money left to me wouldn't be used for the things I'm most against."

"That was last fall. But what of last month? When he had his back to the wall? Surely you could have changed your high-and-mighty position then. You knew what your father had done for you. In spite of all that resistance your precious Wendy had, he was able to make her see that her five-year-old son Bruce needed a father as well as a mother, that he was entitled to his Stockwell birthright as well as his MacTavish roots."

"It's beyond me how Dad convinced her."

"That's right. It is beyond you, Matt. You told me Wendy was a zealot, but sure and you're the fanatical one. That's why it's beyond you. The picture of your father in her mind was of a plutocratic stereotype. Then she met the man, and wasn't it him she related to and not the stereotype at all? While you, Matthew Sykes Stockwell, have known the man—your father!—all your life, and to this day can't deal with anything but your own cardboard picture of him."

Matt set the colt's hoof down gently and got to his feet. "I don't understand what you're so angry about," he said mildly.

"Don't you now?" Kathleen shook her head, the bright red cloud of her tresses shimmering with the movement. Unexpectedly, she changed the subject. "So you've got joint custody of your son Bruce now, and he'll be spending time at Riverview meeting all his fine Stockwell relatives."

"That's what Dad got Wendy to agree to. Yes." Matt was perplexed. What was she driving at?

"Well, if you won't be going up to Canada to see your son, then where will you meet with your Wendy?"

"Why should we meet?"

"You've been meeting, haven't you? Contrary to what you said that day at Purchase."

"I had to see her," Matt explained. "After Dad got her

to share custody of Bruce, I had to go up there and work out the details."

"Which you're telling me now, but didn't bother telling me at the time."

"Because I knew you'd react just the way you're reacting. I didn't want the hassle." Matt took Kathleen by the shoulders. "Look," he said, "there is nothing between Wendy and me. Sometimes we're going to have to talk about our son. That's all. Other than that, it's over. Truly over."

"Then why haven't you told me all that's been happening? Why do I have to find it out from gossip? If not for the ball bearings wagging my father's tongue, I'd never know anything of what's going on."

"I wanted to wait until everything was settled. Then I figured we could both give our undivided attention to the matter of you and me."

"Well, send me a telegram care of my loose-lipped father when you're ready to do that."

"No need. I'm ready now."

"Ready for what?" Kathleen wanted to know. "For us to be lovers?"

"Well, I do want you, Kathleen. Very much."

"All right, then. You turn me on, too. I'll not deny it. Lovers it is, then. Will tonight suit you?"

"Well, sure..." Matt studied her. "Why so cold-blooded about this?" he asked finally.

"Not at all. You'll find my blood every bit as warm and passionate as you could wish."

"But without sentiment," Matt realized.

"Ah, sentiment. Well, now, you have to give to get. And sometimes not even then. Ask your father."

"Let's talk about us, not my father. What's going on. Kathleen? If it's just sex you want and not sentiment, then why have you refused until now?"

"Oh, my! Oh, my! " Hand fluttering to her forehead, palm out, Kathleen feigned martyrdom. "There's no pariah so despised as the virgin in this the last half of the twentieth century, now is there?"

"I never said that."

She ignored his disclaimer. "But here, now, comes a lad willing to save the poor colleen from a fate worse than

382

death—meaning, of course, not ravishment, but chastity. How then can I ever thank you, Matthew Sykes Stockwell?"

"Forget it." Anger flared in Matt's brown eyes. "I don't just want to go to bed with you, dammit! It was never only sex. I thought you knew that. I want to marry you."

"Marriage, is it? Well, now, that's another matter entirely. No thank you kindly, Matt. I'll pass on that offer."

"Let me get this straight. You're willing to go to bed with me tonight, but you're not willing to marry me?"

"That's right."

"Why not?"

"I don't want a hardbitten man for a husband. I want to have children, and I want them to have a tender father. I want a tender, loving husband. I want a man who can bend with me, not one so stiff I'll always have to worry that opposing him might snap him. I want a man whose family means more to him than his principles."

"How can you think my family wouldn't come first?"

"Your father doesn't. With you, principle always comes first and him second. Or is it that you don't love him?"

"Of course I love him. Very much."

"And will you love me and the children in the same way, then?" she inquired sarcastically. "Keeping the news of it to yourself like the miser you are?"

"Kathleen, what is it you want me to do?" Matt asked.

"Tell him how you feel, Matt. Tell your father you love him. Tell him you're sorry you stood against him. Tell him how much you appreciate him talking Wendy around."

"All right."

"What does that mean?" Kathleen eyed him suspiciously.

"It means I'll do what you want. I'll tell him."

"When?"

"Right now. Come on in the house and I'll call him up. You can stand right there and hear the whole conversation."

"Is it my bluff you're calling then? Well, I won't back off. I don't embarrass easily, and I've little shame about eavesdropping—a quality I get from my own father, no doubt." Kathleen allowed herself a small smile. "Well, come on, then." She took his hand and tugged him out of the barn toward the house. "If you're not all wind, let's hear you do it."

"I will. But I want two things in exchange. First, stop putting on that brogue. You know you only do it to keep me off balance when we argue."

"And the second thing?"

"Stop beating around the bush. Say you'll marry me."

"Well, we'll see about that."

"See?" Matthew was suspicious. "What will we see?"

"Why, how tonight turns out, of course. Brogue or no brogue, no self-respecting Killarney girl buys a pig in a poke, you know." Her tone and her words were light, but Matt recognized the love in her eyes.

Matt was still shaking his head in wonder at Kathleen as he picked up the phone and dialed his father.

54

FEW THINGS DURING his years of fatherhood surprised and affected James as much as the call from his son Matt. After their autumn horseback ride together and his successful trip to Canada, James had looked forward to a new closeness with his oldest son. He had even dared to hope that Matt would reexamine his position both in terms of building a future for his own son, Bruce, and taking over some of the Stockwell business burdens.

Instead, James had returned from Canada to find Matt withdrawing his inheritance from the estate because Buffy had offered to match dollar for dollar any contribution he made to the fight against U.S. intervention in Central America. He understood that Matt was acting out of principle, but even so, James had been bitterly disappointed. He felt that a son should have been there for his father when the chips were down.

And now came this call—an unsolicited declaration of love and respect couched in simple, straightforward terms. Although Vanessa had helped put James in touch with his emotions, and he was more receptive than he had been throughout most of his life, he was overwhelmed by Matt's words. His oldest son loved him! Respected him! Appreciated what he'd done!

Nothing had changed. Matt would go right on squandering his money on liberal causes. He would continue to fiddle around with horses, and never be willing to go into business with his father. James knew all that, but it no longer mattered.

Nothing had changed. Everything had changed! He knew that his son Matt loved him and accepted him for what he was. And, in turn, James loved and accepted Matt. Once James had thought that closeness, love, and acceptance could only be attained if they worked together for the same goals—in business. Now he knew that they could be father and son without any reason—any common goal or ideal—except love.

Yes, nothing had changed; everything had changed! He couldn't wait to see Vanessa. He couldn't wait to tell her he finally had his son back from his years of exile in the only way that counted—because Matt wanted to be back with his father!

Vanessa didn't answer the downstairs buzzer, so James let himself into the Tompkins Square apartment with the key she'd given him. She wasn't there. The apartment was empty and strangely quiet.

James roamed around for a few impatient moments before he noticed the letter propped up on the kitchen table. His name was on the envelope in Vanessa's handwriting. He picked it up, opened it, and took out the handwritten sheets inside.

My dearest James,

I am such a coward. You know that about me. I can never face hurting someone I love, and that is, perhaps, one of the greatest cowardices of all. Cowardice, as every anthropologist knows, leads to brutality. And so I am being brutal.

For some time now I have known that I would be leaving for Greece tonight. A colleague, an archeologist, has made some exciting new discoveries in the fourth layer down of a Minoan ruin. It is not an opportunity I can afford to pass up.

That's why I didn't tell you about it. You would have tried to talk me out of it, and you well might have succeeded. If you had, the day would surely come when I would hate you for it. I know that sounds a cliché, but I believe it is really true.

Do I love you? Oh, yes, James. Much more, I'm sure, than you believe as you read this now. But more than my career? I can hear you pinpointing the issue in that way you have of zeroing in on problems and dealing with them directly. Well, then, ask yourself this: Would you give up your career for me? Oh, right now, perhaps, you think you would, but would you really?

We will see each other again. The world—our world, yours and mine—is too small a place that our paths should fail to cross. And when we do meet, will it be as lovers still? I fervently hope so, James. I treasure our lovemaking so very much. I want it to be as lovers that we meet in future. But if, when we meet, that is not your wish, I understand. In this spirit I offer you symbolism. Keep the key to my apartment, James, for as long as you think you would want to use it if I were there. Some day I will return. But when you no longer feel that way—meet someone else. I'll scratch her eyes out! No I won't, I'll understand—just mail the key back. Until that day, I shall go on considering us as lovers.

And so, James, good-bye. You are a good man— the best—loving, tender, kind. Whatever you may think of me, do go on thinking well of yourself.

I love you.

As always,
Vanessa

James read the letter over twice in the twilight drifting through the window from Tompkins Square. He wiped away some tears, then put the letter in his pocket and took out his key ring. He checked the snap holding the key to Vanessa's apartment to be sure it was secure, then put the key ring back in his pocket.

He continued sitting. He thought of his love for Vanessa, and he couldn't bear to think of not holding her tonight. What a day. First the call from Matt, and now this letter from Vanessa. He felt sad, and at the same time introspective. He thought of Vanessa and then his children. And he made a startling discovery. Vanessa had underestimated his ability to change his life for her. He had made so many discoveries in the year since his father died, and changes that had brought him closer to all of his family. And they bound him to Vanessa in a way that only the two of them could understand.

Finally James left the Tompkins Square apartment, hailed a taxi, and gave the driver his daughter's address.

55

WHEN THE DOORMAN buzzed up to announce her father, Patrice swept through the sunken living room of her Upper East Side apartment like a whirlwind. There wasn't time, however, to pick up all the incremental mess of single living. Patrice hadn't been expecting anybody, least of all her meticulous father.

She was still struggling to button her blouse with one hand while trying to stick a tortoise shell comb into her muss of chestnut hair with the other when James entered. They embraced and pecked cheeks. Patrice was gratified when James didn't purse his lips with disapproval at the clutter of the apartment and her personal dishabille, as he usually did.

"What a nice surprise," she greeted him.

"I'm not intruding? I mean, if you have a date, or—"

"You're not intruding. I have no date. Let me give you a scotch," Patrice offered.

"That would be nice. A quick one and then I'm going. I don't want to miss the train back to Riverview."

"A quick one it is." Patrice poured him a drink. "What's new, Daddy?"

"Vanessa has left." He accepted the glass from Patrice and took a long, slow sip of scotch.

"Oh." Patrice couldn't think of anything to say. She was relieved. She thought her father's involvement with Vanessa Brewster had been unwise, to say the least. But she sensed that the last thing her father wanted to hear right now was how much better off he'd be without her. Finally she came up with a combination of words that was both neutral and showed concern. "Is there anything I can do?"

"No. Thanks for offering, though." James looked at his eldest child for a long, silent moment.

It was a very intense, searching sort of look, and it made Patrice uneasy. "Daddy?" she finally said.

"What do you want, Patrice? From life, I mean. What do you really want?"

"The same as everybody, I guess." Patrice shrugged. "Self-fulfillment. Satisfaction. Success. Recognition."

"You're talking about business?"

"Well, yes."

"And that's what's important to you." James sighed. "Well, why not? It's what's been important to me all of my life." Again he pondered. "Ambition." He spoke again. "The last time you and I talked about your ambition was just before the Governor died, wasn't it, Patrice? Yes. More than a year ago. You had plans for moving up at Bartleby and Hatch." James smiled. "You were going to take over the industry. And now you're on your way. Heading up Bartleby and Hatch is a very impressive start." James sighed again. "But you still want more than that. Right?"

"Oh, yes. I want it all. I like the business world. I like competition. Most of all"—Patrice grinned—"I like winning."

"You said the business world. Not just the advertising world, then?" James asked.

"What do you mean?"

"Your success is impressive, Patrice, but Bartleby and Hatch is small potatoes. Would you be interested in utilizing your talents on a somewhat larger scale?"

"Such as?" Patrice was staring at her father again, not daring to anticipate his answer.

"Such as Stockwell Enterprises."

"Are you offering me a job, Daddy?"

"No." James looked at his daughter very seriously. "I'm offering you the whole enchilada. I'm almost fifty-three years old. It occurred to me tonight that I don't want to trot all the way to the boneyard in harness. I'd like to spend some of my life on something besides business. See the world. Maybe even to go Greece."

"Greece?"

"Yes. Well, why not? Anyway, I want to start turning things over to someone I trust, someone I know to be capable. What I'm saying, Patrice, is I want you to come in with me for a year or two, and then step into my shoes."

It was happening too fast. Patrice felt dizzy. "What about Matt?" She blurted out. "Isn't it him you always wanted to take over? The eldest son and all that?"

"Matt will never take over. I've finally accepted that. He is what he is, and I feel pretty positive about that right now. You can't live your children's lives for them. You have to learn to take them as they are." James drained his drink. "How about it, Patrice? Would you like to come in with me and learn how to run Stockwell Enterprises?"

"Are you sure you wouldn't be more comfortable with a man?" Patrice couldn't resist saying it, and she couldn't keep a certain amount of bitterness out of her voice either.

"More comfortable? Probably. But there's no man I could have more confidence in than I do in you." James looked at his watch.

"Well, all right, then." Heart thumping, Patrice accepted. "You've got yourself a deal. Have the signs changed to 'Stockwell and Daughter.'"

"We'll work out the details." James got to his feet.

"I'm really flattered, Daddy." Patrice went to peck his cheek again.

The hug James gave her was surprisingly warm. "One thing, Patrice," he said. "There's more to life than business. Maybe you should think about that."

After her father left, Patrice did think about it. She was lonely. She faced the fact. She wanted to share the news, and she needed to feel close to someone. She thought of Jack Houston and sighed. She still wanted him. She picked up the telephone and dialed.

"Hello." A male voice answered.

"Hello, Miles. It's Patrice." She identified herself to her ex-husband. "How'd you like to have dinner with an old roommate tonight?"

"Gee, I'm sorry, Patrice. I have a date."

"Oh, well . . . a rain check then."

There was a brief pause before Miles responded. "I'm involved with someone, Patrice," he said. "We're talking about getting married."

"Congratulations." Patrice made a fast recovery. "When you nail it down, give me a ring and I'll buy the two of you dinner to celebrate."

"Will do, Patrice."

They chatted a while longer, then exchanged good-byes and hung up. Patrice didn't so much mind about Miles, it was just— Damn Jack Houston anyway! she thought, staring at the phone. She dialed again—slowly.

"Hello. Craig Burrows here." Her old lover sounded the same as always—a little overbearing and a little unsure of himself. It was the way he made love, too.

"Hello, Craig. It's Patrice. I was wondering if you were free for dinner tonight." This beau wasn't her favorite, not even her second favorite.

"Why yes." Caught unawares, Craig sounded like a man who couldn't believe his luck. "Why yes, Patrice, I am."

Not even her second favorite, but it was the beau at hand. "Eight o'clock," Patrice told him. "My place."

Damn him! Damn Jack Houston! Well, if she couldn't have what she wanted, she'd have to settle for what she could get.

Settling—it was one answer to loneliness.

56

"LONELINESS," Holly was saying. "I'd been alone before, but that isn't the same. Loneliness isn't just the condition of being solitary. It's a..." She groped. "It's a *comparative* lack. It's having someone and then not having them. That's what I faced last week when I saw you in the crowd and heard the gunfire. I faced what my life would be like without the person who was filling it. That was much worse than the state I'd been in before I became involved with you. Much worse. I faced real loneliness."

Her words—what they implied as well as what they said—moved Meyerling as he had not allowed himself to be moved very often in his life. "I love you," he said. "I love you so very much."

Holly's composure dissolved in the face of his naked emotion. "I am so damn glad you're alive!" she blurted out.

"Then it's a good thing that unlike the President, I did not forget to duck." He couldn't stop smiling at her, and it made him feel foolish. Her words were unexpected. That Holly cared enough for him to let him know how much she cared was truly wonderful after he'd steeled himself to be rejected by her. Having been sure she was letting him down gently, he now dared to hope again. And that hope made him smile so widely, he was sure he must look like an idiot.

Although they had spoken on the phone, it was the first time they'd seen each other in person since the day of the assassination attempt. They sat facing each other at a small table in the hushed, padded-for-silence VIP lounge at Dulles International Airport. Meyerling was still unable to tear himself away from Washington, and so Holly had flown down to see him.

"I've been so worried. I had to see you for myself to be

sure you really are all right. Damn you, Zelig! It was six hours before you called that day. That was really too much. Six hours of not knowing whether you were alive or dead. If you ever do that to me again, Zelig, I swear I'll kill you myself."

"I couldn't help it. It was complete chaos. Nobody knew how badly the President had been hurt. Alexander was out of control. The Vice President was in the clouds. I had to do what I could to help restore order." As he spoke, Meyerling's eyes were filled with love, and he could not take them off her.

His exquisite sense of timing had deserted him. He desperately wanted to ask Holly the only question that really mattered. He hadn't the foggiest notion of whether this was the propitious moment to ask it or not. And so, like a lovestruck schoolboy with trembling knees and calf's eyes, he finally blurted it out.

"Will you marry me?" He spoke with a rush of anxious breath. "Have you decided yet, Holly?"

"I love you," she said. "I've decided that." In the face of his uncharacteristic stammering, she felt herself blushing. "You Machiavellian Casanova, I love you! Do you hear me?"

"I hear you." No Russian diplomat sitting across from Meyerling had ever guessed that his face could be capable of assuming the pleased expression spread over it now. "I hear you, Holly."

"God, how I love you! When I thought you might be dead . . . Oh, Zelig, the hell I put myself through because I wouldn't admit to myself right away when you asked me to marry you how much I love you!"

"And now? Will you marry me?"

"Oh, Zelig, I—I—"

"I'll go on a diet." He patted the small bulge of his stomach. "I'll give up olives immediately." He pushed the martini glass on the small cocktail table far away from him. "You've no idea how many calories there are in martini olives. I love them. I really do. But no sacrifice—"

"Will you shut up, you idiot!" Holly was laughing, and half crying, too. "Oh! People really aren't supposed to talk to the great Zelig Meyerling this way, are they?"

"Only people who agree to marry him."

"All right, then. If you can give up your olives, I can give up my freedom. I'll marry you."

"Really?" His eyes opened wider than Holly had ever seen them. "You'll really marry me?"

"You'll have to give up all your long-stemmed ladies, too."

"No sacrifice." He shrugged. "Olives—now that is a sacrifice. That proves real love. But other women—what a relief it will be not to have to play that game anymore." He cupped his hand around hers.

"Oh? And what game will we play? After we're married, I mean?" Holly held his hand tightly.

"No game at all." He surprised Holly by being completely serious. "We'll have love. We won't need games."

"Oh, Zelig." Holly found herself brushing away a tear with her free hand. "You are the most surprising man."

"I will make a superb husband." Just as quickly, he wasn't serious at all anymore. "When shall we marry?"

Holly thought a moment. "Autumn. I think," she decided. "It's my favorite season. Late autumn. It's a time for new beginnings." She found herself grinning. Still holding hands, they leaned forward to kiss.

57

MANY WEEKS LATER Jack Houston walked down the corridor of the nursing home to room 316 and knocked. "Come in." The voice that answered was old and querulous.

Jack entered the room and shut the door behind him.

"Hello, Grandpa," he said, then walked over and deposited a package of sundries beside the old man on the bed.

There were magazines in the package, a *Wall Street Journal*, a box of Kleenex, a tin of lozenges, a six-pack of underwear, and six pairs of socks. The old man ignored the package and its contents. He had something else on his mind. "You married?" he demanded of Jack.

"Yes, Grandpa." Jack had told him he was married on his last visit. Memory ran in and out of the old man's mind like water filling and draining from an unstoppered sink. "I'm married."

"The Stockwell woman?"

"Yes, Grandpa."

"His wife? The Governor's?"

"Yes, Grandpa."

"Don't jerk me around, boy!" the old man glared. "Maybe I don't have all my marbles, but I've got more than enough. How could you marry her if she's his wife?"

"He's dead, Grandpa," Jack said patiently. He'd told him at least half-a-dozen times. "The Governor's dead."

"Dead." The old man grinned from ear to ear, a nasty razor slash bisecting his face. "Ha! Seventeen years younger than me and I outlived him! Who was it said, 'Living long is the best revenge'?"

"I don't know, Grandpa. But it's 'living well,' not 'living long.'"

"Don't contradict me, boy! And don't nitpick!"

"I was just trying to clarify."

"Oh, it's all clear, boy. The sonofabitch is dead and you've latched on to the widow. What's she like, Jackson? the widow? Is she..." The old man made lewd movements with his hands, outlining a voluptuous female figure.

"She's very beautiful, Grandpa."

"Yes, well, I'll say that for the dead old bastard—he could pick 'em. Yessir. Still, this widow must be long in the tooth for a lad like you, Jackson."

"She's older than I am. Not enough to bother me."

"Yes. Well, now that you've married her, the thing to do is...the thing to do is...the thing to do is..." The water drained out of the sink. The vacancy sign went up in the window of the blue eyes. The old man squeezed them shut as if squeezing hard would restore his train of thought.

Jack waited. He was used to the old man's sudden losses of concentration, but today he didn't have the patience to wait. "The thing to do is get even." Jack supplied the words.

The old man's eyes focused sharply on his grandson. "Yes, yes. Get even. You get that money back. Use the Governor's widow. Revenge—them Stockwells deserve it. They ruined me, ruined our family. Matthew Stockwell destroyed me. I spent six years in jail and now he's dead. Now it's our turn."

"Sure, Grandpa." Jack looked away from the old man, unable to face the meanness and hatred in his eyes. He had heard these vitriolic words so many times before. He loved the old man; the old man had raised him, but for only one purpose—to get even with the high and mighty Stockwells, the family that had robbed them of their fortune and their good name.

"Boy, don't you humor me. Don't you go back to that nothing life of yours—bellhop, jungle bum, gun for hire. Yes, and gigolo, too. You make the last count for something, Jackson! Don't be softhearted. Don't let your emotions get in the way of doing what you have to do."

"I have to leave, Grandpa." Jack opened the door. "My emotions are in the way. Something happened that neither one of us could have figured. I fell in love with her."

"What's that? What did you say, boy?" The old man lurched forward.

"I love Buffy, Grandpa. I really do." The door closed behind Jack. "I love my wife."

58

"I LOVE MY HUSBAND-TO-BE," Holly still aglow with the lovemaking they had concluded only a short while before whispered to Meyerling. "He is the most satisfying lover who ever held the office of Secretary of State of the United States of America."

"And I love my wife-to-be because she is the unrivaled queen of non sequiturs."

They were in the bedroom Holly maintained for privacy in the rear of her studio above the library at Riverview. It was a warm September evening and she and Meyerling were sitting up side by side in Holly's bed with robes on, going over the arrangements for their upcoming wedding. Although the date had been set some months earlier, this was the first chance he'd had to go over the guest list with her. His involvement with the Reagan administration had kept him very busy and in Washington much of the time.

Meyerling reached across Holly for the wedding invitation list so that he might add a name. "Alexander," he explained. "If we invite Caspar, then we must have Alexander."

"But won't that be awkward? With the Vice President there, I mean."

"It's been more than six months." Meyerling shrugged. "The statute of limitations for political grudges has run out. And I am sure it is clear to Alexander that he is not now and never has been in charge of the country."

"Six months." Holly sighed. "When I think how frightened I was that you'd been shot—"

"Never fear, my dear. I was born a Swiss. Neutrality is my birthright. Not even a madman shoots at a Swiss."

"The missions you undertake are for the United States, not Switzerland," Holly reminded him. "And that makes you fair game for the Basques, the IRA, the Red Brigades, and the PLO."

"Not to mention the far right, the far left, and the radical center," he observed dryly.

"Danger but no glory," Holly protested. "You not only don't have a cabinet post, you aren't even a government official. The President won't trust you with authority, and you aren't in tune with his policies. You tell me you're not a part of the administration, and yet when I ask you what's happening, you tell me you're consulting with them about missions. Missions! What missions?"

"Diplomatic missions that will be undertaken."

"Undertaken by whom?

"Different people."

"You? Will you be undertaking a mission for the administration?" Holly demanded.

"It's possible, Holly. I can't be sure."

"Zelig! We're going to be married in a month. How can you be so evasive with me?"

"I'm not being evasive, Holly. I'm being truthful. I really don't know what I'll be asked to do. I don't know if I'll accept either. That will depend on just how much in sympathy I am with administration objectives in a specific situation."

"So you'll go on consulting with them, but not work for them officially."

"Yes."

"And you won't be on the payroll?"

"Yes."

"Then how will we live?" Holly was ironically dramatic. "How will we eat? Who will support your poor wife and her child?"

"The same people who support them now," he told her. "The Stockwells. I receive a rather handsome stipend from the Stockwell Institute while I donate my services to the country. It should be enough to keep you and Nicholas in cornflakes and caviar."

"And will I see any more of you after we're married than I have up to now?"

"Yes." His eyes softened as he kissed her on the lips. "You'll be with me. I promise." He pulled away. "That is, if you want to be."

"Why wouldn't I want to be?" Holly wondered.

"Well, there is your own work. Your research project. How is that going by the way?"

"All right, but it's so sad."

"Sad?" His tone was lightly mocking. "The fruits of adultery?"

"The fruits of war and revolution," Holly corrected him. "Inevitable fruits."

59

F ROM SPRING OF 1779 through the summer of the following year, Ursula and Roger continued to meet secretly as lovers at Hanging Rock. Their passion was so intense that the rest of Ursula's life degenerated into a dull, gray, tedious waiting period between rendezvous. The time spent with her husband and her father and mother had little reality for her. She was deaf to the meanings of dinner-table conversation filled with the whistling in the dark of Loyalist platitudes.

Ursula heard clearly, however, in her rebel lover's arms. Wrapped in his cloak, lying naked against his nakedness, their bodies still dewy with the perspiration of their passion, she listened contentedly as he spoke of his ideals and his hopes, and of his admiration for the man he prized above all others—his commander, General Benedict Arnold.

"He is the very embodiment of our cause," Roger assured Ursula, eyes shining. "Every officer who serves under him takes Benedict Arnold for his model. You wait and see, Ursula. When we have won, Benedict Arnold will be the name posterity will never forget."

Roger's hero-worship was but a small part of the history taking shape all around Ursula. The very way of life of the patroons—the life-style into which Ursula had been born, which had shaped her from the first, and into which she had married—was at risk. And yet, mesmerized by love, she barely noticed.

She could not help noticing, however, when Mrs. Benedict Arnold, heretofore known to the van Bronckels as the staunch Tory maiden Peggy Shippen, arrived at the van Bronckel manor house where Ursula and her husband still lived with her parents. As a noncombatant, Peggy had passed easily through rebel and British lines. Patroon hospitality demanded that she be received, although the new

398

wife of the Colonial hero of Saratoga was surely the most compromising of guests to a Loyalist household.

There were no other guests at dinner. The van Bronckels' Loyalist neighbors, recalling Peggy's oft-voiced Tory sentiments, regarded her treachery in marrying Arnold as unforgivable. Even with only the family present, the atmosphere was strained. When the meal was over, Meinjeer van Bronckel and his son-in-law, Hans Hoek, rose gladly to leave the ladies for their pipe and brandies. They were surprised when Peggy Arnold thwarted their departure.

"Might I see you two gentlemen privately on a matter of the greatest urgency?" she asked. Her request was bold, and verged on being insulting to Ursula and her mother. Nevertheless, the gentlemen retired to the privacy of a parlor with Peggy Arnold.

Later that night, as Ursula watched her husband arrange his nightcap against the evening chill, she asked what Peggy had wanted. Hans answered obliquely. He said that he feared the patroon community had grievously misjudged the lady. Misguided emotion may have led her to marry a rebel, but her heart was still true.

"And you look so delicate," Roger marveled when their lovemaking was finally over.

"I am a tigress!" Ursula laughed happily. "I scratch and claw. Just look at you, my poor darling."

"Wounds to treasure."

"But how will you explain them to your precious General Arnold?" she teased him.

"I won't have to. He is as enamored of his love as I of mine. No doubt he will have his own wounds."

"And perhaps some he never anticipated."

Roger looked at Ursula questioningly. She told him then of Peggy Arnold's visit to the van Bronckel home. And she repeated what her husband had said about the patroon community misjudging her and her heart still being true.

"To the Tory cause? Is that what he meant? That Mrs. Arnold is still true to the Tory cause?"

"It is how I understood him."

"Would she betray the general then?" Roger's face had gone very white. "I must warn him."

"Be careful, my darling. If he loves her as you say, then warning him might be the most dangerous thing you can do."

"Even so, he is on his way here to take command of West Point. He must be told that his wife consorts with the patroons. I cannot stand idly by, Ursula, and let him be betrayed by her."

"Perhaps she is not betraying him," Ursula said slowly. "Perhaps—"

"No!" Roger was outraged. "Do not say it. You do not know the general. In love, yes. But nothing—nothing!— will ever come before his devotion to our cause." He calmed down a little. "As soon as he arrives, I must warn him."

A few nights later Ursula overheard her husband and her father in conversation with a small group of Loyalist men from neighboring estates. "The rebels are planning an invasion of Canada," her father was saying.

"They have been planning that for a long time," one of the British Tories responded. "Since their first early failure to seize Montreal."

"This is different. They are shifting large bodies of troops and moving into position. It will be a major assault."

"But how do you know this, Meinjeer van Bronckel?"

"We have it from one on the most intimate terms with the new commander of West Point, one who speaks with his knowledge and authority."

Ursula knew beyond doubt now. Benedict Arnold was not simply his wife's dupe, but a willing turncoat. She hurried to Hanging Rock the next day to warn Roger.

But Roger did not come. He had made the mistake of advising General Arnold that his wife was conspiring with British sympathizers. Arnold locked him up. All Roger accomplished was to spur Arnold to hastier action.

Arnold dispatched his wife to the van Bronckel estate once again. He offered to surrender West Point to the English in exchange for twenty thousand pounds sterling and a commission as Major General in the British Army. If his plan failed and he had to flee to British lines, then he would settle for ten thousand pounds as payment for his treachery. This was the message passed on by the Hudson River Valley Loyalists to the British.

"West Point is a major fort, and control of it has strategic importance in the New York and Canadian theaters of operation." Meinjeer van Bronckel summed up Arnold's offer. "It could mean the difference between victory and defeat in the north, and that could affect the outcome of the entire war."

"Why is he doing it?" Hans Hoek wondered.

"It is the influence of his wife." Meinjeer van Bronckel was positive.

"Perhaps. Still, history will label him a great traitor."

The British accepted General Arnold's terms on condition he meet with an emissary from British headquarters to work out details of the West Point surrender. The name of the emissary was Major John André, the date they were to meet, September 21, 1780. Major André would enter rebel-held territory under a flag of truce on the pretext of negotiating a prisoner exchange.

Before the flag could be utilized, however, the British warship carrying André up the Hudson was fired upon and forced to turn back. The major rowed himself ashore and traveled on foot through the woods. In British uniform he successfully avoided American patrols and kept his rendezvous with Benedict Arnold.

While they were in conference, Captain Roger Stockwell overcame his guard and made his escape. Even as Benedict Arnold was arranging for civilian clothes for Major André and writing out a pass that would carry him past Colonial sentries and back to British lines, Stockwell was alerting the Colonial command to Arnold's treachery. That done, he rode with an eight-man troop at top speed for the van Bronckel estate with a warrant for the arrest of Mrs. Arnold.

Word of the Colonials' approach, however, preceded them. Meinjeer van Bronckel was able to have Peggy Arnold spirited away before the rebels arrived. Still, Roger's disappointment was tempered by the sight of Ursula standing on the portico with her husband, father, and mother to confront the rebels.

They could not, of course, acknowledge one another.

Still, their glances met and merged like live flames flaring. In the subsequent confusion of reprovisioning his small troop at van Bronckel expense and watering his horses, Roger managed to whisper seven words to Ursula: "One week from today. Noon. Hanging Rock." And then he was gone again in pursuit of the treacherous and elusive Peggy Arnold.

It was the longest week of Ursula's life, but finally it was over. She arrived at Hanging Rock early, impatient. Her stays well undone to ease the passionate heaving of her breasts, and when her lover arrived, she opened her arms to receive him.

With patent reluctance, Roger delayed their embrace. His first concern was Ursula's safety, and so he had to tell her what had happened and—more important—what was going to happen. "Major André was caught in civilian clothes trying to pass through our lines with the pass General Arnold supplied him," Roger began. "The documents he was carrying were absolute proof of the deal between General Arnold and the British for the surrender of West Point. He is to be hanged."

"Hanged." Ursula shivered. It could as easily have been her father, or one of their Loyalist friends, or even her husband, Hans. All had been involved in the West Point affair. "What about Peggy?" she asked.

"Better luck than Major André. She eluded us altogether. Arnold got away, too. He heard of André's capture and took flight. Ironic. He actually made his escape on the very boat the British had dispatched to rescue André. He is at British headquarters in New York City, and there seems little doubt that Peggy will soon join him there. It is said that General Arnold has been authorized by the British to raise and command a regiment of American deserters."

"Poor Peggy. Tories may have accepted his betrayal, but Tory society will never receive such a turncoat as Benedict Arnold."

"Don't waste your sympathy, my love. We must look to your own welfare. Orders have come down from General Washington to seize the lands of any Loyalists in the Hudson River Valley who were involved in the West Point affair. I am sorry, but the van Bronckel family heads the list."

"Our lands." It would kill her father, Ursula was sure. "And what of us? What will happen to us?"

"The men will be interned. Your father. Your..." Roger had a hard time with the word. "...husband."

"And the women? My mother? Myself?"

"You will be free to go where you will."

"And the land? Our property? The van Bronckel estates? What will happen to them?"

"General Washington has already decreed that the patroon's lands will be given as a reward for valor to certain outstanding Colonial officers."

"Someone else will have my father's property?" Ursula spoke from a daze.

"I am sorry, my darling. But I had to warn you. Everything will be in turmoil." Roger took Ursula in his arms and kissed her tenderly. He stroked her cheek to comfort her. "I love you. It is imperative that we make plans so that we do not lose each other."

"That won't be necessary!" The words, cold with fury, came from the shadows to one side of Hanging Rock. It was unmistakably the voice of Ursula's husband. There was a long dueling pistol in his hand.

"Hans, don't!" Ursula tried to get between her lover and her husband.

"You betrayed me," Hans said in a reasonable tone, as if explaining something obvious to a child whose attention had been distracted. "You betrayed our marriage. But what is worse, Ursula, you betrayed our people to the enemy. You cost us West Point... and now Riverview."

Roger pushed her to one side. He eyed the gun that Hans was pointing at him. "I am truly sorry, sir," he said. "I will, of course, give you satisfaction." Slowly, to show his intention of conforming to the etiquette of dueling, he reached with fingertips pointing downward to withdraw his own handgun from its military holster. "Perhaps Ursula should withdraw," he started to say, but never got past pronouncing the name of his beloved.

Hans fired, aiming for the heart. The shot struck Ursula full in the breast. She sank to her knees. She stared in Hans's direction in wonder, her mouth open as if to speak.

Blood bubbled from her lips. She pitched forward on her face in the rich, black soil of the Hudson River Valley.

A split second before Ursula's body was struck by the bullet, Roger had hurriedly raised his pistol and fired. His arm swung wildly as he heard Ursula's scream. He missed. The bullet hit Hans square in the side, knocking him backward off his rocky perch.

Sobbing, Roger threw himself on Ursula's body and carefully turned her over. He lifted her inert form off the damp earth. He kissed her lips; he tried to quench the flow of blood. But it was too late. She was dead, and Roger Stockwell was alive.

60

"HANS LIVED, and he and Ursula's father—along with several other prominent Tories—were arrested and interned later that day. After Riverview and several other neighboring estates were confiscated, Ursula's mother and most of the other wives and daughters left the Hudson River Valley. The van Bronckels would never return. Before the war was over, General Washington gave the Riverview estate for a small sum to Roger Stockwell in recognition of his many services and acts of valor. So Roger Stockwell moved into Ursula's house," Holly concluded the story with a sigh. "He never married; later his brother and his family joined him, and we Stockwells have been living at Riverview ever since."

Beside Holly in her bed above the Riverview library, Meyerling shifted ever so slightly and then kissed Holly fully on the lips. "And all this time I thought the Stockwells stole Riverview conventionally, just like all the other robber barons stole their land." He smiled.

"That sounds suspiciously like biting the hand that feeds you, darling." Holly was not prepared for so quick a cynical reaction. "And where's your heart? What about Ursula?"

"An adulterer." Meyerling shrugged. "A time-honored victim."

"You sound as if you think it's all right to shoot people for committing adultery."

"Of course it is. When you are my wife, I will shoot you and any lover I find you with on the spot. I promise you."

"What am I getting myself into?" Holly wondered.

"I can also safely promise you that given the quality of my marksmanship, I will more likely shoot off my big toe than hit you."

"I am relieved." Still, Holly wondered, shouldn't he have been just a tad more affected by the sadness of the lovers' fate? He was joking, of course, but still—

The ring of the telephone interrupted Holly's train of thought. It was on the nightstand on Meyerling's side of her bed. She reached across him to answer it, listened for a moment, then covered the mouthpiece. "Washington," she told him. "For you."

Trying to give him a little privacy, she angled her back to him. There was a television set on her side of the bed. She turned it on and twisted the dial so she would have a picture but no sound that would interfere with Meyerling's conversation.

His side of it consisted of clipped responses: "The colonels are not retrievable. . . . No. I assure you, the Greek people would never stand for it. . . . It was a stupid policy; it would be even more stupid to back it again. . . ."

Holly looked idly at the TV screen, where *60 Minutes* was in progress.

"Papandreou? He is a socialist, yes. . . . No, he is not a Moscow puppet, and neither has he horns, nor a tail. . . . He is civilized and reasonable—a Greek patriot first, an ideologue second. . . ."

The television screen was filled now with the shot of a freighter plowing through fairly heavy seas. Suddenly, from the right side of the screen, a two-master sailboat cut diagonally in front of the freighter. A long shot showed action on the deck of the freighter. Sailors scurried about and a man in the uniform of a ship's officer came out on the wheel deck with a megaphone. The sound was still off, so Holly couldn't hear him, but he was obviously cautioning the sailboat to stay out of their path. The camera

405

shifted again to show the sailboat ignoring the request. Instead it was crisscrossing back and forth in front of the ship with the obvious intention of either forcing it to change course or halting its progress.

"Yes. Papandreou will make a deal with the communists because that is the only way he will be able to govern.... But that is the corner we pushed him in to with the colonels.... I know we have considerable interests in Greece.... Yes. Yes, political and business... Multinational involvements, yes... No. Papandreou certainly won't deal with him.... I doubt he'd trust him either.... Nor him..."

Suddenly the sailboat cut too closely in front of the freighter. It achieved its objective. The freighter had to change course to keep from hitting it. But when it did, it had no choice but to swamp the smaller craft. The camera moved wildly, trying to keep up with the crew of the sailboat as it was flung into the sea.

There was a sudden closeup of one of the crew members being tossed around in the water. It picked up the lettering GREENPEACE on a long-sleeved sweatshirt. As a wave flipped the wearer over, her face became visible.

"My God!" Holly gasped. Even soaking wet there was no mistaking that apricot hair. The almond-shaped, hazel eyes were likewise unmistakable. It was one of the Tyler twins—either Beth or Carrie.

"Well, yes, I am on good terms with Papandreou. Our economic philosophies are at opposite poles, but personally we get along.... An unofficial mission with a Stockwell Institute cover to discuss investment in Greece, the economy, and maybe—off the record, of course—the political situation.... Oh, yes. I do believe he means to take Greece out of NATO.... I agree. That would be tragic.... All right, I'll get back to you as quickly as possible. Goodbye." Meyerling hung up the phone. He turned toward Holly and started to say something.

She silenced him with a quickly upheld palm. She had already turned the sound up, and now she turned it louder. Pointing, she directed his attention to the television screen.

Mike Wallace was sitting at an outdoor Greek café at dockside. Across the large round table from him sat Beth

406

and Carrie Tyler. They had changed to dry clothes, jeans and sweatshirts with GREENPEACE blazoned on them. Beth was just answering a question.

"Of course, Greenpeace wants publicity," she said. "We don't feel any shame at capitalizing on our family connections. It's all too easy to point the finger at strangers. How can you measure the embarrassment to our family against the survival of the world?"

"Then you do admit that you deliberately chose this ship to interfere with because it is owned by the Greek shipping magnate Spiro Papatestus—your cousin by marriage—and carrying a cargo consigned to enterprises owned by the Stockwells, a prominent family to which you belong?" Wallace followed up.

"My sister and Deke and I did not personally target this ship," Beth replied. "It was selected by experienced Greenpeace staff for three reasons. The first is its cargo—the ship is carrying uranium ore to be delivered to New York harbor for off-loading to three separate Stockwell nuclear plants in the northeast. One of these plants is not yet in operation. Delivery of the uranium will enable it to go on line. We want to alert the American people to the dangers of nuke plants and to the further danger of transporting fissionable materials through the streets of their cities."

"And the other two reasons?" Mike Wallace inquired.

"The second reason is one that should be a matter of conscience to the world. The ship took on its cargo of uranium in South Africa. The uranium is the product of mines run by a subsidiary of the Stockwell Corporation in cooperation with the government of South Africa. We protest participation in the South African economy by Stockwell and all other American corporations."

"And the third reason?"

"The ongoing disgraceful record of Papatestus Shipping in polluting the Mediterranean, Aegaen, Cretan, and Libyan Seas. Papatestus freighters and tankers have accounted for sixty percent of oceanic pollution in the vicinity of Greece over the past five years. Papatestus has virtually lined the floors of the seas surrounding Greece with canisters containing the most poisonous chemical waste, damaging the fishing industry." Sensing that her agitation might be counterproductive for television, Beth calmed herself. She was learning quickly how to convey her message to the public. "Also," she added, wrapping it up, "oil spills from Papatestus tankers have rendered beaches from the Costa del Sol and Casablanca to Crete and Libya unusable."

The camera came in close on the twins' attractive young faces. There was a ten-second freeze-frame—an effective tableau of beauty and commitment shining from identical visages. Then it was replaced by a commercial.

"Those Tyler twins!" Holly shook her head in a gesture of admiration mixed with exasperation. "You have to credit Beth's idealism, but even so, this is really going to embarrass the family."

"It will hurt their cousin Spiro Papatestus more," Meyerling responded.

"I have a feeling that the twins have further surprises planned for us," Holly commented, a frown creasing her forehead.

"Well, you can ask them when you see them," Meyerling told her.

"See them? I have no plans to see them."

"But you will. On our honeymoon."

"On our honey—? Zelig, are you trying to tell me we'll be honeymooning in Greece?"

"Would you like that? We could stay with Spiro and Louise Papatestus on Crete. They're old friends of mine, and their villa boasts the best view in the Mediterranean."

"You've got your mission!" Holly was mildly indignant. "Honeymoon indeed! They're sending you to Greece."

"Do you mind terribly? I could turn it down. Only..."

"Only?"

"Only I really am the best man for the job. And it's a very necessary job."

"Such modesty." Holly couldn't help smiling. "Well, if a honeymoon is supposed to get the newlyweds away from family, this one certainly won't."

"Well in that case..." He drew her back down on the bed, pushed aside the wedding list, and slipped the strap from her nightgown down her shoulder. "Perhaps we had best get an early start." He kissed the tip of the breast he had bared.

"We already did," she reminded him. "Again?" She gasped at his readiness. "Isn't this very, very early for seconds?" Holly murmured. "We haven't had the marriage ceremony yet."

"It's in the Greek tradition," he assured her. "Read the *Iliad*. Or maybe it's the *Odyssey*." He moved against her, hard and eager.

"Ah," Holly said, reaching for him. "The Greek tradition. But this isn't Greece yet, my love. We're still at Riverview."

"Riverview." He kissed her hotly, deeply. "And is there no tradition of romance at Riverview, then?"

"Oh, there is." Holly rose to him. "There surely is."

And they would take that tradition with them, she thought, as they moved together in the act of love. They would embrace their legacy with all the eager anticipation of those who are truly in love. Yes, the romance of Riverview had a long history, and the Stockwell legacy was not one solely of riches, but of passion, for Riverview reflected the passions of all the world.